Someone Like Me

Stephanie Fournet

www.stephaniefournet.com

Cover design by Jena Brignola

ISBN: 9781091045101

CHAPTER ONE

DREW

I don't want to get out.

This place is surrounded on three sides by the Mississippi River. The fencing everywhere else is topped with razor wire. But in the last eight years, I've never needed those to keep me in.

This is where I belong. And everybody knows it. Ma. Annie. Grandma Quincy.

But out of the sixty-three hundred inmates here at Angola, I'm the one being released today.

It's morning, but it's not time for roll call yet. I know because, for Hickory, it's quiet. There's no such thing as silence in a dorm with eighty bunks to a hall. That's eighty men who talk, whisper, snore, fart, cough, jack off, and whatever the hell else they can get away with during lights out. But in the hour or so before dawn, like now, this place is as quiet as it ever gets, so I know I've got a little time left ahead of me.

Just not enough.

The thought of the outside world has my stomach clenching under the thin sheet. In a few hours, they'll process me out, and then I'll walk through the doors of Reception. Annie will be there, and that'll be okay. That's not the part I'm dreading.

We'll get into her car — I have no idea what she's driving; we've never talked about that — and we'll make

3

the two-hour trip down Highway 61 and along I-10. That's not the part I'm dreading either. Because that's just road and sky. There's plenty of sky here. I'm used to it. Nothing to be afraid of.

For the last five years, I've worked in the auto tech shop. Assistant to the foreman for the last two. I know I could swipe a six-inch screwdriver and sink it into a guard's thigh. Buy myself a whole lot more time.

I've thought about it. Really, I have.

But that would only be more blood on my hands, and I have enough already.

Enough already.

I've been able to picture the ride with Annie, I can get as far as crossing the Atchafalaya Basin Bridge, but as soon as I try to see us pulling off I-10 onto University Avenue, my mind shuts the fuck down.

I roll onto my back. The ceiling above me is a washed out gray in the pale, pre-dawn light. Top bunks are a trade off here. On the bottom bunk, you feel like the world is closing in on you. And with a two-hundred-pound man sleeping in the bed above you, on a noisy heap of springs and feathers, it's not hard to imagine all that shit coming down on you every time that bastard rolls over.

On top, there's nothing there to crush you, but it's hot as fuck up here. I may not be ready to get out and face everything and everyone waiting for me, but I'm not gonna lie. I've missed air conditioning. It's September, and September in Louisiana is like the inside of a baked potato. Steaming and still.

Today is September 18th. Eight years to the day the fool I was walked in here.

4

Walking out, I'll still be a fool, but I've learned some things inside. Back when I was eighteen, I had no idea that in the state of Louisiana an aggravated burglary conviction got you one to thirty. My lawyer made sure to tell me that ten years was a sign he'd done his job.

I'd said nothing to that. I would have taken the thirty if it hadn't been for Annie and Grandma Q. My sister said if I went away that long, I'd miss seeing her have kids, miss seeing them grow, and Grandma said I'd miss her altogether. Those are the little details I have to remember.

I shake my head at the ceiling. What's wrong with me? Those details aren't *little.*

But it's hard to remind myself that there are a few people I care about who don't want me to pay anymore for my crimes. And the fact that I disagree with them only makes them suffer more, and that's the last thing I want.

They are the reasons I "good-timed-out" when I had the chance. For them. Not for me.

The creak of springs and rustling of sheets snag my attention. I glance down to the bottom bunk on my right and find A.J. smiling up at me.

"It's here," he whispers, grinning. "Ya big day."

In spite of myself, I grin back. A.J. Lemoine is a goofy ass mother, and he makes me laugh at least six times a day.

"It's here," I whisper back, glad that seeing his smile makes my own show up. A.J. and I are tight, but I haven't told him how I feel about getting out. Like almost three-fourths of the inmates at Angola, A.J's here

5

all day. A lifer. Second degree murder. No possibility of parole.

You can't tell a guy who'll never get out that you want to stay in. That's just cruel. In fact, half the guys I know have been smiling my way all week, happy for me. It gives them hope.

I feel sick just thinking about it, but I can't let on.

"Annie comin' for ya?" A.J. asks, his voice so low I almost can't make it out over the tide of snores that surrounds us.

I nod. A.J. first met my sister six years ago on a visiting day when his son was here at the same time. Since then, A.J. has asked about her almost as much as Annie's asked after him.

"She'll be happy," he says, nodding with approval. Then his eyes lock on mine like he's been seeing through my mask for weeks. "And everythin' else will work out alright."

I don't care what he did. A.J. doesn't belong here. A lot of guys don't. He's been inside since 1997. Last year he graduated from the Bible college old Warden Cain and the New Orleans Baptist Theological Seminary started decades ago, and now A.J. is an ordained minister. An ordained minister who will die in prison.

A.J. and I have talked about a lot — almost everything — but one of the things I've never come out and said is that it's crazy I'm getting out when he never will. If you ask me, it should be the other way around.

See, when A.J. was twenty-one years old, he got into a bar fight with this piece of shit. Piece of Shit started the fight, and A.J. finished it by breaking a bottle over his head. And that's how you can just be minding your own business one minute, nursing your Bacardi and Coke, and doing life without parole the next.

This is not the way A.J. tells the story. It's how I tell it. A.J. tells a story of a young man who took his gift of life for granted. Who needed to let God into his heart. Who needed to bow to love and forgiveness instead of hate and revenge.

But he didn't step into the bar that night intending to hurt anybody. He walked in there an innocent man. And he didn't ask Piece of Shit to hassle him, either. He was law abiding until that asshole touched him.

I cannot say the same for me.

Nothing that led me here was innocent. I'm guilty. One hundred percent. If I weren't guilty, I wouldn't be here. And Anthony would still be alive.

But I'm here. And he's not.

CHAPTER TWO

EVIE

"Evie!" Tori shouts from the bottom of the stairs. "Where's my Jazz Fest T-shirt?"

I press my pencil into the seam of my open book and push myself off the bed. *The Yamas & Niyamas* will just have to wait.

"It's not in your closet?" I ask, calling down from my bedroom door. I can't see my sister from here, but she can hear me better this way.

She makes a noise in her throat, like a little cough. "If it were in my closet, why would I be asking *you?*"

Any answer I give will only piss her off more, so I head downstairs. "I'll help you look for it."

She's standing there with her arms crossed over her pajamas, the beginnings of a sneer curling her lip. "Did you take it without asking me?"

"No," I say gently. "But maybe I washed it with my things." I move past her, heading toward the direction of the laundry room, and she whirls on her heel to follow me.

"Well, did you or didn't you?" Her voice drips acid.

Tori is in a bad mood. If I'm being honest, Tori has been in a bad mood for about three years. Only it's gotten worse over the last month. For that, I blame Jason Watney.

"I washed and dried a load yesterday morning, but I haven't folded it yet."

She follows hard on my heels. "If you shrunk my shirt, I'm going to be so pissed," she seethes.

8

I seal my lips together, declining to point out that she's always pissed. Instead, I force the slightest constriction in my throat and inhale through my nose, taking a barely audible *ujjayi* breath. I feel the balancing and calming effects of the yogic breathing almost immediately. My shoulders drop away from my ears, and I challenge myself to feel the wood floor beneath my bare feet as I make my way to the laundry room.

Tori's glower seems to burn through the back of my slouchy tank as I dig in the basket, but I concentrate on my breath, the crisp smell of Meyer's geranium fabric softener, and the brush of fabrics against the skin of my hands. I spot the electric blue T-shirt and pluck it from the pile.

I attempt to shake it out to assess any damage, but Tori yanks it from my grip. "Give it here." Her jaw is clenched, and she doesn't even meet my gaze as she drapes the shirt over her front and smoothes it out.

It doesn't look like it shrunk at all, but I'm leaving nothing to chance. "I'll buy you a new one if—"

"That's not the point," she snaps, shooting me a scowl.

The look she gives me is so bitter and violent, I want to look away, back away, and leave her alone, but I don't. I have one guess as to why *this* electric blue Jazz Fest T-shirt is the only one she wants.

Jason Watney.

They went to Jazz Fest together to see The Revivalists and Cage the Elephant last May. Jason was over here almost all summer. But I haven't seen him since August. I've waited for Tori to say something — anything — about what happened, but so far, zilch.

Mom keeps pumping me for information every time we Skype, so maybe it's a good thing I don't really know what happened. Mom's too good at getting information out of me.

Tori is still checking the shirt for shrinkage, smoothing it over her front a third time. Lo and behold, it still hasn't shrunk.

"I think it's fine," I dare to suggest.

She narrows her eyes at me. "No thanks to you."

Ujjayi breathing is miraculous. It's faster than a glass of wine and more mellow than a pot brownie. But I think I'm going to enjoy the hell out of my Ashtanga short form class this morning.

I like to leave more than an hour early for each class. This gives me time to get to the studio, settle energetically into the space, and center myself for a few minutes of meditation before my students show up. The more present I am, the better I see and feel what my students need from me.

And what they don't need is for me to be focused on a run-in with my sister.

I finish getting myself ready and tiptoe downstairs. Tori's bedroom door is closed, and I'm relieved I don't have to talk to her before I head out.

I'm also relieved when I step out into the garage and see that she didn't park her Fiat behind Mom's Volvo. I don't have my own car because I don't need one. Mom and Dad are only home twice a year for three weeks at a time so the XC40's almost always available.

My dad is a petroleum engineer for Chevron. Four years ago, he got transferred to the Abuja office in Nigeria. I was still in high school then, and Mom stayed home with Tori and me. But I'm pretty sure it was the worst year of her life. She missed Dad like crazy.

They've been married for twenty-seven years, but they still act like newlyweds. They hold hands wherever they go. They smile and laugh at each other at the dinner table. And they slow dance in the kitchen.

When they sat us down three years ago and told us Mom would be moving to Nigeria with Dad now that I'd graduated, I can't say I was all that surprised. But it's one reason why Tori and I still live at home.

My house — my parent's house — is the most adorable two-story Tudor style home. It's where Tori and I have lived since I was five and Tori was nine, and it's where my parents plan to retire. Mom wouldn't dream of selling it, and I think the thought of renting it out while they're halfway across the world would actually give her hives.

So Tori and I get to enjoy a home right out of *Southern Living* in the heart of the Saint Streets while keeping the house lived in and looked after. And, really, I couldn't pay rent on my yoga instructor earnings. I only finished my 200-hour certification a year ago. I work part-time at the Yoga Garden, and I do about six private lessons a week, but that's not nearly enough to make up a living wage.

People — Tori, my parents, friends — have asked me when I'm going to get "a real job." I was studying kinesiology at UL, but I only finished three semesters because what I really want to do is teach yoga.

I know it's hard to make a living this way, but it's not impossible. The more students who show up to my classes at the studio means the more classes I'll get. And private lessons are hard to come by, but if I could even

11

double what I'm doing now, I could swing a small efficiency, and I wouldn't really need more than that.

And, yeah, I'm twenty-one, but that's not too old to still be living at home. I don't make much, but I save what I can, and it's not impossible to think that one day I could own my own — perhaps very tiny — home.

My only expensive habit is that I like to travel. I want to go to India one day, of course, but I'd love to see other places too. Mom and Dad have taken us to England, France, and Spain, but I'd love to see Scotland... Greece... Italy... Ooh! And Iceland. And those are just the top spots on my list.

When my parents took us abroad to England and France, we stayed in luxury hotels, saw shows, and ate at fancy restaurants. It was great, but I don't need that either. A backpack, a solid pair of shoes, and a Eurail pass would be enough of a start.

Well, and a plane ticket.

But for right now, I'm happy just where I am. I have a great place to live, a car to drive, and the freedom to do what I love. But that doesn't make me I'm complacent. I mean, on Tuesdays, Wednesdays, and Thursdays, I offer free yoga classes at Parc Sans Souci. It's good practice for me, and it's a way to grow a client base. And sometimes my freebie students even tip.

I'm smiling about this when I pull into the gravel lot of the Yoga Garden. But as I step through the entrance and into the tea room, my smile slips.

Drake Jordan.

He's sitting at one of the tea room tables, stirring a cup of what smells like apple blossom tea. And he's leering at me. As usual.

12

"Hi, Evie." Drake Jordan could not look more wolfish if he had pointy ears and whiskers.

"Hi Drake," I say, and because I don't want to seem rude, I stupidly keep talking. "How are you?"

His grin slithers higher on his cheeks. "Better now."

I press my lips together and force a tight smile. Drake has asked me out twice, and both times, I've politely declined. You'd think he'd take the hint that I'm not interested, but he hasn't yet.

"I saw you were on the schedule today, and, lucky me, I have the day off." Drake is a server at Social. I know this because he's tells me almost every time he sees me. He has an employee discount. We can go to Social whenever I want.

I don't want, but I hate turning him down. I get this twisted up feeling inside like my guts are made of pipe cleaners and they're being wrapped around a toilet plunger.

"That's...nice." I step closer to Studio B where I'll be teaching. Jill, one of the teachers who has been here forever, has a beginner class going on right now in A, but B is just waiting for me.

Drake gestures at his tea. "Would you like to join me for a cup?" He lifts his wide brow. "My treat."

I swallow. "No thanks, Drake. I need to set up for short form."

He nods, grinning like he's in on a secret. "Looking forward to it." He leans back in his chair and crosses his arms over his chest. "What about having dinner with me tonight?"

Shit.

There goes that pipe cleaner feeling. The other two times he's asked me out, I've been able to tell him honestly that I was teaching that night. But tonight I'm free. Unfortunately.

"I…" I stretch out the word and then catch my lip between my teeth and gnaw it nervously. *Stall. Stall and think of an excuse,* I tell myself. "I need to check on something. I'll let you know after class."

Drake's face brightens. I've never seen a face look so happy and so wicked at the same time. "Great," he croons.

I suppress a groan. "I have to get set up," I say in a rush, crossing the tea room. "See you in class." I open the squeaky door and shut it firmly behind me. The rattle echoes across the wood floors. In another life, Studio B was someone's back porch. The house that is now The Yoga Garden is at least eighty years old. The doors rattle in their frames, the floor creaks, it's drafty year round, and I absolutely love it.

Studio B, now a sunroom, has picture windows on two sides. Flooded with natural light and facing the back yard, it's easy to forget that this place sits on one of the busiest streets in Lafayette.

I move across the room, drop my bag and mat on the floor, and breathe a sigh of relief. What the hell am I going to tell Drake?

Karma is absolutely real, and honesty is one of my values. Lying to him isn't an option for me. But I really don't want to hurt his feelings with the truth. I'm not attracted to Drake. Like at all. I feel like I need a shower after just talking to him. The way he looks at me… it's like his eyes have hands and they touch me without permission.

14

But he's a person. A being that carries the same divine spark we all possess. And he's a yogi, which means, in some way, he's trying to evolve. I have to respect that. And I have to honor it.

So I need to find another truth to tell him.

I unroll my mat and reach into my bag for my singing bowl, mallet, and bowl cushion. Making myself slow down and focus, I place these near my mat, arrange myself into a comfortable lotus sit, and on a deep inhale, strike the mallet against the bowl.

The soft chime washes through the room, and I close my eyes. I center my attention on my breath. I feel cool air on the edges of my nostrils and in the back of my throat. For a couple of breaths, I manage to stay with that sensation, but then my mind drifts back to Drake again, and I feel my stomach tense.

Okay, so don't fight it, I tell myself. *Focus on the feeling.*

I inhale again, but instead of sensing the rush of air into my lungs, my awareness moves to the tightness in my middle. There's a churning tension just below my diaphram, a nagging burn of unease. It's rare, but sometimes when I sit in meditation and allow myself to just listen to the sensations in my body, an insight will open itself up to me, and something I didn't understand before will become clear.

Watching the feeling, I note its size and shape, the way the muscles in the wall of my abdomen twitch and tense as if they have a mind of their own, as if they are trying to tell me *Pay attention to us. Don't ignore what we're trying to tell you.*

I begin to think about how the gut really is a second brain, full of neurons that are in constant

15

communication with the brain that sits in my skull. And then I catch myself thinking instead of feeling. I take another mindful breath and try to settle in again.

Thirty minutes pass, minutes in which I am thoughts and feelings, breath and heartbeat, muscle, nerves and bone. And life. I open my eyes, at ease, centered, and with one goal in mind: to offer my students what they need from me. Moving slowly and with awareness, I rise to begin preparing the studio. I connect my phone to the bluetooth speakers and start my playlist. The soft notes of harp and flute fill the space, and I open the door to welcome my students.

Class won't begin for another ten minutes, but a handful of yogis have already arrived. We greet each other with smiles and quiet words, as is our routine, and they move through the room, unrolling their mats and setting out their towels. Ashtanga yoga is intense, and in short order, we'll all be sweating.

Drake is among them, and I am aware of his eyes on me, but I remind myself of my purpose, my intention for the day.

Of course, it doesn't help that he positions his mat at the front of the class as close to me as possible.

At noon, I stand at the front of my mat, and close my eyes, feel all four corners of my feet pressing into the mat. I bring my hands to prayer pose, open with chanting mantras, and begin the short form series.

I take the class through the sun salutations, leading from the front of the studio for the first round before moving through the room, subtly adjusting students as I pass. A palm on the back, a whispered suggestion, or an encouraging word. I do the same with the fundamental asanas, joining in only when I feel each yogi is safe on the mat.

It's during the finishing sequence when everything falls apart.

"Aah!" A sharp, masculine cry pierces the room. Everyone is in wheel pose, including me.

This is not good.

I quickly tuck out of the posture and rush to Drake. "My back!" he wheezes, his eyes screwed shut.

I stand with my feet by his hands, bend over him, and brace him behind his shoulder blades. "Tuck your tail."

He tilts his pelvis and hisses.

"Put your weight into your heels and lower your hips."

"Christ!"

I anchor my own weight so I don't collapse on top of him. I know if I did, my face would land in his crotch, and my crotch would probably end up on his mouth. Great. For the half-second it takes to lower him to the ground, I offer my soul to the devil to avoid this nightmare.

By some miracle or dark magic, I keep my balance and then shift to his side. "Your lower back's in spasm. Draw your knees to your chest."

Drake groans, and I sweep my eyes over the rest of my students. Some have come out of the posture and are watching us with concern. Some are still in wheel, plainly ignoring the sounds of a man in pain.

Honestly, I don't know which is worse. By the look on Drake's beet red face, he's mortified.

17

"If you're still in wheel, lower down carefully, rest your back onto the earth, and draw your knees up to your chest," I instruct.

Drake's breath is still jagged, letting me know that the muscles in his back are still protesting. I lower to my knees and lean down closer to him.

"Breathe," I remind him, my voice a whisper. "Then open your legs and clasp the arches of your feet in happy baby."

He opens his eyes and shoots me a glare. "I'm not doing that." He looks angry, but I know he's probably more embarrassed than anything else.

I raise my voice and address the class. "Let your knees fall open to your underarms and reach for your feet," I tell them. "Grab inside or outside. It doesn't matter, but try to let your knees sink down so you open up your lower back."

As the rest of the class follows my instructions, Drake narrows his eyes at me. I can see he's chafing under his humiliation, but there's a spark of something else in his look.

"You owe me a date now."

My heart sinks. As much as I don't want to go out with him, I can't turn him down now. Not after he's whimpered in pain in front of a class full of women.

I grasp at the only straw I have. "Not tonight. You need an epsom salt bath and heating pad."

He raises a wolfish brow. "Tomorrow night."

I chew the corner of my lip. "I teach the next three nights," I tell him, and I'm so glad it's the truth.

A smile breaks over his face. "Perfect. Friday night then."

18

Defeat washes over me. I swallow and nod. "Friday night."

CHAPTER THREE

DREW

Annie hugs me like she hasn't seen me in eight years. It's only been about eight weeks, but I grab onto her like they'll take her away from me if I don't.

My little sister's all grown up now. She was eleven when I went away. She'll be twenty in December. That's one of the hardest things to get over about being on the inside. In prison, nothing changes. You can almost convince yourself time is standing still. And even though Annie and Grandma Quincy have visited me every other month since I've been in, it's still hard to believe Annie's in college now and not middle school.

"Oh my God," she mumbles into my chest. "I thought this day would never come."

I squeeze her tighter because talking's not a option right now. She's happy to see me. I'm happy to see her. And this is probably as good as it's going to get.

As if sensing my struggle, Annie pulls her face away from my chest and looks up at me. "How you doing? You okay?"

I swallow and shrug. The guard who escorted me out of Reception is still standing behind me. The only thing separating us from the outside world is the gatehouse. I cast my eyes around what I can see of the yard. Wide open field and sky for miles.

"It's just weird," I say under my breath.

A slow smile curls around Annie's mouth. "I'll bet it is." Her voice is gentle, low. Her gray eyes are soft with sympathy. Sympathy I definitely don't deserve. "I don't want to rush you, but we should get going. Grandma's planned a little something for you."

I freeze at this. "W-what do you mean?" The question comes out gruff, and I watch her smile flatten a little.

Annie shakes her head to dispel the mood, and her expression brightens. "Don't get all grumpy. It's just a little get together with family." When I don't respond to this, she adds, "She's making a brisket."

I roll my eyes, but I follow Annie to the car. I know exactly what Grandma Q is up to. Her brisket has been the glue in our family for as long as I can remember. My Aunt Josie, my Uncle Nelson, and Ma haven't always gotten along. Throw my cousins into the mix, and things can get heated. And then some. But nobody argues when brisket is on the table. It's the Quincy Family peace treaty.

At least, it was.

By cooking a brisket today of all days, Grandma Q is telling everyone that my debt is paid. Except it's not, and it never will be. And I'm sure most of the members of my family feel the same, judging by just how many of my aunts, uncles, and cousins have written, called, or come to visit me at Angola.

That would be zero.

And then there's Ma. She *has* written to me. Twice a year for the last eight. Every March 11th, Anthony's birthday. And every August 2nd. The day I got my brother killed.

Ma's letters are always more or less the same. Her life makes no sense without Anthony. He was all the gold she had in this world. It's my fault he's gone.

And she's right.

I've kept all of her letters. For years, I taped them to the wall behind my bunk. And then about three years ago, A.J. saw me tacking up another one, and he hoisted himself up there to read them. Without a word, he tore them off the wall, wadded the letters into a ball, and threw it at my head.

"You don't get points for punishing yourself," he told me.

I agree with that. Punishing yourself doesn't count. Because that's a choice. You can start it and stop it whenever you want. That's why I think the punishment others dish out means more. I didn't bother explaining that to A.J., but I still kept the letters.

But Grandma Q is making a brisket. I know where she stands. Impossibly, she hasn't turned her back on me. It'd be so much easier if she had. I don't know why she didn't. I can get why Annie hasn't. Without Anthony, I'm her only brother. Her only living sibling. But Grandma Q has four other grandsons. Three from Uncle Nelson, and one from Aunt Josie.

None of them are convicted felons, and none of them have gotten anybody killed.

But she wants me, and that by itself I can't ignore. If she told me to get lost, I would. Instead, she's putting me up in the apartment above her garage. No matter what, I'm grateful. I need a place to stay. It's one of the conditions of parole. I don't feel like I should be out, but since I am, I need to live somewhere.

And I sure as hell don't have any money for rent.

A job is the next thing I have to figure out. But when I start thinking about that, it feels like a vice is closing around my head. Who would want an ex con on their payroll? Unless they were also ex cons, and I'm not supposed to associate with any of those.

22

And no matter what I think I deserve, I'm not the same person as the kid who dragged his brother into a fancy house we both thought was empty. I'm not going to break any laws. I'm not going to steal from anybody. I'm not going to hurt anybody.

I've hurt enough people. I don't want anymore of that.

Most of all, I don't want to hurt Grandma Q and Annie anymore than I already have. And I won't do anything that would make Anthony ashamed of me. Those have become my three rules. My three guiding questions, as A.J. would call them. *Would it hurt Grandma Quincy? Would it hurt Annie? Would it make Anthony ashamed of me?*

So that means, as much as I think I should still be on the inside, I'm not going back again. And offing myself would break all three of my rules. So I've got no choice but to make the best of it.

"Did they take your tongue in there?"

I nearly jump at my sister's question. We're on I-10, and I don't even remember the last thirty minutes of the drive.

"No," I mutter, clueless as to what else I should say.

Annie doesn't take her eyes off the road, but I see she's laughing at me. "You were pretty lost in your thoughts. I figured it was because you were taking in the change of scenery, but you didn't look like you were even noticing."

I swallow and glance out of the windshield and windows. We're on that wooded patch of I-10 between Baton Rouge and the Atchafalaya Bridge. I shrug. "It looks pretty much the same as it always did."

Annie snickers under her breath. "Yeah, but you didn't even blink when we drove through Baton Rouge."

My sister is chatty. She always has been. And I know my silence is probably driving her crazy. I run my eyes down her profile. Her ponytail is pulled high and her compact, cheerleader arms are braced against the steering wheel like a Nascar driver's. She looks ready to bounce out of her skin. Like a coiled spring. Then I frown.

"Wait. It's Monday. Aren't you supposed to be in school?"

She shoots me a sidelong glance, grinning. "Yeah, but I told my professors I had a family obligation."

I raise a brow, not liking the sound of this. "An obligation? I'm an obligation?"

Annie rolls her eyes. "No. Of course not. I wanted to pick you up."

"Because I could have taken the bus—"

"*Drew,*" she scolds. "C'mon. If the roles were reversed, would you want me taking the bus?"

I shudder at the thought. "What? Hell, no." The idea of Annie going to prison for any reason is absurd and surprisingly painful. I wouldn't be able to bear it. And I wouldn't want her to take the bus on a good day.

"Good. I'm glad we agree on that. No buses for either of us," she says, scoring a point I'm not exactly ready to concede, but I keep my mouth shut.

"Hey, did I tell you I changed my major?"

I blink in surprise. Annie is now a sophomore at UL. Last I knew, she was majoring in business. "No. Did you change your mind about finance?"

She nods. "Yeah. I switched to criminal justice. I want to go to law school," she says, smiling proudly. "I

24

think I want to be a public defender. And maybe even a judge one day."

I feel like I've been hit in the chest. "Why?" I hear myself ask.

Annie gives a shocked laugh. "Because of you, silly! I want to help prisoners and ultimately work on sentencing reform. Do you know Louisiana has some of the toughest sentencing laws in the country?"

I do know, but I listen as she launches into an attack on the state's mandatory sentencing laws, and I feel myself sink lower into my seat. I wanted to get her talking about something so I could lapse into silence beside her, listening and giving the occasional grunt, but I didn't expect her to talk about this.

I want to argue that some people deserve to be locked up and forgotten about — myself among them — but then I think about A.J., and I clamp my mouth shut.

My sister, on the other hand, has been doing her homework, and for the rest of the drive, it's all I hear about.

When we exit I-10 onto University Avenue, I find myself gripping the ceiling handle. We'll be at Grandma Q's in five minutes, and my gut feels like I've eaten steel wool.

The northside of Lafayette looks pretty much the same. The Cracker Barrel and the Motel 6 are still there, right off the exit, but now there's a place called Home Slice where Acme Taco used to be.

I've never given a shit about any of this, but focusing on the scenery is easier than thinking about what awaits me. We drive beneath the underpass for the

25

train tracks and come up at Four Corners, the worst major intersection in Lafayette. The LessPay motel is unchanged, and unfortunately still open. Everything looks the same, and that has the steel wool in my gut morphing to lead.

We turn onto Congress Street, and here absolutely nothing has changed. Aside from Lafayette Middle School, the busy street is lined with old houses and duplexes that look just as I remember them. And while these are a few steps above the Four Corners neighborhood, their sameness nearly suffocates me.

Annie makes a left onto St. Mary, and I start sweating.

"I'm so excited," she says under her breath, completely oblivious to how close I am to puking. "Grandma's going to just scream when she sees you."

I don't have the heart to tell her this isn't what I want to hear right now.

When she turns right off St. Mary, I feel a jolt. A part of me expected her to keep going straight, cross St. Landry, and turn onto St. John. To Ma's house. My old house.

But, of course, we're not going there.

I haven't seen that house since the night I was arrested. The night Anthony died. I never went back home after that.

I'm lost in a blur of memories when Annie makes a left onto St. Joseph Street. Grandma Q's house is on the first block, the two-story creamy yellow house with the detached garage in the back yard. With my heart in my throat, I notice there are two cars in the driveway. I have no idea who they belong to.

It's a Monday afternoon. People work. Would anyone in my family other than Annie take time away from their responsibilities to welcome me home?

"Who's here?" I rasp as we pull into the driveway. Annie comes to a stop and kills the engine.

"Oh, that's Aunt Josie's car behind Grandma's." Annie says this before glancing over at me. Then her eyes go wide "Drew, you're all sweaty. Are you okay?"

I swallow against a swell of nausea, but I can't bring myself to answer.

Annie's hand closes over my wrist. I meet her pitying gaze. "It's going to be okay," she says gently. Then she tilts her head and gives me a weak smile. "I mean, Ma's not coming, but that's probably not a bad thing, right?"

I wipe my brow with the back of my hand and shake my head. I can't just sit in the car like a coward, so I push open the door and step into airless humidity. The thought of fainting hadn't occurred to me before, but now it seems a real possibility.

My legs feel like they belong to someone else as I make my way across the lawn, but before I'm halfway there, the front door swings open with a squeak of hinges I've known all my life.

And Grandma Quincy is there.

"Thank God." Gray headed, plump, and shorter than Annie, my grandmother bustles down the walk and grabs me around the middle, squeezing me just like my sister did two hours ago. My arms fall around her, and when I look down at the top of her head, a swirl of iron gray waves pinned up in a rough bun, I can feel the ground beneath my feet for the first time.

Grandma Q whispers into my shirt. "It's so good to have you back."

Movement catches my eye, and I look up to see my Aunt Josie standing in the open doorway. She's shading her eyes against the glare of the sun, so I have no way of knowing what she's thinking.

Her hair's longer than I remember, falling to her shoulders, and maybe she's a little more full figured than she was eight years ago, but she still looks great. And she looks like Ma, which stings and soothes me all at once.

Grandma Q untangles from me and turns to Josie. "Come welcome your nephew home," she says. It's not an order, just a nudge, but I wonder if being here is really Josie's idea. I don't want any of my family to feel compelled to see me. I'm not the black sheep of the family.

I'm the Black Plague.

But Josie smiles when she steps out, and she approaches me with her arms outstretched. Grandma steps aside, and then my aunt is hugging me, and I'm nothing but confusion.

"Welcome back, Andrew." She squeezes me. I close my arms around her, but I don't hug her as tightly as I did Grandma. I don't understand. If she's happy to see me, why didn't I hear ever from her?

And then she says something that nearly knocks me down. "I'm so sorry, Drew." I hear a catch in her throat, and when she pulls back, Josie wipes her eyes with the back of her hand. "I should have come to see you, but I didn't want to upset Lottie. I should have written at least. I hope you can forgive me."

28

My mouth opens, but no sound comes out. I close it, swallow, and then try again. "I don't blame you, Aunt Josie," I manage. "There's nothing to forgive."

Instead of making her feel better, I see I've done the opposite because my aunt starts sobbing, and she clutches me into her arms again.

"Oh, Drew." She cries against me. "It's like we lost both of you, and now you're back. You don't know how good it is… what it means to see you."

No words come to my aid. I just pat Josie lamely on the shoulder. Because she makes it sound like I'm back from the dead, and while this isn't entirely untrue, it still feels cosmically unfair. If anyone deserves to be resurrected, it's Anthony, not me.

But like Lazarus, this world no longer makes sense to me, and I'm lost in it. I'd give anything to go somewhere and hide for a while.

And it's as though Grandma Quincy reads my mind, because she tugs at Josie's shirtsleeve to get her to release me. "C'mon, Josephine, let's show Andrew upstairs. I'm sure he'd like to settle in and rest before the others show up." Her eyes, merry but watchful, shoot up to mine. "The brisket still has another two hours, so you've got a little time to yourself."

I want to kiss my grandmother's feet, but instead, I follow her around the side of the house to the detached garage.

"Annie and I have had a time getting this place up to snuff," she tells me as we mount the wrought iron stairs that lead to the apartment. "I hadn't touched your grandpa's workshop all these years, and when we finally came up here, it was full of sawdust, cobwebs, and mouse scat."

29

I want to tell her that after eight years without a shred of privacy, anything with four walls and quiet will be a palace as far as I'm concerned, but I shy away from talking at all, much less talking about prison.

She pushes open the door, and the scent of lumber and wood stain punches me in the nose. Grandpa Pete. The space is immaculate. In place of his table saw and workbench is a futon and a dinette table, but the smell and the way the light from the windows warms the exposed tongue-in-groove walls has me choking against a rush of memories.

Grandpa Pete teaching me how to use a lathe. Grandpa Pete letting me borrow his jigsaw to make my own skateboard. Grandpa Pete lighting his pipe and sitting down at the top of the stairs beside me the night after my father left us.

He died six months after I went to Angola. Bone cancer. He and Grandma Q had come to my preliminary hearing and my sentencing, but by then he was in too much pain to make the two hour drive to visit.

I've asked myself if burying one grandson and seeing another thrown behind bars hastened his death. No doubt, it added to his suffering.

And that's on me.

"He loved being up here," Grandma Quincy says, as though she's clued into my thoughts. "There've been more than a few times when I've found myself making dinner, and I actually walk to the back door to call him in… Even after all this time."

I force myself to look down at my grandmother, but her eyes are fixed straight ahead, taking in the light and space and probably seeing Grandpa Pete.

30

"Time is funny that way. Sometimes it feels like ages since I've seen him, and other times it's like he's just up these stairs, and he'll be down in a minute."

I know a whole lot more about time than I did before Angola, and I nod in agreement. Time is more like a pool than a river. Deep in one spot. Shallow in another. Able to swallow you whole.

My grandmother seems to remember herself, and she turns to me, her face alight. "Of course, now when dinner's ready, I'll have you to call down."

She says this like it's good news, like having me here is restitution. And all of the sudden I feel sick again.

Moving past me, she steps into the open room. "The futon flattens out into a bed with just a little fuss." She pats a folded pile of bed linens. "I can make it up for you now if you'd like or you can leave it just so until tonight."

I shake my head and find my voice. "I got it, Grandma."

She nods and points to an armoire on the far side of the apartment. "Annie and I took your clothes and things down from the attic and washed them to get rid of the musty smell, but..." She screws up her face and sizes me up. "I don't think too many of them will fit. You've grown quite a little bit."

I feel myself crack a smile. They aren't joking when they say eight years of hard labor. And when the work day is done, exercise is one of the better ways to spend the rest of the time between dinner and lights out. Damn near everybody in prison works out. It keeps you from going crazy.

"I've put on about thirty pounds," I confirm, keeping the details to myself.

31

Grandma Q raises a brow. "And it's not around your middle, either."

This pulls a laugh from me, my first as a free man. When I processed out this morning, Angola gave me the sum of my commissary balance, a whopping $212; $10 gate money — as if ten bucks would get anyone much of anything on the outside — one set of clothes to wear out (underwear, socks, a knit polo shirt, and my prison issue shoes), and an identical set as a change of clothes. They also gave me a three day supply of Zoloft, which one of the prison doctors prescribed for me years ago. If I want to keep taking it — and I do — that's another thing I need to sort out.

Aside from a few books, one a Bible from A.J., and a few personal effects, this is all I have with me. But looking around the room, I begin to notice some familiar sights. On the bookshelf next to the armoire and beside the bathroom door is a collection of CDs from my old room. And on the shelf above them are pictures.

The one of Anthony and me on my seventeenth birthday has me sucking in my breath through pursed lips, and I have to look away.

Focus on something else. Anything else.

Across from the futon on a makeshift shelf is the TV from my old room and a now ancient PlayStation. Clearly, Annie and Grandma Q have no idea that both of these are stolen property.

Shit.

Pinpricks of black dot my vision. I wonder what would happen if I popped all three of the Zolofts right now. I brace my fingers against my forehead and turn back to Grandma Quincy.

"Um… Is it okay if I lie down for a while?" The words rasp like tearing paper, and my grandmother steps closer to me. I narrow my eyes in a squint so I don't have to meet her gaze full on.

She raises a hand to my cheek, and when she speaks, her voice is so gentle, I almost collapse at the sound. "It's a lot to take in. You get some rest, love. I'll send Annie up to get you when it's time to eat. Your cousins will want to see you as soon as they get here, but I'll hold them at bay."

In the tornado of my thoughts, this is one more mobile home that now spins out of control. But I manage to nod and follow her to the door. She presses a kiss to my cheek before letting herself out.

I turn and move back to the futon. I grab the top sheet off the pile of linens, and without letting myself study them, I pick up each of the framed photos on the bookshelf. I tuck them at the base of the TV and cover the whole shameful pile with the bedsheet.

All of that shit will have to be dealt with. But I can't face it now. I stagger back to the futon, which is about three inches too short for me, and fall face first. And I weep for the next half hour.

CHAPTER FOUR

EVIE

"Thanks so much for doing this. I just need a few minutes to take my mind off everything," Janine says, following me out onto the back porch. Janine Mayfield and her husband James bought the house across the street two years ago, and we've been friends ever since. "James is watching the baby, so I only have about a half hour, but I just feel like I'll die if I don't—" Her voice chokes off, and I watch her eyes fill.

I shake my head, gripping her hand and wanting to soothe her. "It's all right. I'm happy to help. I actually did a postpartum series at the studio last year, and the moms in the class said it helped a lot." I set down the two mats in my arms and unroll them.

And that's the moment my Rhodesian Ridgeback, Gemini, whooshes out of the doggy door and bounds up to us. He immediately aims his black nose at Janine's crotch before I shove him aside. "No, Gem. Go lie down." I point toward the other end of the porch where his outdoor bed sits, and with a drooping of his head, Gemini obeys.

A startled laugh escapes Janine, and her tears seem to be forgotten. "He's such a good boy—"

The words haven't even left her lips before Gemini jerks his head in the direction of my neighbor's yard and bounds across the lawn, barking with excitement. I peer over to find what looks like a party at Mrs. Vivian's house. About a dozen people are scattered around her lawn. A handful are sitting at her picnic table, empty plates in front of them. A couple of guys stand near the barbecue pit, sipping beers, and, at

Gemini's continued welcoming bark, two kids — a boy and a girl who can't be more than five — streak over to the chain-link fence that joins our yards.

I turn back to Janine and raise an ironic brow. "You were saying?"

She *tsks* and rolls her eyes. "He's still a good boy," she insists, watching Gemini wag wildly and lap at the fence, trying to greet the children with canine kisses.

"Yeah, whatever you say," I tease, and then I lower into a cross-legged sitting position. "C'mon, we'll start like this."

"Oh! Just a minute," Janine says, trotting back toward the door to take off her shoes. A high-pitched squeal sails across the yard, and I look back to see the giggling, dark headed boy standing with his pudgy hand through the fence. Gemini licks it with gleeful abandon. My guess is the plump little fist is covered with ice cream or popsicle juice or some other treat.

Mrs. Vivian has always been our backdoor neighbor. She still works in her garden almost every day, but she's starting to slow down. I don't know how old she is, but I know those little ones aren't her grandchildren, but her *great*-grandchildren.

I quickly scan the yard for my elderly neighbor, but I don't find her at the picnic table or in the cluster of people lounging in lawn chairs. At first, I think she must be inside, and I hope she's all right.

But then I spot her on the right side of her yard, near the garage, talking to a tall, dark haired man. I don't recognize him, but he has the look of Vivian's grandsons. Except younger. And leaner around the middle. Better looking.

35

From my angle I can tell they are out of sight from the rest of Vivian's guests. And this is when the stranger looks up and straight into my eyes, almost piercing me with his gaze. I suck in my breath. He's caught me staring at what is probably a private moment. I jerk my face away and focus on Janine. She joins me in *sukasana,* and I start us off with a few measured breaths, willing my mind to return to the present. I ask Janine to softly close her eyes, and then I take her through alternate nostril breathing, or *kundalini.*

Within a few exhales, I can feel my own body ease and unravel, and I hope it's working as well for Janine. I bat my eyes open and see that already she looks less tight in the shoulders. But we only have about thirty minutes, so I need to make each one count.

"Okay, let's move forward onto all fours," I tell her, taking the position on my mat as she follows suit. "We'll start with a flat back, and do a few cat-cow stretches."

After a quick, but yummy hatha session, I walk a completely relaxed and supple Janine through the house and to the front door.

She gives a deep sigh and looks at me in gratitude. "You are a miracle worker. I think I could actually face a night ruled by cholic."

I wince through my smile. "I hope you don't have to."

She shakes her head. "You know, I have a feeling I won't. I'm so relaxed now, I think Aaron will feel the difference in me." Janine blinks in surprise as if her own words startle her. She scrunches up her nose. "Does that sound crazy? I hardly trust myself to talk to people these days. Maybe it's the hormones, but I say the weirdest things."

I clasp her gently on the elbow. "You don't sound crazy," I reassure. "Of course little Aaron will be more relaxed and at ease if you are. He can feel tension in your body. And he's aware of your breath and heartbeat. How could he be okay if you're not?"

Janine closes her eyes and smiles, looking almost prayerful. Then she opens them. "What do I owe you?"

I shake my head. "First lesson's on the house."

"Well," she says, narrowing her gaze. "What if I want to come back?"

This, right here, is probably the highlight of my whole day. I've helped my friend by introducing her to yoga, and she wants more. I can't even count the number of times I offered a lesson before she got pregnant, but that obviously wasn't the right time, and now this is.

I can't hide my smile. "I'll give you the Saint Street discount. Fifteen an hour."

Janine eyes me like I'm crazy. "I know it's more than that to take a class at your studio, and that's not a private lesson."

"Yeah, but I'm teaching you in my own home," I say, gesturing to the house around me. "No overhead, and I don't even have to drive anywhere. Seriously, that's what I charge all my neighbors."

The look she gives me is skeptical, but I just smile. "Well, the first chance I get, when Aaron isn't crying loud enough to shake the shingles off the roof, or he's not nursing me dry, I'm making you some lemon squares."

"Ooh…" I croon appreciatively. Janine's lemon squares are the best ever. "When you're ready, I won't turn you down."

After I tell my neighbor goodnight, I walk through the front room back to the kitchen, brimming with happiness. Tori's at the counter by the sink, chopping an onion.

"So, are you going to help me, or am I cooking by myself?"

The smile on my face freezes. My shoulder blades draw together, but I will myself to breathe evenly. Tori and I share dinner-prep duties on the days I don't have a late class. Tori earned a chemistry degree, and she works as a lab tech at United Blood Services, testing blood samples, so she's home pretty much every day right after five o'clock. But that means she's usually the one to start dinner, and she never lets me forget it.

"I'm going to help you," I say gently, not taking her bait. I've given it a lot of thought, and I think my sister craves an argument. I have a theory that feeling embattled — believing that others have wronged her — brings her some relief. If someone else is to blame for her unhappiness, then she's off the hook. It's not her fault. And then maybe the universe owes her for damages, and one day in some cosmic righting of wrongs, she'll get this huge settlement that will make it all better.

But that's not how karma works.

What I resist persists, so I hold back the sharp retort at her oh-so-very-annoying jab, and I reach under the counter for the stockpot. I grab the olive oil and drizzle some over the bottom, but I know my one act of non engagement won't be enough.

"I can't believe you didn't charge Janine," Tori hisses. "So, people can just call you up out of the blue now, and you'll teach them for free?"

I make an effort to shrug casually as I turn on the burner. "Free trials are pretty common in business, though, aren't they?" I say, my voice light, my tone genial.

Tori snorts. "Yeah, but then you're only going to charge her fifteen an hour. And don't try to lie. I heard you."

Lie?

When was the last time I lied to her? Seventh grade? Tori knows — she has to know — how important honesty is to me. So this swipe draws blood. I can't bring myself to say anything as I move to the fridge for minced garlic and ginger. We're making coconut curry over cauliflower rice, and it's going to be amazing — if I don't lose my appetite first.

"I mean, fifteen dollars an hour? Why bother?"

Maybe I could try a change of subject. My mind grabs the first straw within reach. The handsome stranger who was talking to Mrs. Vivian.

"It looks like Mrs. Vivian is having a party out there."

Tori *tsks.* "You know why, don't you?" Her disapproving tone catches me off-guard, but at least she's dropped the topic of my yoga lessons.

"No. Why?"

"Because." Tori coughs in disgust. "Her criminal grandson got out of prison today. And he's going to be living with her!" Indignation swells in her voice, and she looks at me, clearly expecting me to share her outrage. I can only frown.

39

"Grandson? Mrs. Vivian had a grandson in prison?" Mrs. Vivian Quincy is one of the most vibrant souls I know. She's been a widow for about as long as I can remember, but she's never seemed sad. This piece of news makes me sad for her.

"You didn't know that?" I look over my shoulder to find Tori wrinkling her nose at me. I shake my head, almost afraid of what she'll say next. "Oh my God, it was all over the news. This grandson and another grandson — I think they were brothers — broke into a house in Bendel Gardens. Apparently, they thought it was empty, but the guy who owned it was home, and he, like, charged in with his gun and shot one of the robbers."

My eyes bug. "One of Mrs. Vivian's grandsons? Was he okay?"

Tori's forehead screws into a frown. "No," she sneers, eyeing me like I'm crazy. "He died, like, right there."

This news lands in my middle like a sucker punch. Poor Mrs. Vivian.

I think about the man I saw talking to her. I didn't recognize him. The other adults there had familiar faces I'd glimpsed over the fence enough times throughout the years.

His is not one I know.

I wonder if he's the one who has been in prison. I close my eyes and remember his image. He was tall. Toned and fit. Healthy looking. Nothing about his appearance would give away his past.

Except maybe the shadows around his eyes. I remember the troubled look he wore when he was talking to Mrs. Vivian and the piercing stare he gave me before I glanced away.

If he had smiled, I would have smiled back and waved. But I'd looked away because he'd eyed me with suspicion. I had felt like I was intruding.

And now, all I can think is, *That man watched his brother die.*

"So now this low-life is going to be our neighbor," Tori snipes, jarring me from my thoughts.

I can't explain why, but my reaction is knee-jerk. "Maybe he's not a low-life. Maybe he just made a mistake."

Tori's mouth falls open. "You mean to tell me you're okay with a violent criminal living practically in our back yard?"

Dammit. I've done it again. Fallen into her trap. I may as well have stepped into a bayberry bush. No way out of this without a few scrapes.

I put on a curious frown and take the cutting board of sliced onions from my sister. "*Is* breaking and entering considered a violent crime?" I muse aloud. I really have no idea, but it doesn't seem like it to me.

My sister scowls at me. "Well, it's a *felony*, and it *sounds* violent."

I resist the urge to point out — with no small amount of sarcasm — how very logical she sounds. Instead, I pull out my phone and Google it, but all I get are a bunch of ads for law offices and a definition of the various degrees of burglary.

"What are you *doing?*"

I shrug. "I'm looking it up, but I'm not finding anything helpful. My guess is it's not a violent crime."

41

Tori shakes her head. "It doesn't matter. I don't want him living right next to us."

My brows lift, and I can't help the edge of condescension that creeps into my voice. "Tori, what could you possibly do about it?"

She raises her chin and crosses her arms over her chest. "I could tell Mrs. Vivian I don't appreciate her harboring criminals, and if I get even a whiff of anything remotely illegal coming from him, I'll call the police immediately."

"Victoria," I sigh, slouching. It feels like weights hang from my shoulders. "You don't have to be like that."

Her mouth tightens. "Someone does. It'll put him on notice."

I roll my eyes. "It'll offend our neighbor — a woman we've known since we were kids." She stares at me, unmoved. I try a different tack. "And think about it. If he *is* a violent criminal — and I'm not saying he is — do you really want to piss him off?"

"I won't be bullied in my own neighborhood," Tori declares with a tight shake of her head.

I sigh again. "I'm guessing he won't be either," I say softly.

Tori's eyes bug. "Are you saying I'm a bully? Is that what you're saying?"

A bayberry bush has thorns pointing in every direction. Only a fool would walk straight into one. Clearly, I am such a fool.

"Tori, let me talk to Mrs. Vivian." I hear myself say. "I'll find out more about him and what's going on. Maybe the situation is temporary. Maybe... I don't know… maybe he's found God or something. It might not be as bad as you think."

She *hmphs* and rolls her eyes. "That's so like you," she mutters. "Ever the idealist. But fine, whatever. You talk to Mrs. Vivian and find out what the hell is going on with that jailbird grandson of hers. And you can casually mention that I'm thinking of buying a handgun."

CHAPTER FIVE

DREW

My first night on the outside seems as long as December.

I can't remember ever being so fucking cold. The futon mattress may be softer than my plastic-covered, prison-issue one, but if I lie straight, my heels stick off the end, so instead, I stretch out corner to corner, which feels risky after so long on a top bunk.

The AC blows straight through the afghan bedspread like a cold front. I try to keep my eyes shut and dig into my pillow against the blast, but the strain gives me a headache. After about an hour of this, I get up, cross the room, and shut the damn thing off.

Without the noise of the window unit, silence falls over the apartment. Absolute silence. But at least it's not freezing. I turn back and stop to glare at the futon. My head fizzes with the chatter of my cousins, aunts, and uncles. And my stomach groans against the glut of food Grandma Q served up. Brisket. Buttered corn. Fig preserves over ice cream. Like nothing I've had in years, and I've got the heartburn to prove it.

I might as well face it. I'm not going to sleep anytime soon.

Especially not after working out my grandmother's plans. I love her more than life, but I swear, that woman is a master manipulator. She may have been wearing a look of loving innocence, but she knew exactly what she was doing when she cornered my cousin Chip.

Apparently, Chip and his buddy Cody own a garage. Grandma Quincy asked Chip — in front of everyone — if he'd hire me. We were all sitting down to the feast she'd made, and Chip had just sunk his teeth into brisket-on-French-bread when she did it. I've never seen a picnic table full of people get so quiet so damn quick.

My cousin's startled eyes had cut to mine before he'd looked back at Grandma Quincy, but I saw the wariness in them. He wanted to hire me about as much as he wanted a rabid dog to kiss him full on the mouth.

With that memory, the apartment's silence seems to close around my throat. I yank open the door, practically bolt outside, and lean against the stair rail.

The buzz of locusts crowds my ears, and the familiar noise is a relief. Locusts clamor at Angola all summer long. Hot nights and the drone of their music go hand in hand. I sink down onto the landing and let my legs dangle over the edge. The middle rail hits me right at my chest, so I cross my arms on it and rest my chin, just listening.

Chip doesn't want to hire me, and I don't blame him, but I need a job, and working in a garage is something I can do.

Hell, I'd be good at it.

At Grandma Q's pointed question, Chip had mumbled something about looking into it, but he hardly sounded enthusiastic. Even though his feelings were obvious, Grandma Q still pulled me aside after dinner, telling me — not suggesting — but telling me to go over to the garage tomorrow to put in an application.

And I think I have to do it.

I don't want to put Chip in a tough spot, but who else would hire me? And maybe it wouldn't have to be for very long. Maybe if I work there for sixth months or a year until my probation is over, I could look for something else. With some experience on the outside, maybe another garage would take me on.

I close my eyes because trying to picture that far into the future is a mind fuck. Picturing tomorrow is only just bearable. I can barely handle getting from this moment to the next.

A flash of light behind my eyelids makes me lift them. I'm facing the back yard and the house behind Grandma Q's. I see what's caught my attention. A light in a second floor window.

A feminine shape moves behind thin curtains, and I remember the yoga lesson. And the girl next door.

She'd been staring right at me. I'd felt eyes on me all day from everyone, but sidelong glances. Furtive looks. My family trying to size me up — without acting like they were sizing me up. It had felt like ants crawling all over my skin.

But this was different.

I was talking to Grandma in the side yard right by the stairs of the apartment — right under where I'm sitting now — when I felt like I was being watched. I glanced behind Grandma Quincy to see her neighbor across the yard, eyes on me searching and curious.

It lasted only a second, but her stare seemed to lay me open. Like she was seeing everything I was trying to keep locked down. When she looked away, I felt released. Like a fish suddenly freed from a hook and dropped back into safe water.

Until she started the yoga practice.

And then my head might as well have been on a swivel. I'd find myself watching and yank my eyes

46

away, but they'd just travel back to her again. And again.

Maybe it was because I hadn't seen a woman who wasn't family or prison guard in eight years, but I don't think I'd ever watched anything so beautiful. Her body as a moving masterpiece. Her limbs were firm and toned. They flexed and lifted and stretched like she moved through water.

The shape flickers behind the curtain again, pulling me back to the now, and I'm certain it's her. I catch myself staring hard, trying to see through the gauzy fabric before I shake my head in disgust. One day out of prison, and I'm already committing a misdemeanor. Revised Statute 14:284. Peeping Tom.

Swinging my legs to the left, I shift myself ninety degrees, so I'm now facing a ligustrum hedge and the roof of Grandma Quincy's next door neighbor. Last I knew, Mr. Hardesty lived there, and he was at least seventy back then. Even if someone new has the place, there's not an unshuttered window in sight, and no lights burning either.

I cross my arms again over the railing and breathe in the night. The air is humid and still, but compared to the unnatural chill of the window unit, I welcome it. Nothing feels familiar but this. I recognized my aunts and uncles, and, of course, Annie and Grandma Q. But today I kept seeing Anthony in the faces of my cousins, and it was torture.

I used to see Anthony at Angola. In the west yard. In the mess hall. In fields harvesting soybeans. He'd flicker past the corner of my eye, and I'd do a double-take. I'd spot him a hundred yards away, and I'd take off in his direction, slowing as soon as I saw the

47

truth, but unable to turn back until I proved to myself it wasn't him.

I knew it wasn't him. It couldn't be him. But I would have been happy then to talk to his ghost.

I still would.

So seeing his face on my cousin — here at Grandma Quincy's where everything is both familiar and strange —might be enough to drive me crazy. Chip's grown up to look so much like him — except for the hair. Anthony's was curly. Unruly. And Chip's, though thick, is stiff and straight. And Chip's eyes are brown.

Anthony's were gray. Like mine. Like Annie's. Like Ma's.

But it doesn't matter. I sigh against the hot September night. If I go work for Chip, I won't be able to look him in the eye anyway.

My driver's license expired in 2012. I want to work on cars, but, at the moment, I can't even drive one. Not that I have one to drive. So unless I want my grandmother or my baby sister chauffering me all over town, I'm taking the bus.

I only rode it a handful of times when I was a kid, but I don't think the experience has improved much over the last eight years. It's running about ten minutes behind schedule, and by the time I climb aboard, after standing on the corner of St. Mary, my shirt is soaked through.

But if I'm telling the truth, it's not all because of the heat.

I don't know Chip anymore. He's three years older than me, and, yeah, we used to play as kids, but once he was in high school, he didn't need anything to do with me. Other than the occasional Sunday dinner and holidays, we never really saw each other.

If we'd been tight, this would be different. It wouldn't feel so much like asking for charity.

But charity — or maybe mercy — is what I get. Because when I arrive at C & C's Auto, it's not Chip I have to face, but his business partner Cody.

I recognize him from the old days. He was always hanging around with Chip. And he was always smiling.

The guy is smiling now.

Wearing blue coveralls and a wide grin, he gets up from a desk littered with papers and clipboards and walks toward me with his hand out.

"Drew! Great to see you, man!"

I blink, a little shocked at his welcome, and take his hand. The creases of his knuckles are lined with grease. That and the smell of tire rubber and WD-40 reminds me of the auto shop at Angola. Cody pumps my hand, meeting my gaze in a way most people in my own family didn't yesterday. And I'll admit, it's disorienting.

"Good to see you, too," I mumble. I hear the sound of a ratchet drill over my shoulder, and I resist the urge to turn toward it.

He drops my hand and folds his arms across his chest. Casual. Easy. "Chip said you'd be dropping by. Said you're looking for work." It's only now that his grin slips. "I'm afraid we don't have anything full-time. And I really only need somebody for small jobs... oil changes and battery replacements and that sorta thing."

49

I blink again. Is he already offering me work? Or is he trying to get me to find something better?

"I've gotta give the bigger jobs to my regular guys. At least for right now." Cody shrugs. "Low man on the totem pole. You know what I mean?"

Frowning, I find my voice. "Y-you mean you'll hire me?" I realize as I ask just how nervous I am he'll say no. Because I don't have any idea what I'll do if he does. And in the two minutes I've been in the garage, I've figured out I don't want to leave.

For the first time since I got out yesterday, I feel like I might be able to relax. The sights, sounds, and smells of this place feel like home. I'm itching to pick up a socket wrench and duck under the hood of any of the cars in the garage bays. Get to work and get out of my own head.

Something about my question makes Cody's grin stretch wider. "Well, yeah, I told you Chip and I talked about it. And you're Chip's family, right?" he asks, looking at me like I'm slow but in a way I know he means no insult. "And family helps out family."

I swallow, confused. I should just thank him, but I can't let it go. I clear my throat. "Is that what Chip said?"

His brows shift into a frown for just an instant, but the glimpse tells me all I need to know. "That's what *I* say."

No one's told me who has the controlling share of the garage, but now I'm guessing it's Cody. And I'll bet money it's Cody, not my cousin Chip, who's okay with me working here.

"So," he asks, the frown clearing and that unstoppable grin taking over again. "When do you want to start?"

Cody spends most of his morning with me. After I fill out employment forms, he gives me an old set of coveralls with the name *Danny* stitched over the chest, and puts me to work. He watches me do two oil changes before turning me loose on the steady stream of customers that run through the garage.

Chip gets back sometime around one — startling me again with his resemblance to Anthony — but other than giving me barely a nod when he first moves through the garage, he pretty much ignores me and goes about his business.

At five, I clock out, cross Johnston Street, and catch the bus back.

And I'm half-starved. Grandma Q made me a giant breakfast of eggs, bacon, and toast before I left on my job hunt, but that was hours ago.

I don't expect my grandmother to cook for me, but I know there's leftovers from yesterday. I've been fantasizing about a cold brisket sandwich for about the last two hours.

But when I open her kitchen door, the smell of smothered pork chops nearly brings me to my knees. Not only do I find Grandma Quincy at the stove with three saucepans going, but she's not alone. At first I assume the woman by her side is one of my cousins, but then the visitor turns.

And it's her.

The girl from yesterday. The yoga girl. She's standing in Grandma Q's kitchen, stirring a pan of sliced apples in what looks and smells like butter, sugar, and cinnamon. And she's smiling at me.

At *me.*

It's a smile so warm and open that I feel it. Like a hand on my bare chest.

"Oh, good," Grandma Q says, drying her hands on her blue apron and tilting her head toward her guest. "You're just in time. This is Evie Lalonde. She's our backdoor neighbor. Evie, this is my grandson, Andrew Moroux."

Evie Lalonde. I repeat her name to myself, wanting to save its music for later. It's a trick I learned in prison. Holding something in your mind is better than not holding it at all. Holding something beautiful in your mind can carry you a long way. Her name is beautiful. *She* is beautiful. Tomorrow, when I'm waiting to meet with my probation officer, I will hold Evie Lalonde in my mind.

Evie sets down the wooden spoon and offers me her hand, still smiling. "Hi Andrew. Nice to meet you."

For the second time today, I'm stunned someone wants to shake my hand. But that surprise is quickly replaced when her small palm presses against mine. Soft, warm, and grasping, this is the handshake of a sincere person.

That's another thing I learned in prison. Handshakes, fist bumps, hand clasps, hi-fives, hugs. The way a person presses flesh says everything. Either they do it because they have to, and they're pulling away even before they get there, or they're all in. They press. They seal. They make it mean something, and even if

52

you know they're bad news — I've known murderers who knew how to shake hands way better than drug dealers — with a real handshake, you know where you stand.

Evie Lalonde presses. Evie Lalonde seals. Her handshake is all in.

"It's Drew." I hear myself say, lost in the feel of her hand in mine.

"Drew," she echoes, her smile growing. Her eyes are a pale green. Like the underside of oak leaves. Her hair is as dark as Steen's syrup, a mass of tight curls pulled back into a ponytail. She nods. "That suits you better."

She must not know who I am or what I've done. She wouldn't be smiling this way if she did. And with this thought comes a heady buzz, because all of a sudden, I realize that this is bound to happen. Countless times. With hundreds of people.

Everyone from my old life knows about me. But there's a world of strangers who don't. Temptation, a beast with claws, digs deep into my soul. What could happen if she never knew about me?

With that thought, I drop her hand and rock back on my heels. My heart's pounding from the battle I've just won against myself, and I breathe in and out before I speak. "Yeah, Drew sounds a lot more like a guy who deserved eight years behind bars."

I watch as she blinks in shock and catches her plump bottom lip between her teeth. I've scared her, and I'm sorry for that, but it had to be done. She needs to know exactly what I am. More importantly, I need her to know.

But Evie surprises me when she shakes her head, her smile returning. "Nah. The name *Andrew* means *manly* or *masculine*. *Drew* is just a friendlier, more playful version of that."

Now I'm the one who's shocked. Either she isn't easily rattled, or she already knew about my time on The Farm. I shift my gaze to Grandma Q and find her grinning like a kid.

Oh, yeah. Master manipulator.

My focus shifts back to Evie in time to see her give a little shrug. "I have this thing about names. I love knowing what they mean."

I can't help it. I have to know. "So what does *Evie* mean?"

Her eyes light with amusement, and she bounces a little on her toes. The gesture is so sweet, I want to pat myself on the back for winning it before I shove the thought away. *"Evie is short for Evangeline, which means good news."*

I resist the urge to shake my head. She is definitely not good news. Not for me. Evie Lalonde is decidedly bad news. I've been in her company for less than five minutes, and she's made me forget who I've been and who I need to be.

It's time to say goodbye.

As hungry as I am, dinner will have to wait. I turn to Grandma Q. "I'm gonna go up and have a shower. You don't need to wait on me for dinner."

Grandma rolls her eyes. "Oh, pooh. As if I'd eat without you. But wait," she says, holding up a hand to stay my exit. Then she turns on her heels and fusses with something behind her. "Here, before you go up, try some of this zucchini bread. You must be starved."

She shuffles back and hands me a thick slice of baked bread dotted with chocolate chips, a pat of butter melting seductively across its center. Forgetting everything but my empty stomach, I grab it like the animal I am and bite into it.

"Mmm..." I moan, unashamed. The bread is spiced with cinnamon, and the sweetness of the melted chocolate chips paired with the salt of the butter has me closing my eyes like a drunk man. "Grandma, this is *the best.*"

She titters. "Don't tell me, Andrew. I didn't make it. Evie did."

My eyes fly open and land on the beautiful girl in my grandmother's kitchen as this slice of heaven melts on my tongue. As I look at her, I see two bright spots of color rise on her cheeks. I feel a powerful and unwelcome urge to taste them.

"Of course, I will take credit for the zucchini," Grandma Q says, jiggling her head with pride. "I gave Evie some over the fence this morning, and she just whipped that up this afternoon."

I swallow the bite and dip my head at the two of them. "Well, I guess I have you both to thank," I manage. I need to get out of here. I know this because leaving is suddenly the last thing I want to do. I let myself meet Evie's gaze, and I nod again, holding up the remaining scrap of zucchini bread. "Really. The best I've ever had."

And then I make myself walk away.

I take my time in the shower, all the while praying that Evie Lalonde will be gone once I head back to my grandmother's kitchen.

When I do, I have to admit to myself I'm disappointed my prayers were answered.

CHAPTER SIX

EVIE

His eyes are gray. Not light blue. Not hazel. Gray.

I've never seen anything like them. I want a closer look, but I don't think he'd like that. In fact, I don't think he's all that happy I'm here. When we shook hands, he looked like he wanted to beat a path to the door.

Maybe he doesn't like strangers. Or maybe he knows why I'm really here. Because I feel awful about questioning Mrs. Vivian this morning to satisfy Tori.

And Mrs. Vivian was really sweet about it. I told her I'd seen the family out in her yard yesterday and asked if it was someone's birthday.

Later, I keep thinking about that question. Didn't I know it wasn't someone's birthday? And if so, didn't my pretend ignorance constitute a lie? To make matters worse, she'd been so honest with me. She told me all about her grandson's homecoming. His time in prison. Even his crimes.

And I'd listened, feeling almost sick for prying into their private lives. All for what? To shut up my sister?

When Mrs. Vivian picked the three zucchini for me while we talked, all I'd wanted was to make amends. Does a loaf of zucchini bread make up for nosiness and duplicity?

I doubt it, but Drew seems to like it.

Drew Moroux is a big guy. And those coveralls don't really cover all that much. He's in amazing shape.

That much is obvious. And he's aptly named. He's masculine and then some.

Which is why when he closed his eyes just now and moaned over the taste of my zucchini bread, I had to stifle a giggle. It was just so cute.

I want to know more about him.

Like does he like all sweets or just spice breads? Why do the coveralls say *Danny* instead of *Drew?* And why did he say that about his name? About Drew being the name of someone who *deserved* eight years behind bars?

But I don't get the chance to ask any of this because he's gone too quickly.

Once the door shuts behind him, I turn and face Mrs. Vivian, who's smiling like she's in on a secret. I blink and smile back.

"I think he liked the bread," she says *sotto voce.*

I laugh. "It's my mom's recipe."

Mrs. Vivian narrows her smiling eyes. "I'm pretty sure your mama is still halfway across the world, right?"

"That's right. She won't be back until December."

"Mmm-hmm," she says with a nod. "Thought so. So why are you letting her take credit for the quality of your baking?"

A nervous laugh escapes me. "I'm not," I deny.

Mrs. Vivian turns the flame down on her smothered pork chops before she crosses her arms and eyes me. She nods her head toward the door where Drew just left. "That boy is having a hard time of it — even after eight years of hard time — and in the thirty seconds he was scarfing down your zucchini bread, it looked like he got to forget about all that." Mrs. Vivian

58

clucks her tongue. "You, young lady, did that. Not your far-flung mama."

I smile, conceding victory. Who am I to argue with Mrs. Vivian Quincy? Besides, what she says and the gratitude I see in her eyes makes me feel as though I've atoned for my prying. "Fair enough," I say, peeking at the cinnamon apples she asked me to stir. They look so good. Gooey and golden brown. I'll have to try making them myself.

"Would you like to stay for dinner?"

I snap my gaze up at her. "Oh, thanks, but I have a class tonight." As good as the apples look — and smell — I wouldn't accept even if I were free. Because, judging from my brief encounter with him, I don't think her grandson would really want me to join. "In fact, I really should be going."

"Another time then," Mrs. Vivian says, shuffling toward me before hugging my neck. "It's nice to have young people around."

The plump softness of her embrace reminds me of childhood and safety. Both of my grandmother's are gone, and I haven't hugged my own mother in months, so I cherish the feeling.

"It's always nice to see you, Mrs. Vivian."

My yoga-in-the-park class is small, but satisfying. I have two repeat customers and two newbies who both take my card, so I drive home wreathed in peace and grateful for the day's events. I pull into the driveway and see that Tori is home, but I'm not going to let that weigh down my fluffy mood.

And as luck would have it, when I step into the kitchen, the air still redolent with the scent of zucchini bread, I find it empty, but as I reach the top of the stairs,

59

intent on grabbing a shower before fixing some dinner, I freeze outside of Tori's bedroom door.

Because I hear her crying.

At once, I raise my fist to knock, but I hold myself back before my knuckles meet wood. I know my sister, and she won't like me knowing she's upset. Tori hates being vulnerable. I want to find out what's wrong, and I want to ask how I can help, but my intrusion now will only make things worse.

As quietly as I can, I step back from the door and close myself behind my own.

Ten minutes later, after I've showered and wrapped my hair in a towel, I find a text on my phone.

Tori: Mom called. She wants you to Skype.

My blood ices over. Is something wrong? It's almost two in the morning in Nigeria. Something's wrong. Is this why Tori was crying? If Mom wants me to call her this late, then something must have happened to Dad, and it's then that I notice the missed call on my phone from Mom.

"Oh shit."

I dart around my room, tripping my way into underwear, tugging a stubborn racerback bra over my still damp skin. I throw on a top and shimmy into one of my many yoga lounge pants, open up my laptop and mistyped my password twice before I force myself to go still. I close my eyes and take a full, slow, deep breath. My exhale is shaky, but at least the breath has quieted my racing mind.

I open my eyes, type the password, and Skype call my mother. It takes so long for her to answer, my mind starts running through terrible scenarios. But then her smiling face takes up my laptop screen.

"Hi, angel! How ya doing?" She squints at the screen through her glasses. "Is your hair wet?" She's in her silk blue and white striped pajamas. She looks tired, but I can tell she's curled up in her favorite chair, the lamp glowing beside her. The windows that look out onto their gorgeous garden are dark.

"Mom, what's wrong? Why are you calling this late? Is Dad okay?" I can see just looking at her there's no emergency, but I can't help asking.

Mom tilts her head to the side, pursing her bottom lip with a regretful smile. "Everything's fine. I didn't mean to scare you." She shrugs and shakes her head, wrinkling her nose. "I just can't sleep. I think it's hormones."

Mom turned fifty in March, and the way she tells it, she got her first hot flash from blowing out her birthday candles.

The tightness in my belly unspools. I let go a sigh. "Sorry you can't sleep." I scoot back against my headboard, tuck my legs into a lotus pose, and prop the laptop on one knee.

"Honey, tilt the camera up. I'm staring at your neck," Mom says.

I laugh and do as she asks. "So other than insomnia, what else is going on?"

Her hazel eyes turn owlish behind her glasses. "I think I should be asking you." A small crease appears between her brows. "Tori says you're going on a date Friday with a boy you despise and baking for an ex-con?"

I palm my forehead. Leave it to Tori to dramatize the most mundane of events. "Ugh. Is that what she told you?"

61

I see her fighting a smile. "Pretty much. Want to sort out fact from fiction?"

That's when it hits me. It's all fact.

"Well… Drake is one of my yoga students, and I sort of…" I make a face, "owed it to him."

Mom arches a thin, perfect brow over the rim of her glasses. "You *owe* someone you don't like *a date?* I feel sure your father and I raised you better than that," she says in her teasing tone, but she leans closer as though to look me in the eyes, but really, she's just looking at a screen. And I'm looking at her image on the screen in front of me, not directly into the camera.

So neither one of us is really seeing the other.

"How, exactly, did that happen?" she asks.

I sigh. "He's been bugging me to go out with him, and Monday he hurt himself in my class, and I felt bad for him, and I guess also a little responsible, and…" I shake my head and roll my eyes. "I guess I couldn't say no."

Mom studies me, a smile curling one corner of her mouth. She's always been so beautiful. Her platinum blonde hair has lost a little of its luster to a light gray, but she's as glamorous as ever. Even at two in the morning.

Tori got her coloring, but I look like Dad. Dark eyes, curly brown hair.

"My soft-hearted girl," she says with a sigh. "You'd better be careful. You'll find yourself married to some poor slob just because you felt sorry for him."

"Mom."

My tone, which really comes out sounding like the one I used at sixteen, makes her laugh. I miss that laugh. I miss her.

Her laugh ends in a kind of humming lilt I've known all my life. "Just promise me you won't let this Drake character take advantage of your good nature."

"It'll be fine, Mom." But if I wasn't looking forward to Friday night before, I'm all out dreading it now. I already know it's going to be awkward, and now I'll probably have to tell her all about it when we have our family Skype on Sunday.

Thanks a lot, Tori.

Then her gaze sharpens with interest. "And what's this about baking for criminals? Is this a new charity endeavor of yours?"

"Tori," I mutter under my breath. "I made a zucchini bread for Mrs. Vivian and her grandson, that's all—"

Mom shoots up so that the top of her head is out of frame. "Her grandson? The Moroux boy? He's been released?" Her hazel eyes are wide now, magnified by her bifocals.

Her surprise throws me. As does the fact she knows his name. "I — yeah, I mean, I guess so." What kind of answer is that? Of course he's been released. It's not like he escaped.

He didn't escape, right? Mrs. Vivian wouldn't be harboring an escaped felon.

Mom's focus drifts off screen. "I guess it *has* been that long. My, how time flies," she says distractedly. She blinks and looks back at the camera again, frowning. "You said you made the bread for Mrs. Vivian and her grandson. Was he visiting her or..." She stops, seeming to be waiting for me to finish her sentence. I do.

"He's living in the apartment above the garage," I supply.

63

Her soft *Oh* and the way she draws her bottom lip between her teeth unsettle me. "Mom, what?"

Her frown deepens. "What was his name again? Started with an 'A.' Alex? Andre?"

"It's Andrew," I say, and then because I can't help it, "Drew."

Her focus sharpens again, and I swear, it's like we're in the same room. It reminds me of being sixteen, when she used to grill me on Friday nights before I was allowed to leave the house. *Are you going to Tracy's? Will her parents be home? Will boys be there? Do you know you can call me anytime, and I'll come get you — no questions asked?*

"Evie, you know I adore Mrs. Vivian, but as I recall, those boys were a heap of trouble before all of that happened," Mom says, a no-nonsense look on her face. "I can't say I'm pleased to hear the Moroux boy is living there."

I think of the man I met this afternoon. The one who couldn't seem to get away from me fast enough. The one who let his guard down for about five seconds to enjoy a chocolaty slice of zucchini bread. The one who wore shame like a weight around his neck. He didn't look like trouble.

He looked like a wounded animal. Or a lost boy. Skittish. Untrusting. Hungry.

"I met him today." My voice is casual, but I'm aware that I want it to sound casual. "I don't think you have anything to worry about."

"Evangeline." Mom eyeballs me over the rim of her glasses, one brow arched. "Do I need to remind you about the raccoons?"

I give my mom the stink eye. "Mom, please. I'm not nine."

She's still pinning me with her stare. "You're not nine, but some aspects of your personality have not changed. Those raccoon kits would have torn you to shreds if your father hadn't stopped y—"

"*Mom,*" I drone, growing embarrassed. And irritated. Mom — and Dad, and Tori, for that matter — are always bringing up this story.

And despite my protests, she doesn't stop. "We let you and your sister explore the woods for ten minutes while we got the tent set up and—"

"And, yes, I know," I edge in, my tone flinty. I tilt my head from left to right as I regale her with the details. "We found the dead mama raccoon. Then we heard the kits crying in the hollow of a water oak. And I wanted to rescue them. I remember, Mom."

My mother has been nodding with each remembered fact. "Yes, and you would have crawled into that hollow to fetch them, even though they were hissing and spitting at you like a pair of bandit-masked demons."

"I was going to throw a camping blanket over them like a net," I say in my defense. "They wouldn't have hurt me—"

Mom's sudden laughter interrupts me. "Do you hear yourself?"

Humorless, I cock a brow at my mother and wait for her laughter to subside. "I honestly don't know why we're even talking about raccoons, Mom," I level.

"Oh, no?" She's still smiling, but there's an edge to her expression I can't at first decipher. And then I do. Exasperation. That's what it is. She sighs. "Well, I'll spell

65

it out for you, kid. You are too tender-hearted for your own good, and one day, it's going to put you on the path of someone who's going to tear you up a whole lot worse than those baby raccoons would have."

"Mom," I grumble, speaking through clenched teeth. "Give me a little credit. I'm twenty-one, and I'm a pretty good judge of character—"

"Then promise me you'll stay away from that Moroux boy."

"Oh my God, Mom." My voice pitches higher. "I made Mrs. Vivian a loaf of bread. And do you know why?" The words ring with a shrill edge. "Because Tori was so freaked out that Mrs. Vivian was letting her grandson live in her garage, I was afraid she was going to say something rude to her."

Mom looks surprised at my outburst. She opens her mouth to speak, but I keep going.

"Do you have any idea what she's like these days? She's horrid to *everyone*. You're on another continent," I snap. "But I'm living under the same roof, and I'd rather not have all of the neighbors giving us the evil eye because she's made an ass of herself by sticking her nose where it doesn't belong or saying something absolutely *vile* to someone."

The look of exasperation is gone. Now Mom looks concerned. "Evie—"

"So I took it upon myself to find out what the deal was with Mrs. Vivian and her grandson. So I could reassure Tori that he's not, in fact, likely to break in during the dead of night and slit our throats." As I say this, there's a part of my mind — a detached, observant, and completely grounded part — that notes the sarcasm dripping from my words. And the pulse pounding in

66

my neck. This unwavering and timeless part recognizes that I have left it's centering guidance and am now going rogue. "And guess what, Mom? He's not. He practically scurried out of Mrs. Vivian's kitchen when he found me there this afternoon. The guy had *zero* interest in talking to me whatsoever."

The grounded observer in my mind notes a root of disappointment attached to these words in particular.

And that is the thought that rises through my outrage and flashes across the forefront of my mind.

I wanted Drew Moroux to talk to me.

I clamp my mouth shut as if there's a risk I'd say this aloud.

Holy crap. Did I really want that?

At the speed of thought, I catalogue the memories of Drew Moroux I've gathered. The moment our gazes locked yesterday. The way his gray eyes pierced mine as he shook my hand today in Mrs. Vivian's kitchen. The thrill that feathered up my middle when he asked what my name meant.

Oh, yeah. I wanted him to keep talking to me. I can't deny I was disappointed when he walked away.

Mom eyes me for a minute, clearly waiting to see if there's more to my invective. But I'm done. I'm now marinating in the chagrin and regret that follows nearly every mindless release. I can't help but mentally scold myself. I should have paid better attention to the current of my emotions as Mom and I talked.

In a flash, I recall everything I've just said, and close my eyes, wincing. If Tori heard, she'll—

"Well, I have to say, I'm relieved to hear that."

My eyes snap open. "What?" I ask, thrown.

67

Mom gives me an arch look. "That the Moroux boy wasn't interested in talking to you." Her expression turns purt as she mutters, "Though I can't imagine why."

"Mom," I mutter, unamused.

She giggles. "At least I don't have to worry about you getting mixed up with him."

"Mom." I am more than ready to end this conversation, but she narrows her eyes at me.

"I don't have to worry, do I, Evie?"

A tempting voice in my ear urges me to tell her exactly what she wants to hear. But I can't. I know innately that I can't give my mother the reassurance she wants.

I was in Drew Moroux's company for less than five minutes today. And that's not enough. I know — like I know the way to the studio and how to execute a flawless crow pose — that I want to talk to him again.

"Mom, worry is a waste of consciousness," I tell her. Not a lie, but also not the answer she wants to hear.

She sighs. "You always say that."

"Well, it's true."

She lifts her chin, looking mildly affronted. "Well, I do worry. About you. And your sister. What else can I do from so far away?" Her affronted look morphs into one both sad and guilt-ridden. "Speaking of Tori… what's going on?"

As if on cue, my phone pings. I glance down and read the text.

Tori: Since I'm obviously so HORRID and VILE, please don't feel compelled to speak to me. In fact, I'd rather you not. I might say something rude and offend my perfect sister.

68

My stomach plummets and blood rushes to my cheeks.

"Oh, shit."

CHAPTER SEVEN

DREW

It's less than a five-minute walk from the Patterson Street bus stop to the probation office on West Willow, but I feel like a neon sign the whole time.

I was used to being one of only a few white guys in the dorm or the mess hall or the yard. But I belonged there. Sure, I had to take my share of licks the first year or so and then dish out some of my own to earn my place. Make it clear nobody needed to mess with me to prove a point. But after that, I belonged. Nobody thought twice about it.

But as I walk up West Willow Street, every single pair of eyes that passes me, whether in a car on the road or in the skull of that old lady crossing the street headed to the Health Unit — is staring at me with one question.

What the hell is he doing here?

Don't get me wrong. White privilege is real. And it's everywhere. Especially in Louisiana's penal system. I don't for a minute think I know what it means to be a minority.

I just know that right now, I stick out like a trail of toilet paper out of the back of some schmuck's pants.

And that scenario doesn't sound so bad once I meet my P.O., Mr. Alan Overton.

The guy is about fifty-five. His hair and skin are one color — a color I could only describe as sand. He's unsmiling. Maybe because his office smells like vinegar.

By way of greeting, he slides a specimen cup across his desk. "Mandatory drug test. Tell me now. Are you going to pass?"

"Yes, sir."

Angola has no shortage of drugs. And, yes, I've taken them. Eight years is a long time, after all. But I haven't done anything in forever. Not since Annie, who was sixteen at the time, *casually* asked me in one of our phone conversations what I thought about marijuana.

I told her to stay the hell away from it, and then I took my own advice.

Overton follows me to the restroom and stands behind a partition while I face the urinal.

Now, I've heard guys on The Farm talk about beating the system by taping a Ziploc bag of clean piss right by their junk and tearing a hole in it at the right moment. Hell, one guy smuggled a vial up his ass to keep the stuff body temperature.

I think about this while I'm trying to take a leak. How the hell did that guy get it out with some dude watching over his shoulder?

Back in Overton's office, we sit across from each other, and he stares at me in silence for what seems like ten minutes.

"You good-timed out, but before that you never sought parole."

This isn't a question, so I don't feel the need to answer. Most people don't believe me when I say I deserved to stay right where I was. But Louisiana prisons are crowded. Guys who've done three-quarters of their time can get out for good behavior. Even if they don't particularly want to.

Overton lowers his pale blond brows. What they lack in color, they make up for in volume. "Does that mean you *liked* prison?"

"No, sir. I did not like prison."

His frown deepens. "So, then are you *lazy?* Too lazy to meet with your attorney and seek your parole hearings?"

The accusation chafes. Even as a thief, I wasn't lazy. Anyone who wants something has to work for it. I like work. I like problems that need to be solved. A car engine is a great place to solve problems.

"I'm not lazy, Mr. Overton."

He leans back in his desk chair, which issues a squeaking protest. "Good. Because one of the conditions of your probation is employment."

I nod. "I got a job yesterday, sir."

"Where?"

"C & C Auto. On Johnston Street."

He shifts his gaze to the dinosaur of a computer on his desk and grunts. "Worked in auto tech," he mutters under his breath, to whom I'm not sure. Then he glances at me. "Are you familiar with the terms of your probation?"

I nod again. "My lawyer went over them with me last month."

He looks unimpressed. "Well, I'm going over them again."

So he does. No drugs. No alcohol. No weapons. No associating with known felons. I must maintain employment. I must maintain housing. I must not commit any misdemeanors nor felonies. I must not leave the state of Louisiana. I must meet with my probation officer once every thirty days here in his office. I must submit to drug testing at each visit. I must submit to his unannounced visits and search of my dwelling. Should I follow all of these terms for one year from my release date, I will be cleared from probation.

72

"You understand, Mr. Moroux, that the violation of any of these terms of your probation means that you would be returned to Angola or any other state facility to serve out the remainder of your ten-year sentence?"

I nod. "Yes, sir."

He raises a bushy brow. "Tell me now. Am I going to catch you in violation of any of the above."

"No, sir, you will not," I tell him, speaking truth. "I have no intention of violating any of these terms or returning to prison."

He still looks unimpressed. "Why should I believe you?"

I stare at him and decide to tell it straight. "Mr. Overton, I live with my eighty-three-year-old grandmother." He doesn't blink. The look on his face would have me believe every ex-con lives with his granny. "I don't wish to disappoint her again. And I'm pretty sure if I did, she'd skin me alive."

Five minutes later, I'm walking back to the bus stop.

Because of my meeting with my P.O., Cody told me not to come in today, and now that the meeting's over, I have no idea what the hell to do with myself. The bus ride only takes about thirty minutes, and after a sweaty, three block walk, I'm back at Grandma Q's.

But I can't bring myself to head back up to the apartment, and if I go inside the house, Grandma will just fuss over me.

I need to make myself useful. I scan Grandma's yard. The grass is cut, the edges trimmed, and her vegetable garden is well tended.

I know she spends at least an hour in her garden every day, and that is most definitely her territory, but I

73

wonder who's mowing her lawn. If she's paying for a service, that needs to change. I should be doing it. Of course, I'd need a mower.

With that thought, I check the side door of the garage, find it open, and push my way inside.

And all thought of looking for a lawn mower vanishes when I see it. Anthony's 1992 Toyota Supra turbo. Black. Liftback two door.

I lean against the door sill as the floor rolls under my feet. A buzzing that sounds faintly like a tornado siren peals through my head. The last time I saw this car — rode in it — was that night.

My vision tunnels, and I back out of the garage. I stagger to the picnic table in the yard and practically collapse onto it. With my face pressed to the wood and my heels digging into the ground, I try to will the dizziness away. Instead, a sinister nausea swells inside me.

Anthony worshiped that car. He worked two summers at Sonic, squirreling away every penny to save for it. He bought it at the end of his senior year and took me everywhere in it.

He worked for it. When Anthony wanted something, he fucking worked for it.

Unless he was with me.

Why couldn't that old guy have shot me instead? I was standing right there, stuffing his wife's jewelry into my backpack. Anthony had been at the window, about to toss his bag — with the guy's laptop, Rolex, and 9mm tucked away inside.

We would have been out of there in twenty seconds.

Why couldn't he have shot *me?*

The old guy had fired once. Later, he'd said he hadn't meant to hit either of us. A warning shot. Just to keep us from running. Well, that warning shot landed in my brother's neck, and he'd dropped like a stone.

With my head pressed to the wood of the picnic table, I can feel the midday sun beating down on the back of my neck. My eyes are in line with a gap in the table between the red-painted planks. I can see my feet and the hard-packed dirt beneath the table. A carpenter ant moving at top speed tears first over one shoe and then the other before veering right and disappearing beneath the bench.

If I would have been the one who was shot and killed, would Anthony be sitting right here? Wishing he was dead?

Well, he wouldn't have picked up a lamp and thrown it at the old guy the way I did. That bumped my charges up from simple burglary to aggravated. My lawyer had tried to claim it was self-defense, seeing as my brother had just been shot in the neck and was bleeding out on the floor.

I wasn't even thinking when I threw it. Not really. I just needed it for cover. Something to distract the guy long enough so I could get to Anthony and try to stop the frantic spurting of blood.

I didn't think he'd die. Not then. Not when he lost consciousness seconds later. Not even seconds after that when the blood stopped seeping through my fingers.

The guy had called 911. The ambulance — and police — were on their way. They'd save him. Of course, they were going to save him.

I mean, this was Anthony. My big brother. He couldn't die.

When I heard the sirens approach, I was relieved. I knew we were in a shit ton of trouble. And we'd probably do time, but we'd live to tell about it.

One of the counselors at Angola — Jerry Gunderson, the one I liked best — once told me that denial protects us.

I must have been in the throes of some pretty fucking serious denial to think my brother could survive getting his neck blown open.

I lift my head and rub my eyes as if I could wipe away the image. It used to be all I'd see. Every time I closed my eyes.

Ergo, Zoloft.

"Shit," I mutter aloud. My supply runs out tomorrow. "What the hell am I—"

"Drew?"

I freeze, my hands still covering my eyes. It's her. Even though I've only heard it once, I recognize her voice.

Evie Lalonde.

I drop my hands and blink at the vision of her crossing her lawn, flanked by a sleek, golden dog. And her legs — long, lean, and mostly bare in those light blue shorts — move in fleet strides.

"Are you okay?" she calls across our yards, and now I can see she's frowning as she approaches the fence.

How do I answer that? No, I'm definitely not okay. That's probably obvious.

She reaches the fence, her eyes sweeping over my face. I compose my most stoic expression. Prison is the

76

best place for honing a stoic expression. Unless it's anger, any other emotion is a liability.

Except humor. Laughter is its own shield, but there's no way I could summon a laugh right now. And if I could, I'd probably look insane. Hanging my head one minute, and cracking up the next.

Evie tilts her chin to one side, seeming to scrutinize me. "Bad day?"

And it's the shape of her mouth that undoes me. She's not smiling. Not really. But there's something soft and friendly about the line of her mouth. A compassionate concern that's disarming.

Yes, *disarming*. That's a good word for her. The look of her takes away not only any weapons I might carry but any protections as well. She's dis*armoring*. dis-*shielding*. I feel like I've been left wide open.

I shrug. "I've had better."

Her eyes brighten. I wonder if she's questioning the likelihood of that. I mean, I just got out of prison. Exactly how many better days could there have been?

A smile spreads over her face, and she tucks a springy, dark curl behind one ear. "Tell me. What constitutes a good day for Drew Moroux?"

The question takes me completely off guard. On so many fronts. For one, I'm almost knocked over sideways by the fact that she's asking. For another, I have no idea anymore.

I could tell her what made up a good day at Angola. That's easy. First of all, the best days would have to be between late October and early April. Anytime when the lows dip below seventy. When you can work in the auto shop without sweat running into your eyes. Because then you've got to wipe your eyes to clear them. And there's always, and I mean always, grease on your hands.

Every day in the summer, I'd leave the shop looking like barbecued raccoon.

Another mark of a good day on The Farm was gumbo. It might turn up on the menu when there was a nip in the air. The kitchen crew at Agnola doesn't mess around. Cooking is serious business. And The Farm is called The Farm for a reason.

People on the outside pay high dollar for farm-to-table cuisine. Well, inmates raise and grow almost everything they eat. Of course, our farm-to-table was nothing fancy. Beans and rice made up a good chunk of what we got. Still, I never minded beans and rice.

"Nothing special," I answer finally. "A day that's not too hot and good food on the table."

In response, Evie Lalonde shades her eyes, glances up at the noon-day sky, and wrinkles her nose. "I guess today doesn't count as not too hot."

I shake my head, feeling the sweat trickle down the back of my neck. "Nope." I'm sure my T-shirt is darkened with perspiration. Some of it's from the heat; it's as humid as dog breath, a typical September day in Louisiana. But some of it, I know, is from the shock of seeing Anthony's car. That Supra in the garage is like a finger pointing right at me.

You. You did this, it says.

I shudder with the thought, and Grandma Q's neighbor doesn't miss it.

A line appears between her pretty brows. "You sure you're all right? How long have you been sitting out here in the sun?"

78

I wipe the heel of my hand across my slick forehead. "Not that long," I say, wanting to brush off her concern.

But Evie Lalonde is not easily brushed off.

"You should move over here," she says, gesturing to the two plastic Adirondack chairs someone dragged beneath the live oak in Grandma Q's back yard. They're just feet away from her.

I know better. I tell myself I know better, but I move anyway.

The two chairs are facing our house, their backs to her, but I grab one and whirl it around. I perch on the end, elbows on my knees, and look up to find her smiling. We're under the shade of the same tree, the roots of the oak spreading out and warping the base of the fence that separates us.

She's watching me, and, I swear, it's only her smile that makes it bearable. I don't even deserve to be talking to someone like her. To any girl. To anyone.

But her smile — soft, natural, like the opening of a flower — makes me forget that.

"What are you grinning at?" I hear myself ask, while my own grin, foreign and unpracticed, rearranges the planes of my face. My cheeks feel rubbery, like I've just had a shot of novocaine in the gums.

When she answers, her voice is low, almost inaudible. "I asked you to sit down, and you did."

My eyebrows climb. "And that's a surprise?" Wouldn't any warm-blooded male on the planet sit if this woman asked him to? Hell, I bet most of the cold-blooded ones would as well. I think she could command even snakes and alligators to do her bidding.

Evie nods, her smile stretching. "It is. I got the feeling last night that you didn't much care for my company."

Regret assaults me. "I'm sorry I gave that impression. It wasn't your company I disapproved of." My voice drops lower of its own accord. "It was mine."

She seems to absorb my words before tilting her chin to the right and assessing me. "Your grandmother's right about you."

My insides shrivel. *Good God, what did Grandma Quincy say?*

"Oh, yeah?" I put on my best prison yard stare. Who's interested? Not this guy.

"Yeah." Evie's smile turns teasing, and her green eyes light with mischief.

We stare at each other, and I see she's calling my bluff. If I want to know what my grandmother told her, I've got to ask.

"Well, aren't you going to tell me what she's right about?"

Evie narrows her smiling eyes as if she's debating whether or not she should share. I feel like she's dismantling me with her gaze. Taking me apart bit by bit, the way I might take apart a carburetor.

It's a look that makes me feel like a rare commodity. Maybe even like I'm the only man on earth.

And if I were, it wouldn't really matter what I'd done. Would it?

Her next words pull me out of this mini-fantasy.

"She says you're hard on yourself. And, yeah, I agree."

A splash of cold water in the face couldn't have sobered me better. Too hard on myself? I wear my

80

brother's blood on my hands. There's no such thing as too hard. But, obviously, talking to Evie Lalonde is a sign I'm going soft. I get to my feet.

"Grandma Quincy's getting old. She doesn't remember everything like she should. Have a nice day, Evie." And I'm moving away from her as fast as I can without actually breaking into a run.

"Drew! Wait!" She calls after me. "I-I'm sorry. I didn't mean to offend you."

I turn back to her because I can't help it. "You didn't offend me. You just reminded me I shouldn't be talking to you."

Her face screws into a frown. An adorable frown. "But why not? What did I do?"

She looks so distraught — this girl I've just met but can't stop thinking about — that I actually take two steps in her direction. It's not her fault I'm unfit company. I need to tell her as much so she'll stop looking at me that way.

"You didn't do anything. I'm the problem, and you're better off keeping your distance."

Evie executes a slow nod. "Oh, I see," she says, crossing her arms over her chest. "That dangerous are you?" There's no missing the sarcasm in her voice.

What can I say to this? I'd never hurt anyone. Not again. I don't even want to pretend that I would. But she needs to stay away.

"Just because I wouldn't hurt someone doesn't mean I'm safe."

Her green eyes flare with amusement, and I know she's trying not to laugh at me. Dammit. No one in Angola laughed at me. Except A.J., of course. But he laughed at everything.

81

Evie holds my gaze as she takes an exaggerated step backward. "Am I safe now?"

I roll my eyes, but I work hard to keep my mouth a flat line. "How old *are* you?" I ask with censure.

"Twenty-one." She ignores my tone. "How old are you?"

I shake my head, refusing to take her bait.

She brings an index finger up to her sensual lips and taps it lightly against them. I swallow. It's so fucking pretty.

"Let's see." Her eyes take me in, assessing me from head to toe. "You're in your twenties. That's obvious. Too young-looking to be thirty… "

She watches me for confirmation, but I give nothing away. That doesn't mean I feel nothing. Behind my wooden exterior, my heart is racing. Heat flames my cheeks because, for the first time in eight years, a woman is checking me out.

And not just any woman.

A goddamn beautiful, fearless, zucchini-bread-baking, yoga-posing, legs-that-start-on-terra-firma-and-stretch-all-the-way-to-heaven woman who knows I've just gotten out of prison and wants to talk to me anyway.

Jesus Christ, I should totally walk away, but I fucking can't.

"And, as everybody knows, you've been gone for awhile." She keeps that sharp focus right on me as she says this. No glancing away. No dropping her voice to a whisper.

My ab muscles jump as though she's touched my middle.

She narrows that gaze on me still. "Mrs. Vivian said it was eight years?" Her statement comes out a question. When I nod in spite of myself, something softens in her expression. And this time her voice does drop. "You must have been a baby."

"I wasn't a baby," I say, shaking my head. "I was a grown-ass man."

"Hmm," she mutters doubtfully, the softness gone. "Did you know that the male brain doesn't reach full maturity until age twenty-five?"

I blink. "Where the hell did you hear that?"

Evie gives me a half shrug. "I read it in *Psychology Today.* You can look it up online." She watches me for a reaction, but I give her none. "So, basically, you were still a kid, still making decisions the way a kid does, when you—"

"I was eighteen when I broke into that house and got my brother killed," I spit out, my voice venomous. "Not a kid. Totally legal."

Her expression doesn't change at my biting tone. She looks completely calm. Not startled. Not even offended.

Who is this girl?

"So that means you're like twenty-six or twenty-seven right now," Evie says, and she smiles with self-congratulation, completely ignoring my outburst.

I give up. She's too adorable. "Twenty-six."

She lifts her chin, sizing me up further. "And when's your birthday?"

I debate not telling her, but I have a feeling she'd figure it out on her own anyway. "April 28th."

She throws her head back and laughs at the sky. "Oh my God!"

My brows drop. This is not the response I expected. "What's so funny?"

83

Evie frames her forehead with her hands, still laughing as though I've just made the best joke ever. I'd be embarrassed, but I'm sort of mesmerized watching her laugh. Her all-out smile is brilliant. Radiant.

She's wearing her hair pulled back again, those dark curls just barely tamed by a light blue elastic band. What would happen if it just snapped under the pressure, and her curls fell around her shoulders?

What the hell am I thinking?

I shake my head, irritated with myself. "Yeah, April 28th is hilarious, isn't it?"

"No." She gives a sigh, recovering her breath and meeting my confused gaze. "You're a Taurus."

"A Taurus," I repeat, picturing the Fords specifically designed for grandmothers and school librarians. "As in the *car?*"

This sets her off again, and she laughs with abandon. She's laughing *at me,* and for the first time in my life, I don't care.

"No. Your sign. Taurus. The bull."

I give her the side-eye. "Oh, you're one of *those.*" My tone is light, teasing, but really? My sign? Give me a break.

Still grinning, she rolls her eyes. *"Such* a Taurus," she mutters.

"You say that like it's a bad thing. What's wrong with being a Taurus? If any of that stuff were real, I mean."

Evie *tsks.* "It's not a *bad* thing. It's just so obvious now that you're a Taurus. I should have guessed it before."

I shouldn't ask. I just shouldn't. "Why?"

She looks almost giddy. "Because you're clearly very stubborn—"

"What?! I'm n—"

"And once you make up your mind about something, it's almost impossible for anyone to convince you you're wrong." She lifts her shoulder in a shrug. "Like a bull."

"What if I'm not wrong?" I ask, sensing she's referring to the warnings I've given her about me.

"Well, that's just the thing. A typical Taurus usually doesn't bother to question. They're very fixed in their beliefs, so they tend to be pretty conservative and narrow-minded and—"

"Wow, this keeps getting better and better."

She frowns at me. "Don't get offended. That's just one side of the spectrum. Tauruses have some wonderful attributes."

I nod, mocking. "Sure. Bull-headed. Closed-minded. What could be better?"

Her eyes snap with a kind of green ire. "For one, they're very rational and pragmatic..."

"Mmm-Hmm. Too logical to buy into any horoscope bullshit," I mutter, beginning to enjoy myself. And that enjoyment doubles when her jaw cocks to the side.

God, she's gorgeous.

"And being an earth sign, they're very grounded. Stable. Reliable. That kind of thing." She speaks through gritted teeth, but she's not fooling me. There's a smile just waiting to show itself behind the taut lines around her mouth.

"*Earth sign* sounds like crap, but I'll take *stable and reliable.*"

85

The nostrils of her pretty, straight nose flare. "Because of this, they are very loyal and can be great friends." She gives me a pointed look. "If they ever manage to make any, of course."

Laughter erupts from me, sudden and loud. I think it startles her, but not half as much as it shocks me. I can't remember the last time I laughed like this. It's different, laughing on the inside. Inmates laugh, of course. But there's nowhere for it to go. Every burst of laughter is weighed down by the knowledge that no one there is free.

I've forgotten what it feels like to really laugh on the outside. Until now. And it feels fucking great. I fix my eyes on the beauty that is Evie Lalonde and laugh my ass off.

By the time I'm done, she's beaming, giggling right along with me.

"So, be honest," I say, once I can speak. "Is Taurus the worst one? The worst… sign or whatever?"

She rolls her eyes. "Hardly. That would be Leo." Evie shakes her head. "So full of themselves."

I chuckle. "You're really into this stuff."

She shrugs. "It's interesting. It certainly doesn't explain everything about a person, but it's surprising to me how dead-on it can be."

I should leave it at that, leave altogether, but I really just want her to keep talking. "So, what's the opposite of Taurus? The least grounded, least rational?" I stop myself from saying *most irrational* when I see that ire return to her eyes.

"Not my sign," she says tartly.

"Oh?" I tease.

Those nostrils flare again.

86

"Actually, the direct opposite on the Zodiac, which would be the sign directly six months apart, is Scorpio, but Scorpio and Taurus actually have some traits and values in common, so they aren't contrasts of each other if that's what you mean."

I feel the corners of my mouth turn up, and I really can't help it.

"Don't laugh at me!" But her scolding falls flat when she can't even yell at me without laughing.

I shake my head, wanting to show contrition, but unable to keep a straight face. "I'm sorry. I'm sorry. You just take this so seriously. I'm..." I search for the right words. Words that will leave room for my extreme skepticism while still showing her respect "I'm not used to considering things from... a less than scientific perspective."

"A *scientific* perspective," she echoes, and the way she emphasizes *scientific* actually makes me a little nervous. Like I've just entered a debate I haven't really prepared for.

"Yep." I sound far more confident than I actually am.

She nods as if agreeing with me. "Well, *science* really just means *knowledge*, right?"

I side-eye her, cautious now. "Sure..."

Evie nods again. "And science is really just the knowledge people gather after making observations, right?"

"I guess so..."

"Mmm-hmm. Well, I think our ancestors, the ones who looked up at the night sky for answers to how the universe worked, were scientists in their own way," she says, wearing a thoughtful expression. "I think they

87

made observations and noticed patterns, night to night, season to season. Year to year."

She steps closer to the fence and carefully leans her forearms between the chain-link spikes. "And, yeah, they made up stories based on what they observed that are not technically scientific, but it doesn't mean they don't hold truth." She gives me a half-smile that actually makes my heart thump harder for three whole beats. "I mean, mythology has been around for a long time. People retell the same stories over and over again. And even if they aren't empirically true, they still may have something to teach us."

I think she must be onto something because I want to keep listening to her even if nothing she tells me is true.

So I ask, "Okay, then, which one of these magical, astrological signs were you born under?"

Her mouth firms as she tries not to smile at my question. "I'm a Pisces." Then she gives me a conspiratorial wink. "It's the best one in case you didn't know."

And I'm laughing again. "Oh, really?" I think of the guys in Hickory dorm. If they could see me now, talking and laughing with this beautiful girl, wouldn't they call me a fool? I can just hear it.

Look at that bimbi. Who does he think he is, talking to an Alexia? Ain't he got more sense than that?

"Mmm-hmm. Pisces are generous, compassionate, intuitive, and gentle," she says, the note of pride clear in her tone.

I should tell her goodbye and go inside, but instead I move closer to the fence and stand just a couple of feet away from her. "Let me guess, then. If those are all the traits about being a Pisces, then what could go wrong?" I study her, and I know without even having to think about it. Everything about her tells me she's vulnerable. This girl might as well have a neon sign above her head blinking "Take Advantage of Me."

"Someone who's too generous and compassionate and gentle gets stepped on and used," I tell her. "They don't see danger when it's staring them right in the face."

I watch her swallow, but she doesn't take her eyes off mine.

"A person like that would be too trusting for her own good."

Evie swallows again and straightens her spine. "I did say we were intuitive, which means we're good at reading people."

I frown. "But you don't deny being stepped on and used."

Color rises to her cheeks. "Well... I mean... it's not like that never happens. That's bound to happen to everyone at some point."

Holy shit.

I suddenly want to pound flesh. Who has been walking all over this girl? A boyfriend? A boss? I rake my eyes over her, seeing her anew. She's long-limbed and lean, maybe five-foot-seven. But I'll be damned if she weighs over one-twenty soaking wet. What could she do if someone tried to hurt her?

What if I wasn't who I am? What if some other asshole got released from Angola and lived in the house behind hers. Some of those fuckers on the river aren't there for life, but they should be. And when those guys get out, they'll hurt people.

89

People like Evie Lalonde.

I step closer until the spikes of the chain-link fence dig into the skin of my abs. Evie has the good sense to step back, though her hands still grip the metal that separates us. Her green eyes are wide and watchful, and I silently hold her gaze for a long moment.

"Now listen up, Evie. All that compassion and generosity and gentleness you got by being born under the right sign? You just keep that to yourself until people you meet prove they're worth it." I stare hard to make sure she's listening. She doesn't blink, and I know I've got her full attention. "I've spent time with real monsters. The kind that would cut you open, reach inside of you, and steal your soul if they could sell it for one bump. And as packed to the gills as Angola is, it might as well be empty for all the bad guys who walk free every day."

She holds my gaze but says nothing.

"You shouldn't be talking to *anyone* like me. Including me."

Something flashes across her eyes. That ire.

"What if my gut tells me you're not a monster?"

I push away from the fence. "You'd be wrong."

As I walk away from her, it's hard as hell not to look back, but I don't.

CHAPTER EIGHT

EVIE

"We should share the Wood Oven Roasted Merguez for two," Drake suggests, smirking at me over the glowing votive on the table. "It's incredible."

I frown down at the menu and stifle a shudder. "Um... I don't eat lamb. I was thinking about the Gulf Tuna Melt."

I hear Drake shift against the leather upholstery of the booth where he insisted the hostess seat us. I get the distinct impression he's waiting for me to look up at him, so I do, and I find him leaning back against the rich leather, his arm draped possessively across the back.

"Evie, I've taken you to one of the best restaurants in Lafayette." He shakes his head, wearing a pitying smile. "You can't order a tuna sandwich."

I take a sip of my water and swallow the urge to comment. If Social is so posh, why do they serve tuna sandwiches? As a matter of fact, why would they have a whole section of the menu dedicated to "sammies?"

But I resist. It is a great restaurant. I haven't been here in awhile, and I don't want to be rude to Drake. We can have a nice meal, say goodnight as friends, and be pleasant to each other the next time we're both at the studio.

"What about the Ora King Salmon?" I ask.

He glances down at the menu, and his eyes widen. Only then do I read the price. It's thirty-two dollars. The twelve-ounce ribeye is the only item more expensive, topping out at a steep thirty-six.

"That's... that's an incredible choice." I think he's gone pale, and I feel terrible. Sure, I don't really want to be here, but I'm not planning to bankrupt the guy.

"On second thought," I blurt, scanning the menu quickly. "I think I'll have the mushroom flatbread. That black truffle salt sounds really good."

"Oh." Drake almost sags with relief. "Yeah, that is good. The wild mushroom ragout is delicious."

I smile, equally relieved, and when our server arrives, Drake orders for us, including asking for two Pickup Lines.

At my confused expression, he chuckles. "You'll see."

The drinks arrive a moment later, and I learn that a Pickup Line is a whiskey cocktail. I take a sip, and quickly decide it's about eight parts whiskey, one part simple syrup. The stuff burns all the way down, and I can feel the blood vessels in my throat dilate with just one swallow.

I am not a whiskey drinker, so I nudge the glass away from me and wait for the ice cubes in the tin cup to melt and water it down a little. Silently, I wish I'd had the chance to order a glass of sauvignon blanc instead.

Fifteen minutes down, I tell myself. It's really twenty-five if you count the ride over here, and I do. I've got at least an hour to go.

"So, you know I'm getting my MBA, right?"

I nod. "You've told me." About five times.

Drake chuckles again. "Two more semesters, and then I'll be ready for the big time."

I smile politely. I should say something nice. I mean, obviously, it's not easy waiting tables to put yourself through grad school. Drake is driven. I'll give him that.

"A lot of hard work," I offer, and his face lights up.

92

"You're damn right. I thought getting my BA was tough, but man, those graduate level professors aren't messing around. You have to be cutthroat. On your game day in and day out. Just last week... "

I wonder what Drew Moroux is doing right now.

My guess is he's home, maybe eating dinner with his grandma or helping her with the dishes by now. He's probably had a shower after a day of working on cars. Working with his hands.

Such a Taurus.

I smile to myself and have to bite down on my lips when Drake gives me a funny look.

"You've heard of it before? Disruption theory?" he asks.

"No, I don't think so. Please go on."

And he does.

I'm terrible. I know I'm terrible, but while he talks, I find myself picturing those hands. Drew Moroux's hands are huge. They're paws, really. Rough, calloused, and lined in grease that night when we stood in his grandmother's kitchen.

He was cradling his head in those hands when I saw him outside the other day.

God, he looked so miserable. If there wouldn't have been a fence between us, I would have gone and put my arms around him.

He tried to scare me away, but, really, there's nothing scary about him. Sad. He's shrouded in sadness. But I don't think he's a danger to anyone. Except maybe himself.

It's been two days since he tried to spook me, and I haven't stopped thinking about him. Hell, every time I pass my bedroom window or take Gemini out back, my eyes are searching for him.

I know virtually nothing about Drew, but I have this unshakable certainty that if we went out on a date, he'd let me order a tuna sandwich. And a glass of white wine.

Come back to the now, I nudge myself.

I reach for the tin cup and try the whiskey again. The ice melt makes it easier to swallow, so I do.

"Good, huh?" Drake says, smirking with pride.

"Not bad," I admit, grateful now for the almost instant fuzziness the whiskey lends to my surroundings.

"Next time we come, we'll get the Sazerac. Now, that'll put hair on your chest." As if on cue, his eyes fall to my cleavage, and I lift the whiskey to shield it from view.

Next time?

At that moment, thank all the gods, our food arrives. The mushroom flatbread is heavenly, and I can sink into savory pleasure of the fontina cheese and the unami goodness of the mushrooms. Meanwhile, Drake eats every bite of the Wood Oven Roasted Merguez for two, and I can't help but wonder what would have happened if I'd agreed to share.

By the time he takes me home, I've succumbed to two whiskeys, which, in hindsight, was a bad idea. Now that we're sitting in my driveway, Drake is trying to nail down another date, and I really could use a little less fuzziness right about now.

"So, we should do this again." Drake has one wrist draped over the steering wheel, but the other rests on the shoulder of my seat. I press the release button on my seatbelt and slide the strap off me.

"It was a nice dinner," I say noncommittally. It turns out even after two Pickup Lines, I still suck at saying no.

"Really?" The pinky of his right hand straightens and brushes a curl away from my face. My breath halts, and I reach for the door handle.

"Mmm hmm. Great food," I mutter, opening the door.

Drake opens his as well. "I'll walk you in."

"Oh, you don't have to do th—"

"It's no trouble." And he's out of the car and by my side before I can even clear the door.

I'm not afraid of him. Drake, I know, may be a cheese ball, but he's not a sex offender.

At least, I don't think he is.

Besides, I tell myself, *Tori's home.*

My sister may not have spoken to me since Tuesday night, but she wouldn't turn a deaf ear on me if I started screaming on our front porch.

Drake takes my hand as we walk up the steps, and while I don't return the grip, I can't bring myself to pull away. It would be rude, and it might hurt his feelings. We reach my front door, and I'm pretty certain he's going to try to kiss me.

Would one kiss really be so bad? I mean, there won't be any chemistry. I'm sure I'd feel like a mannequin to him. That might take care of this whole crush thing without me actually having to tell him—

"Do you think I could come in?"

Coming in means more than a kiss goodnight. I force myself to look up and meet his gaze. Drake looks confident. And eager. I bite my lip.

"It's... really late."

95

Leering, Drake gives a slow shake of his head. "It's only ten-thirty."

"Yeah, but I have a ten o'clock class in the morning."

He raises his hand and grazes a thumb down my cheek. My heart thumps higher in my chest than it technically should.

"I'll make sure you sleep soundly afterwards."

My too-high heart drops somewhere around my liver. "Drake, I don't... I don't think—"

"Jesus Christ."

The curse cuts through the night air. I jerk my head toward the street where the sound issued, but the glow of my front porch light has thrown everything beyond the steps into darkness. Still, I see a shadow, broad and swift, move across my lawn.

"The word is *no*, Evie," the shadow growls. "Two letters. One syllable."

I fast blink. I can't believe what I'm seeing, yet nothing else makes sense.

"Drew?"

He mounts the steps and is towering over Drake, his eyes like a viper's, slitted and unblinking. I watch Drake swallow and take a measured step backward, but then he squares his shoulders.

"Who are you?" Drake asks, irritation ringing in his voice.

"Andrew Moroux, Evie's neighbor. I just got out of Angola on Monday."

Drake splutters a laugh. "Bullshit." Then he turns to me. "Evie, let's go inside."

"No."

Again, the word is Drew's, not mine.

I glance back and forth between the two men. Drake looks confused and harassed, but Drew looks ice cold. Glacial. Like nothing in the world could move him off my front porch. Did I say there was nothing scary about him? I need to revise that. Because standing beside me, casting a shadow over Drake, he looks pretty scary.

And yet I don't feel scared. Not for me. Not even for Drake.

But he's being a bully, and that's not cool. "Drew, this is my friend Drake." My voice is cordial, even, hopefully reminding everyone to be civil. "He takes classes at the yoga studio where I teach. Drake, Drew lives in the house behind ours."

With this polite introduction, both men shift on their feet, seemingly unsure where they stand. But I know where I stand. Drew's intrusion, bullish though it was (*such a Taurus!*), has given me the opening I need to end this date, and I'm taking it.

"Drake, thanks again for a lovely dinner." With a speed and deftness that surprise me, I insert the key in the deadbolt and unlock it. In the next moment, I'm standing in the open doorway facing them both. "I'll see you at the studio." Then I shift my gaze up to Drew's, but his gray eyes are masked in shadow. All I can tell is they're pinned on me. "Drew, have a good night." And with that, I slip inside and bolt the door.

Gemini is at my knees, whining and pawing with excitement to see me, and I drop my bag and reach down to rub a hand along his sleek back, but I don't move otherwise. Instead, I peer through the peephole at the fishbowl image of two men glaring at each other. The standoff lasts just a few seconds, and then Drake breaks right, heading back to his car. But he keeps his eyes on

Drew as he goes. Drew, in turn, pivots to track Drake and doesn't move until Drake's ignition fires up and his reverse lights come on. Then he slowly stalks back into the night.

And that's when I bolt through the front room. "C'mon, Gem." The dog tears across the floor, hard on my heels until we reach the hall closet where we keep his harness and leash. Excited that we're going for a rare late-night walk, Gemini leaps and twirls, making it almost impossible for me to loop the harness around his long forelegs.

"Hold still, buddy," I hiss whisper, not wanting the noise to attract Tori's attention or wake her if she's sleeping.

Once he's harnessed and leashed, I stuff a roll of poop bags in my pocket, and we dash back to the front door. Drake's car is gone, and the street in front of our house is empty, but I don't think Drew could have gotten far.

Pulling Gemini with me, I take off in my midi dress and lace-up espadrilles, running through the grass in the dark. At the street, I look right towards Souvenir Gate and the lights of Champagne's Grocery, but I see no one. Spinning left reveals a hulking shadow moving with ground-eating strides toward Howard Avenue.

"C'mon, Gem." And with that, we break into a run. My dog and I are not the stealthiest pair, so I'm not surprised when the shadow stops moving. He's facing me when I slow to a walk about fifty feet from him.

"What are you doing?" he asks, his voice accusatory.

"What am *I* doing?" I scoff, closing the distance to ten feet. "What are *you* doing?"

The light from the streetlamp at the next house only illuminates his silhouette, but his shrug is unmistakable. "Going for a walk. What does it look like?"

"In the middle of the night? Right in front of my house?" Gemini strains on the leash, eager to meet this new friend, and even though I try to anchor him with my weight, he pulls us until he can sniff Drew's shoes.

This close, I can make out more of his features. He doesn't look any happier to see me than he has every other time I've encountered him. But, in spite of my irritation, I'm secretly glad to see him.

Elated, really.

After thinking of him all through dinner, the moment I heard his voice from my front porch, I'd felt like I'd won a prize. *First Prize for Daydreams Coming True goes to Evie Lalonde!*

Yeah, maybe he was an ass to Drake. I'm not about to ignore that. But out of all the things I could be doing at ten-thirty on a Friday night, talking to Drew Moroux has suddenly become number one.

He crosses his arms over his chest. He's wearing a white T-shirt — maybe it's just an undershirt; I can't tell — jeans, and what appear to be work boots. Whatever they are, it's a good look for him, especially the T-shirt.

"I needed air, so I took a walk around the block," he says, his voice flat. "Yours isn't the only house on it, guppy."

My eyes bug. *"Guppy?!"*

I hear rather than see him snicker, and he shrugs again. "It sounded better in my head than *Pisces.*"

I want to laugh, but I shake my head instead. "No. It doesn't."

This time he laughs for real, and for the life of me, I can't help it. Laughter ripples from me.

This. Even just this feels better than my entire date with Drake.

I let myself take a step closer, and my laughter settles. "You needed air?" My tone is light, as though I'm only mildly interested, but that's not true. Despite the banter, I know he's likely to slip away any second, and I want to keep him talking.

Drew doesn't answer me, but he reaches down with one hand and scratches Gemini on the head. Gem opens his mouth with what I think of as one of his canine smiles and wags with gusto.

Drew's squats down and smoothes both hands along Gemini's neck, petting and stroking.

"Hey, boy," Drew coos with such gentleness, I'm almost jealous. Scratch that. I *am* jealous. It isn't just the soft tone of his voice or even the touch — though I'd be lying if I said both didn't tempt me — it's the way Drew's guard comes down as he pets my dog.

When he speaks again, he sounds a long way off. "I can't remember the last time I touched a dog. Any animal, for that matter."

And with that, I'm no longer jealous. I'm heartbroken.

"Oh, Drew." I sink to my knees. Right there on the street. In my dress and everything.

I watch him, but he doesn't meet my gaze. He just keeps petting Gemini. I want, more than anything, to reach out and touch him. To acknowledge the pain that anyone who's been through what he's been through

100

must feel. But I know, even though I know little else about him, he'd reject that.

So, instead, I lay a hand on Gem's back and follow the stroking rhythm Drew has set. A moment later, Gemini heaves a great doggy sigh and sits on his haunches between us, clearly lavishing his good fortune.

"I think he likes you," I say, seeing that the lines of Drew's shoulders have relaxed.

"Hmmph." Drew grunts, still moving his big hands in long, even strokes. "He's as bad a judge of character as you are."

"I was talking to Gemini."

The night air quakes with his laughter, and I silently congratulate myself.

He shakes his head. "You have to admit, your friend Drake is a hamflower."

"A *what?*" I snort, laughing already.

"An asshole."

I open my mouth to argue, but no words come. "Um… Yeah. Yeah, he kind of is."

Drew blows an amused breath out his nose, but he shakes his head again, eyeing me sharply. "Then why did you go out with him?"

I close my eyes, shrinking under his stare. The thought of giving him all the details is almost painful. "It's a long story," I say with a sigh.

I peek at him, and though it's still dark, I can make out the frown creasing his brow. "And what was going on when I walked up?"

I remember Drake's awkward proposal and wrinkle my nose in distaste. "He just wanted to come in," I say quickly, ready to brush the topic aside.

"That didn't sound like all he wanted."

101

My neck heats. "Well, he wasn't going to get more than a goodnight kiss, that's for sure."

Drew is silent for a moment, watching me. "But did you *want* to give him a goodnight kiss?"

The question hangs on the night air as though suspended by late summer humidity.

"No," I admit finally.

"But you would have let him kiss you." He's not asking. He seems sure this is fact, and I can hear he doesn't like it.

But since he's not asking, I feel no need to respond, so we stare at each other. His hands have stopped moving on Gem's coat and those shoulders look strung tight again.

"My God, you would have let him kiss you?" The censure in his voice makes me squirm.

I shake my head like it doesn't matter. "It's just a kiss. What's the big deal?"

His voice pitches higher, startling the night. "Because you didn't want it!"

A porch light of the house nearest us comes on, and we both scramble to our feet.

"Shit," Drew mutters. "I can't get arrested for disturbing the peace."

I grab his wrist and tug him in the direction of my house. "C'mon. It's no crime to sit and talk on my front porch."

He halts and pulls out of my hold. "I'm not going to sit and talk on your front porch."

I cock a brow at him. "Oh, but yelling at me in the street is okay?"

"I'll walk you home," he says, ignoring my jab.

We set off in the direction of my house, but I'm only moving to put distance between us and any neighbors who might be thinking of calling the police to report a man and a woman arguing in the street.

He stops in front of our house and nods toward my front door. "Go in and lock up."

I shake my head. "No thanks, Gem and I aren't finished our walk."

Drew glares down at me. "It's not safe."

I give him an innocent smile. "I have Gem to protect me."

He regards my Rhodesian Ridgeback with doubt. "That goof?"

"H-hey," I defend, laughing, because it's true. Gemini is a goof, but he's a big goof. At his last check up, he weighed in at eighty-six pounds. "He may be friendly, but he's big. Anybody who'd want to mess with me would think twice before trying."

Drew crosses his arms over his chest but says nothing. I take this as agreement, and I make two strides before he steps in front of me.

"Creeps are one thing. Drivers are another," he says with a scowl. "People like Douche-Bag Drake have been out drinking, and it's dark. Gemini can't protect you from that."

I grin. Opposing him shouldn't be fun, but it is. I reach down and run a finger over this side of Gemini's harness. "He's got reflectors," I say. Then I shrug. "But if it makes you feel better, I'll walk against traffic, so I'll see any cars coming and step into the grass."

I can't be sure, but I think I hear a low-pitch growl. Gem perks his ears and looks around. I have to fight so hard not to giggle.

I start walking, and as I expected — as I intended — Drew falls into step beside me.

"And you say *I'm* stubborn," he mutters.

CHAPTER NINE

DREW

I should turn around and walk in the opposite direction. I should. But I don't.

I tell myself I want to make sure she's safe, and that's true. I do.

But, really, I just want to be near her.

Yesterday and today, I put in extra hours at the garage after my shift. Off the clock, of course. I told Cody it's because I want to familiarize myself with makes I didn't see in the auto shop at Angola, and he said that was cool.

It keeps me busy. And it keeps me from thinking about the two people I don't want to think about. My sanity depends on holding too many thoughts of Anthony at bay. Seeing his Supra nearly cleaved my head open. When I'm in the apartment, it's like I can feel it beneath me. Like a pulse.

Like a fucking tell tale heart.

I haven't been able to bring myself to ask Grandma Q what the hell it's doing there. Frankly, I'm afraid to. None of the reasons I can come up with are ones I'd like. Like, maybe she keeps it as a memento of him. And I wonder how many other mementos there are. Upstairs in the unused bedrooms. In the back of her closet. How much square footage is taken up by grief?

Or maybe she's keeping it for Ma.

Anthony didn't have any dependents. No one to inherit his stuff. So she would have been left with it all. And maybe she couldn't bring herself to sell it, but she couldn't bear to look at it every day either.

Given her semi-annual letters, this seems to be the most likely reason.

"You've gone quiet all the sudden," Evie says beside me. We've turned the corner onto Souvenir Gate at the end of the block, and I wonder how far this dog walk will go.

As much as I want to be near her, I have no intention of filling the silence that stretches between us. I'm already giving myself enough rope to hang us both with.

But silence doesn't seem to be Evie Lalonde's favorite thing. "Did you work today?"

"I did."

The dog, who has been nearly pulling Evie's arm out of socket in his forward assault, catches the scent of something interesting near a storm drain, and we stop walking to humor him.

"How's that going?" she asks.

Staying busy at the garage the last two days has also been my only relief from thoughts of her. After I walked away on Wednesday, she stayed with me. Like smoke that clings to clothes after a bonfire. Or the heat of a sunburn on skin... long after the sun has set.

I kept seeing her laugh. Hearing the lilt of her voice when she called me a Taurus. I'd find myself imagining what it would feel like to bury my nose in those dark, lustrous curls. And that would inevitably lead me to wonder about other dark curls. The secret scent they might hold...

"Overtime," I hear myself mutter.

"What?" I look down to see her frown of confusion.

I clear my throat. "I've been working overtime. It's good. Keeps me busy."

Her dog gives a loud snort and jerks forward, pulling Evie with him.

"Here," I say, grabbing the leash. "Let me hold that."

"He usually isn't such a handful," she says, but she unloops the handle of the leash off her wrist and offers it to me. "Walking at night excites him. Ridgebacks are hunters and trackers, and I guess there are different smells out here at night."

The dog strains against the leash, and I have to firm my arm to keep him in check. I glance down at Evie. How the hell did she keep him from dragging her like a ragdoll?

She smiles up at me as though she's read my thoughts. "I'm stronger than I look."

I sniff to cover a laugh. That's another thing I've kept reliving. The way she has of making me laugh. This lighter-than-air feeling that seems to fill the space above my diaphragm.

I didn't leave the apartment to go in search of her. Really, I didn't. Sleep was a long way off, and that Supra was right below me. And I had to get out. But when I turned onto St. Patrick Street, I knew I wanted to see the front of her house. Just see it. Just to fill in the landscape in my mind.

Because I know exactly what the back of her house looks like.

When I saw the car pull up, my heart had started this heavy chugging in my chest. The night she came over, Grandma Q told me that she lives in that house with her sister. That their parents are somewhere in Africa or something like that.

So when I saw the car, I guessed I had a fifty-fifty chance of catching sight of her. But I didn't plan on her seeing me. In fact, I hung back a good thirty yards. Until I heard them. Heard that coddletwat hint he planned to fuck her silly. And she was definitely not giving him the checkered flag.

But she wasn't telling the assnut to go choke on his own dick, either.

Honestly, I don't even remember deciding to step onto her lawn. I was just there.

A little voice in the back of my head tells me this should alarm me, but it's her voice I tune into.

"I don't like disappointing people." This lone confession seems to come out of nowhere, but the way she says it feels like it's an answer to a question.

"You don't like disappointing people," I echo, testing out the statement and measuring it against what I know of her. My mind flicks through the images I've collected of her. Leading some woman through a yoga lesson on her back porch; baking a zucchini bread for her elderly neighbor; asking if I was okay the other day; going on a date with a bona fide buttmunch.

"I can't imagine that happens often," I tell her. "You're a people-pleaser."

We're under the halo of a streetlamp, and I see her clearly when she looks up at me with a rueful smile. "It happens all the time."

I frown. "What? People-pleasing?"

She shakes her head. "No. Disappointing them."

I look at her like she's crazy. "How?"

Her chest inflates, and she blows out a breath. "Oh, gosh, let's see. My parents wish I'd stayed in school. My father is sure I'll live in poverty because a

108

career as a yoga instructor is only for the independently wealthy or River Ranch trophy wives." She ticks these offenses off on her long, delicate fingers. "My sister Tori currently isn't speaking to me because she overheard me complaining about her to my mom…"

She meets my eyes with a little nod. "I'm actually pretty disappointed in myself for that one, too, because I totally lost control, and I hate when I do that…"

We turn onto St. Joseph, my street, and I eye her, my brows lowered. "Not to sound like a dick," I begin, making a point to speak gently. "But I know something about disappointing your family. Evie, what you're talking about? That ain't it."

She jerks to a stop as though she's struck a wall. She spins to face me, her eyes wide. "Oh my God, Drew, I didn't mean — I must sound — I can't imagine what you must thi—"

I raise a staying hand. "Calm down, Guppy."

The nickname has the desired effect. Her look of horror quickly dilutes with startled amusement. "Seriously," she says, fighting her grin. "I apologize for being so obtuse. For someone who prides herself on being sensitive, I really needed that lesson on reading the room."

I shake my head at her. "You know, you're pretty hard on yourself. Is that like a hobby, or do you work that shift full-time?"

She tries to glower at me, but the lift at the corner of her mouth ruins the effort. All she manages to do is look even cuter.

Lord, give me strength.

The night is thick around us. And while the occasional car has passed by, the streets are sleepy and most of the houses dim. There's no one out here to see us. If I were someone else, I'd seize this moment, so ripe for the picking, and drag her to me. I'd kiss that lush mouth and hold that lithe body against me.

And I wouldn't stop until she begged for mercy.

Just the thought has my pulse thrumming and insistent, so I tug on Gemini's leash to get us moving again. "C'mon, boy."

We're approaching Grandma Q's house, and the sight of the garage hits me like a cold shower. I pull my gaze from the garage door and focus on the darkened asphalt instead. If I need a reminder of why I should leave Evie Lalonde alone, I don't have to look far.

"What's that about?" she asks, yanking me from my thoughts.

"What?"

"That look you had a second ago. You were wearing it the other day. At the picnic table," she clarifies.

I take in the alert cast to her eyes and shake my head before glancing back down. "Not going there, Evie."

From the corner of my eye, I see her nod in profile. "Got it. But I can see you're thinking about something. Something bad." She makes a smacking noise with her mouth. "I don't think it makes you very happy. And since anyone's suffering is everyone's suffering, I need to try to change that."

This girl is too much. My gaze slides to her, and I arch my brow in challenge. "And just how will you manage that?" By the tone of my voice, she should take the hint this will not be an easy — or even manageable — task.

110

"Well, let's see..." She swings her arms lightly as she walks, the bangles on her thin wrists making their own music, light and playful. Just like she is. The bottom of that turquoise dress hits her just past her knee, but the thin pleats in her skirt swirl and ripple like water as she walks. The dress is modest, innocent. But the way she moves in it is sensual.

Like a touch.

I have to admit, being with her — thinking of her — puts the pain on hold for a while. She makes me stop thinking of all the ways I've ruined everything. All the people I've hurt.

The problem is I shouldn't stop. I don't deserve to stop.

"Tell me one thing that happened today that you're grateful for."

I don't know what I was expecting, but it's not this. One thing I'm grateful for? We walk in silence for a moment, and I break it so she doesn't get the wrong idea.

"There are a lot of things." I don't tell her I'm grateful I had a roof over my head this morning when I woke up. That I had a job to go to. That Grandma Q is always happy to see me. That she's had breakfast and dinner on the table for me every day. I'm grateful for all of these things, but also feel guilty for enjoying them.

And then the right answer arrives. "I went the the health clinic and got my Sertraline refilled."

She gives me a blank expression.

"Generic Zoloft."

"Oh." Realization, not judgement, washes over her face. We walk for a long moment in silence. When she speaks again, her voice is so soft it's unsettling. "Does it help?"

The tenderness in her words sends a shiver through me. Like the tickle of a feather. "It..." I begin, trying to recover but keenly aware of the gooseflesh down my arms. "It does."

I don't tell her it makes it easier to keep living, but I have a feeling that I could. That she would hear that without freaking out. Without looking at me differently.

"I missed a dose yesterday and couldn't get more until today, and it messed me all up." I have no idea why I volunteer this. The words seem to leave me on their own.

"Did you..." She's looking at me closely, but I don't feel like a curiosity. A freak. "Were you depressed before you went to prison?"

I snort a laugh of derision. "Hell, no." I think about the witless asshole I was back then and taste metal.

"So..." Evie seems to choose her words carefully as if she's afraid of offending me. I don't know if it's because of the cover night gives me or because she speaks so softly, but her questions don't rankle. Not at all. "Did living in prison make you depressed?"

I shake my head. "No. It was what I did to get there."

I can tell she's not looking directly at me, and I'm glad because I couldn't meet her gaze now if I tried. But maybe the reminder that I'd actually committed a crime has spooked her. A ridiculously foolish part of me hopes it hasn't.

But we turn the corner onto Howard Street in silence, and I grow more certain that she's had enough of my company, finally, and is ready to keep her distance.

And then she slips her hand into mine.

It's not a come-on. Far from it. But a buzz of awareness wraps around my hand and climbs up my arm before sluicing over my whole body. Her touch is like a gust of wind scattering ashes. Or sweeping clouds from the sun.

It wrecks me.

Because I can't do anything else. Lost as I am in the depth of her kindness, I just hold on. Until we turn the final corner onto her street.

When I'm able to release my hold on her fingers, she lets go as well. Her house comes into view.

"Have you ever tried yoga?" she asks. "For your depression, I mean."

I arch a brow at her. "There's not a whole lot of yoga in prison, Guppy."

She rolls her eyes. "You calling me *Guppy* is not a thing."

My smile is automatic. It stuns me, considering where I was a moment ago; I couldn't have spoken past the knot in my throat. "Oh, it's a thing."

"And there *should* be a lot of yoga in prisons. It would make a huge difference."

I nod in pretend agreement. "Yep. It would mean a lot more inmates would get *cabiared.*"

A line appears between her brows. "What does that mean?"

I palm my forehead, trying not to laugh. "Forget I said anything. You don't want to know."

Evie glares at me, looking a little impatient, and she sighs. "Whatever. But you're not in prison anymore." Even though it's dark, I can see some of that ire I spotted the other day. "I could teach you the basics, and then we could go over some poses that help with anxiety and depression."

I begin to shake my head. "That's just not—"

"Do you work tomorrow?"

I shift my jaw back and forth, not wanting to outright lie. "I have stuff to—"

"Can I come see you?"

My mouth hangs open like a stupid Christmas nutcracker. I need to tell her no, but the word won't come.

A smile like sunlight on water claims her face. "I'll be there a little after eleven." And before I can say anything else, she grabs the leash and takes off for her front door.

"I-I might be busy," I call after her.

"You'll be there," she hollers back without turning around.

I watch the swish of her dress as she skips up the steps, the way her hair — pinned up in a barrette — spills down her back in dark springs.

And she's right. I will be.

I'm up at six-thirty, but not because Evie Lalonde is coming to teach me yoga. I've decided during the night that's not happening. I've suffered plenty of humiliations in the last eight years, but this is one I haven't earned. So, no. No, thank you.

114

I'm up because Grandma Q rises by dawn to make breakfast, and if she's going to go to so much trouble, I might as well be there to eat it.

After I get up, shave, and dress, I find Grandma at the kitchen table in her housecoat. She's sipping a cup of coffee, and I can smell biscuits in the oven, but she looks a little washed out. She's rubbing a hand to her side as though she's stiff.

"Morning, Grandma. You okay?"

Her face brightens when she sees me, and she drops her hand, but in this moment, she looks her age. "Just moving a little slower today, is all." She sets down her coffee cup and shifts to push back from the table. "Here, let me pour you some cof—"

I place a staying hand on her shoulder. "I can get my own coffee, Grandma Q." And then I get busy doing it so she won't think she needs to wade in. When my cup is made, I take a seat at the table across from her.

"Did you sleep alright?"

She scrunches up her nose, her way of saying she'd rather not talk about it. "A spot of bother and a touch of a headache kept me up, but I took my blood pressure medicine when I got up, and I feel better."

"You have high blood pressure?" I hear myself ask, feeling dumb the moment the question leaves my lips.

Her eyes dance. "I'm eighty-three years old, Andrew." She chuckles. "I've got that and a lot more."

I smile, but her words make my insides feel weighted. One thing being released has made me realize is just how much she's aged. The first morning I was here, I noticed the days-of-the-week pill dispenser on her kitchen counter, but I guess I just chose to ignore what it

115

meant. I'm not ready to live in a world without Grandma Quincy.

"What are you doing today?" I ask, keeping my voice casual.

She takes a sip of her coffee. "I'm puttin' up my okra."

"Putting it up?" I glance around her kitchen. "Where?"

Grandma's mouth twists to the side, and I can see she's laughing at me without actually laughing.

"I'm gonna pick what's ready and add it to what I've picked this week. Half of that I'll chop and put in the deep freezer for gumbos. The other half'll get pickled."

I have no idea what I'm signing up for, but I don't hesitate. "I've got all day," I tell her. "Put me to work."

Her smile tells me she's pleased. "Alright."

The oven timer buzzes then, and I get to my feet. "I'll get that."

"Oh, pooh," she fusses, struggling to stand. "You don't have to do all that."

"Yes, I do," I say, slipping on a pair of oven mitts. "I need to help out more around here. You don't need to be doing everything."

I open the oven and pull out a tray of golden, hand cut biscuits, and set them on the stove.

"Well, I've been doing all the same things in this house for the last fifty-two years," she grumbles, but I still hear affection in her voice. "I don't see why that should change now that you're here."

I move to the cabinet and take down two plates. "Grandma, I've got two people in my fan club." I point one of the plates at her. "You're the president, and Annie's the vice president. I can't afford to lose either of you. So let me keep you from working yourself to the bone."

Grandma Q gives me a simpering smile. "I'm not going anywhere anytime soon, love."

After we've halfway filled what Grandma Quincy calls her "chipwood bushel basket" with okra, we wash and sort the yield, plus what she's stocked in the fridge, into two piles. Anything shorter than Grandma's index finger or my pinky gets chopped for the freezer. All of the longer pieces will be pickled.

The chopping and bagging goes quickly, but when Grandma transforms her kitchen into a makeshift cannery, I get the feeling we'll be here awhile. I'm ordered to take down all the eight-ounce Mason jars from the upper cabinets while Grandma fills a stock pot and sets it on the stove to boil.

We're about halfway through sterilizing the jars and lids when someone knocks on the kitchen door. My eyes dart to the Bakelite wall clock above the stove. As soon as I see it's half-past eleven, I know exactly who it is.

What I'm unprepared for is how amazing she looks in yoga wear.

Sure, the first time I saw her across both our yards, she was dressed in similar tights and a tank. But this is up close. This is just feet from me. And, this time, she's also aiming that smile my way.

117

Grandma Quincy is the one who lets her in since I've insisted on holding the tongs and fishing jars and lids out of boiling water.

Grandma invites Evie in before joining me at the stove and handing over another jar to be sterilized. As she does, she stretches up on her tiptoes, aiming her mouth toward my ear.

"You might have more than two people in your fan club," she whispers.

CHAPTER TEN

EVIE

The sight of Drew Moroux dressed in an apron and oven mitts, bearing a pair of tongs has officially made my day. And it has not been the greatest day.

Mom texted me this morning asking if I knew why Tori was talking about moving out. Of course, I knew nothing about it since she hasn't spoken to me in days. I've given Tori her space, but as soon as I read this, I confronted her.

It did not go well.

And then, naturally, Drake was in my class. Before we got started, he made a big show of saying what a great time he had last night. In front of all my students. But when he cornered me afterward, he pelted me with questions about "that Neanderthal who showed up at my door last night."

Did he really just get out of prison?

Is he a stalker?

Is he a sex offender?

I only managed to get out of there when I told him I had plans with a friend. I just didn't tell him who the friend was.

But as soon as I see Drew like this in his grandmother's kitchen, I forget all of the crap from this morning.

"Andrew's helping me pickle okra," Mrs. Vivian says, wearing a proud smile. Drew's face is flushed, and I'm not sure if it's from his proximity to boiling water or if he's just a tad embarrassed to be seen like this. "Would you like to help?"

I take another look at Drew's blush and know there is just one answer to this question. "Absolutely!"

Mrs. Vivian snatches another apron off the hook by her pantry door, and before I know it, I've washed my hands three times as instructed, and she's walking me through the assembly of pickling brine. I measure out a concoction of salt, water, and vinegar into a waiting soup pot on her stove.

Meanwhile, Drew is tasked with the job of filling eight Mason jars with chilies, mustard seeds, sprigs of dill, and, finally, okra pods.

"Put the first one in stem down," Mrs. Vivian tells Drew. "Then the next one goes in tip down. And then stem down and so on."

"I got it, Grandma," he responds softly, grasping the first okra from the colander on her counter.

"Try not to let your fingers touch the mouth of the jar."

"Grandma, my hands have never been this clean," he says. "It'll be okay."

"You want to get botulism?" she asks, making both of us laugh.

"No," he answers on a chuckle.

"Then don't let your fingers touch the jar."

Drew doesn't take his eyes from the task. It's like watching a game of Operation. Only a whole lot better. I love Drew Moroux's hands. That's an established fact at this point. They're huge and rough and beautiful.

"There," he says, stepping back from the first jar and effectively ending my hand-gazing trance. "Pour it on."

Mrs. Vivian leans forward, frowning over her glasses, to inspect his work. She leans back, facing at me with a nod. "Pour it on. Just be careful not to burn yourself."

By now, my brine has come to a boil, so I dip the ladle in and carefully empty it into the jar. Another ladleful brings the liquid to about an inch below the glass threads.

"Good. That's enough," Mrs. Vivian says. "Now, Andrew, without touching the inside of the lid, place it on top and screw it on tight."

He follows her instructions, and I delight in watching those hands grip down on the jar and lid. "One down," Drew says, setting the freshly sealed preserves on the counter. "Seven to go."

Mrs. Vivian watches us closely while we complete the second jar, but this time she says nothing. No warnings about bacteria or burns. When this one is complete, she shuffles back from us.

"I think you two have got the hang of this. Would y'all mind if I go put my feet up for a few minutes?"

At this, Drew turns to face her. "You feeling okay, Grandma?" His forehead is creased with concern.

"Just a little tired, love," she says, batting him away. "Glad for your help in here."

His frown deepens as he watches her waddle out of the kitchen.

"Everything okay?" I whisper when I'm sure she's out of earshot.

Drew's eyes cut to mine. I watch his chest fill and then he lets go a breath. "I'm just worried about her."

"She's slowing down," I say, "but she's in great shape. I see her in that garden almost every day. Not many people her age could work that hard."

"You think?"

I nod.

121

Drew moves back to the empty Mason jars, shaking his head as though trying to shed worry. "I guess it's just because it's all catching up with me," he says, reaching for the jar of mustard seeds. "After being gone for so long, I mean."

It must be so strange for him, I realize, coming back to a life he left for such a long time. "I can only imagine," I say softly.

I don't want to pry or make him feel like he's some sort of curiosity, but even as stoic as he is, I think Drew Moroux needs someone to talk to. I bite my lip, but then I remember he trusted me enough last night to talk about his depression. That's not small.

"I-I hope you've figured out by now," I begin, my voice tentative and low. "That you can say whatever's on your mind, and you won't get any judgment from me."

He's midway through stuffing the jar with dill, and his gaze slides over to mine. He doesn't look worried anymore. Instead, he looks kind of amused. "No judgement, huh? This from the woman who burst out laughing at the mention of my birthday."

A giggle escapes me before I can lock it down. "That's different," I defend, but I'm sure I'm blushing. "That's not personal stuff."

He grabs a chili and tosses it into the jar. "I know, Guppy."

I make a face. "Oh, we're still doing that? It's so yesterday."

Drew laughs a big, window-rattling laugh. "Oh, yeah," he says, chuckling. "We're still doing that."

While he loads the jar with okra pods, I wrack my brain for an equally horrible nickname for him.

122

"Let's see," I muse aloud. "Taurus… Bull… There's that story about Ferdinand. I could call you Ferdi—"

"Hell, no."

"No, really. Don't dismiss it out of hand," I urge, trying not to laugh. "He has lots of friends, and I think he likes flowers." And then I do laugh because the thought of Drew sniffing flower blossoms is almost as cute as Drew in an apron stuffing okra in a jar for his grandmother.

He gives me a mock-menacing frown and pushes the prepared jar to me. "Pour."

I scoop a ladleful from the simmering pot. "Whatever you say, Ferdi." It's the sound of his smothered laugh that sets me off again. But this time, I'm pouring boiling brine with one hand and steadying the base of the jar with the other. And as I laugh, brine sloshes over the mouth of the jar and onto my hand.

"Ow! Shit!" I scream, leap back, and spill the rest of brine on the counter and the floor.

"Evie! Jesus!"

"Ow! Ouch!" I hop around, flapping my hand before Drew grabs me by the elbow and hauls me to the sink. He turns on the faucet and jerks my hand under the cold stream. I hiss with relief, but it still burns like hellfire.

"Shit, Evie," Drew mutters, frowning at the burn. The little patch of flesh between my left thumb and forefinger is already an angry red. I can feel my pulse in my hand, and even with the flush of cold water, the heat compounds with each heartbeat.

I press my lips together, grunting. I don't want to seem like a wimp in front of him, but this frickin' hurts. I take a long, deep breath through my nose.

123

"You okay?" he asks, his voice right at my ear. That's when I realize it's Drew's left hand cradling mine under the spray of the faucet, and that's his right hand rubbing slow circles in the middle of my back.

I nod, not trusting my voice. It's bound to come out a squeak — either from the pain or the sheer surprise that he's touching me.

"Stay here," he says, laying my hand on the divider between the two wells in Mrs. Vivian's sink. "I'll be right back."

And then he's gone, out the kitchen door, leaving me with the distinct loss of his touch. Oh, yeah, and a throbbing hand.

The kitchen door swings open a moment later, and Drew enters, bearing a spiny sprig of aloe vera. "Hang on a sec," he says before tossing the broken succulent onto the counter beside me and leaving again.

I really hope he's not bothering his grandmother. The burn hurts, but I'll live. And I don't want her to have to get up from her rest.

But when Drew returns, he's alone, carrying a hard plastic first aid kit. He sets it down on the counter next to the aloe and grabs a clean dish towel from one of the cabinet drawers.

"Did you wake Mrs. Vivian?"

He makes a face I don't recognize. "No. She's sitting up in bed watching *Ellen.*" Then I swear I hear him murmur something that sounds like *little manipulator* under his breath. But I don't get the chance to ask about it because he shuts off the water and when he starts patting my hand dry with the towel, my eyes nearly roll back in my head.

"*Mother Kali,*" I groan through gritted teeth.

His brows pinch together. "What'd you say?"

I shake my head tightly, bearing the last of his ministrations with the towel. "Kali," I grunt, squeezing my eyes shut. "Hindu goddess."

I hear a disbelieving chuckle. "Are you a Hindu?"

Opening my eyes, I find him watching me with naked curiosity as he rests my hand on the edge of the counter.

"No... At least no more than I am anything else."

Drew turns to the first aid kit and snaps it open. "What does that mean?" he asks, rifling through its contents. He pulls out a tube of Aspercreme. I resist the urge to make a face.

Lidocaine. Well... just this once.

"Just that I don't really believe in any one religion," I say with a shrug. "But I also don't believe in nothing. Most religions have aspects that intrigue me. Parts that I honor."

He unscrews the cap to the ointment and squeezes a dab onto the tip of his right index finger. "So, you're a cafeteria-style believer."

I crack a smile. "Well, *belief* is a strong word."

With his left hand, Drew picks up the aloe frond and scrapes it with his thumb, opening the skin and revealing the shiny green gel within. He globs this onto the tip of his right middle finger, and then he takes both fingers and skates them — one coated in Aspercreme and the other in aloe — over the burn.

It stings and soothes at the same time, and I shake with the effort not to pull away.

"So what word would you use?" he asks, pulling me out of my fugue of pain.

125

"What?" I ask, blinking in confusion and searching his gray eyes for clarity. They are the exact color of a leaden winter sky. As I study him, a barely-there smile forms on his lips. At the same time, the searing in my hand cools by degrees.

"Instead of *belief,* what would you call it?" We are standing quite close, my injured hand resting on his broad palm. We are so close, I can smell his shaving soap. Fresh lumber and sundried cotton. He smells clean, natural.

Male.

I indulge in another inhale before getting a hold of myself. His question is an interesting one and deserves a thoughtful answer.

"Observance," I say finally.

His eyes narrow in mock scrutiny as he nods almost imperceptibly. Drew's mouth this close is a dangerous distraction.

He needs a friend, I remind myself. *Stop objectifying him.*

"And this Kali character, the Hindu goddess. What's your... *observance,"* he stresses the word before tightening his mouth against the pull of his smile, "... about her?"

It's the knowledge that he's trying not to laugh at me again that clears my head. Of all the deities in the global pantheon, Kali would be among the last any mortal should dare mock. I give him a warning glare.

"Kali, the great mother, is both creator *and* destroyer."

Drew quirks his brow. "Destroyer? A mother?"

"Well, sure." I love the expressiveness of brows, dark slashes that paint his moods. When he lets them

126

move, that is. Though, I have to say, I haven't seen his stone-faced stare all day. "Most of the time, to create something new, something old has to be sacrificed or abandoned. Even if it's just a way of thinking or the road not taken."

His frown eases. "So this Kali mother isn't killing her children, then?"

I shrug. "Well, she does that too."

Drew's mouth drops open slightly. "And Hindus *worship* her?"

It's so hard not to laugh at his appalled expression. "Think of it like Mother Nature. Nature destroys as well as creates, right?"

He blinks twice before his look of horror eases. "Good point." Drew reaches into the first aid kit and plucks out a roll of adhesive tape and a pack of gauze. "Still, why call on something so... *risky* as a mother who destroys her young?"

This time I do laugh, imagining what he must be picturing. "Actually, Kali is partial to women and children," I explain. "If they call on her during times of danger or distress, the results are said to be quite powerful."

Drew gives me his look of amused skepticism, just like he did when I tried to explain the Zodiac. I'm sure he thinks I'm a nut, but looking at him right now, I'm also pretty sure he likes it.

He likes me.

And with this thought, our eyes lock, and a current of electricity seems to crackle between us.

It's Drew who breaks the standoff, shuffling a step or two away from me to tear open the packet of gauze. He affixes the end with a strip of adhesive tape

127

and carefully secures it to my palm before wrapping the gauze around my hand. He makes a few passes, covering the medicated burn completely. A snip of scissors and one more piece of tape, and the job is done.

I turn my hand over and wiggle my exposed fingers. "Thanks a lot."

He shrugs off my thanks and opens the cabinet above Mrs. Vivan's sink. He grabs a plastic bottle and shakes it. "Want some pain reliever?"

I glance at the blue and white Ibuprofen bottle and shake my head. "No thanks. NSAIDS mess with your gut biome."

Drew's eyes widen slightly. "Gut biome," he echoes with a slight nod, and I know he's thinking I'm a nutter again.

"You know." I shrug. "Your probiotics and good bacteria that live in your intestines."

His surprised look grows and a single laugh escapes him. "Guppy, I had a lot of time for reading in prison, but nothing I came across had to do with intestines."

"Well, trust me on this, Ferdi," I say, fighting my grin with everything I've got. "Steer clear of that stuff. I'll take some white willow bark when I get home."

He gives a low whistle and shakes his head. "Boy, you really *are* one of those."

"If you mean informed, health-conscious, and homeopathic," I say, setting my hands on my hips and squaring off with him. "Then, yes, I am one of those."

He bunches his lips in consideration, hiding his smile. "I wasn't thinking of those exact words, but—"

I swat his elbow with my good hand, setting off another booming laugh. Somewhere in the middle of it, I

128

hear him stammer something that sounds like *hippy guppy*, and I completely lose it.

I laugh the kind of laugh that is completely airless, a suffocating laugh that nearly takes out my knees. I list against the counter on a graceless slide toward the floor, and Drew, red-faced and glossy-eyed, lost in his own hysteria, comes to my rescue, gripping me by the elbows and holding me against his quaking body.

His massive, wood-sinewed, utterly miraculous body.

Tingles, like waves of liquid pleasure, coast down every nerve where we touch. Some even make a detour and gather in a region that is definitely not touching him but is damn keen about the idea.

He likes me, my ego squeals.

He needs a friend, my conscience counters.

For a timeless instant, I ignore this war waging in the center of my consciousness, and revel in the feel of his body against mine. We are both still laughing, still coming down from the moment of hilarity, but I am so present that I am aware of the humor… and the touching… and the turmoil all at once.

And I feel so alive.

And I know I've felt some semblance of this aliveness, this vitality, each time I've been near Drew Moroux. And it's not because he has sexy, car mechanic hands. Or that his eyes are the color of night clouds. Or that his body is as hard as a live oak.

It's because he makes me laugh just like this. Because he lets me see a side of him I suspect the rest of the world does not share. Because, even when he teases me, he makes me feel rare and intriguing. Like a jewel.

129

Our eyes meet, and for a split second, I see a yielding in his. A flash of hunger and need. And just as quickly, it's gone. Then, like a shot, Drew stands bolt upright, taking me with him. Clasping me by the shoulders, he steadies me on my feet for the shortest of instants, and then he drops his hands, stepping away from me.

I stand there, half-stunned, as though someone has splashed me with ice water. Perhaps only three feet separate us, but he now feels so far away.

Suddenly ashamed of myself — for what, I'm not entirely sure — I look down at my feet.

Drew clears his throat. "Would you like me to walk you home?"

Glancing up at him, I frown. He looks shame-faced, too. I swallow and cast my gaze over my shoulder to the unfinished pickling project.

"We... we still have a few more jars to fill." I look back at him and find that his stoic facade has replaced his look of self-blame.

"I think you're out of commission," he says, tilting his chin the direction of my hand and not quite meeting my eyes. "Besides, it's not really a two-person job. Grandma Quincy usually does it alone. I can finish."

He's basically telling me to leave. The sting of this realization draws a hot blush to my cheeks. And for the first time, I can't get away from him fast enough.

CHAPTER ELEVEN

DREW

On the Friday of my second week at C&C, Cody hands me an envelope, and it takes me a second to realize it's a paycheck.

Real money. Earned the old-fashioned way.

It's less than five hundred dollars, but, I swear, it's the richest I've ever felt. I have to walk out back to the alley behind the shop while I choke down the knot in my throat and get my shit together.

Grandma Q will be proud of me. Annie will be proud, too. But it's Anthony's approval I wish I had the most, and he's not here to see me making my way on the straight and narrow. And that thought does nothing to clear my throat or dry my eyes.

At five o'clock, I cross Johnston Street and walk along the edge of Moncus Park until I reach Regions Bank. They close at five-thirty on Fridays, so I have just enough time to open two accounts, one checking and one savings, deposit my check, and put a little cash in my wallet.

But when I get home just after six, Grandma Q is not at the stove like she has been every other night I've come home. The kitchen looks just how I left it. Grandma's oatmeal bowl and coffee cup, both still half-full, sit on the table. Definitely not normal.

"Grandma?" I clear the kitchen in two strides and pick up speed in the dining room, my heart punching the interior walls of my chest. "Grandma?"

"Ohhh." The feeble moan comes from the living room, and I take off at a run.

I find Grandma Quincy on the couch, lying on her side, her face twisted in pain.

"What? What's wrong?" My first thought is heart attack, and I drop to my knees beside the couch. Does she need CPR? How do you do CPR?

"It burns like *fire*," she says. She's on her left side, her arms crossed around her middle, and she gestures to her right. "Oh, my lands…"

"What does? Your kidney? Your stomach?"

"My skin," she answers, closing her eyes and wincing. "I think maybe it's shingles."

"Shingles?" I echo, stunned. I know what shingles are. At least, I think I know. Like chicken pox or something, but in the nerves. A few years ago, one old guy in Hickory came down with shingles and gave chicken pox to three other inmates. "Can I take a look?"

She nods tightly, eyes still closed. Her face is ashen, her brow creased. Carefully, I take the hem of her shirt at her hip and raise it, exposing her where belly meets back. She makes a muffled noise that just kills me, and I move as gently as possible.

I see nothing. No sign of rash, no redness. But when I lay the shirt down and place my hand on her forehead, I feel fever.

"Grandma, I'm gonna call Aunt Josie," I say softly.

She moans in protest. "Don't do that. It's late."

"It's not late. It's not even six o'clock."

"She'll be trying to get dinner on the table."

My eighty-three-year-old grandmother is lying on the couch, moaning in pain — a sight I've never seen and one that strips me down to nothing but terror — and she's worried about being an inconvenience.

"Grandma, that's not important."

She makes a noise in the back of her throat, but she doesn't open her eyes, so I go to the kitchen. A phone — a cheap one — is one of the first things on my list now that I've got money. I grab the cordless off the charging station and find Aunt Josie's number in the call history.

"Hey, Mama," she answers, a smile in her voice. Just hearing her on the other end of the line brings relief.

"Josie, it's Drew. Grandma's sick."

Twenty minutes later, Aunt Josie and I are both standing over Grandma Q, arguing with her.

"I'm not going to the emergency room. I'll be there all night." She's still lying on the couch. Her eyes are still closed, but her will is stronger. "I won't sleep a wink. They'll put me in a room with a flu patient, and I'll never come out."

Josie and I eye each other over her. Even in this condition, she's a pro at emotional manipulation.

"If you would have called someone earlier, we could have gotten in to see Dr. Sullivan or at least taken you to a walk-in clinic," Josie counters. "We can't leave you like this all night."

Grandma Quincy cocks one eye open and aims it at her daughter. "I didn't feel this poorly earlier, Josephine, and you can and will leave me here tonight."

The eye shuts again.

I shake my head at my aunt. Grandma had to be feeling bad all day. She would never leave breakfast dishes unwashed otherwise, but I don't dare admit this oversight aloud.

"Have you taken anything for the pain, Mama?"

Silence.

"I'll take that as a no," Josie mutters.

I leave them and head to the kitchen. I open the cabinet where Grandma Q keeps her pills and feel a stab of regret at the sight of the Ibuprofen bottle.

Evie.

The afternoon we spent in this kitchen washes over me, as it has a thousand times since Saturday, but I don't have time to sort through it all again. But unwilling to ignore Evie's advice on pain relievers, I reach for the red and white Acetaminophen bottle instead.

I fill a glass of water and take it and the bottle back to the living room. Aunt Josie stands over Grandma Q with arms crossed at her middle. Grandma hasn't moved. I set down the meds and water on the coffee table and lean in.

"Grandma, can I help you sit up to take some medicine?"

She makes a noise of assent, but moving her leaves me a little sick. Her strained breath and stifled moans make it clear that even sitting up is agony. By the time we get her upright and propped against the arm of the couch, my forehead is damp with sweat, and my hands are shaking. And it's not from the effort.

Aunt Josie uncaps the medicine bottle and shakes two pills onto her palm. "Mama, you don't want some Advil instead? It'll last longer."

"Nope." Grandma Q shakes her head. "It'll mess up my gut biome."

My mouth falls open. I narrow my eyes at her. "What did you say?"

134

She purses her thin lips, forcing a poor show of innocence. "Isn't that what your girlfriend said?"

"You were watching *Ellen*," I accuse, forgetting for a moment that she's ill. "And she's not my girlfriend."

My aunt looks back and forth between us, a smile slowly spreading across her face.

"She's not my girlfriend," I tell her.

"Clearly not."

Aunt Josie's obvious amusement has me glaring back at my grandmother. "How could you possibly have heard that with the TV on?"

Her lips draw down in apparent disinterest. "My remote has a mute button. Same as everybody's."

Josie snickers, and I shake my head. "I can't believe you."

Grandma Quincy closes her eyes and frowns. "Don't fuss me. I'm sick."

At this, Aunt Josie tips back her head and laughs with abandon. "Drama Mama," she mutters.

My grandmother opens her eyes and gives her daughter a scowl. "Now that I'm sitting up, I think I need to move to the bed."

I almost protest. Getting her to sit up was torture enough.

"My legs don't hurt," she says. "Just my trunk."

We help her up and, she's right, the worst part is getting her to her feet. Once she's on them, she moves on her own, albeit slowly, across the house. Even so, I stay by her side in case she loses her balance. She's still feverish. Plus, she's eighty-three.

135

When we get to her room, Grandma Q stops at the foot of the bed. "Josephine, I think you'll need to help me into a nightgown."

I look at my aunt. "You can manage from here?"

She nods, but before I can leave, Grandma Quincy grips my wrist. "Do me a favor, Andrew. I haven't eaten all day. Walk down to Champagne's and get me some boudin and a dinner roll, would you?"

"Of course, Grandma. Anything else?"

She presses her lips together in a moue. "Maybe some ginger ale?" Then she releases my wrist and pats my hand. "And get something for your dinner while you're there. You can take my card. It's the green one in my wallet."

I'm grateful I had the chance to go to the bank. There's no way I'm going into her purse for her card.

"I got it, Grandma."

Once outside, I'm relieved to be alone. The mention of Evie left my nerves raw and exposed. I sent her away on Saturday, but that doesn't mean I've stopped thinking about her.

Or looking for her.

Every time I'm on the stairs, coming to or from my apartment, my eyes are trained on her house. At night, probably four times a night before I collapse in bed, I look out my window for the light in hers.

When it's on, it feels like someone's lit a sparkler in my chest.

Two nights ago, sometime after ten, I was about to turn in and checked it one last time. As I looked, her light went out, and the knowledge that she was climbing into bed less than an acre away set me ablaze.

I stretched out on the futon, and God help me, I let myself picture what she wore to bed. Nothing frilly. Nothing out of a Victoria's Secret ad. Evie doesn't need lace trim or a satin cami set to make her feel beautiful.

Not that she doesn't deserve it. She deserves everything fine. Nothing's too good for her.

But she wouldn't choose fancy. She'd choose simple. Comfortable. And, yeah, probably organic cotton or some shit like that. And no matter what it was — an old T-shirt or a tank top and shorts — it would look fucking amazing on her.

And, no, I did not toss off in bed thinking of Evie in her pajamas. Watching her bedroom window and then jerking off would feel like I'd violated her. It would feel like I'd stolen something from her.

And I don't want to take anything from her. Even if she'd never know it.

That doesn't mean Evie doesn't cross my mind when I'm in the shower, taking matters in my own hands. She does. I'm not a monk. Even when I try to think of nothing, just feel, something of hers will flash through my mind. The fall of her curls... the pale green of her eyes... the weight of her laughing body against mine...

And I'm gone.

I don't need to walk into Champagne's with a tent in my coveralls, so I shove these thoughts aside, make my way to the end of the block, and cross Souvenir Gate. I push open the door to the corner grocery and deli. This place has been here forever, and though this is my first time being inside since getting out, little appears to have changed. It's small, and it smells like what I'd

137

imagine 1950 smelled like, and the Saint Streets wouldn't be the same without it.

I can see at once I'm the only customer. An older woman with long, white hair smiles at me from the register, and I can hear a radio coming from the kitchen behind the deli, but otherwise, the store is empty. They'll close in twenty minutes, but I take my time. Grandma Q wants boudin, and I don't, and if this is the first meal I get to buy for myself as a free man, it's going to be something I actually want.

The chalkboard sign by the first deli case announces hamburger steak as the plate of the day. But after walking over here and working all day in the garage, I'm too hot for hamburger steak.

Then again, I definitely need a shower before I sit down to dinner. I'm filthy. Maybe after I'm clean, I'll be able to stomach something heavier.

Without any further prompting, thoughts of a shower bring Evie to mind, and I close my eyes and smother a groan.

The bell over the door chimes, announcing another customer, and I remind myself where I am. I focus on the coolness of the air conditioning on my skin and the sound of the store clerk greeting whoever has come in.

"Hi," the customer greets back, and I open my eyes. I stare blindly at the glass case in front of me, and my heart rate climbs.

It's her. I know it's her without even turning around.

In fact, I don't turn around. Instead, I hold perfectly still and listen to each of her footfalls as she walks without hesitation to my side.

138

I look down at Evie. She is all the beauty. All the beauty in the entire world.

She aims a timid smile up at me, half hopeful, half wary. She is so innocent. I feel like one of Satan's bastard sons standing beside her. Like I've climbed up from the large intestines of hell and belly-crawled out of the sewer to stare up at an angel.

Someone like me should not have the power to hurt her. But I do. I have. I can see by the way she looks at me that I left her bruised the other day when I sent her away.

I want to fall at her feet. I want to beg her forgiveness. I want to stand outside her door as her bodyguard so no one else unworthy can get close enough to touch her.

At the same time, I want to erase all memory of me from her mind.

I want to remove all her curiosity. All her compassion for me. And, yes, this crush of hers I can't begin to understand.

And I want to grab her. I want to crush her against me and kiss her hard. And long. I want to tell her how goddamn good it is to see her. How seeing her is torture, and not seeing her is torture.

How as much as I want her to forget me, I never want to forget her. I want to worship her, and tuck her image — her perfection — deep inside of me. Carry it with me and make it my own, so I can believe that something within me is good.

"What are you doing here?" My voice is low, hoarse. I know she's not here to shop. She's not picking up dinner or a bag of chips.

I watch her swallow. "I was on my way home from class. I saw you cross the street," she says, her eyes widening with that wariness. "I parked my car at home and walked—" she stops, bites her lip, and begins again, "—ran over."

I'm about to tell her I'm not worth crossing the street for when the deli clerk emerges from the back.

"Can I help you?"

"Just a minute," I tell him without taking my eyes off Evie. He watches us stare at each other for a long moment before taking the hint and stepping away.

"Go home, Evie." It takes all of my strength to speak those words.

She shakes her head. "I don't want to go home."

"Go home, Evie."

Her expression hardens, and she tilts her head to the side. "I will if you come with me."

It's like a punch in the gut. The temptation nearly takes me down.

"I can't. Grandma's sick. I'm getting her something to eat."

At once, her hard stare falls away and her brow knits in concern. "What's wrong with Mrs. Vivian?"

I shake my head. "Not sure. She thinks it's shingles."

Her eyes widen before she presses her lips together in sympathy. "I've heard that's really painful."

I just nod.

Evie glances around the shop. "What does she need? What would help?"

"She just wants boudin and ginger ale," I say with a shrug.

And with that, the tension of a moment before disappears, and Evie cracks a smile. "Well, we should get her some."

Before I can argue, Evie darts off toward the drinks cooler.

"Hey pal, we're about to pack up for the night," the deli server says, approaching me again. "You want anything?"

I order the boudin and two dinner rolls. Then I scan the case. Food is the last thing on my mind right now. Maybe I'll just skip dinner tonight. Or make a sandwich later when my insides aren't tangled in knots of regret.

While the clerk packs up my order, Evie reemerges at my side. She's carrying a plastic shopping basket bearing a six-pack of ginger ale, a box of townhouse crackers, and a small jar of orange marmalade. I frown, wondering if the last two items are for her or Grandma, but whatever.

"I'll have a round of the camembert," she tells the clerk when he hands me the to-go box.

I should just grab the soda from her, head to the checkout, and leave, but I can't.

I'll walk away when we get outside, I tell myself.

The clerk wraps up her cheese as we wait in silence. When he goes to hand this to her, I step in front of Evie and claim it.

"Hey," she scolds, making a grab for her cheese, but I lift it out of her reach and move toward the checkout.

"Give that back," she says, fast on my heels.

I reach the counter, set down the groceries, and then pluck the items from her basket.

"What are you doing?" she asks. The woman at the counter starts ringing up everything, and Evie reaches for the small purse that hangs from her shoulder.

"Let me," I say. It's not a plea. It's a command. She must hear the strangled edge in my voice as clearly as I do because she doesn't argue. If buying my own food is an achievement, providing hers is a sacrament. There's nothing better I could do with my paycheck than feed her.

The pleasure this gives me goes bone deep, and I feel lighter, less burdened when I hand over the cash.

"Put those in a separate bag," I tell the woman, indicating the crackers, jam, and cheese. As she bags the items, I glance down and see a small frown on Evie's brow, and I wonder why it's there, but I know better than to ask.

I take the receipt and the bags and then hold the door open for Evie. We walk side by side to the corner where I should go left to Saint Joseph Street and she right to Saint Patrick Street. I hand her the plastic bag holding her items.

"Here you go."

She looks up at me, the frown etched deeper. "Those aren't for *me*," she says. "They're for *us*."

"Evie—"

"Please," she says, pinning me with the life-giving green of her eyes. Her voice is low, strained. "Please just let me be near you."

Thank God I'm filthy. Thank God I'm covered in sweat and grease and brake fluid. Because if I were clean enough to touch her, my tongue would be in her mouth

142

right now. My hands in her hair. Her breasts crushed against my chest.

But I am not clean. Hell, I will never be that clean. So I stand stockstill and feel her words slice me open. I have the will to keep from kissing her within an inch of her life. But any power I have to turn her away has vanished.

I'll have to search for it later, but for now, I grab her hand, and we cross the street.

CHAPTER TWELVE

EVIE

When we get back to Drew's house, he leaves me in the kitchen to see to Mrs. Vivian. I stand there, fidgeting with one of the plastic bags, not wanting to unpack the remaining groceries because I'm holding out hope.

I want to be alone with him. Up in his apartment. Sharing a meal.

It's shameful how much I want to be with him. I've never felt like this with anyone. I tell myself I'm not the kind of girl who pines over guys who don't want to be with me, but I sure am pining over Drew Moroux.

And I want him. I want him like I want to keep my own skin. But I meant what I said a moment ago. If all I can have is just to be near him, keep his company — be his friend — that's all I'll ask of him.

I know he doesn't trust himself. Not with friendship, and sure as hell not with more than friendship. And he's stubborn, but so am I. I didn't think I could miss seeing someone so much in just a matter of days.

I mean, I haven't hugged Mom and Dad in months. Yeah, I miss them, but it doesn't feel like a giant fish hook has me caught under the ribs.

So if he tries to push me away tonight, I'm going to push right back.

I'm squaring my shoulders and frowning with determination when he walks back into the kitchen. A flash of surprise crosses his face when he sees my expression.

"What?" he asks.

I fast-blink, feeling like an idiot, and clear my face. "How is she?"

Drew winces. "Hurting. And there's nothing I can do to help."

"You brought her food," I tell him, hoping to cheer him up. "That's helping."

He shakes his head. "My Aunt Josie says she's going to stay the night. Grandma refuses to go to the emergency room, but she's running a fever, and if she takes a turn for the worse, Josie wants to rush her to the hospital. Which means I'm basically no use at all."

"What do you mean?" I ask, frowning.

A look of naked disgust claims his face. "My driver's license is expired. And I'm uninsured now. Neither one of them wants me to get behind the wheel until I'm covered and legal."

I see his disgust for what it is. Shame. Self-loathing. I'm about to offer myself as an emergency driver, but I clamp my mouth shut. That's not what he wants. He wants to be able to help his family on his own.

Still, I might be able to make that easier.

"What's keeping you from getting your license and insurance?"

His glowering brow lifts, and his expression lightens a little. "Nothing after today," he says cryptically.

At my blank stare, he grins, turning my heart to butter. "I got my first paycheck today."

All hint of self-loathing is gone. In fact, he looks so proud, I want to hug him. "That's awesome!"

His grin grows, and his cheeks, high-boned and gorgeous, flush pink. "You're the first person I've told."

145

Little fireworks of joy burst in my chest. Then an idea strikes that makes me feel like a helium balloon. "Monday — i-if you like, I could drive you to the DMV to renew your license," I stammer, wanting so much to do this for him it's almost embarrassing. "I have classes in the morning, but we could go in the afternoon."

For a moment, his stoic stare is all I see, and I'm sure he's going to turn me down.

"That would be... That would be great."

Yes!

It takes all the restraint I have not to cheer, but I bounce a little.

"You're weird," he says, his gray eyes lighting with the hint of a smile.

No point in denying that. "Yes, I am. But why do you think so?"

He splutters a laugh. "Because no one else looks that excited about going to the DMV."

I rock my shoulders side to side in a pathetic dance move. "Long lines? Awkward pictures? What's not to like?"

He laughs, raw and free. Seeing this is worth making a fool of myself. He looked so sad at the store. So unbelievably sad.

I grab the loops of a shopping bag. "Have you ever had soft French cheese and marmalade?"

His expression is priceless. "What do you think?"

I cock my brow at him. "Well, you're in for a treat. How about we grab some plates and go upstairs?" I try to sound super casual. I don't want him to think I mean Netflix-and-chill.

Of course, I'd totally Netflix-and-chill with Drew. That would be... *wow...*

146

I'd better not think about it.

But when I look up at him, I'm pretty sure he knows I'm thinking about it. And he doesn't approve.

"I don't think that's a good idea, Evie."

Even though it's the reaction I expect, it still feels like an elbow in the gut. "Sure." I nod, shaking it off. "Sure, we can stay here. I just didn't want to disturb Mrs. Vivian."

Something shifts in Drew's eyes. He looks over his shoulder toward Mrs. Vivian's dining room and then back at me.

"On second thought," he says, grabbing a couple of dirty dishes from the table and ferrying them to the sink. "Let's go up. Grab a couple of napkins."

He nods over his shoulder to the wooden, rooster shaped napkin holder in the middle of the table, and I pluck some. Drew rinses out the dishes before claiming two plates and a couple of knives from the cabinets and drawers.

"C'mon."

Afraid to say anything lest he change his mind, I follow Drew out of the kitchen, around the side of Mrs. Vivian's house, and up the stairs.

I have never been to the apartment above the garage, but when he pushes the door open for me, I recognize his smell. Split lumber. Clean cotton. I immediately smile.

"I love that smell." I take a deep inhale, and turn my smile on him. Drew's mouth turns up a little, but no light reaches his eyes. I see something like regret in their depths.

"This was Grandpa Pete's workshop."

"Is that a bad thing?" I know his Grandpa is gone, and maybe what I'm seeing is grief, but I don't think so.

Drew closes the door behind him and drops his keys on a kitchen counter that runs along the west wall. "It's not a bad thing that it was his space…"

I think he's pausing, preparing to finish his thought, but he doesn't. Instead, he moves to the small kitchen table in the center of the apartment and carefully lays out the plates and knives he carried up.

I take my cue and set down the grocery bag and napkins. If he doesn't want to talk about this, I'm not going to push.

I reach into the bag and set out the crackers, marmalade, and cheese. When I look up, Drew is leaning against the counter watching me. He looks exhausted.

"Are you okay?"

His expression is unreadable. "I really need a shower."

I straighten, rethinking my intention to stay. I want to be here, but I don't want to make him uncomfortable. "Would you rather I go?"

I watch him swallow. He crosses his arms over his chest. "Honestly?" he asks, lifting one brow to survey me. He's not smiling. My heart sinks, but I nod.

"I always want honesty."

The left side of his mouth draws up in a reluctant smile. "You would," he mutters. Drew shakes his head. "If I'm being honest, I don't want you to go."

My smile is unstoppable. "Then go take a shower," I say, gesturing to the bathroom door across the apartment. "I'll wait."

A measure of surprise shows on his face. "You will?"

"Of course."

Without another word, he crosses to an old wardrobe next to the bathroom and pulls out fresh clothes. He looks at me over his shoulder. "I'll just be a minute. Make yourself comfortable." And then he steps into the bathroom and shuts the door behind him.

And I'm alone in his apartment. It doesn't feel weird, and that's... *weird*. The space is austere, but it has its own warmth. The fading sunlight through the windows on three sides of the apartment paints the wood walls a kind of rosy gold. Besides the little kitchen table and chairs and the wardrobe, the only other furnishings are a bookshelf and a futon.

The futon is clearly where he sleeps. The mattress is outfitted with bed linens and a pillow, and the bed is made. This makes me smile. Drew lives up here, alone, with no one here to see and yet he makes his bed in the morning.

I hear the sound of the shower, and I still. This sound is followed by a muffled, metallic *chink!* Like the sound of the zipper on a pair of coveralls hitting the floor.

I grab the back of one of the kitchen chairs. Because behind that bathroom door, Drew Moroux is naked. Naked, and washing away the sweat that clung to him when I approached him at the deli. The grease on his hands. The exhaustion from his muscles.

I'd like to help with that. With all of it.

I'd like to brush soap against a washcloth and rub it over his skin. Take away everything that makes him feel unclean. Weighted down.

149

I'd like to shampoo his hair, running my fingers against his scalp until he closes his eyes in pleasure.

I'd like to hold him against me, skin to skin, so he would know that there's nothing about him I'd reject.

Nothing at all.

I release the chair back and pace the floor, trying to put distance between me and these thoughts. That's when I notice a yellow sheet draped over a wide rectangle across the room from the futon.

I frown at it, wondering what it might be. I step closer, curious, but I'm not about to snoop. Maybe it's just a dust cover over something that's been up here for a while, though it doesn't look dusty.

Turning my attention away from this mystery, I check out his bookshelf, which forms a kind of privacy wall at the foot of his bed. But since it faces the door and his dining area, it seems the least private of his possessions, so I don't feel like I'm spying on him. The bookshelf must serve as a kind of dresser or end table because one shelf holds a spill of change, a pocket knife, and a smooth wooden box I tell myself I'm not allowed to open.

The shelf above this holds just three books, a red hardcover copy of the American Standard Version of the Bible, a worn paperback copy of Dante's *Inferno* that looks older than both of us, and a newer, but not brand-new, copy of *Atonement*.

"Jesus Christ, Drew," I whisper.

I've never read Dante, but I know enough to guess it's not the feel-good book of the Renaissance. I didn't read *Atonement*, either, but I saw the movie. Everybody dies. And the one who's to blame can never really atone. Drew has a copy of the Bible, but, honestly, the first half of that is all about a pissed off patriarchal deity.

A trip to the library for more cheerful reading material is definitely in order.

I hear the shower cut off, and I let my eyes travel lower to the collection of CDs. As anyone might expect, most of them are at least ten years old. But a younger Drew Moroux clearly liked Jay-Z, Fall Out Boy, and Kings of Leon. I pull out the last one, *Only by the Night*, and look at the familiar red and black cover art.

The bathroom door opens with a whoosh of steam, revealing a breathtaking sight. Drew — his wet hair curling in dark waves, his clean face red from the shower — dressed in a plain white T-shirt and worn jeans.

His feet are bare, and from head to toe, he is masculine beauty embodied.

He sees me holding the CD case and gives me a questioning lift of his brow. I show him the cover. "You have good taste in music."

He steps out of the bathroom and drags a towel over his head, catching the gathering droplets in his hair. "Had," he says. "The incarceration station plays exclusively Christian songs, so I'm way out of touch."

"Incarceration station?" I hear myself ask.

Drew's perfect lips shape into a grin. "KLSP. The radio station at Angola."

I blink in surprise. "So, you heard no other music? Like, at all?"

He shrugs. "Sure, yeah, but it was harder to come by. There's a music collection in the prison library. You can put on headphones and listen to that, but most of it is old shit. Perry Como and Elvis." He tilts his head to the side like he's confessing a secret and whispers. "And there's contraband music, of course. Just like there's contraband everything."

I want to hear more, but is it rude to ask? To be so curious? I can't imagine living in prison, but as I've come to know Drew, it's not hard to picture him there. He wears its effects like a second skin. I read discipline in his posture. Restriction in his muscles. Deprivation in his eyes.

"Christian music?" I say, unable to help my grimace at the thought of listening to gospel for eight years.

"Whether you wanted to hear it or not," he says, executing a slow nod. "There are speakers all over The Farm, so the warden can reach all sixty-three hundred inmates at once."

"What would he say?"

"*He* didn't say much, but he also liked to play recorded sermons. A couple a day."

My mouth drops in horror.

Drew's laugh is bitter. "Guppy, there's far worse things to happen in prison than listening to sermons and Christian rock."

I close my mouth, suddenly ill. He's smiling at me, sort of, but he's watching my expression, too. What worse things happened to him at Angola? Did someone hurt him?

Or worse?

The thought nearly tears my heart out of my chest, and I want to hug him.

"Don't look at me like that, Evie." His voice rasps with something I can't name. It's not warning. Desperation?

I tear my eyes away, blushing. Still carrying the CD, I move back to the table. "Are you hungry?" I ask, unwrapping the cake of cheese.

"Starving." His voice behind me is low, almost feral, and I can't help but feel he's not talking about hunger. Not normal hunger, anyway. But the word isn't an invitation. I know this. So I ignore the stirring it triggers in me.

Taking the knife, I slice the camembert in half before cutting small wedges of the butter soft cheese.

"Come sit," I tell him.

But he doesn't. Instead, he goes to the mini fridge and pulls out a green apple and a ceramic pitcher. He rinses the apple at the sink before drying it on his shirt, and then he picks up a lone glass in the otherwise empty draining rack.

He turns back to me. "I just have the one glass," he says, his tone apologetic. "You can have it."

I smile at him because the gesture is immeasurably sweet. "We'll share."

With a shrug of acquiescence, Drew fills the glass with a purple liquid.

"What's that?" I ask startled.

Before my eyes, color rises to his cheeks. "Grape Kool-Aid," he says with chagrin. "Grandma Quincy makes it."

I stifle a laugh. "Why does she make you grape Kool-Aid?"

Drew sets the apple and the glass on the table and sits across from me. "Because it was my favorite as a kid, and I don't have the heart to tell her it's too sweet for me now."

This time, I do laugh. *He's* too sweet.

153

"I cut it with a little water to make it bearable," he says wryly, and this makes me laugh harder.

Putting on a harrassed look, Drew takes the knife I've abandoned and slices the apple. I open the box of crackers and serve us each a generous handful. With care, he lays apple slices on my plate, like a row of crescent moons.

"Thank you," I murmur.

He just nods, not meeting my eyes.

We sit silently for a moment before I realize he's waiting for me. And as polite as that is, I quickly understand it's not out of politeness. He's looking at the cheese wedges like they're about to sprout legs and walk off the table.

"Despite appearances," I reassure, "it's really good."

He narrows his eyes just slightly. "Do you... do you eat the white stuff?" He looks embarrassed, uncertain, and for the world, I would not laugh at him.

"The rind. Yes, you eat it. Here." I pick up an apple slice and top it with a creamy wedge of camembert. The walk outside and the time out of the cooler has left it gooey and irresistable. I bite half of the little stack, the tart crispness of the apple with the creamy, earthiness of the cheese is sinfully delicious.

"Mmmm."

Drew's eyes widen, and he looks between me and the cheese. "That good?"

"That good," I answer with my mouthful.

"What do I have to lose?" he mutters, taking a piece of apple and following my lead. As soon as he bites down through the cheese and its tougher rind, he

154

frowns. But as he chews, the frown morphs from one of suspicion to one of concentration.

A short noise of surprise leaves his throat. "That *is* good."

And at his words, I beam.

"Try it on a cracker," I say, layering cheese on a townhouse wafer before handing it to him. If he'd let me, I'd feed him, but I know he wouldn't let me.

Still, this is the most fun I've had in months.

"God, it's like butter," he says, smacking his lips.

"I know, right?"

I go to open the orange marmalade because the combination of cracker, cheese, and bitter orange is going to blow his mind. But the lid won't budge. I struggle for a moment, twisting the base and the lid with no results.

"Here, hand it over," he says.

I could just as easily tap the lid with the butt of the knife, and it would pop open with a good, stiff turn. But why would I do that when I have a chance to watch Drew work with those hands? So I give it to him, and my only complaint is that the show is over too quickly. The instant he has it by both ends, the lid gives a satisfying pop, and the orange marmalade is free.

He watches with interest as I spread it on a cracker before dressing it with cheese. I hand the bite to him.

"Your life will never be the same."

Smirking, he takes the treat from me and pops the whole thing in his mouth. I watch. One bite. Two bites. Then he closes his eyes and sighs.

"I didn't even think I liked orange marmalade," he says almost reverently.

I giggle.

He opens his eyes, looks at me, and then sweeps his gaze around his one-room apartment. "This is the first time I've actually enjoyed being in here."

Laughter dries up in my throat. "Why?" My shock is unmistakable. "Why haven't you enjoyed being here?"

He takes a deep breath and lets it go in a jagged sigh. "It was my grandfather's." A lost look comes over his eyes. "He died not long after I went inside. Cancer. The last time I saw him, I was being sentenced."

His shame is a tangible thing. It's so painful, my own gut twists with it. So I let myself feel it, like the edge of a pose, difficult and uncomfortable. Maybe if I share it, his burden will be lessened.

And then again, maybe it's something he can let go.

"Do you think he was ashamed of you?" I ask evenly, my voice soft but steady.

Drew looks at me, shocked. "H-how could he not be?"

I let the question echo around the room.

"I mean," Drew continues. "I was a felon who cost him the life of his grandson."

This I can't let slide. "But you were also his grandson."

He clamps his mouth shut, and I see by the workings of his jaw that he's clenching his teeth.

"Let me put it another way." I try again. "Why would he have gone to your sentencing if he were ashamed of you?"

"To see justice done." He bites off the words. He's not talking to me. We may both be in the same

156

room, but while I'm sitting in a chair at a small table with a miniature feast, he is wrestling a demon.

My words are gentle and low. "Is that something a dying man does? Goes to his grandson's sentencing out of spite?"

Everything — his whole posture and the muscles in his face — goes slack then. Drew thumps his elbows on the table and stares at his outstretched hands. He closes his eyes. "No."

Maybe he's thinking it already, allowing the knowledge to penetrate, but I want him to hear it aloud.

"My guess is he went there to be with you on such a terrible day," I whisper, "because he loved you."

He opens his eyes and gives me a wary look, and I'm afraid I've gone too far. He watches me for a long time. Long enough for my heart to pound like an obnoxious snare drum in my chest.

If I could just touch him now, maybe he'd trust me. Maybe he'd trust himself.

I slide my right hand across the table to take his, but as soon as my fingers brush his knuckles, he pulls away.

He hides the intention by picking up the glass and taking a swig of its purple contents, ignoring the stinging blush that rises to my cheeks.

When he sets the glass down, I'm the one who needs to hide, so I take it up and follow his example. Watered down, artificial grape coats my tongue and slides down my throat.

"Good God," I rasp. "That's awful."

It's weak, but my effort draws a crooked smile from him. Again, he watches me for an endless moment.

I can tell he's debating his words. I see in his eyes when he makes up his mind.

"That was a nice thing to say."

Relief courses through me, and I swallow hard. "You mean about the Kool-Aid?" I tease, wrinkling my nose.

A chuckle escapes him. "You're a goof."

That, right there, is worth the rejection, I tell myself.

Okay, yeah, the rejection is pretty bad. I don't like it one bit. But I love seeing him laugh. Still, I'd better go before I make an even bigger fool of myself. The last thing I want is for him to tell me it's time I leave.

"I should get going," I say, getting to my feet. "I need to feed Gemini."

He rises with me, a look of alarm flashing over his features and disappearing just as quickly.

"How is everything at your place? Your sister still mad at you?"

I roll my eyes and snort a bitter laugh. "Only every day." It's true, but I don't tell him about the fight we had when I came home Saturday with the burn on my hand. Or the late-night Skype-lecture that followed hours later. "At least she's not talking about moving out anymore."

Drew's brows draw together. "Evie, your sister sounds crazy."

This time my laugh is genuine. "Why do you say that? You haven't even met Tori." Of course, I can't fault him for his opinion. Tori is… well… Tori.

"She'd have to be," he says, still frowning. "Who wouldn't want to live with you?"

And I don't know who is more startled. Me, suddenly awash in what feels like a warm bubble bath around my soul, or Drew, who looks like he could swallow his tongue.

"I-I mean... You know," he stammers, walking us over to the door. "You're easy-going a-and considerate. And you have great taste in cheese."

He's making light of his admission, but all of his bluster makes up for pulling his hand from mine. He likes me. He may not be able to accept everything I want to offer him — everything I am — but he likes me.

And maybe, after tonight, we can really call each other friends.

Drew opens to the door to a charcoal sky, the frayed ends of dusk. "It got late," he says, sounding surprised. He looks at me with a frown. "I should walk you home."

I step past him and out onto the landing. "Nah. I'll be okay."

His frown deepens. "But it might not be safe."

I cock a brow at him. "It's not even eight o'clock. It's perfectly safe." Still, he advances, looking determined, and I hold up a hand. "If it makes you feel better, I'll just cross through the yard and jump the fence. You can watch for assailants from up here."

He mirrors my arch look. "You're going to jump the fence? Who are you, Wonder Woman?"

"Just watch," I say, no shortage of sass in my tone. And then I turn to go, but I spin back to face him, the impulse irresistible. "I had fun tonight."

And before he can step back, I grab him around the middle in my fiercest hug.

CHAPTER THIRTEEN

DREW

Her arms close around me, and I fight for breath.

Not because she's hugging tightly — though she is — but because it feels like heaven. And since I can't help it, I wrap my arms around her, pulling her into me.

"Me too."

I close my eyes and dip my nose into her soft curls, grabbing what I can of the moment. She smells like lavender and patchouli. Like the free spirit she is. Free and innocent.

Inhaling her is almost as dangerous as holding her, and doing both at once threatens to shatter my control.

I'm trying to muster the will to let her go when she drops her arms and steps out of my reach, giving me her megawatt smile. She starts down the stairs, but points her finger at me.

"Monday. The DMV. It's a date."

A laugh breaks from me. Going to the DMV could never and will never be a date.

Which I guess is what makes it safe for me to agree.

I nod. "Monday."

I will see her again on Monday.

The thought feels too much like oxygen. Fresh. Vital.

With one more flash of that smile, Evie trots down the stairs. When she reaches the bottom, she looks back up at me. The world is one color, the closest gray to black, but there's still just enough twilight to make her out against the shadows.

"Watch me," she calls, reminding me of her promise to jump the fence. I laugh again, shaking my head.

"Be careful. You're going to tear those leggings." A memory surfaces of Ma yelling at me and Anthony. I'd torn the seat of my shorts trying to climb a chain-link fence in our neighborhood. And maybe it's because I'm looking at Evie, but the memory of Ma and Anthony doesn't bring me to my knees.

"No, I'm not," she sing-songs, sounding cocky.

She flits across the yard and past Grandma's garden. I'm prepared to see her gingerly grasp the fence post and slowly work her toes into the chain-link to scale the fence, but as soon as her hands hit the top frame, Evie vaults herself in one fluid motion over the fence.

I blink.

"What the fuck?!" I whisper, not believing my eyes. And then I shout, "Damn!"

Her delighted laugh rolls over the yard. She turns and gives me a wave. "Told ya!" She pumps a fist in the air. "Yoga power, baby!"

I clap and whoop, and she executes a dramatic bow. My laughter echoes through the night, a foreign but welcome sound.

She cups her hands around her mouth. "Goodnight, Drew."

I wave to her and watch as she turns, speeds across her yard, and slips inside the house. I shake my head. Why am I even surprised? She's lighter than air. In every way. Gravity doesn't apply to her.

Who wouldn't want to live with you?

I can't believe I said that out loud. But it's the truth. I turn and re-enter my apartment, a space that has

161

been redefined with her presence. I run my eyes over the tongue-in-groove panels my grandfather measured and cut himself. I look down at the planks beneath my feet that he sanded, stained, and sealed.

If Evie is right... if Grandpa Pete came to my sentencing to... well... to be there for me...

I didn't think about it at the time, but he must have known it would be the last he'd see of me. I swallow at the thought. I'd spotted him and Grandma sitting with Annie a few rows behind me in the courthouse when the bailiff had brought me in. Annie and Grandma Q had been crying. I only looked at him once, but Grandpa Pete's eyes had been dry. Empty. I hadn't been able to face him after that one glance.

But I also hadn't been able to imagine it would be the last time I'd see him.

I look back at the small table in my apartment. Only the apple core and a few slices of cheese remain. She left the crackers and marmalade, and the sight of them makes me smile. I wrap up the leftover cheese, determined to have it for breakfast in the morning, and then I wash the dishes.

As I do, I can't help but wonder what Grandpa Pete would think of the evening I'd shared with Evie in his old workshop. I roll the thought around in my head, seeing it from every angle. And I can't find any from which he'd mind.

I've felt him in this space since the day I got out, but this is the first time that feeling hasn't crushed me.

I brush my teeth and strip off my jeans and T-shirt. Before I turn off the light over the sink, I pick up the CD Evie left on the table, load it into the portable player on the bookshelf, and select Track 4. As Caleb

Followill sings about how he could use "someone like you," I replay the feel of Evie Lalonde in my arms and the sight of her sailing over a four-foot fence as if it didn't exist.

CHAPTER FOURTEEN

EVIE

"Where have you been?" Tori frowns and looks toward the back porch. She's curled up on the couch with a copy of *Self* in her lap. "I heard you pull up a couple of hours ago. Have you been sitting out there this whole time?"

Gemini races up to me. I reach down to pet him, giving myself time to weigh my words. In all honesty, I'd hoped Tori would have been in her room when I came in, ignoring me as usual. I pat Gem on the rump and then follow him to the kitchen. This isn't going to be pretty, but I'm not about to lie. Stalling while I feed the dog is all the reprieve I'm going to get.

I walk back into the den and meet her gaze. "I was at Drew's."

Her eyes bug. "What?! Again?" She slaps the magazine down onto the coffee table.

"Again," I say with a nod, but I also can't help crossing my arms over my middle. It's a defensive gesture, I know, and I shouldn't feel as though I have to defend myself. "I really like him, Tori."

Disgust washes over her face. "You've got to be kidding me. So, what, you're dating the ex-con now?"

Her question burns like acid. Not because of her tone and her intent to hurt me, but because I'm *not* dating Drew, although I'd like nothing better. I'd also love to be able to tell my sister how much it hurts that he doesn't want that. But I can't share this with her either.

There's almost nothing I can share with her these days.

Tori shakes her head. "I just don't get what's the matter with you."

164

I hope with all my heart she can hear the love in my voice. "That makes two of us."

She gives me a withering glare and then shocks the hell out of me. "You are the most selfish, self-absorbed person I've ever known."

My mouth falls open. It's like she's slapped me. Selfish? I have no words. This is so much worse than calling me a liar. All I want is for the people in my life to be happy. To give them what they need. How can she not see that?

"Tori, *what* are you talking about?" My throat has gone dry, so my words come out parched and feeble.

She stands, eyes blazing, shoulders rigid. "Oh, please, Evie. Are you really that obtuse?" she sneers. "It's one thing to waste your family's sacrifices by becoming a yoga instructor. But then to chase after an *ex-con?* Well, that's just an insult to all of us."

If she'd struck me with a bat, I couldn't feel more shocked. And wounded. "Tori... I don't know what you mean. What... what sacrifices?"

Her glare singes my skin. "If you don't know what I mean, you're not only selfish. You're stupid."

She spins on her heel and is out of the room before I can summon another breath. Sweat has broken out above my lip and under my arms. I want to believe she's being irrational, saying things to hurt me because she — for reasons I don't understand — is hurting. But something in the lines of her face, in the heft of her words, fills me with doubt. And fear.

Sacrifices?

I'm suddenly terrified that her accusations are true.

What could she possibly mean?

I want to rush up to my room and call Mom, but a quick glance at the clock on the mantle tells me it's not even four in the morning in Nigeria. Trembling and hugging my elbows, I let Gem into the back yard before locking up. While I wait for him to do his business, I look up at Drew's apartment, yearning suddenly for the comfort of his company. But the glass panes in the door and his one window facing me are dark. I can't imagine he's already asleep, but I won't bother him.

If he has a phone, he hasn't bothered to give me the number. And going back there would, indeed, be selfish. He's dealing with his own troubles. I don't need to burden him with mine.

I lock up, turn off the lights downstairs, and trudge up to my room. Gemini follows closely at my side, and he stays by me as I wash my face, brush my teeth, and change into pajamas. I text Mom and ask her to call me as soon as she's up. I tell her we're fine, but I need to ask her something important.

It doesn't matter when she calls. I know I'll be awake.

I try to settle myself in meditation, but anxiety leashes my mind and runs wild with it. I give up sitting still and unroll my yoga mat. Seeking solace in my favorite YouTube channel, I find a *Yoga With Adriene* twenty-seven minute stress relief video. Seeing Adriene Mishler's friendly smile and hearing her familiar voice gives me a measure of ease. I've been a devoted subscriber to her channel for four years now, and putting on a YWA video is like meeting up with an old friend.

Starting in a seated posture, Adriene takes me through a breath cycle of shoulder squeezes and neck stretches. A sequence of alternate nostril breathing morphs into cat-cow rotations, and then I move with her to downward dog and into a warrior series.

As I move, my anxiety lifts, but in its place, I become aware of a heavy sadness. And I realize this is what has driven the panic, what my mind really wanted to avoid. The sadness at being responsible for someone else's suffering.

My certainty of this is rooted deep. No matter what answers Mom can give me, I've hurt Tori in some way. Intentional or not. And I can't stand it.

I come to the end of the video, roll up my mat, and turn off my light. I stretch out on my bed, calmer but not comforted.

When my phone rings an hour later, I'm relieved Mom hasn't chosen to Skype me. I don't want to face anyone right now.

"Hey, baby, what's the matter?" The concern in her voice makes my eyes sting. It's so good to hear her, I want to cry. I hold it together, though, briefly recounting the scene Tori and I had downstairs.

"Mom, why would she say that? Why would she say I'm being selfish?"

"She said that?" Mom asks, sounding, to my relief, just as shocked as I am.

"*Yes*," I say, stressing my confusion. "She said I was wasting my family's sacrifices. And then she called me stupid for not seeing that."

"Oh dear," my mother says on a sigh. Her response makes me feel better for about five seconds. "I had no idea she felt that way about it."

My stomach pitches. "About what?"

Mom makes a noise deep in her throat. Even from halfway across the globe, it sounds like regret.

"About what, Mom?"

For a moment, she doesn't answer even though I'm hanging on her every word.

"About putting off pharmacy school."

"What?!"

Pharmacy school? Tori? This is the first I've ever heard of it.

"Oh dear," Mom says again.

"Mom. Tell me what's going on." She'd better hear the edge in my voice because I sure can.

"Well, your sister finished her chemistry degree the same year you graduated high school…"

This I already know. "Yeah, and?"

"And she wanted to go on to pharmacy school, but she was going to have to borrow to help cover her tuition and living expenses," she says as though this clears up everything. It doesn't.

"So… why didn't she go?" Even as I utter the question, I cringe inside. The answer is already wrapping its tentacles around me.

Mom sighs. "We offered to pay for the program if she waited to go and stayed home with you."

My mind blanks for a second. Why in the hell would they ask her to stay home with me?

"I don't understand."

"Well, it just made sense, honey." Her voice rises with a note of pleading. "I mean, we didn't want you to be alone. You were barely eighteen, and we also didn't want Tori to overwhelm herself with so much debt. We couldn't help her out much then, but after a few years we knew we'd be able to put aside—"

"But Mom, I was starting college. Why would that even be necessary?"

I hear her sigh over the line. "Honey, your father and I just felt like you weren't ready to be on your own."

I feel like someone's dropped a cannonball on my stomach "You mean you asked my sister to put her dreams on hold so she could stay home and *babysit me?*"

"Evie, don't think of it like that." Her voice takes on a sing-song quality. My nostrils flare.

"How else am I supposed to think about it, Mom?" I reimagine the last three years and my head spins. "I was eighteen. What did you think I would do?"

"Evangeline," Mom says, and dammit if my name isn't marinated in condescension. "You *know* how you can be. Like that time you gave that vagrant a ride, and he stole your wallet?"

It was a week after I'd gotten my driver's license. It was pouring rain, and the man was dripping wet, holding a sign that read *Will work for food.* "I was *sixteen.* And he was hungry—"

"He was an addict. And you could have been been abducted," she says, her voice going throaty with drama. "You have no idea the human trafficking problem there is here in Abuja."

I rolled my eyes. The man I'd picked up was so emaciated, I probably weighed more than he did. "Mom, this is Lafayette. Please." I'd lost my wallet, and I'd never offered rides to strangers after that. Lesson learned.

"What about when you were seventeen and you gave all of your senior trip money to Invisible Children?" she asks, saying the words slowly as though I have trouble understanding.

169

"What's wrong with being passionate about stopping warlords who enslave children?"

"Passion is one thing, honey. Making a twelve hundred dollar donation — all of your babysitting and birthday money from every year of high school — without talking to your parents or anyone?" She makes a little noise of offended disbelief. "You were going to use that money to go to Universal Studios with your friends. They were so disappointed."

I resist the urge to growl. I've never regretted that decision. I still don't. My three friends, girls I never even see anymore, still went. They still had a great time without me. I mean, yeah, I absolutely *love* Harry Potter, and I still would like to see The Wizarding World at Universal, but I think both J. K. Rowling and Harry Potter — and most definitely Hermione — would have supported my choice to save children from being stolen from their homes and forced into a terror campaign. That has much more lasting value than getting a butterbeer at Honeydukes with my high school besties.

"Evangeline, it's those sort of things that make us worry for you. And we, your father, your sister, and I, just thought it would be best to give you a few more years to grow up."

"Oh my God." I'm horrified. And not only that but betrayed. Humiliated. "No wonder Tori hates me, Mom. How could you do this to her?"

"She agreed with us, Evie. It was to her benefit as much as yours—"

"It didn't benefit either of us." My raised voice bounces off the walls. Tori can almost certainly hear me now, but I don't care. "And the fact that you didn't even tell me — didn't include me in this decision—"

"Well, in hindsight, that might have been a mistake, but you were a really young eighteen."

I push myself off the bed. Sitting still is no longer possible. It may never be. "And now, Mom. I'm twenty-one. How about now?"

Her silence says everything.

"Oh my God," I mutter, feeling ill.

"We just worry about your judgment, Evie. That's all."

I laugh, but the sound is humorless. "Oh, that's all? Just my judgment? Just the decisions I make about how to live my life?" I have never been this angry. Not with Mom. Not with anyone. "Decisions like my career? Who my friends are? Who I date? Things like that?"

"If you think about it from our perspective, honey—"

"No, Mom. I'm an adult. It's my life—"

"First your drop out of school, and then you work in a field with no future, and now you're spending all this time with that Moroux—"

"Don't you dare." I snarl the words through gritted teeth. "Don't you dare speak his name."

Out of all the insults I've endured tonight, this is the one I will not abide.

I hear my mother's quick intake of breath. "Evie." She's startled. Scandalized. Hearing the disappointment in the way she says my name has brought me to my knees again and again.

But not tonight.

"Enough," I rasp, almost choking my anger. "I've heard enough."

I manage to end the call without breaking down, despite my mother's repeated pleas to *just listen*. But

171

even in the relative silence of my racing thoughts, I find no peace.

I try again to sit in meditation, but one thought keeps cycling through my mind.

I can't stay here.

I can't stay here.

I can't stay here.

If there's anything that conversation with my mother revealed — and it revealed *everything* — it's that I have to. HAVE TO. Move out.

There is no other option. My entire family still sees me as a child. They have orchestrated all our lives, in secret, based on that belief. And it has cost my sister's happiness. Her freedom.

It's also cost mine, though I'm only now realizing it.

I know I will not have peace until I can at least prove to myself that the way they see me does not define who I am. So I have to move out.

Right now.

I spring up from my meditation bench and change out of my pajamas into clean clothes. I grab a duffle bag from the closet and hastily fill it with clothes and toiletries. As I do, I consider my very short list of options.

I have money. Well, a little. I could stay in a hotel one night. A very cheap hotel. Probably a motel if I'm being honest. And go in search of a second job and a miniscule apartment tomorrow. I can Uber or take the bus because I'm definitely not driving Mom's Volvo.

No way.

Once I find a place — a pet-friendly (because I'm going to take Gemini. He's mine after all), super-small, and affordable place — I can move out the rest of my stuff and slowly assemble the other things I'd need to outfit a home of my own. Dishes... towels...

Pretty much everything.

Maybe I can find someone who just needs a roommate. Someone who'd be willing to accept both me and Gemini.

I'm not going to lie. My spirits flag when I think about how hard this is going to be. And it will be hard.

But not impossible.

I can do this. And now that I know what needs to be done, I can't stay here a minute longer.

Except, if I stay in a hotel — or even a motel — tonight, I would put a dent in my savings. And that's the bulk of what I have for a security deposit. And a pet deposit. And first month's rent.

I sigh.

This realization leaves me two options. I can either stay here and pace the floor until morning. Or I can reach out to a friend.

Drew.

His name rises like a phoenix, glorious and aflame. But as much as I'd love to turn up on his doorstep with an overnight bag and attempt to convince him to share that futon with me, I know he'd just try to talk me out of my plan.

And as far as sharing a bed? Well, who am I kidding?

So that, at the moment, leaves Janine, my friend and neighbor across the street. I saw Janine just yesterday, pushing the stroller out her front door while I was heading to a class. It was almost ten in the morning, but she looked exhausted. She mustered a smile and a wave, but there was no mistaking the shadows under her eyes and the fatigue in her posture.

I won't call and wake her up. I'll text her. If she doesn't answer, I'll… Well, I'll figure that out then.

Me: Are you guys up? I know it's late, but I need a big favor.

I send the text and watch my phone. It's almost eleven-thirty. But it is Friday, which means Janine's husband James won't have work in the morning. For all I know, they've hired a babysitter and are out.

Janine: The baby and I are up. Again. What's wrong?

A sigh of relief escapes me. Thank you Baby Aaron for all your sleepless infant ways.

Me: I know it's a lot to ask, but I need a place to sleep tonight. I can't stay here any longer.

My friend's response is immediate.

Janine: OMG! Of course. Come right now!

And then:

Janine: Is it Tori? Did she cross the line?

I bite my lip. There have been a few times I've gone over to Janine's after a blowout with Tori. None since she's had the baby, but Janine has always been a sympathetic ear. Naturally, she's a Cancer.

She's also getting her master's degree in counseling, so, yeah, I guess talking to her is free therapy.

Me: It's not just Tori. It's a lot of things.

And that's the truth. In fact, I can't really blame Tori for this one. Or, at least, I can't lay all the blame on her. My parents hold some responsibility.

But, I now realize, so do I.

174

I shake my head like a dog after a bath. It's all so convoluted. I need time to reflect and self-examine. And at some point, I'll need to face my family again, but that can't happen until I've gotten my life together.

Janine: Come over. Now. I just unlocked the front door.

I press a knuckle to my lips, debating. And then I go for it.

Me: Could I bring Gemini with me?

If she says no, I know he'll be fine here. I'll come back first thing in the morning to let him out and feed him. It's not a big deal.

Janine: OF COURSE!!!

A lungful of relief leaves me in a rush. Okay. Okay. I can do this.

Me: Thank you. Thank you. You are the best!

I tuck my yoga mat in its sling and loop the bag I've packed over my shoulder. As quietly as possible, I creep down the stairs with Gemini running ahead of me, excited and curious about what we're doing in the middle of the night.

Working soundlessly, I pack Gem's food and his dishes into a sturdy paper sack, and he twirls and leaps at my feet the entire time, thinking he'll be getting a midnight snack.

"No, buddy," I whisper, and then I text Janine again.

Me: Walking over now.

And then I snap on Gem's harness and leash, gather up all of my bags, and head out the front door.

Before I even reach Janine's porch, I hear Aaron's sustained and impressive wailing. The door swings open

175

as Gem and I approach, and the moment I see my friend, I stop in my tracks.

"Oh God, Janine. If this is too much—"

"No, no. Don't even think that," she says, cradling her squalling infant in one arm and gesturing us inside with the other. She's wearing a giant T-shirt, a pair of what I am pretty sure are James's pajama bottoms because the cuffs drag the floor, and a burp rag over her shoulder that bears a suspiciously milky-white streak. About fifty percent of her hair is tied back in a band, but the rest of it falls in a light brown aurelia around her face.

She is the picture of new motherhood.

"He's going to cry all night whether you're here or not, and the way I see it, at least now you can hold him while I run to the bathroom."

I drop my bags inside the door, divest Gem of his harness — even though he hasn't moved from the door and is eyeing the tiny, deafening human with caution — and hold out my arms to take the baby.

He's bigger than he was eight weeks ago when Janine and James brought him home from the hospital, but he still can't weigh more than a dozen pounds. I clutch him to me as though a gust of wind threatens to carry him away.

He rails and squirms and cries real tears. His little body is hot with the effort, his face as flushed as a nectarine.

I immediately start bouncing and swaying. "Every night, Janine?" I look at her with sympathy to find her fairly sagging with relief. I can't help but ask. "Why isn't James helping?"

176

A gentle smile claims her mouth. "He does. We've just decided to take it in shifts. If we can each get four interrupted hours, it doesn't feel like the roof is caving in."

"Well, tonight you are both getting more than four hours," I vow. "There's no way I can sleep after the night I've had. I'll stay up with Aaron. Just tell me what to do."

She's shaking her head before I even finish. "No, I couldn't ask you—"

"You're not asking," I interrupt. "In fact, I'm telling. This is how it's going down tonight."

She stares at me for a moment, and only the sound of Aaron's cries pass between us. Crossing her arms over her chest, she eyes me hard. "Let's try something. I haven't bathed in two days. I'll go grab a shower and come back. If you are still able to take it, I'll lie down for a little while."

I nod. "Sounds good. Though we'll be fine." The staccato of Aaron's cries hasn't eased at all, but I take it as a good sign that it also hasn't gotten any worse. I can do this.

But Janine just stares at me, worry plain on her face.

"We'll be fine. I promise."

She covers her mouth in obvious horror. "I'm a terrible friend," she says, shaking her head. "You came here needing a place to stay in the middle of the night. I haven't even asked what happened. How can I think of leaving you with my inconsolable infant? What's wrong with me?"

She looks so distressed, I don't know who's more upset, her or the baby.

I hold Aaron against me with one arm and use the other to pull Janine in for a hug. "Nothing's wrong with you. You're the perfect friend." When I draw back, I see she's close to tears, and that makes three of us. And this thought, as sad as it is, makes me laugh a teary-eyed laugh. "You're taking me in in the middle of the night without demanding an explanation. You're giving me a way to help you in return. Plus—" I press a kiss to Aaron's scrunched up brow. "Looking after Aaron means I can focus on something besides my own problems. What more could I ask?"

Janine rolls her eyes, but she does it smiling. "How do you always know the exact, right thing to say?"

I think about the fight with my mom and the run-in with Tori that led to it all, and I can't agree. Still, I might have gotten a few things right when Drew and I talked about his grandfather earlier tonight. But two out of four is still pretty weak.

And maybe Aaron likes what I have to say, too, because his cries seem to downshift to serious whimpers with a few hiccuping sobs. Janine looks down at him.

"Poor darling. We've changed formulas. We've seen two different pediatricians. We've tried baby massage." She draws in deep sigh and lets it go. "He just seems to need to wear himself out every night. Twice a night."

The fight seems to be going out of him even as we talk. "Go take your shower." I gesture toward the back of the house. "I'll rock him and see if he'll settle down. And if not, we'll both have a good cry."

She gives me a sympathetic smile. "I'm not going to demand an explanation, but I'm ready to listen when you want to talk."

I nod. "Maybe in the morning."

"Okay," she whispers before kissing Aaron on the back of the head. "I'll just be a few minutes."

"Go." I shoo her away and carry the baby to the recliner. Sinking into it is like landing in an upholstered hug, and something inside me lets go. Tears rise, and one or two fall, but I don't come close to rivaling Aaron's downpour.

But soon we fall into a steady rocking rhythm, and more of his whimpering turns into shaky breaths, his eyes losing focus. Sensing that we'll be here a while, Gemini flops on the floor in front of my feet, heaves a resigned canine sigh, and rests his chin on his paws.

Memories of the past few hours flash through my head, but I don't try to hold onto them. I'm in no condition to think about my next move or question my decision to leave. I know if I would have stayed at home tonight, I'd have climbed the walls. But here, as Aaron slowly drifts to sleep in my arms, I feel a sense of peace and rightness.

In a way, I see it as proof. My parents and sister have been engineering their lives to… to what? Take care of me? Supervise me? Control me? None of those terms seems exactly right, and yet they all fit in one way or another.

But if the first thing I do after leaving home is take care of someone else, albeit a tiny human and for just the span of one night, then I'll take it as a sign. They're wrong about me. They've been wrong all along.

179

I'm not incapable. I'm not irresponsible. Sure, I might be impulsive. Deciding to move out of my childhood home at eleven o'clock on a Friday night could be categorized as impulsive, I realize. But there are worse things to be, right?

Manipulative, for one, *Mom.* Embittered would be another, *Tori.* And even if I haven't actually talked to him about it, I'd have to assign Dad the label of *complicit,* and I'd rather be impulsive over complicit any day of the week.

Wrapped in a towel turban and dressed in fresh pajamas, Janine returns a few minutes later to find Aaron asleep in my arms.

"Let me take him and lay him down," she says, stepping forward. "He might wake up when we move him, but you could get in bed."

I shake my head. "No, no. You go on. We're good right here."

Janine looks at me like I'm crazy. "Are you sure?"

"Very. If I get sleepy, I'll just lean the recliner back a little."

My friend's brow creases in concern. "He'll probably only sleep a couple of hours. He usually wakes up at one for a bottle, and then it starts all over again."

"Tell me what to do. I'll be ready."

I can see her reluctance, but Janine finally goes over his feeding routine. Warm the bottle in the sink. Change him if he's wet. Feed and burp him. Change him again if he poops. Commence baby comforting protocols.

I got this, so I order Janine to bed.

Around midnight, I actually do drift off, taking advantage of the reclining comfort of the rocker and it's lovely extendable footrest. Aaron squeaks and snuffles as I adjust us, but he quickly settles. Almost exactly an hour later, he begins to stir, and I don't wait for him to cry before I'm up and heating his bottle.

The diaper changing ends whatever patience Aaron has with me, but he's soaked. I manage to get him out of the wet one before James finds us in the nursery looking exhausted. He doesn't seem surprised to see me, so I let him know I have everything under control and send him back to bed.

It's two a.m. before Aaron's back asleep, and by then I'm wide awake, but the events of the early morning have only solidified my sense of competence.

When Janine takes the baby from me at five in the morning, smiling at me like I'm a saint of God, I follow her orders to go lie down in the guest room.

The blessed aroma of coffee and the sounds of a cooing newborn wake me around seven-thirty. I lie there for a moment, gathering my bearings, and weathering the pitch in my stomach as I recall everything from last night.

But the sky hasn't fallen, and the feel of Gemini's rump against the curve of my knees gives me the reassurance that all is, in fact, well.

When I shuffle into the kitchen, Janine greets me with a wry smile. "You are officially James's favorite person."

I rub sleep out of my eyes and blink at her for explanation. Aaron is in her arms, suckling the bottle he clasps in both hands while gazing adoringly at his mother. Baby Aaron is obviously a morning person.

"The both of us are so rested today that we actually feel human." Janine's cheeks turns pink as her smile grows. "We even feel like a couple."

I'm halfway to the coffee pot before the meaning of her words sinks in. I gasp, coming fully awake, and gape at her in mock scandal. "Ja-nine!"

She giggles, and Aaron, amused, coos around the nipple in his mouth. I fill a coffee mug, splash a little of the Half-N-Half from the carton she has left on the counter, and join her at the table. Janine's kitchen is sunny. Her cabinets and walls are a crisp white, her granite countertops an indigo blue, and her backsplash is a yellow ceramic tile with cobalt accents. It's a place I've always felt welcome.

Janine's smile sobers a little as she eyes me over her coffee cup. "Ready to tell me what happened?"

I take a restorative gulp of hot coffee and spill my guts. I tell her everything. My budding friendship with Drew. Tori's accusations. My late-night call with Mom. And how foolish I feel as the apparent baby of the family who can't be trusted to lead her own life.

And Janine listens. Nodding with encouragement and asking the rare question. I plow through a bowl of granola and finish off a second cup of coffee before I'm done. Janine has moved to the kitchen floor where Aaron kicks his little legs and squeals at the shiny mirrors and brightly striped shapes that dangle from his activity gym.

"If you don't mind me saying so, Tori has a little pseudo-martyr thing going on," she says, arching a no-nonsense eyebrow.

I blink. "What does that mean?"

Janine brushes her ponytail over her shoulder. "A pseudo-martyr is someone who makes a sacrifice, perhaps for a number of reasons, but makes a show out of their suffering. In some cases, the reason they make the sacrifice may be simply to make a show of their suffering."

I exhale a sigh. "That's Tori, alright."

Janine nods. "If that's her M.O., then despite what she says, she's getting something she wants out of this arrangement, beyond the payoff your Mom and Dad have offered her."

Payoff. The word make me shudder.

I press fingers to my temples. "It all sounds so shady. How could they be so secretive and... and... underhanded."

Janine's smile is gentle. "I know you feel manipulated, and there's probably a sense of betrayal too—"

"Uh, yeah." My words drip with sarcasm.

"And you have every right to." The cast of her eyes tells me she means it. "But in terms of family dysfunction, this is pretty mild."

I know she's right, but I still—

"But you still feel like the rug's been pulled out from under you," she says, naming the experience perfectly.

"Yes. And I'm angry," I admit.

"Good," she says with an encouraging nod. "Anger is a boundary-building emotion. Your family has disregarded your boundaries and your autonomy in some pretty fundamental ways. Your feelings are absolutely normal. And necessary."

183

I wrinkle my nose. "So you don't think it was impulsive to leave in the middle of the night."

She stifles a laugh, but I can tell she's not laughing at me. "I would have been disappointed in you if you'd stayed. Especially if you felt that your well-being and sense of self required you to leave."

I think I've made the right decision, but it's good to hear that Janine agrees.

She frowns, leans over Aaron, lifts one of his legs, and sniffs his diaper. "False alarm," she mutters before looking back at me. She waits for me to stop laughing before she moving on. "So, do you know what comes next for you? What your next move is?"

Despite my confidence in this decision, my stomach tightens at the thought. "Well, I need to find an apartment. Or a roommate," I qualify. "And I need to find a second job. Soon."

Janine chews her bottom lip, nodding slowly. "James and I actually talked about that this morning." A bashful smile lights her face. "Well... *after...*"

"Aaron close your ears," I whisper, making us both laugh.

"Actually, we talked about Aaron, too," she says, her face sobering.

I frown. "What do you mean?"

"Well..." She draws her shoulders up in a kind of self-conscious shrug. "What do you think about staying in the guest room and helping out with the baby... you know... until you find something more permanent?"

My breath catches. "What?"

Janine grimaces. "I told James you'd never want to. I mean, who wants to spend their nights with a screaming infant?" She slaps her hand over her mouth,

184

realizing what she's just said, and her gaze falls on Aaron. "Oh, my angel, Mommie loves you so much. I'd spend every night with you no matter how much you scream—"

"Janine—"

"I didn't mean to sound like—"

"Janine, I'd love to."

She halts her maternal guilt-induced apology and looks up me. "What?"

I sink down from the kitchen chair to a spot on the floor beside her and Aaron. "If the rent's not too high, I'd love to stay and help—"

"Rent?!" Her eyes bug, and her mouth quirks in an odd line. "We wouldn't charge you rent. We'd *pay* you."

Now my mouth falls open. "Janine, you couldn't — I wouldn't feel—"

Her hand lands on my knee. "Do you know how exhausted we've been? I can barely stay awake in my classes. I had to drop down to nine hours. And James said he was so tired during a client meeting this week, he almost wept when it was over." Her own eyes fill with tears. "Evie, he's a first-year CPA, he can't cry in front of clients. They'll leave him."

"I get it but, you don't need to pay me if I get to live here for fr—"

"It's a write-off, Evie. James says it'll actually help us with our taxes."

"I — But—"

"Evie, just say yes. We can work out the money tonight when James gets home." She squeezes my knee again. "And we won't take advantage of you, I swear.

185

We'll split shifts so each of us gets enough sleep every night. And of course you'd have nights off."

I give her a wicked grin. "Or y'all could take a night off. And go somewhere fun. Maybe New Orleans or a bed and breakfast?"

Her eyes round with wonder. "Oh... really?" Her chest heaves. "That would be *so* great..."

She looks so awestruck I have to laugh. I push myself up from the floor. "We'll work it out. But right now, I need to get ready. I have class at ten."

Janine seems to come to herself, blinking away visions of room service and do not disturb signs. "Oh, right. I have some reading to do before class. But—" She points a finger at me and gives me her own wicked grin. "Sometime this afternoon, I want to hear more about this Drew guy."

CHAPTER FIFTEEN

DREW

Evie's light has been out for two nights.

She didn't mention she was going anywhere. I know it's none of my business, but I can't help but wonder where she is. It's Monday morning, and we're supposed to go the the DMV this afternoon.

Which is definitely not a date.

But we didn't really settle on a time. And we never swapped numbers, so I can't call her. Of course, even if I had her number, I still don't have a phone. So I'd have to call from the cordless in Grandma's kitchen.

How pathetic is that?

Still, something tells me I don't need to worry. When it's time to go, Evie will turn up. It seems like she's turning up all the time. Even if I haven't been able to catch a glimpse of her all weekend — not since I watched her disappear inside her house after clearing the fence like an Olympic gymnast.

I keep thinking about Friday night. How having her in the apartment left a permanent change. How I still feel Grandpa Pete everywhere, but now the feeling is lighter, warmer. How Evie is a living, breathing pain reliever. A laughing, teasing pain reliever.

Knowing I'd clock out early, I got to the garage at seven this morning, and I've spent three hours so far replacing the motor mounts on a Nissan Versa. And that's where my cousin Chip finds me.

"How's Grandma?"

I pull my head out from under the hood and peer around the engine sling. Chip stands there with his hands on his hips, his eyes not meeting mine. My guess is he's focused somewhere around my collar.

This is actually the first time he's spoken to me about anything personal in the two weeks I've been here. Before now, he's just given me orders. And that's okay by me. I follow his orders and give him no reason to feel like he's made a mistake in offering me this chance. If I have a question, or need to go over a repair with a manager, I try to find Cody. I know my cousin doesn't want to talk to me, so I'm surprised to see him now.

"She's in a lot of pain, but she's trying to be tough about it." Grandma's self-diagnosis was spot-on. Shingles. A mean case of it, too.

Chip winces, and in this moment of distraction, he brings his gaze to mine. "Aunt Josie called my mom and told her this weekend."

I nod. "Yeah, Aunt Shelly and your dad came over this weekend to look in on her." Shelly and Nelson are Chips parents. He's the oldest of their three boys. And like I said before, he's the one who looks most like Anthony. Standing this close, talking to him, is a mindfuck. I want to stare at him, look at him from all angles. Just to pin down all the ways he's like my brother.

And I want to hide my face and cry. The way I do when Anthony visits my dreams.

"They're glad somebody's at the house with her," he says, keeping his eyes on mine. "I am too."

To say I'm shocked would be an understatement. It takes me a second to marshal a response. "I'm lucky to be there," I tell him, and we both know it's the truth.

He nods, whether in acknowledgment or agreement, I can't tell. Then he walks away. But before he's out of the bay, he calls over his shoulder, shocking the hell out of me again. "Keep up the good work."

I look back at the Versa, but it takes a moment of blinking and throat clearing before I can get on with it.

After the mounts are replaced and the ticket's written up, I clock out. Evie said she had class in the morning, but her afternoon would be free. I don't want her waiting on me, so I catch the 11:49 bus back home.

When I get there, I check on Grandma. She's sitting in her easy chair in a sleeveless cotton nightgown. Anything tighter than a smock hurts, she says, so I'm making sure she has a clean one every day.

"How you doing, Grandma Q?"

She raises the remote and pauses what appears to be a soap opera. I don't think I've ever seen her watch a soap opera.

"I," she says with no shortage of dramatic flair, "do not like being sick."

I stifle a laugh. She would not appreciate laughter. "No, Grandma, I'm sure you don't."

"I have watermelons to rotate, beds to till, and seeds to buy for my winter garden." Her mouth is tight, and I can see her hands grip the arms of her chair. "No time for this at all."

"I can do all of that. You just tell me what you want, and I'll do it."

Her answering sigh is one of exasperation, not relief. "Well, where's the fun in that? That's like seeing a picture of an ice cream cone when you could be eating one."

This time, I can't help it. I laugh, and I earn myself a stern look.

"Have you had lunch?" I ask, sobering as best I can. "I can fix you some of that chicken salad Aunt Shelly made."

189

Seeming placated, Grandma nods. "That would be lovely."

I fix sandwiches for the both of us. The plates look a little bare without a side, so I take a couple of apples from the crisper. At once, I'm back in my apartment, sitting across from Evie.

I'll see her soon.

At the thought, liquid fire runs through my veins.

The ride in the car all the way to the DMV in Abbeville... the long wait... the ride back. After years thinking about it as punishment, time, I now realize, can feel like wealth.

With these thoughts buoying me, I carry the sandwiches and sliced apple into the living room, and I eat lunch with Grandma.

"How are things at the garage?" she asks before sinking her teeth into her sandwich.

I remember my near-miraculous conversation with Chip and the light feeling I have lifts a little higher. "Good." I munch an apple slice. "Chip asked how you were doing."

Grandma flattens her lips together. "Hmmph. He should come see for himself."

I hide my grin with a bite of sandwich.

"Evie's taking you to get your license today?" she asks, her voice layered with a kind of manufactured innocence.

I frown. "How do you know *that?*" Listening in on us when she was supposed to lying down, watching *Ellen* is one thing, but when Evie and I discussed going to the DMV, Grandma was in the throes of illness. "You couldn't have been listening Friday night. You were almost delirious with pain."

"Maybe, but Josephine wasn't." Grandma shrugs. "What can I say? Quincys have good ears."

It's official. I am done underestimating Grandma Quincy and her minions.

"And big mouths, apparently," I mutter into my sandwich.

"I heard that," she levels. "And you didn't answer my question. Is she taking you today?"

Why bother avoiding the interrogation? Grandma will find out no matter what. "Yes, Grandma. Evie offered to take me today to renew my driver's license."

I expect her to look satisfied, even smug, but the lines on her forehead form a V. "Something odd is going on over there."

"Where?" I look behind me to see what she means, but it's the same old living room.

"At the Lalonde's."

I face my grandmother, immediately on alert. The image of Evie's darkened room springs to mind. "What do you mean?"

Grandma sets her jaw to one side. "Trudy Troxclair came over this morning to see how I was doing. She has a vegetable garden too, but it's not quite as big as mine." Grandma holds up a hand in a gesture that says Trudy Troxclair can be forgiven for such an outrage. "And she said she saw one of the Lalonde girls rolling suitcases out of the house and across the street."

I have so many questions, I shake my head, frowning. "W-who is Trudy Troxclair?"

191

Grandma glares at me with disappointment. "Trudy." She jabs her thumb over her shoulder in the direction of the back yard. "The Troxclairs have lived behind us, next door to the Lalondes for thirty-odd years. Don't you remember? Trudy and Bud?"

I open my mouth to argue that I don't, but what's the point? "Sure. Right. The Troxclairs. How could I forget? And she saw what, now?"

"Haven't you been listening? What? You have axle grease in your ears?" Grandma scolds gently. "She saw one of the girls moving suitcases into the house across the street from them."

"Which girl?" Evie mentioned that her sister was talking about moving out, but if she did, then why are Evie's windows dark?

Grandma shrugs again. "Trudy doesn't know which is which. But those girls look nothing alike. And they act nothing alike." One of Grandma's eyebrows lifts higher than the other. "Trudy said the other one was in the front door, yelling at her sister. So if you ask me, it was Evie with the suitcases." Grandma wrinkles her nose. "That other one's always yelling."

I narrow my eyes. "And Trudy Troxclair told you all this?"

"All but the part about the other one always yelling. I've seen that with my own eyes."

Clearly, Grandma's eyes see plenty, but not nearly as much as her ears hear. Her network of spies, both within the walls of her house as well as beyond it, is impressive.

And a little scary.

I finish my sandwich, and when Grandma is done with hers, I clear both plates and head up to my apartment. On the way, I scan Evie's back yard for any sign of her. It hits me then that I haven't seen Gemini in the yard the last few days either.

It's just after one, and I decide that whether or not I have time for a shower before Evie shows up, I need one anyway. If I'm going to be with her for the rest of the afternoon, I don't want to make her sick.

But after a shower and then a shave, there's still no sign of her.

What the hell happened between her and her sister? Did she leave willingly? Did her sister force her out? Has Grandma got the wrong idea, and it's Evie who's still at the Lalonde residence?

I don't really care about the driver's license. Sure, I need it, but whether I get it today, tomorrow, or next week doesn't really matter. But I want to know what happened to Evie. And I'm more than curious.

I'm concerned.

I've only known her a few weeks, but I just can't imagine her throwing someone out. She might yell at her sister. She's feisty enough. And she's emotional. But she's also compassionate. To a fault. And she's unfailingly kind. She'd never do something as hateful as throwing her sister out of their home.

Which makes me suspect it's the other way around.

And Grandma's friend says she saw her taking luggage across the street? Is that where she's been the last two nights?

Is she okay?

With that one question in mind, I leave the apartment and head down the stairs. I doubt I could clear the fence the way Evie did the other night. Scale it, sure. But I'm not going to do that either. The last thing I need is for her sister to call the police on my ass.

So I walk around the block. I've only seen the front of her house at night, and even then, it looked perfect. Daylight does nothing to change that impression. It's the most charming house on the block. The sloping gable, slate roof, and circular window make it feel like something out of a storybook.

A part of me envies Evie for growing up here.

Of course, it's nothing more than she deserves, and I deserve nothing close. And I can't blame the house I grew up in on the way my life turned out. Ma did the best she could with the three of us. She's a nurse. I don't think she ever liked the job much, but for a single mother, it's about as good as it gets. Our home wasn't fancy, but it was clean, comfortable, and safe.

She gave the three of us what she had to give. Happiness just wasn't among her possessions. Not when we were growing up, and definitely not now.

Still, that doesn't mean we grew up without happiness at all. Even as a toddler, Annie danced and sang all day. It may have been annoying as hell at times, but it was always cheerful. And Anthony could make our mother smile even after her longest day at the hospital. As the oldest, he'd fix dinner on the nights we didn't eat with Grandma and Grandpa. Nothing fancy. Tuna and macaroni and cheese. Hot dogs. Sloppy Joe's.

But when Ma would come home to see dinner on the table and the three of us bathed, our homework finished, she would beam at Anthony like he was her guardian angel. I guess he did whatever he could to make Ma feel like Dad taking off wasn't any great loss.

She will never forgive me. Not ever. That's just something I have to live with.

I won't forgive myself either, but as I stand at the foot of Evie Lalonde's front steps, I realize that I *want* to be forgiven.

Maybe it's the sight of this house, brimming with welcome and the promise of family. Maybe it's living with Grandma Q and feeling every day the grace she gives me. The grace that is possible. Maybe it's the way Evie made me see my last exchange with Grandpa Pete with new eyes. Maybe it's the moment I had with my cousin this morning.

I want to be forgiven. I want to belong to my family — my whole family — again. I want to grieve Anthony *with them*.

And I want Evie.

With that thought cresting above all the others, I climb her front steps and knock on her door. At first I hear nothing. Gemini's excited bark is a now-familiar sound. I hear it when he's in her back yard, chasing squirrels. But it's absent now.

But then, the clop of heels across a wood floor issues from the house. The bolts clack, and the door opens to reveal an attractive blonde. A blonde who's scowling at me.

Definitely not Evie.

I know at once this is her sister. Tori. I narrow my eyes in suspicion because if my guess is right, she's kicked Evie out of the house. But I'm not sure, and I need to be sure.

"Is Evie home?" I ask.

Her scowl sharpens. "Who wants to know?"

I feel my jaw set, imagining this person talking to Evie like that.

"I'm —"

But she holds up her hand, recognition blazing in her eyes. "I know who you are." Her nostrils flare and her top lip curls with disgust. "You're that lowlife felon who's freeloading off Mrs. Vivian."

Her words are like a pop to the jaw, shocking, but effective. Familiar shame rises like smoke. How can I respond? What she says is true.

I am that lowlife felon.

I am freeloading off my grandmother.

She jabs her finger at me, and I back onto the steps. "You. Stay. Away. From. My. Sister," she spits. "She doesn't know what's good for her. Evie would pick up a stray rat if she thought it needed help. She's got to be just *crazy* about you."

Shocked as I am, my first impulse is to defend Evie. "We're just friends —"

"Right. *Right.*" Her head nods with violent sarcasm. "'Cause ex cons make such *good* friends." But as she says this, she leans to her left to peer past me across the street, a sudden wariness in her eyes.

I swivel on my feet and look in the same direction, the brick house across the street a silent witness to our scene.

I turn back to Tori Lalonde. "That's where she is." It's not a question. What Mrs. Troxclair told Grandma must be true. The need to check on Evie conquers all else, even the assault of her sister's words.

I descend one step before her sister grabs my arm.

"Leave her alone." She sounds vicious. But when I meet her eyes, I'm surprised to see an etching of both fear and doubt.

I recognize the look. I've seen it in the mirror.

"I won't let you go near her," she snarls. "She's too trusting. Too soft. You'll only take advantage. You'll only hurt her."

I pin her with my coldest stare. "You mean like you?"

At Angola, I stared into the faces of hundreds of murderers. No lie. Hundreds. None of them looked as dangerous as Tori Lalonde does in this moment. Her eyes narrow on me as if all she sees is my death.

"You listen to me, you shitbag. We are nothing alike, you and I." She is hissing. Actually hissing. "I'm hard on Evie, but I'm always looking after her. I'd never put her in harm's way—"

I'm shaking my head before she's even finishes. "I'd never let anything hurt her," I swear, the words coming from a place so deep inside me it hurts.

She just raises a hateful brow. "Oh really? What would your brother have to say about that?"

CHAPTER SIXTEEN

EVIE

I tiptoe out of the nursery with one thought in mind: Little Aaron Mayfield has his days and nights confused. The kid sleeps like the dead all afternoon.

But with me here today, Janine took the opportunity to get her first haircut in months. Thank goodness. She needs a little time to herself. I told her to get a mani-pedi while she's at it.

And now I have the house to myself. Well, me and Gemini have the house to ourselves. He's been following me around nonstop for the last three days. At first, he kept standing by the front door, clearly wondering when we were going home. And, yeah, that left me with a lump in my throat and tears in my eyes more than once.

Because I don't know how to feel. Or maybe it's just that I feel too many things.

I miss my home. I miss feeling at home. It's only been a few days, and so far this little arrangement I have with Janine and James couldn't be better, but I still feel like a guest. I'm trying not to take up too much space, and when they're both home, I don't want my presence to make them feel awkward, so I've been spending a lot of time in the guest room.

And that doesn't feel like home either.

It's nice, of course. A little Laura Ashley for my taste, but nice. I feel weird about leaving dirty clothes on the floor or taking a nap in the afternoon, even though I'm pulling a baby shift every night, and after the third night, it's not so easy.

So now that Aaron's down and Janine is gone for a while, I take the advantage of the quiet and sit in meditation in Janine's sunlit front room.

I'll admit, this is my favorite room in Janine's house. The floors are a ruddy glazed brick, and while it's cool under my bare feet, the wide bay window and its view of the live oak in Janine's front yard keep the room from feeling cold. Sunlight filters through the leaves, giving the room a greenish hue, and the pale blue of the walls seems to drink it in.

I sit on Janine's white loveseat facing the window and tuck my feet into a lotus pose. I lay my hands, palm-up, atop my knees, symbolically releasing anything I don't need and accepting what the universe has to offer me, and I close my eyes.

The sound of Gem's toenails across the brick lets me know he's come to find me, and I hear him walk in a quick circle before lying down on the little tight weave jute rug in front of me. He gives a huff of acceptance. He knows if I'm sitting like this, nothing exciting is going to happen for a while.

Following my breath as it travels through my nose and down my throat, I try to anchor into the present. The sounds of the house around me play a different music than the one I am used to. The light behind my eyelids is brighter. The cushion beneath me both foreign and firm. I accept all these differences.

I accept that I don't know what I'm doing or where I am going.

And as soon as I accept this, I let myself feel the current of fear that has swept through me from the moment I knew I had to leave home.

The fear is there. Right in my middle. Like a ball of tar. Dark. Sticky. Opaque. And as much as I'd like to pull away from it, deny it exists, I focus on the feeling, my breath shaking out of me as I do.

What am I afraid of?

The grounded part of my mind, the endless observer, poses this question, and without hesitation, I see a kaleidoscope of answers. Mom, Dad, and Tori. All disappointed in me. All disapproving of what I've done. I see my leaving as not only an exodus from the house, but as a diaspora of my family, the separation and dissolution my own fault.

I don't question how realistic or rational this fear is. It just is. Its presence in me makes it real enough. This is what I must deal with.

More fears come. The weariness of my welcome here with Janine and her husband. The erosion of their goodwill and friendliness. The awkward distance that comes of a friendship that has been asked to bear too much. And beyond that, the gaping mystery of what next?

A shabby apartment. Light brown stains in ceiling tiles overhead. German cockroaches creeping under dingy baseboards. Three different locks on the one door.

Loneliness.

I breathe in and explore this new arrival. I can't find the darkness at its center. But it doesn't feel deep. It feels… shallow. Ephemeral.

Because contrasted with the fear of loneliness is the certainty of an antidote.

At the sound of Drew Moroux's voice, I open my eyes.

200

Meditation can bring on a host of sensations. Phantom touch. An Aurora Borealis behind the eyelids. Even the feeling of levitating in mid air.

Surely the sound of Drew's voice has come from within me, my mind's proof of the impermanent nature of loneliness.

But then, Gem and I both hear Tori's strident tones echoing across the street, and we stand at the same instant. A quick glance through the bay window only shows me oak branches, so I bolt for the door.

I swing it wide and see them. At once, the lines of their bodies tell me everything. Ugly words have been spoken.

I hesitate for a moment, not wanting to leave the baby, but I have to stop whatever is happening across the street.

"Gem, stay," I command. And as if he understands the urgency, my dog's body goes rigid, alert for any danger across the street or in the house.

I set off at a run in time to see Drew tear from the front steps, his face a mask of misery.

"Drew, what are you—" Before the question is out, I gasp. "Oh my God! The DMV. I was supposed to pick you up. I completely forgot."

He looks at me and shakes his head. "It doesn't matter." His voice is gruff, almost strangled. "Goodbye, Evie."

He veers right before I reach him, moving in long, quick strides away from me. His *goodbye* hangs in the air, sounding hauntingly permanent.

"Drew, wait. I'm so sorry—"

He lifts the back of his hand, waving me off. "I've got it. I don't need you," he calls without looking back.

I don't need you.

The words land like launched darts in my chest. My shoulders bow with their impact. With my mouth hanging open and useless, I watch him until he turns the corner. But because he moves so fast, I don't watch long.

Still the whole time, I feel Tori's eyes on me. I turn to face her.

"What did you say to him?"

Her shoulders square in defiance, and I know this can't be good. "Only what he needed to hear."

Shit. Definitely not good.

I fold my arms across my chest, the second thoughts I'd grappled with during my meditation rapidly fading. "What exactly did you say?"

Tori's lips tighten, and I notice that even though her usual hostility lines the skin around her eyes, she also looks a little unsure of herself. This is rare. But then she blinks, and the look is gone.

"He needs to stay away from you."

My jaw clenches. "That's not for you to decide."

"I'm only looking out for you, Evie."

I shake my head. "That's not your place. I can look out for myself."

Tori rolls her eyes. "Evie, come back home and stop being ridiculous. Mom and Dad are so upset that—"

I hold my hands up to stop her. If I focus on their disappointment, I'll waver. "No one's more upset than I am." And this must be true. My hands are shaking with anger. What else could she have said to Drew? Would her rudeness be enough to send him away with that devastated look on his face?

The trust growing between us is still new. But I feel sure deep inside me that it's real. He would trust me over her, wouldn't he?

"What else did you say to him?" I press.

Tori blinks. A chink in her armor. She said something else. Something hateful and awful. I know it. I turn toward the direction where Drew disappeared, wanting to go after him, but I can't. Not now, anyway. Not until Janine gets back.

"He's worthless, Evie. Just let him g—"

My gaze whips back to her. "Shut up, Tori."

The words stun us both. I don't think I've ever said them to her. To anyone, really. Her face morphs from shock to outrage.

"What the hell is wrong with you? I don't even recognize you."

My anger, now a rolling boil, threatens to froth over. "Because you don't know me."

I want to rail about how my whole family has seen me as a helpless child. How insulting that is, and how invisible it makes me feel. But before I can draw breath to deliver this invective, Gemini gives one sharp, insistent bark.

And then I hear them. Aaron's cries.

The last thing I want is for Janine to return home, finding me in the street yelling at my sister while her infant son cries in the house alone. Without another word to Tori, I turn and run back inside.

"You've been moping around here for a over week." Janine pats Aaron's back, burping him, as he's perched over her shoulder. "At first I thought it was just

203

the adjustment to this little guy's night shift, but now I'm worried about you." Judging from her face, she's telling the truth.

Drew won't see me.

After Janine got home from her hair appointment last week, I went straight to his apartment. It had been too late to head to the DMV, so I planned to offer to take him any day he was free.

But he wouldn't even open the door.

I could see him in there through the blinds. He sat at his little kitchen table with his back to the door, unmoving. I called his name, and when it was clear he had to have heard me, known it was me, the humiliation burned me inside and out.

I went back the next day to see if he'd calmed down, but the blinds were drawn, and I could make out nothing of the inside. I went down to Mrs. Vivian's kitchen door to see if he was with her and, if nothing else, to find out if he was home. But when she came to the door, it was clear I'd woken her. The angry flush of blisters covering the left side of her neck and her cheek made guilt swirl in my stomach.

I haven't gone back.

But I miss him. I miss him, and I want to heal whatever damage Tori did to him. Whatever damage anyone has ever done to him.

And short of setting up camp at the foot of his apartment stairs, I don't know how to make him listen to me.

"Is it because of things with your family?" Janine asks, but before I can answer, Aaron roars a lusty belch that startles us both and sets us laughing.

I use the moment to dodge her question. "Is he eating more? I swear, he's grown since I moved in."

Janine nods. "I think he's going through a growth spurt, but don't change the subject."

I wince. "That obvious?"

She gives me a knowing smile.

"I talked to my mom last night. She wants to come in to *clear the air*," I say with a shrug. "She seems to think I'll move back if she just explains their reasoning one more time."

Janine studies me with scrutiny. "And that bothers you?"

She's going to be a really good therapist one day. She can see right through my avoidance tactics. I shake my head. "It doesn't bother me, but it's unnecessary. I mean, she and my dad will be back in December. No need to come now," I say this with conviction. "Especially since it'll change nothing."

And that's true. I told Mom as much. So far, my arrangements with the Mayfields is going pretty well. It doesn't feel like home yet, but I've lost that sense that I'm an interloper. I'm not exactly sure what I am — something between a friend and live-in domestic help — but things are going smoothly.

I can tell what we're doing is benefiting everyone. James and Janine are getting more rest, and they seem happy about that. Aaron has three people to take care of him. And I have a place to stay, a little more money in my pocket, and no rush to figure out what comes next.

And I think we are all doing whatever we can to give each other privacy. When James is home in the evenings, I still stay in my room so he and Janine feel

205

like they have the place to themselves. They've invited me to join them to watch TV. Sometimes I accept, but more often than not, I'll watch something on YouTube in my room or take Gem for a walk.

And, yes, when I do that, we walk past Drew's house. It's a little pathetic and juvenile, but I can't stop thinking about him.

Janine settles Aaron back in her arms to give him the rest of his bottle, but she doesn't take her eyes off me. At last, she shakes her head.

"There's something else."

I give her an arch look. "Are you sure psychology is the right field for you? What about interrogation? Surely, the CIA has need of your talents."

She laughs, making Aaron smile up at her. He makes joyful noises of adoration, and we both laugh harder.

Janine shakes off her amusement. "You don't have to tell me if you don't want to, but I do have a guess."

I smirk at her. "Of course you do."

Her all-seeing eyes don't blink. "Drew Moroux?" Her tone suggests she doesn't need confirmation.

My sigh is answer enough.

"What do you want to do about it?"

I shrug, but the motion is meant more as a shield against what I say next. "What's there to do? He doesn't want to see me."

Her brows lift, but her tone is mild. "I doubt that very much."

I pull a face. "He walked away from me. He's avoiding me. The last words he spoke to me were literally *I don't need you."* I shake my head. "Not a lot of room for misinterpretation."

I can tell she wants to laugh at my ironic tone, but Janine gives me a sympathetic smile instead. "But where was he when he said that to you?"

She's heard the whole story, so she's just making me say it aloud.

I roll my eyes. "He was at my house. Presumably looking for me."

Clearly satisfied, she nods. "From everything you've told me, it sounds like seeing you is something he desperately wants." The softening in her voice and the implications of her words make my throat close.

Seeing Drew is what I desperately want. Does he want it this much?

Just imagining he does — that he wishes to see me but won't let himself — makes me want to run to him. But I have no idea what I'd do once I got there. He has made up his mind about me.

"Well, I think we should throw a party and invite him," Janine says as though I've spoken.

"What?"

"You know. A block party. Like we always do." The Mayfields have been known to throw great parties. Halloween. Mardi Gras. UL Homecoming. "We could invite the whole neighborhood. His street. Our street. Do you think he'd come?"

My laugh is mirthless. "Hell, no." Drew is not the party type. Not at all.

Janine shrugs. "Well, I still want a party. We haven't done anything since Mardi Gras."

I eye Aaron pointedly. "I can't imagine why not?" I tease.

207

"Exactly. I was huge and aching for the Fourth of July, and then I was sleep-deprived and tearful for Labor Day." Janine's eyes flash with a kind of excitement I haven't seen since the first half of her pregnancy. "And there's supposed to be a bit of a cool front this weekend. James could grill... I could make lemon squares and brownies... Ooh maybe we could do a Tex-Mex theme—"

"You had me at lemon squares."

She laughs. "Good. It'll cheer you up." Then she looks at me with a tender expression, her tone all gentleness. "You could use a little cheering up."

CHAPTER SEVENTEEN

DREW

I tuck my new driver's license into the sleeve of my wallet. "Thanks for taking me."

My sister smiles up at me as we cross the parking lot of the DMV. "Of course. I would've done it sooner if you'd asked."

I grunt. She'd do pretty much anything I'd ask, so I try not to ask. But the city bus doesn't go all the way to the DMV office in Abbeville, and while Grandma's feeling a lot better, she's still not quite herself.

And I wasn't about to ask Evie Lalonde.

Think about her? Sure. Speak her name aloud in the dark echoing of my apartment? That too. Hold myself back from going to see her? Every damn day.

Her sister Tori may be the wicked witch of the Saint Streets, but we are of one mind when it comes to Evie. She doesn't need to be anywhere around me.

It doesn't matter at all that I'm beginning to believe I might need her just so I can keep breathing.

"Errmmgg," Annie says, her brow furrowed into an exaggerated frown.

I eye her with concern. "Excuse me?"

Her frown holds, and her voice comes out gruff and gravelly. *"Me imitate you, Grumpy,"* she says, sounding like a bad imitation of an old *Tarzan* movie. *"No words. Just grunts and growls."*

I stare at her, prison-grade stoic face locked and loaded. "You look like you're shitting your pants."

Startled laughter decimates her frown. Watching my kid sister laugh chips away at the mask. I give a grudging smile. She points at it.

"There. That's better." We reach her car, and she holds up the keys. "Wanna drive?"

I freeze. I hadn't expected her to offer. At Angola, every once in a while, I would need to test-drive a prison vehicle to check the alignment or listen for a timing misfire, but that meant driving maybe a quarter mile around the auto shop. My heart pumps faster at the thought of the open road.

"You sure?"

Annie looks at me like I'm crazy. "What? You think I'm a chauffeur? Drive you all the way out here to get your license so you can ride shotgun all the way back?"

"Alright, sassy," I say, giving her a fake glare and opening my palm. "Gimme the keys."

And driving might as well be flying. The power to choose the path in front of me, to rev, to slow, to tune the damn radio is as sweet as honey. My time at Angola seems to slip a little further into the past as my hands rest easy on the steering wheel.

Who knew?

Annie must sense my absorption in the experience because, for once in her life, she doesn't chatter for a whole ten minutes. But we're just past Maurice, listening to Atlas Genius when she drops a bomb.

"Grandma says you have a girlfriend."

"I do not." The denial fires off like a bullet. I feel Annie's eyes on me, but I keep mine on the road.

"Aunt Josie says so too."

I groan. Do all the women in my family have the meddling gene? "They're both wrong."

"Anyone I know?"

210

I speak through gritted teeth. "I do not have a girlfriend."

She's undeterred. "Then who's the girl in question because, I mean, there's obviously a girl," she reasons. "And whether or not she's your friend or your girlfriend, there's a story."

"No girlfriend. No story."

"Oh, *come on*, Drew."

I give her the side eye and see she's wearing a look of impatience.

"I'm not buying the no-story story. Spill."

I don't want to concede and prove her right. But the urge to talk about Evie, to visit her in words, to bring her to life in my mind again is sudden and potent.

"Do you know the people who live behind Grandma?"

Annie gasps. "It's Evie!"

I blink, managing to keep my eyes on the road, but just barely. "There are two girls who live there. Why do you assume it's Evie?"

Annie makes the noise of a deflating balloon. "Easy. Because Tori Lalonde is a bitch."

I glance over at her, all stoicism gone. "How do you know that?"

"Evie is just a couple of years older than me. We used to play together sometimes when I stayed at Grandma's. Evie's the nice one. Always has been. Tori is the mean one. I don't see you going for a mean girl."

I ignore her comment about what kind of girl I'd go for. The revelation that Evie and Annie know each other makes sense, but I would've never imagined it. I want to know more.

211

"How old were you when you used to hang out?"

For some reason, this questions makes Annie laugh. "Hang out? The first time I climbed the fence to go to Evie's I was probably six years old."

I rack my brain trying to even remember Annie at six, but I can barely picture her. I would have been thirteen or fourteen at the time. Busy cutting up with my own friends.

"It's been years since I've talked to her," Annie says, sounding thoughtful. "But I can totally see y'all together."

The comment gives me whiplash. "We're not together."

"Why not?" Disbelief rings heavy in her voice. "She's funny... easy-going... beautiful... She's perfect for you."

She *is* perfect. I won't argue with that. But not for me. I shake my head.

"I'm not looking for a relationship."

I feel Annie's eyes as though they are boring into the side of my head, but I keep my focus on the road.

"Why the hell not? Unless you've been hiding some secret love affair with one of your cellmates, you've been single for a *really* long time, Drew. Have you become a monk?"

I haven't, but maybe I should.

"I'm not a monk," I mutter.

"Then why not Evie? I'm not saying you have to marry her, but you should at least try dating again. Get back out there and start living a real life—"

A flash of Evie in a white dress and veil rattles so hard, I grip the steering wheel with white knuckles. "Not Evie."

"Not Evie," she mimics in a grunting voice, and I know without looking that she's making that constipated face again. "But *why not* Evie?"

God, I miss her. Just hearing her name wakes up my skin. The memory of her in my arms ripples down my torso like warm rain. I miss her company. Her happiness. Her depth.

Her laugh is weightless. Her good heart bottomless.

It's Tuesday. I haven't seen Evie in over a week — when she came to my door, and I had to grip the edge of the table to keep from standing, ripping the door off its hinges, and dragging her to my bed.

Hell, I can't even imagine being the kind of man she deserves. Even in my fantasies, I play the villain. Keeping my distance is clearly the best I can do.

Beside me, Annie heaves an audible sigh, bringing me back to the now. My sister is obviously annoyed that I'm giving her the silent treatment, and since she's done me a favor by driving me all over town, I feel a twinge of guilt.

"I *have* started to live a real life," I defend, dodging her question about Evie.

Annie shifts in the seat beside me. When she speaks, her voice is low, but still betrays annoyance. "Working at the garage and taking care of Grandma don't count."

I cough, offended, and shoot her a glare. "How can they not count?"

"Because," she drones. "That's no fun."

213

"Horse shit," I say. "I love fixing cars, and I love Grandma."

Annie *tsks*. "You know what I mean."

I shake my head. "No. I don't. I like my job at the garage. I'm good at it." This is true. I don't have any secret aspiration to go to college and learn how to do something that would require a starched collar and a laptop. That kind of life was never meant for me, and it certainly isn't now. "And you and Grandma are really all that matters to me."

As soon as the words leave my mouth, I taste their falsehood. Evie matters to me. Her happiness... her safety... her needs.

A new fantasy emerges. One in which I'm not the villain, but still an outlaw. A vigilante who stands guard, in secret, at her door while she sleeps, keeping her safe from anyone who would harm her. Anyone unworthy. A sentinel who is gone by morning...

"But that's what I mean."

I feel like a dog on a leash, jerked away from this path that leads nowhere. We've come to the light at Johnston and South College, and, still lost in my head, I turn to look at my sister. Her eyes are pleading.

"Drew, that's not enough. That's not enough to build a life on."

I stare at her. Build a life? She's not even twenty years old. Where does she get this stuff?

"Don't look at me like that," she scolds. I face the road in time to see the light change. "I've been worried about you for almost as long as I can remember. I just want you to be safe and happy, okay?"

Even without seeing her, I can hear the strain in her voice. It stuns me. I mean, yeah, I know she wants

214

me to be safe. To be happy. But I never imagined she worried over it. The realization has me frowning.

"I'm safe, Annie," I say softly.

"But are you h-happy?" The strain in her voice has become a catch. I glance over at her to see her lips pressed tightly together, but the quiver in them is unmistakable.

Oh, Jesus. Don't cry.

How do I explain to her that happiness doesn't factor for me? After what I let happen to Anthony, I cannot live a happy life. I can know moments of joy. I can be happy for other people. But the best I can ask for myself is to live in peace.

"I'm satisfied with what I have."

Annie lets that hang in the air for about five seconds. "And why don't you want more? Better?"

I know I shouldn't say it. It'll only upset her. But I can't help it. "Because Anthony doesn't have better."

"Drew." I can't look at her, but I can sense she's completely deflated beside me. Her voice is the sound of heartbreak.

I just drive. It's all I can manage. Signal. Take the turning lane at St. Julien. Wait for the green arrow. While we are at the intersection, though, Annie's hand settles on my forearm.

"It wasn't your fault."

I choke out a mirthless laugh. Annie knows the whole story. And she's lived with Ma her entire life. She knows it's my fault. She knows as well as I do.

"I'm not saying what you and Anthony did wasn't wrong. You know it was wrong," she says. And even though her voice is soft, it's steady. "But you *both*

215

knew. Neither of you expected what happened to happen, but he wasn't inno—"

I pull my arm from her touch. "Stop."

She ignores me. "He wasn't innocent."

When I turn onto St. Joseph Street, I have to force myself to go the speed limit. We seem to crawl over the three blocks. I pull into Grandma's driveway and kill the engine. I stare straight ahead at the house, unable to look at my sister.

"Thanks for your help." And I'm out of the car.

It's late afternoon. I should go check on Grandma, but I'm about to lose it. I need to be alone so I can get a grip.

Behind me, I hear Annie's door open.

"Drew, why won't you listen to me? He wouldn't want this for you," she calls after me. "Anthony would want you to be happy."

I can still hear her even after I clear the side of the house. I'm glad the wrought iron stairs make such racket as I jog up them so I don't have to focus on Annie telling me how much my brother would want me to live enough for both of us.

I force myself to go down to the house about an hour later. I need to make sure Grandma has something to eat. Since her illness, she seems only to want a little breakfast and maybe a sandwich at lunch, and I've been trying to make sure she eats some dinner every night.

Annie's car is gone, and that's a good thing, but I'm no fool. If Grandma didn't hear our little exchange — and with her uncanny ability to pick out a conversation across the house, I have no doubt she did — Annie probably told her anyway.

To my surprise, the mouth-watering scent of bacon hits me as I step into the kitchen. Grandma Q is at the stove, her back to me as the frying pan hisses and spits.

She looks over her shoulder. "How about BLTs for dinner?" She's in her housecoat. The same one she was wearing when I left this morning. I wonder if she stayed in it all day or if she decided to change before cooking.

"BLTs sound great." I'm glad to see she's up, but I can't help but think it's taking a toll. I approach her and reach for the fork in her hand. "How about you let me finish these?"

She waves me away. "If you want to help, slice that tomato," she says, nodding to the deep red beefsteak on the counter. "That's harder on my arthritis than this is."

Okay, then. I thin-slice the tomato, rough cut a little lettuce, and spread mayo on slices of bread.

Grandma forks the crisp strips of bacon out of her cast iron skillet and onto a stack of paper towels. She turns off her burner and pats the bacon dry.

"Cut up two of those peaches for us," she tells me, pointing to her fruit bowl. I obey, of course, and a moment later, we are sitting at the table to the simple meal that is pure heaven.

My first bite — the marriage of the soft Evangeline Maid bread, the salty, still-steaming bacon, and the garden-fresh tomato — is better than any narcotic I've ever tried. I consume the sandwich in a few bites and eat the sun-ripened peach as my dessert, all thoughts of my conversation with Annie forgotten.

Until Grandma pipes up, of course.

"So, you can drive again," she says, commenting, not asking.

I nod. "Yes, ma'am." I'm still enjoying the post-meal haze, and I don't immediately pick up on the alertness in her voice.

"You need a car."

It's the way she says it that pricks my ears now. It's not innocent commentary. My eyes narrow on my grandmother, but she looks down at the uneaten half of her BLT.

"I'm doing okay without one," I tell her, keeping my voice even. "And I'm saving what I can. I'll buy one eventually."

She picks up her sandwich, takes a bite, and chews slowly. "No need to buy one when there's already one here for you."

The fine hairs on the back of my neck stand erect. Holy shit. The Supra.

God dammit.

"Grandma—"

"Let's go take a walk outside," she says, pushing herself up from the table. I don't move.

"Grandma, I know what you're trying to do."

"You always were my smartest grandbaby," she says, sounding unimpressed. She shuffles to a narrow drawer beside the sink, with her back to me and rifles through it for a few seconds. I hear the tell-tale jangle of keys, and my stomach free falls. Sweat mists my temples, and the BLT I just enjoyed becomes a cinder block in my gut.

218

Without looking at me, Grandma Q turns, tucks the keys into the pocket of her housecoat and heads for the door. "Come with me."

When I show no sign of moving, she wraps her fingers, gnarled with age and arthritis around my bicep. She says nothing until I look up to face her. And of course I look up. I have to. She's my grandmother.

"Andrew Quincy Moroux, get out of that chair and come with me. I am *not* asking."

And what other choice do I have? She's my grandmother.

I follow her, no surprise, out of the kitchen and around the back of the house to the detached garage. I haven't been inside since that day Evie Lalonde found me shaken and sweating at the picnic table.

The feeling I have now is not much better. Grandma points to the catch at the bottom of the old fashioned garage door. "Hoist that up for me, Andrew. I can't lift that much these days."

Smothering a groan, I do as she says. The panelled, wooden door lifts with surprising ease, making me wonder which of my cousins or uncles has kept it greased and in use all these years. The force of our entry stirs a meager belch of dust and grass clippings, but the space is fairly tidy, if musty and, with the sun setting behind the garage, almost completely dark.

Still the shadow of the Supra lurks like the spectre of a boogeyman under a child's bed. As though it could pounce on me like an animal, my whole body is strung tight. Grandma ambles into the darkness, and with the *chink* of a pull-string, the garage is lit in yellow incandescence.

Maybe it's the jacked up state of my nerves, but the overlapping of images — my tiny, housecoat-clad grandmother and my dead brother's muscle car — are both darkly funny and oddly mythic, like an allegory. I don't know whether to laugh or cry. The gyroscope holding my own sense of balance spins wildly for a second, and I reach for the garage door above my head to steady myself.

My heartbeat is all I hear.

I blink and refocus on the sight in front of me. Grandma Quincy opens the driver's side door, but no interior light comes on. She disappears into the car, her slippered feet jutting out the open door the only sign that anyone is there. I hear a *thunk* followed by a *click*, and then I watch her feet kick for purchase before my grandmother rises out of the car, holding something.

"I kept up the registration," she says, handing a slip of paper to me. "It's in your name—"

"I don't want it."

Grandma stares at me for a moment before dropping her knuckles to her hips. "And why not?"

My tongue sticks to the roof of my mouth, dry as ash. I try to swallow, lick my lips. Then I shake my head, my gaze falling to her flowered polyester slippers.

"I can't," I croak.

She pads over to me and lays a hand on my elbow. "You can." When I begin to shake my head, the hand on my elbow squeezes. "You *must.*"

A sound like a dry laugh escapes me, but my throat aches and my eyes sting. I make myself meet her gaze. Her old eyes aren't gentle, but fierce, and for this I'm grateful. Gentleness now would ransack me.

"Grandma, I couldn't bear to drive it."

One brow lifts under a rainbow of wrinkles. "That's okay. It doesn't drive anyway," she says, an impish smile shaping her mouth. "Chip says mice have chewed through the wires in the starter. And the battery corroded long ago. Hell, all the belts have probably dry rotted."

In the back of my mind, a tiny voice whispers something about how pissed Anthony would have been about this.

That's my fault, too.

A sigh escapes me. "If it doesn't even start, then why are we out here. Why are you doing this to me?"

Both brows climb now, and she looks at me with ironic surprise. "To you? You think I'm doing this *to you?*" Those eyebrows drop to the stern, scolding expression I've recognized my whole life. "Andrew, I'm doing this *for you.* You gotta stop dragging your guilt around like it's a boulder tied to your neck."

At this moment, it feels like that boulder is in my throat. I can't make her or Annie understand. Separating myself from this guilt is impossible.

And who would I be if I did?

I'm choking on the violence of emotions, but I manage to force out two words. "I can't."

Her mouth sets. Her shoulders rise and fall with her breath. Suddenly, my grandmother looks very tired again.

I swallow, my own distress receding in the face of worry for her. "Are you alright?"

She blows a breath out her nose and shakes her head. "No, I am not. I am worried about you, and I refuse to watch you waste the life you've been given."

Disappointment seems to weigh down the lines around her eyes. It gives the heft of my guilt a run for its money.

I feel so heavy I want to sit down. I want to lie down. I want to collapse on the ground and form a sinkhole so dirt caves in on top of me, filling it up until there's nothing left but a bald patch of dry earth.

"There's nothing I can do," I tell her, and my voice already sounds like its coming up from underground.

At this, I swear, if lightning bolts could shoot from Grandma Quincy's eyes, I'd be struck dead. "Nothing you can do? I will *tell* you what you are going to do." She points a weathered index finger at me as though the gesture alone could poke a hole in my chest. Then she jabs at the Supra with the same force. "You are going to fix that goddamn car so it runs like new. And if you're not going to drive it, you're going to fetch the best damn price for it you can—"

"I don't want the car or any money—"

She reels back as if I've spit on her. "Who said anything about *you* getting the money? You can put that straight into my IRA," she snaps. "I love you more than life, Andrew, but you live here rent free, eating from my table for breakfast, lunch, and dinner. I've held onto this wreck all this time for you. The least you can do is make it worth my while."

I know what she's doing. In my head, I call this what it is. She's manipulating again, saying everything she needs to say to make me do what she wants. But, my God, it works. Even though I see right through her, I can do nothing about it. I don't want to touch Anthony's car. I can barely stand to look at it.

But how can I tell her no?

CHAPTER EIGHTEEN

DREW

The next day, after work, I'm in Grandma's garage, facing down the Supra.

It takes me twenty minutes just to make myself touch it. *It's just a car.* I tell myself, over and over. But after staring motionless at Anthony's car for so long, I decide I need to trick myself into tackling it. I find a dusty transistor radio and tune it to the station they're always playing at C & C. I open the garage door, the side door, and the two windows to give the place fresh air and better light.

I'd give anything to tow the Supra to the garage to make it feel more anonymous, but that would be a waste of money, and without even looking inside her, this job is going to cost a bundle anyway.

A bundle and then some, I decide when I finally pop the hood. And it's only when I see the damage, a set of individual and interconnected mechanical problems, that my hands stop shaking. The smell of rodent piss is unmistakable, and if I ever get this thing running, adding heat to that stench is going to be sickening. I need to look up ways to neutralize it without using anything corrosive.

But the smell is the least of my problems. Grandma was right. It's hardly a clean job, but the starter wiring is stripped and gnawed up and down. A total loss. My first step is to remove the shot battery and clean the corrosion of the connectors before I do anything else.

And then I take stock of everything. At least, everything I can see.

The radiator is bone dry, and the greenish stain on the concrete under the Supra would suggest it leaked out a long time ago. Everything I can see that is rubber — valve cover gaskets, hoses, belts — is porous at best and crumbles to dust with my touch at worst.

I can only imagine that the resin in the brake pads is in just as bad a shape. And I'm going to need a frickin' swimming pool of Metal Rescue to remove all the rust. From the rockers, to the cylinder heads, to the engine walls themselves.

And then once I get it started, if I can get it started, I'm sure a host of other issues will show themselves.

"Jesus, Anthony," I whisper before I back away and head upstairs for a shower.

I walk home from the bus stop the next day carrying everything I could afford from AutoZone. A battery, a terminal brush, a socket wrench, and a gallon of Metal Rescue. I brought a backpack to carry everything, but even with that, this shit weighs a ton — especially after three blocks.

I switch shoulders, wondering if Grandpa Pete has the Phillips head I'll need to disconnect the starter's wiring. I'm cursing myself for not at least making a better inventory of his old tools when I notice the poster.

It's neon green and tie-wrapped to the stop sign at the corner of Howard Avenue and St. Joseph Street. Giant, swirling letters in orange, blue, and red seem to shout:

FALL FIESTA BLOCK PARTY!
609 SAINT PATRICK

SATURDAY, 8PM-TIL
COME FOR THE FAJITAS!
STAY FOR THE MARGARITAS!

A multicolored — if simple — drawing of a sombrero takes up the top left corner of the poster while a pair of red and yellow maracas appear to shake on the bottom right.

Nothing about the sign gives me a second thought except the address. Grandma's number is 609 Saint Joseph. The house behind hers, Evie's house, is on the even side of the street. I don't know the address, even though I've been in front of her house twice now. But the house across the street from Evie's, the one where I last saw her, might be 609.

If it is, is Evie still there? And are her friends throwing a party?

This is the first hint I've had of her in days, and I'm stirred like a roux. I know Evie's not back at her house. Her darkened window mocks me both night and day. And if she is still just across the street, then even if I've got the wrong house and one of her neighbors is hosting this party, I can only imagine that Evie will go.

I hate parties.

I didn't even want to attend the welcome home gig Grandma Quincy threw for me. But I know without even thinking about it that Evie loves parties. The chance to meet people… watch people… make them laugh… dance and sing… She'd be in the thick of it.

Unlike me in every possible way. And now, whether she's still in the neighborhood or not, I content myself with this image. It is her I see as I replace the battery and clean the terminals.

225

Friday, after work, I get to the bank in time to deposit my check again, and then I borrow Grandma Quincy's car for a trip to Wal-Mart. The load of materials I need is much greater than I can manage on the bus, and while I'm sure I'll have to resort to Pull-A-Part in the future, for now the discount warehouse is my best option for hoses and belts, and two more gallons of rust remover.

After two days of doing little more than staring at her innards, I've decided to let the cylinders soak in Metal Rescue while I change as much rubber as can be managed. It might take a day or two of flushing before I can even tell if the engine looks sound. And if she isn't, well, I'll just have to tell Grandma that the Supra is good for nothing but parts.

There's a side of me that would like nothing better than to declare the job a wash. Walking into Grandma's garage every evening hasn't gotten any easier. It's only after I get my hands dirty that I can stand being in there. Until then, I still shake and sweat and curse myself.

But once I get to work…

I don't know. Time seems to skim like a speed skater on ice. I pull myself back from inside the hood to find all trace of daylight gone, moths and mosquitos crowding the air in the garage, the former trying to mob the overhead light, and the latter mobbing me.

C & C closes at two on Saturdays, and I'm on duty until then, so I don't get back to the Supra until a little after three, but the quality of the air has changed. A shift in the breeze this morning has brought in a dry north wind that makes it easier to breathe. This breeze even smells different, more like the tang of fall instead of the hot breath of summer.

I stand in the doorway of the Grandma's garage, picturing Anthony behind the wheel and wondering what the hell he'd think if he could see me messing with his baby. This is the ritual, or at least part of it, I have to pass through just to approach the hood.

And when I do, I see that one of the cylinders, by some miracle, has run clear.

I thump the engine with one side of my fist. The other cylinders don't look like they've drained at all, but one out of six is better than none.

I work on refitting hoses for a couple of hours and stop when Grandma calls from her kitchen door to say dinner is ready.

Over a meal of baked ham and biscuits, Grandma Quincy proceeds to tell me that I should go to the party around the corner.

I finish off a buttered biscuit dressed with ham and Steen's syrup before responding. "Well, I would, Grandma, but since I live here rent-free and eat from your table, breakfast, lunch, and dinner," I wave my hand over the meal she's made to illustrate my point, echoing the words she threw at me days ago, "I need to be sure I'm making it worth your while. And you've given me a job to do."

Grandma Q eyes me, her mouth a flat line. She's clearly unimpressed with my little speech, but I think she gets the message. I'm only going to fall for one manipulation tactic at a time.

What I don't tell her is that working on Anthony's car, as hard as it is, scares me a hell of a lot less than wading into a crowd of strangers to face Evie

227

Lalonde. Just because I don't want to encourage Evie doesn't make me a masochist. In the mix of her friends and neighbors — all free of felony records — I'd stand out like a bruise.

She needs to see me for who I am, but that doesn't mean I want to watch it happen. Watch the look on her face change — growing awkward and embarrassed, and maybe even a little sick — when she realizes I was never fit for her company.

It's with this cheerful thought that I return to the garage after dinner. Maybe it's this promise of Evie's eventual rejection and maybe it's the escape from Grandma Quincy's disappointment, but despite the evidence of my guilt, the garage feels like a retreat. I get back to work.

I'm replacing the radiator hose when I catch salsa music in the distance. It's around eight o'clock. I look up to see the graying dusk in the sky and make out the sounds of Marc Anthony's "I Need to Know."

I wonder what she's wearing.

The temptation just to walk down the side street to catch a glimpse of her assaults me like a rogue wave. I shake it off, knowing it's madness, but I go to the old radio and turn up the volume on "This is America" just in case.

And I keep working... for hours.

At least my hands keep working. In my mind's eye, I imagine the lengthening hours and the slow trickling away of party guests. What if I let myself loose tonight when the streets go quiet? Would I find her after midnight, cleaning up red Solo cups and paper plates?

Could I approach her then like a stray dog looking for scraps?

She'd take me in if I were that stray dog. I know this like I know my own name. And then I'd be able to watch over her night and day. Make sure no losers like that Drake asshole could get within groping distance of her. Lay down at the foot of her bed and never want anything more.

I'm so deep in this ridiculous stray dog fantasy, I don't hear the footsteps.

In fact, I notice nothing until a shadow falls over my left side, and I look up with a start. I'm bent double under the hood, and I straighten up so fast at the sight of her I nearly take my head off.

We stare at each other for a moment. Me, shocked as hell because I feel like I've conjured her. Evie, more beautiful than I've ever seen her and looking, I quickly realize, seriously pissed.

Her dress is a pale blue cotton, off-the-shoulder with a wide ruffle that wraps all the way around her. It's so short I feel a gut-check when my eyes skim her bare thighs.

I swallow and then blink when I take in the thermos dangling from her left hand and the two plastic cups she carries in her right.

My eyes meet hers. "What are you doing, Evie?"

She blinks then, and I notice her eyes are a little glassy, her eye makeup smudged. Just barely. She's been drinking. Not a lot, if my guess is right, but enough.

"Coming to find you. What does it look like I'm doing?" And the way she says it confirms she's pissed at me.

She has every right to be. I've been an asshole to her. But obviously not enough of one because here she is.

And, God, it's so good to see her.

She looks amazing. And like nothing that belongs in here.

I glance around the garage and then let my eyes sweep over her. "It looks like you got lost..." I do a double-take on the sexy-as-hell suede booties that show off the scarlet tips of her toenails. I force myself to look up "... on the way to a party."

She shakes her head, her eyes narrowed with ire. "No, I made it to the party, but the person I wanted to be with the most wasn't there." She sets down the thermos on the Supra's chasse. "So I decided to bring the party to him."

The person I wanted to be with the most.

The words run over me, searing me all the way down. That is exactly how I would describe *her*. She is the person I want to be with the most. The only person. I've missed her with a longing I've never known. One I don't want to be cured of.

But this is torture because she shouldn't be here, and I don't know if I can find the will to make her go. I glance at the wall clock and get a jolt when I see it's almost eleven.

I frown. "How did you get here?"

Evie stares at me like I'm daft. "I walked."

She walked. Looking like that. At this hour. I grit my teeth. "That's dangerous."

Tilting her chin down and looking up at me under her lashes, Evie bats her eyes with unmistakable irony. "It's just around the block, and, well, I couldn't exactly drive," she says, patting the top of her thermos with one hand.

If I want her to leave — and I don't — I'll have to take her home myself. She sure as hell isn't walking back alone.

Evie sets the two cups side by side on the edge of the Supra's frame and unscrews the lid of the thermos. She pours, and a slushy frozen margarita spills into the first cup, a little splashing over the side and onto the car.

"How much of that have you had?"

She raises a hand to silence me, and it's this motion that shows me she's had more than one. Evie fills the second cup before replacing the lid. Then she lifts both and her eyes meet mine.

"Here. Drink with me." She thrusts one toward my chest. "And I'll accept your apology."

Alcohol is off limits while I'm on probation, but I don't know if I've ever needed a drink more. I take the cup. "My apology?"

Evie lowers her lashes. This time there's no irony in her demure expression. I see hurt etched around her eyes.

"For pretending I didn't exist the other day." Injury is layered in her voice too. "It was cruel and humiliating."

In prison, the threat of being stabbed with a shiv was low, but still real. Sometimes, I'd wonder what it would feel like. To be cut open with something usually innocent and harmless. Like a toothbrush or a comb.

With Evie's words, I don't wonder anymore. I'm gutted.

If someone else hurt her the way I've hurt her, I'd want to kill the bastard.

"I'm sorry."

At my words, she raises her gaze to mine, and I tell her the truth. "You deserve better."

One of her delicate brows lifts. "From you?" she asks, not missing a beat and teasing out my ambiguity.

"*Than* me." I chase the words with a slug of margarita. It's cold and strong, but too sweet for this moment.

Evie narrows her eyes. "I won't drink to that."

I set down the cup. "*And* from me," I say because it's true.

She drinks, keeping her eyes on mine the whole time.

Because I have to know, I ask. "How are you?" My voice is low, but I'm afraid she can still hear my need. "You moved out."

Evie nods, looks down at her cup. "It was time. I needed to make a point."

"What point was that?"

Her gaze knocks back to mine, determination steely in her green eyes. "That I can take care of myself."

The argument I shared with her sister rushes back to me. The protectiveness she showed for Evie mirrored my own. But now, facing the memory tilts me off balance. I agreed with Tori then. About me. But the look of resentment on Evie's face makes me wonder if allying with her sister is really a good thing.

I know it's fucked up, considering everything I've done and said to push her away, but I don't want her to hate me.

I bring the cup to my lips and drain it. The taste of tequila is stronger this time. It's been a while since I've had its smokey nectar on my tongue. Or in my blood for that matter. And with the emptying of the cup, I can feel the liquor hit my system. It's been a hell of a long time.

As soon as I set it down, she tops off the cup again.

"Evie, I don't think—"

"I told you I was bringing the party to you," she says, but the lack of festivity in her tone is almost funny.

I give her a hard stare. "It doesn't look like you're having such a good time."

Her tense expression wavers. Anguish and vulnerability peek out. I clench my hands against the urge to reach for her. Comfort her.

"Because you don't seem glad to see me."

It's as though my chest unzips, and my heart falls to the floor. It may even bounce a few times. I want to drop to my knees.

I ache to tell her how it is.

Seeing you's the best thing that's happened to me all week.

I've missed you so much I'm ready to bash my head against a wall.

If I were a different man, I would have carried you upstairs already.

The ache is so bad, I can't bring myself to do what needs doing. Tell her something ugly and untrue that would keep her away for good.

Hell, I probably couldn't pull it off if I tried. And then what? Walk her home afterward?

You don't do it for me... but I have to walk you to your door to make sure you're okay or I won't sleep tonight. Or any night after that...

Yeah, that would be a disaster.

So I tell her something true. "I'm glad to see you, Evie." I try to keep my face even, detached, but she must hear some of the understatement in my voice because she lets go a breath she was holding, and those lovely bare shoulders settle lower.

"I've missed you," she says, and I have to close my eyes. God, the ways she's looking at me. I might die.

My only refuge is in the cup in my hand, so I drain half of it again. I open my eyes, but I can't meet hers. Instead, I stare at the Supra's rusted cylinders.

"Mrs. Vivian is okay?" she asks a moment later.

I nod, relieved she's moved to something else. Something besides what lives and breathes between us. "She's better." Then I shrug. "Not quite back to full steam, but better."

"She'll be back to normal in no time." The smile I hear in her voice makes me look up.

Big mistake. That sweet smile is kryptonite. I may never be able to look away again.

"Oh, she's still got it where it counts," I say, tapping the side of my head. Evie's smile grows, and without even thinking about it, I take a step closer to her. The corner of the Supra's front end is still a wedge between us, and even though that must make up hundreds of pounds of steel, it may as well be nothing.

"The two of you are so adorable." When she says this, her eyes glint with joy. "The crone and the warrior."

This catches me off guard. "Excuse me?"

A giggle escapes her. "They're archetypes. Strong masculine energy. You help and protect her. Wise feminine energy. She helps and guides you. It's a powerful mix."

I crack a smile. "Energy," I mutter, shaking my head. "Guppy, you're somethin' else."

A playful scowl claims her face. "You're just ignorant. It's not your fault." She throws back the rest of her margarita. "You're lucky you have me to teach you about the mysteries of the universe."

My laughter booms through the garage. I suddenly feel lighter. Younger.

Better than I am.

"Go ahead, Guppy. Teach me."

She licks her lips, preparing to school me, and at the flash of the tip of her pink tongue, my mouth goes dry.

"Well, you—" she gestures to me with an upturned palm, "are obviously the warrior archetype—"

"Hold up." I raise my own hand to stop her and just manage to keep from grabbing her outstretched fingers. "What's an archetype?"

Her eyes bug. "Oh my God, you poor baby!" She shakes her head dramatically. "You really do need me more than you realize."

She's teasing me, but her words hit home anyway. I'm not supposed to need her, but there's no denying it. It feels like I need her just to stand upright. I need to know her. I need to be near her. I need to protect her. But, most of all, I need for her to be happy and whole.

Which is why I also need to stay away. Because how could someone like me give her what *she* needs? I'm an ex-con with blood on his hands. I work in a garage for fuck's sake. Ex-con grease monkey. That's what I am.

"An archetype is… well, it's like a pattern. A recurring pattern or figure that exists everywhere." Her

235

silvery green eyes have gone wide with wonder. "Throughout time. Among all cultures. In art. In stories. In dreams…"

My brow creases. I have no idea what she's talking about, but I'm glad she's giving me something else to focus on besides her nearness and that awed look in her eyes. "Like what. Give me an example."

Her gaze sharpens. "Like a symbol or a type of story or myth." She looks so excited to be telling me this I have to keep my smile in check. She's shining. Absolutely fucking stunning. "Like a coyote, fox, or wolf. How many stories can you think of where one of those animals is a trickster?"

I blink at her. "You mean like fairy tales? Or cartoons?"

Her smile widens. "Both. Either. Doesn't matter."

Little Red Riding Hood. Wile E. Coyote. *The Fantastic Mr. Fox.* "A lot," I say, unimpressed. "But what does that matter? Foxes and coyotes are sneaky bastards. Everybody knows that. They were always finding ways of raiding the hen houses at Angola."

She laughs again, nodding. She sets down her drink and makes two fists, gesturing emphatically. "Exactly, but the power of the archetype is not only in what it symbolizes but what it reveals *to* us and *in* us."

I don't think I've ever seen her this animated. I can't take my eyes off her.

"Take the fox, for example. Think of the words and phrases we use to describe people that have to do with foxes. *Outfox… crazy like a fox… sly as a fox.*" She rattles these off so quickly I can't help but smile. "Even though the fox is small, he can evade and best his enemies because of his cunning. Even if they are bigger

236

and more powerful. The fox archetype reminds us that might doesn't always win. That wits matter more. For better or for worse."

She pauses, and her smile softens. "So those stories aren't really about foxes. They're about us. And the neat thing is, they are found all over the world. Existing simultaneously in cultures that had no common language or connection during ancient times. Isn't that amazing?"

"It's..." It's over my head is what it is. Even though my view of life and mankind grew and unfolded while I did time, I didn't give much study or consideration to anything she's describing. Patterns that connect us. Symbols that mean the same thing to all people. And as I stand here, staring at the most beautiful human being I've ever known, I realize she's made the world — the whole universe — bigger and more mysterious. *"... incredible."*

"I know, right?" She nods, beaming. "The more you know about archetypes, the better you can understand who you are and where you are in your life's journey. And there's so many really cool ones. Like the Green Man."

"Green Man?" I sound so stupid. What is she even doing here with me?

"Yeah, like in *Sir Gawain and the Green Knight.* Or Peter Pan. Or Shrek."

"Shrek?" I laugh. I can't help it. What the hell is she talking about?

She laughs at me laughing but recovers to educate me. "The Green Man — who is usually green all over or dressed in green — symbolizes life, the natural world. The wild." Her eyes, their own vivid green, shift between mine as if she knows a secret, and she's going to share it. "The Green Man's job is to remind us that we are wild, too. If we forget that — if we think we are so civilized and cerebral and *rational* —" She rolls her eyes as if being rational were the most ridiculous thing in the world. "We fall out of balance, and we wind up making fools of ourselves."

She stares into me, and her voice drops. "For all of our fancy clothes and planet-destroying ambitions, we're still animals, after all."

There's no chance I've forgotten this. The heat in her gaze stirs the animal within me. He's powerful. And hungry.

Our eyes are locked, though hers now are dark-pupilled and half-lidded. Mine, I'm sure, as feral as any beast's.

Evie takes one step in my direction, and I lunge for her, the animal I am breaking free. Our mouths collide as though our whole lives have unfolded for this moment. Every day. Every decision. For this.

As though the touch of her lips, the taste of her has been wrought by time and evolution and divine intent to be mine. My mouth. My body. My heart hers.

My hands tangle in her curls as I crush her to me, and I dive into her mouth. She welcomes me as she has always welcomed me. Eager. Open. Loving.

Evie.

Her kiss — the pressure of her soft body against mine, the heat of her mouth as it captures my tongue — pulls me farther and farther away from any hope of redemption.

With this kiss, I claim her like the criminal I am.

CHAPTER NINETEEN

EVIE

My head spins. I can't feel my feet. And it has nothing to do with the three and a half margaritas I've knocked back tonight.

Drew is kissing me like he's wanted me his whole life.

Like I'm perfect just the way I am. Like there's nothing he would change about me.

And he shows no sign of stopping. His stubble scrapes against my chin as he tilts my head back to delve deeper into my mouth. His tongue tells me everything he's been hiding behind that careful stone facade.

He feels what I feel. As strongly as I feel it. And with each surge of his tongue and suckle of his lips, he erases the shame and the doubt of every step I took in the dark to find him here.

It was right to push him. This is what he needed. What we needed.

My hands climb his arms, up over his wide shoulders and along his neck until my fingers glide into his dark hair. Everything about him is so rough and coarse, but his hair is as soft as down. It reminds me of what I've known all along.

He's not as tough as he seems.

I smile at the thought, hair tickling my fingers as I caress him.

"What's so funny?" he murmurs against my lips between kisses.

But I just giggle and kiss him back, hard and long, jealous for this closeness he's finally giving me. Talking can wait.

"You laughing at the way I kiss?"

239

I shake my head, lips brushing against him. "I love the way you kiss." He sucks in a gasp before claiming me again, sending a surge of pure pleasure straight down between my legs.

We lose ourselves in each other for another long moment. All tongues... lips... hands... fingers. Our bodies pressing into each other.

"Good," he mutters. "Was worried I'd forgotten how."

I giggle again and let my teeth close on his bottom lip before releasing it. "Well, we can practice as much as you want."

One hand grips me behind my neck, the other at the small of my back, and with a thrill of pleasure, I feel one of Drew's legs wedge between mine. The top of his thigh meets me right where I need it, and a soft cry escapes me.

He echoes me with a moan. The sound is both need and satisfaction. Passion and pain. It calls to me. I run my hands down again until they grip either side of his waist, hard as lumber but thrumming with heat. My thumbs glide over the front of his gray T-shirt, and his abs twitch beneath it. And the way he pulls me tighter against him, pressing that thigh harder against me, let's me know my touch hasn't tickled but tormented...in the best possible way.

God, I want to make him feel good.

How long has it been since he's known a loving touch? I'm aching to be the one to give it to him. And not just tonight, but every night. With this thought, I let my hands slip under the hem of his shirt and flatten against his scorching-hot skin.

"Mmm, Evie," he moans in pleasure, but shakes his head, rocking against my mouth. He brings his hands to mine, clasps me around each wrist, and moves my touch to his back — outside his T-shirt.

"But I want—"

He silences me with another kiss and a firmer press of his thigh.

For a moment, all I know is his touch, the feel of him against me. But my awareness, my experience of pleasure circles back to wanting to give it to him. And if, for right now, I'm only allowed to touch his back, I can work with that.

His muscles on either side of his spine shift beneath my palms as he moves with subtle grace against me. I feel the heave of his breath through his ribs. I paint him with my touch, learning his terrain, feeling the sheer strength of him. And then I move to trace it all over again, but this time with the light scrape of my nails.

A deep, throaty growl rumbles from him, and his mouth slides to my jawline. Teeth close gently around my right earlobe.

"God, you feel amazing," he whispers. The hot fog of his breath sends chills down my neck.

"I want to make you feel good," I confess. I don't tell him it's something I need. What I feel for him is too big to manage any other way.

He kisses my neck, and my thoughts unravel for untold minutes. Then I move my mouth to his neck, wanting him to know how this feels, and I taste salt and man.

He even tastes sexy. How is that possible?

I don't think I've ever felt this much pleasure. I want to live fully in this moment, but even as we are in the throes of discovering each other, I know this is Drew. And at some point soon, in a few seconds or a few hours, he's going to pull away and bring up that wall of his.

I have to destroy it. And the only way I can do that is with proof of what we can be together. Proof that he can trust himself with me. Which means I need to give myself to him.

I *want* to give myself to him.

I bring one hand around to his chest and grip the front of his T-shirt as I raise my lips to his ear. "Let's go upstairs."

Drew stills, and for a terrifying moment, I think I've already spooked him. Panting, he presses his cheek against mine.

"We can't."

He's not pulling away. And I know I'm not imagining the regret I hear in his voice. So I try again.

"We can," I whisper. "I want to."

Drew's arms close around me so tight. I don't think anyone has ever held me this close. I hug him back as tight as I can.

"I shouldn't tell you how much I like hearing that," he mutters against my neck, almost like he's talking to himself. "I'm not... *prepared* for that."

I can't help my grin, and I turn my smile against his ear, trace the shell of it with the tip of my tongue. He shivers. "I think there's something pressing into my belly that says otherwise."

I feel his rasping laugh throughout my whole body. But instead of throwing me over his shoulder like I want him to, he draws back just enough to look me in the eye.

The smile is still there, but it's wary. "Evie, baby, it's not safe."

I blink. Where else could I be safer than with him? "Why not?"

His brows lower, and his smile turns jaded. "Babe, I've been in prison."

I watch him for a second. Then my eyes bug. "Oh my God." I place my hand on his cheek. "Are you — Are you okay? Do you have an—" I stop, unable to make myself say *STD*. Not because I'm squeamish, but because I know admitting it would be painful. Because someone in prison must have hurt him.

He grips me by the shoulders and looks me dead in the eyes. "I know I don't HIV, Hep C, or TB. They test you a month before you get out," he says, and as the meaning of his alphabet soup sinks in, I let go a sigh of relief for him.

"Thank God," I say, more thankful about this news than maybe any other I've ever heard in my life. "Well, then… we can—"

"No." Drew shakes his head, and his stoneface is back. "No condoms. We can't."

I grip his shirt harder. "But I'm on the pill and you just said—"

He raises a brow and aims a stern glare at me. "I said I didn't have the deadly shit. I didn't say I didn't have shit." His smokey eyes blaze. "And I'm not letting any shit that touched me touch you."

I meet his unrelenting stare with my own. I want to ask what happened to him there. I want him to share it with me so he'll know — whatever it is — it won't scare me away. But I also don't want to ask. Knowing for sure someone hurt him might tear me open.

243

But then another thought occurs to me, and I want to make this alright too.

"Eight years is a long time to… be alone. If you had someone—"

His hands on my shoulders become vices. "Evie," he says my name through clenched teeth. Old fury glows in his eyes. "It didn't go down like that."

It's like a blow to the stomach. I stagger, and Drew wraps an arm low around my back. But I shake my head, planting my feet and gripping him right back. He needs to know I'm strong enough. For both of us.

"I-I teach a class," I say, then swallow, trying to master the tremor in my voice. Drew frowns, confusion playing in his eyes. "It's called Yoga for Trauma. It can hel—"

"Baby." His eyes narrow, and one side of his mouth curls up. "It happened. One time. Before I knew how to look after myself on the inside."

I watch his face, stunned silent that he's giving me so much truth. This is as open as any man could ever be.

One brow comes up. "I'm not saying it wasn't a fucking nightmare. It was." The smile is a ghost now. "But it isn't what defines me. As soon as I got the chance, I beat the shit out of that fucker, and I was done with it."

At first, I have no idea what to say. And then, "That's something a Taurus would do." I don't mean it as a joke, but he bursts out laughing.

Drew shakes his head, his laughter dying away, and he just looks at me. And the way he looks at me, like I'm someone he'll never see again, turns up my fear again.

"Please don't send me away."

244

His eyes narrow with what I now see is anguish. He runs his gaze up and down our bodies, pressed together as they are, arms around each other. "Does it look like I want to send you away?"

I hold his gaze. "That hasn't stopped you before."

His eyes close, and when they open, slowly, he's mastered the anguish, his expression hard again. "I should walk you back."

"No." My voice is low but firm. "Don't tell me what you *think* you should do. Tell me what you *want* to do."

"Evie—"

"You've given yourself all these bullshit reasons why you shouldn't be with me," I say, fisting my hand in his shirt. "But I've never felt like this with anyone else, and I think the same is true for you. Am I right?"

Drew's jaw sets and his nostrils flare. "You don't know what's good for you—"

"Jesus!" I push against his chest, but his arms firm around me. "Why doesn't anyone believe in me?!"

Surprise at my outburst flashes in his eyes, but my own rage burns brighter so I barely see it.

"I'm not an idiot, Drew," I spout, balling my fists and bouncing them off his chest. I'm too close to do more than tap, but I'm so fucking angry, I could scream. I nearly do. "I know what I want for my life. The kind of job... the kind of future..." And then I scowl at him because it hurts so much to say it, knowing it won't matter at all. "The kind of man."

His brows lower, the look of surprise gone. Now he just looks pissed. Seriously pissed. Well, he can join the club.

245

"I am *done* with letting other people tell me what I can and can't have. Telling me I don't know what's good for me. Newsflash: I'm the fucking world-class expert on me, and I'll take what I want, goddammit." I shove him, hard this time, and he has to brace against me to keep his feet. It's not much, I know, but it feels fucking great to set him off balance. "What about you? What do you want?"

He grabs my upper arms, and I'm sure he's about to march me down his driveway to the curb. Instead, he gives me a shake that rattles my bones.

"You know what I want?" he growls, bearing teeth like animal. But before I can answer, he's on me.

His kiss is violent, demanding. My breath goes at the shock of it, replaced with his. Hot. Angry. Fierce. One of Drew's hands leaves my back and the garage echoes with a clatter as the car's hood slams shut.

That thigh is between my legs again, but instead of pressing into me, Drew uses it to walk me back. I clench his shoulders when I start to tip backward, but he hooks his arm low, clutching me to him. His free hand braces, and then I'm lowered, gently, to the hood of the car.

Half his weight settles on me, and Drew deepens the kiss. Anger and shock give way to heat and hunger. On top of me, Drew feels incredible. He kisses me hard, and I kiss right back, tangle my fingers in the soft waves of his hair, and grip him to me.

Drew tears his mouth away, panting, and he presses his forehead against mine. My whole world becomes his eyes.

"I want *you*, dammit." He grinds his pelvis into mine, and I arch my back in answer, a cry escaping me. "I've wanted you since my first day as a free man."

"Take me." I want to give him myself and in exchange, I want to take all his pain from him.

A growl of frustration tears from his throat. With a look of torture, Drew raises up on his elbows and glares down at me. And I see the moment he breaks. The moment he surrenders to his desires.

His right hand grips the top of my off-the-shoulder dress, and with one deft tug, my left breast is free.

His hot mouth closes over it. I gasp and arch up into him, pleasure shooting through me.

"Drew... oh God..."

He moans against me in answer.

Before this moment, I used to wonder what all the fuss was about. Whenever a man found his way under my top, I was content to patiently let my partners grope their way beneath my bra in anticipation of the moment they would eventually take their attentions south.

But the fever of Drew's mouth and the worship of his tongue are twin revelations. It has never felt like this. Spikes of pleasure and longing have me lifting off the hood of the car. All I can think about is how close he is to my heart. As though he is discovering what it holds for him. Discovering. And welcoming.

And it's the most erotic experience of my life.

I close my eyes, drowning in the sensation, dimly aware that I could come — actually come — from this alone. And then he pushes down my dress, freeing my right breast now, and the ecstasy begins all over again.

But this time, his work-calloused hand claims the left with a jealous touch.

"Drew," I gasp his name, uncertain how much more I can take. I want to reach for him, pull him into me, but the sleeves of my fallen dress now have me pinioned by the arms. All I can do is clutch his hair at the roots.

"I need you," I whisper.

My honesty feels like a gift I want him to accept. My words could not hold more truth. It isn't just his touch I need and crave, though I do. It's him. What I hold for him in my heart may be new, but it also feels like it's always been his to claim.

We're supposed to be together. There's just no doubt in my mind. I only have to show him.

"Oh, I need you," I say again, and this time the words come out louder, more plaintive.

His mouth leaves my breast. "Right here, baby," he murmurs, and then he's kissing me again. But this time one hand glides down my side until his fingers reach the back of my left thigh. He strokes me lightly from the top to the back of my knee, coaxing a high-pitched hum from me.

Drew echoes it with his own deep rumble.

I free my right arm and stroke his cheek. His jaw is chiseled, stubbled. My fingers trace his beauty as we kiss. His breath deepens against me as the hand on my leg glides up again. This time all the way up to the edge of my panties.

My free hand rides down the line of his jaw to his neck where his pulse is racing. This proof of his excitement undoes me. He palms the side of my hip, running his hand up and down over the elastic of my panties. Drew's breath is jagged, and I realize he's waiting. Waiting for a signal from me.

I close my eyes and bring my lips to his ear. "Oh, God, yes."

Drew yanks my panties down to my thighs. His weight leaves me and silk slides off my feet. I open my eyes to see him standing between my knees, but when I try to sit up to reach him, he presses a hand against my shoulder.

Our eyes lock as he wraps a hand around my right ankle and anchors it to the front bumper of the car. He grabs my other leg and tugs me toward him. I slide free down the hood with such momentum that I throw my arms out to the side to catch myself.

But before I can go ass first off the front of the car, Drew drops to his knees and throws my left leg over his shoulder.

"*Drew,*" I squeak. My slide down the car hood has rucked up my dress, and now Drew meets my gaze over the tangled fabric.

"You're so fucking beautiful."

The two lights in the garage aren't bright by any means, but spread out on the hood of this car with my dress bunched at my middle, there is absolutely no hiding. Yet when I take in the heat and longing in his dove gray eyes, I decide I don't want to hide.

His hand on my ankle makes a slow journey on fingertips up to the peak of my knee and down the valley of my thigh. My breath goes shaky. He grips my inner thigh, but even this doesn't prepare me for the press of his lips that lands between his thumb and forefinger.

I exhale a hard breath.

He's just inches from me — from my root chakra. The place of grounding. Of stability. Of the most basic needs. I close my eyes and feel its red glow. In this moment, I have no doubt I'm right where I need to be.

Drew's right hand comes to my left inner thigh, and his lips follow suit, greeting the soft skin there. I feel the tip of his warm, wet tongue. The scrape of his two-day beard.

This red glow seems to spread down my legs, anchoring me to him. Because his touch, both gentle and eager, tells me I'm safe. Wanted.

And I should be ready for it, but the explosion of orange behind my eyes takes me by surprise when his mouth lands on my sex. His tongue opens me like a lotus blossom. He moans, and I feel it all the way in my womb.

I feel everything.

Drew's hands and mouth. The car hood beneath me. The narrow ledge of front bumper under my heel. The tiny hairs on my arms that stand at attention in the rush of so much bliss. My sacral chakra pulses with pleasure. With life.

I reach for Drew, and his left hand catches my right in a tight squeeze, but he doesn't stop. His lips, tongue, teeth reign over me. And then fingers find my entrance, and my gasp echoes through the garage.

The world turns yellow.

I am consumed in fire. Power radiates from my center. His fingers move inside me, creating ripples of energy and sensation. I feel like there is nothing I can't do. Together, there is nothing *we* can't do.

I open my eyes to find Drew watching me. Energy surges higher, claiming my heart, the fourth

250

chakra. Nothing even close to this has ever happened to me. Yet I know it for what it is.

This is love.

The sparks flaring behind my breastbone are surely green with heart chakra energy.

And with this awakening, sensations catch fire in my throat, the joining place between heart and mind, and I have to speak.

"Drew, Oh God, Drew—" I close my eyes to the blue that has now ascended all the way up to my neck, opening me. Making room for the words. "You have no idea—"

But I do. Energy ignites the sixth chakra, right between my eyes. And I see. I am the universe's gift to Drew, and he is its gift to me. I can almost feel the cosmos, with its deep indigo eyes, seeing through me. Witnessing this divine intention as it is fulfilled.

The blade of Drew's tongue moves over and over me with such tender violence. His fingers surge into my slickness, giving and claiming my arousal. His other hand clenches mine like he'll never let go.

Just as he is meant to.

And with this earth-shattering thought, I shatter too, with the rush of an orgasm I feel clear through my crown. Loving Drew with all I am and the knowledge that we are infinite.

CHAPTER TWENTY

DREW

For the first time in nearly a decade, I have no doubts.

I've just made Evie come on the hood of Anthony's car. My brother would definitely approve.

But for the first time in nearly a decade, I don't care. My one concern as I get to my feet is Evie.

The garage door is, as it has been all night, wide open. I scan the street and am relieved to see no one. No cars. No old lady out walking her dog. But just in case, I lift one hand from Evie's thigh, reach forward, and tug down the hem of her dress, covering her intimate beauty. The narrow thatch of dark, fragrant curls.

Her sexual scent is my new addiction.

Claiming her wasn't a choice. I chose it as much as I choose to draw breath. I shouldn't have been so weak, but I have no regrets. How can you regret the greatest moment of your life?

As I adjust her skirt, Evie seems to come to herself, her half-lidded eyes focusing on me standing above her.

"I think you should come down here," she says, beckoning me with the one hand that's not flung over her forehead. The hand I held as she came.

The vision before me is the sexiest damn sight I've ever seen. Or imagined. Evie, looking like one of her Greek goddesses, lays across the hood of the Supra, breasts still bare, wild curls fanning out around her. Cheeks and lips flushed from climax and rough kisses.

Any red-blooded man — and a good many women — would give their right eye for the invitation she's just handed me. I'm red-blooded, and I could make it in the world one-eyed. But I meant what I told her.

No way in hell I'm taking a chance with her safety. If I had a condom, I'd cave. There's just not enough will power in the world.

But when I shake my head no, I reach for that hand again. Give it a squeeze. "Not gonna happen tonight, Guppy."

She snorts a laugh at the nickname, and it's no use to fight my smile.

"Stop calling me that," she says through her laughter.

I can't help what I say next. "I'll have to stop. Because right now you look just like a mermaid." And she does. With her perfect, white breasts and her riot of curls spilling around her as though she's floating on the ocean. All she's missing is tail and scales. And I'm as hard as Poseidon's trident just looking at her.

Her smile grows, and the effect is so stunning my breath hitches.

"We could always make a trip to the drugstore," she says, her brow arching and that smile turning wicked.

Why couldn't I have met her before I got hooked on stealing? Hell, even just right before that ill-fated night. Yeah, I realize I was eighteen then, and she would have been like twelve or thirteen, so it never would have happened.

But I wish I would have known her or known she'd find me one day. It would have been enough to make me clean up my act. The promise of her — of just this moment right now — would have changed my whole life.

I shake my head again. "No drugstore. You've been drinking. How do I know you're even in your right mind?" I'm teasing. Mostly. She seems a little buzzed, but no more than that. Still, I'd slit my wrists if I slept with her and she ended up regretting it.

But Evie's brow lifts higher with mock menace, and she pushes herself up onto her elbows. If it's possible, the move only makes her look sexier.

Jesus, I need a shower.

"Drew Moroux, don't think I'm not onto you."

I tilt my head, studying her. "Oh?"

She shakes her head. "You're not pushing me away. Not now. Not ever."

"Evie..." I'm not ready to admit she'd broken me in a way I don't want to be fixed. I don't know what to do. I only know I can't hurt her anymore.

She sits up and fixes her dress, watching me the whole time. "Nope. Don't *Evie* me." Despite her words, her voice is calm, level. "We're done with that."

My brows drop. "Done with what, exactly?"

Evie runs her hands down the front of her dress, trying to smooth it, but given the last half-hour, it's pretty rumpled. And her hair is bigger, wilder than I've ever seen it. God, she's gorgeous.

I *really* need a shower.

"You," she says, "acting like there's nothing between us." She pins me with her stare, and she looks confident. Certain. Or like someone who's trying to fake it.

I swallow but keep my expression blank. What I just showed her can't even come close to all I feel, but she doesn't need to know that.

"Maybe it's time I walked you home," I manage.

Her look of confidence wavers a little, and I see what it's costing her.

"I don't want to go home. I want to stay with you."

She wants to stay with me.

I've been fighting so hard to deny what's here that I haven't let myself feel this. How it feels to have Evie's affection.

It's like flying without wings. Exhilarating. And fucking terrifying.

When I say nothing — because this freefall makes it impossible to speak — her frown deepens.

"Why do you do this? You run hot and cold and—"

"Stay," I blurt.

But her eyes flash with ire. "You give me these mixed signals, and—" She stops. Blinks. Tilts her head to the right. "Wait. Did you just say I could stay?"

I grab her hand and tug her off the hood of the Supra. Dragging her with me, I yank down the garage door, turn off the lights, and lead her upstairs.

I flip on the overhead in my apartment, and my eyes fall to the futon. She'll be sleeping there with me in short order. I tear my gaze away. I can't handle that just yet. I still haven't recovered from what just happened downstairs.

She's said nothing the whole way up, so maybe she hasn't quite recovered either. The thought warms my chest, and I have to push that aside too.

I release her hand and turn toward the fridge. "Want something to drink? Water? Grape Kool-Aid?"

Evie's watchful expression collapses with a startled laugh. Our eyes meet, and I know we're both thinking of our picnic a couple of weeks ago.

"I could use some water."

I take two glasses from the draining board and fill them. I feel Evie's eyes on me, and when I face her, she's wearing an intrigued frown.

"What?"

She lifts her chin in my direction. "You have two glasses. Last time, you only had one."

My face heats without warning. I added the second glass the day after her visit. Before my run-in with her sister, I had pictured her coming back here so we could talk more. As friends.

Yeah, denial is a poor man's opiate.

I shrug, blushing fully now. "It might have occurred to me that I needed to expand my glassware collection," I mumble.

Evie grips my arm, tilts back her head, laughing at the ceiling. Her curls cascade over her bare shoulders and down her back. I forget to breathe.

"By one hundred percent," she says, beaming. "Does that mean I inspired a one hundred percent change in your opinions on glassware needs?

A gruff chuckle rattles from me. "Maybe."

She shakes her head, her perfect, white teeth glinting with her amusement. "Such a Taurus," she mutters. "But still, I'm obviously making an impression."

She's making an impression alright.

I take a sip of water, hoping it will clear my head. Cool my blood. Maybe if we talk for a while, I'll be able to go to bed exhausted instead of on the verge of self-injury.

I pull out one of the kitchen chairs and gesture for her to sit. She does, eyeing me with open curiosity. I move to the chair opposite her and decide at the last moment to drag it around so I sit beside her instead of across as I did the night we ate French cheese and marmalade.

"You aren't my backyard neighbor anymore," I say, needing to talk about anything at all.

Evie smiles, but it's not a real Evie smile. I know because I've only seen smiles that touch her eyes. This one's not even close.

"Yeah, that," she mumbles. She hides behind her lashes as she looks down at her glass. "It was time to move out." She takes a sip of water and says nothing else.

In the weeks I've known Evie, she's been anything but tight-lipped, so I get this is serious. The memory of my one encounter with her sister resurfaces, and I wonder if Evie left because Tori kept getting in her face. The way she got in mine.

I frown in concern. "Was it your sister?" I ask, gentling my voice. The thought of someone hurting her — even being hard on her — has my fists clenching.

Evie raises her eyes to mine, and though she's still wearing that paper smile, I see sadness.

"No." She shakes her head. "It was me."

I frown harder. This I can't believe. But I don't press. If she can't feel at home in her own house, I want her to feel at home here. And I want it with a sense of urgency. We don't have to talk about anything she doesn't want to talk about.

But she surprises me a moment later. "I'm the one nobody trusts, apparently."

"What?" I think a sucker punch would have stunned me less. I don't exactly have a social network, so this may not be saying much, but out of all the people in my life — my life now on the outside — Evie's probably the one I trust the most.

I mean, I love Grandma Q. God knows I do. But I'm onto her. I trust her to have my best interest at heart, at least what she *thinks* is my best interest, but I'd be a fool to think she isn't always working some kind of grandmaternal angle. And Aunt Josie and Annie may not be as bad as she is in that category, but all they lack is experience.

That leaves Chip, Cody, and the guys at the garage. I'm grateful to my cousin and his buddy for the opportunities they are giving me, and the other employees at C&C are good guys, but I can't say I've gotten to know any of them enough to *trust* them.

So that leaves Evie. And I do trust her. With my secrets. With my friendship. And a hell of a lot more.

It's me I don't trust.

"I don't get that," I say, pulling my thoughts away from my merits. Or lack thereof. "How can they not trust you? You're kind and considerate. And honest to a fault—"

Light laughter breaks through my little speech. Finally, her smile reaches her eyes. I keep hold of my own smile and pick up where I left off.

"You go out of your way to help other people, and you're completely selfless," I add with a shrug. "How could they not trust you?"

Wide-eyed wonder has replaced her smile. "You think I'm selfless?" Her voice is hushed with surprise.

I exhale a laugh. "Are you kidding me? Of course you are. You're always offering to help me or Grandma." I jerk my thumb over my shoulder in the direction of her house. "You went out with that Dirk dork—"

"Drake," she corrects, fighting back a smile.

"Drake dork, whatever, even though you don't like him—"

Her giggles peal through the apartment, making it a happier place than it has surely ever been.

"Of course you're selfless," I say again. But when I do, her giggles dissolve, and she just looks at me. I look back. And what I see is a mix in equal measure of doubt and hope. "What is it?" I ask her.

Evie's eyes cast down again before she lifts them to mine. "But do you think I'm foolish? Incapable of taking care of myself?" Now, doubt has won over, ushering in misery in the corners of her eyes. Maybe even some fear.

The look is one I've never seen on her. And I hate it. Without even thinking about it, I grab the leg of her chair and drag her into my space. Her eyes widen a little in surprise.

"Where's this coming from?"

She blinks at me, her guarded gaze shifting between my eyes. "That's what this is all about. My family thinks I'm too naïve. Too *irresponsible*," she says, stressing the word with bitterness, "to make good life decisions."

My shoulders brace, defenses at the ready. "Who said that? Tori?" My dislike for Evie's sister grows by leaps and bounds as I watch dismay pull at her features.

But she gives a rapid shake of her head. "Not just Tori." Her words come out in a rasp, and she swallows against emotion. "She and my parents apparently have felt this way for a while. They decided I wasn't ready to live alone."

I tuck my chin. "Like they tried to stop you from moving out?"

Evie shakes her head, but I watch in horror as her eyes fill with tears. The sight sparks a tiny but white hot flicker of rage low in my chest. No one. No one should make Evie cry.

"No…" Her bottom lip, the one that is now my favorite bottom lip in all the world, trembles. "They cut a deal with my sister to pay for her graduate school if she stayed at home with me until I 'grew up a little.'" She makes air quotes with her fingers as she says this, and though she looks angry, the first tear splashes down her cheek. She doesn't have to say it. This betrayal has devastated her.

Without even thinking, I take her hand and rest it on my knee, covering it with my own. At this gesture, she gives me a watery smile, but her lips press hard so I know she's fighting to keep her composure.

I hate this too.

"That's bullshit," I say, my voice low and steely.

She sniffles a kind of laugh and wipes her eyes with her free hand. "I know—" she halts, looks up at the ceiling, and inhales a deep breath through her nose, "—I know I can be…" Evie shakes her head again, seeming to struggle for words. I squeeze her fingers.

A moment later, she tries again. "I know I am free-spirited, and I don't want the same kinds of things they want. Like money and material things." She blushes and looks down as though she's admitted something terrible. "I know I let my heart guide my decisions...sometimes even when other people would choose something more rational or less messy, but—"

She looks up at me, and I swear she's searching my face, checking my reaction. My expression is stoic on purpose because, in spite of myself, her admission makes me almost lightheaded. Money and material things don't matter to her?

I mean, yeah, if I'd given it any thought, I wouldn't have assumed they did, but hearing her come out and say it makes me want to grin like a fool. Because I'll never have any money. Nothing more than what I can earn as a mechanic, anyway. I can't buy her a house in Bendel Gardens or take her to Colorado for Mardi Gras like some rich guy in town would, and I probably never could. I shouldn't be thinking of a future with Evie, but in this moment, I can't help it. Even though my poor prospects are just one of the reasons I shouldn't be with her, they are now one less.

I can provide a simple life if that's what she wants.

But I shouldn't be thinking like this. No matter how good it feels.

Evie blinks at me, and I realize she's waiting. Waiting for me to say something.

"What?" I ask, lost.

She blinks again. Bites her lip.

I press her hand harder against my knee, wanting to erase whatever doubt is pooling in her eyes.

261

"Evie, what is it?"

She lets out a sigh. "I'm afraid you agree with them."

"What?"

A frown of frustration crowds her worried expression. "I'm afraid you think I'm too innocent to know what's good for me."

Only when it comes to me, I want to blurt, but I don't. I can tell by the look on her face this would hurt her, and God, I don't want to hurt her.

Not anymore than I already have.

"You *are* innocent, thank God." The words, spoken low, leave me without thought or permission. But as soon as I hear them in the air between us, I know they capture just what I feel. "Your innocence — your goodness — isn't a flaw. I wouldn't change it for the world."

Evie's eyes lock with mine. The doubt in them is gone. I've never seen anyone look so sure. In the next instant, I pull her onto my lap and kiss her with everything I'm worth. With a whole lot more than I'm worth.

But this kiss isn't like the half-starved attack I made against her in the garage. This is a joining. A pairing. This kiss carries promises I shouldn't be making, but I make them anyway. Her mouth is sweet, silken, and welcoming. I've never felt so welcome.

It shakes me.

I don't want to leave her mouth, her touch. God, I never want her to leave my sight.

Whatever will I had to stay away from her has dried up and blown away. I'm wrong for her, rich or poor, but I can't find the strength to stop. I kiss her and

262

kiss her, learning her taste, the petal softness of her lips, the flick and dance of her tongue.

And the kissing does nothing for my other problem. I'm hard as a tire iron. And Evie on my lap doesn't help matters. She's light, but not weightless, and the weight of her — the soft and firm of her — is driving me crazy. On my thighs, pressed to my front, she feels amazing.

When I can't deal anymore, I break the kiss. "I need a shower." I sound breathless because I am, and judging by how Evie eyes me, I probably look half-mad.

But she just flattens her hand to my cheek and rubs her palm against the grain of my stubble, grinning a sexy-as-hell grin. "I don't think you need a shower. You smell great."

Even though the corner of my mouth lifts at this, I shake my head. "Nah, I really need a shower." Her expression doesn't change, so I tack on, "Been a long day."

Evie's smile firms in a way that I know she's trying not to laugh at me. I don't care. I don't *want* to leave her to take matters into my own hands. I have to.

Luckily, she slides off my lap without protesting. "Can I borrow a T-shirt?"

I suppress my sigh of relief. "Hell, yes." I rise and find one for her in the armoire drawer. It's a plain white tee that I'm sure will look incredible on her. Feel incredible. I already know one shower may not be enough.

"I'll be right back," I promise, moving toward the bathroom. "Make yourself comfortable." Evie nods, curls bouncing. "I will," she says. I picture her stretched out on the futon in nothing but the t-shirt, and my balls tighten.

Shower. *Now.*

In the bathroom, I close the door behind me and turn on the stream. I catch my reflection in the mirror above the sink before the steam clouds it over. I don't just feel like a wild animal. I look like one.

I strip off my clothes and step under the scalding spray. For a long moment, I just stand there, letting the water wash away the sweat and grime from my hours in the garage. I cup my hands and fill them. But as soon as I wet my face, I smell her, taste her again. It's as though the water has atomized the scent she's left on me, and I am again between her legs.

I moan.

Taking the bar of soap, I brush it over my chest, belly, and thighs. And when I close my eyes, I see Evie. The bare-breasted goddess. The laughing mermaid. The gravity defying gymnast. Teacher… Sage… Friend. Every one of her faces. I am devoted to each.

I am not just devoted to her, though I know I would do anything for her.

I love her.

I'm in love with Evie.

A lightning strike of emotion — pain, ecstasy — zags down my chest. I love her, and I see no way back. No way to reclaim the self-command to stay away from her I had just days ago.

I love her, and it's as though I could burst with it. I want her with such a power that I'm tempted to throw caution to the wind, knock down the bathroom door, and — wet and half-washed — tackle her onto the bed.

This can't happen. Won't happen, but with the thought, I wrap a hand around myself and give one, slow stroke.

Another moan echoes off the walls of the shower stall.

Could she have heard it over the rush of water? I glide my hand up, and the question dies as blood leaves my frontal lobe and runs down, pooling in my primitive brain, where pleasure and need are all that exist.

My erection is wet from the shower, but it's not like Evie's wetness. The heated nectar that signaled her desire for me.

For *me.*

My God, the memories of her saying she wanted me, of her beckoning me on top of her spur my pulse, and my blood rises, roaring in my ears.

So when the door knob clicks, it sounds like it's coming from a long way off. Not right here in the bathroom. It's only when I hear the *snick* of the shower door that I open my eyes.

Shrouded in mist, naked, Evie stands there, looking like a Druid priestess in the middle of a sacred rite. I hold my jutting cock, mid-stroke. Hips tilted, glutes flexed. Her eyes take me in, and I actually watch her pupils dilate.

I drop my hand, flushing with shock and shame. But she leans in, clutching the frame of the shower door, chest heaving.

"Don't stop." Her voice sounds like it's coming from somewhere deep inside her. "I want to watch."

I swallow hard, shame leaving me in rush of lust. I reach for her as she reaches for me, and I pull her under the stream. She lifts her mouth up to mine, and I wrap my arms around her. My cock presses against her belly, as though seeking her, and my mind can only conjure visions of lifting her to the wall and wrapping her legs around my hips.

A sound of suffering leaves my throat. Evie answers it with the force of her kiss.

And abruptly breaks away. "Just do it," she pants against my lips. "Take me."

But I shake my head. "No, I can't." My lungs struggle to fill as steam clouds the air and desire threatens to choke me. "I won't."

"Then let me." She tries to drop to her knees, but I catch her by the elbows.

"I won't risk it." I drag her up, and she raises her gaze to mine. Droplets of water sparkle on her lashes, making her eyes look like twin jewels set in diamonds. She looks me up and down, her gaze full of longing, her cheeks flushed with heat, her lips ripe from kissing.

Eyes wide, but focused, she presses the tip of her index finger to the flesh just below my navel before dragging it lightly down to the edge of my pubic hair. I shudder with the sensation.

"I-is this how you do it?" she asks, a tremor in her voice.

With a will all its own, my cock leaps at the nearness of her touch. I fight to keep still. "Do what?" I ask through clenched teeth.

Fascination and wonder slow dance in her eyes. "Touch yourself." Her voice is soft with something powerful. Curiosity? Arousal? "Like this? In the shower?"

She draws a tiny, sideways figure eight — an infinity sign — through my coarse curls. A rough noise leaves me, but I can't answer her. The head of my cock is nearly purple with strain.

With her fingertip still touching me, she fans her fingers and drags them lightly against me as she turns up her palm.

"Give me your hand," she says, her own open and outstretched. Heart hammering, pulse banging in my throat, I put my right hand into her left, palm up almost reverently. And Evie closes our two hands around me.

I hiss in a breath.

"Show me," she whispers.

I tense, my mind reeling. But then her hand squeezes mine gently and guides it upward.

"Oh, God Evie," I mutter, eyes closing.

I feel her bring our hands up to the tip, gripping just a little tighter, making my knees weaken, before moving back down to the base.

"Jesus, that's the sexiest thing I've ever seen." Her startled rush of words brings my eyes open, and I watch her watch this.

Her hand. Around mine. Around me.

I'll admit it's pretty fucking sexy.

But her lovely fingers aren't touching me where I want them, so — gently, as though asking permission — I open my grip, take her hand, and wrap it around me.

It's her moan now that sings against the shower walls.

I close my hand around hers and pump once.

267

"God almighty—" The back of my head slams against the shower wall, and with my left arm, I encircle Evie's waist and crush her against me. In the crook of my arm, she leans into me, breasts pressed to my ribs. When her thighs close around my left leg, I quicken the pace.

Her hand is soft and alive, her grasp eager and enthralled. My body tightens as she watches us, but then she brings her gaze to mine, and I see something boundless in the green of her eyes. Whatever it is, I want to fall into it and never come out.

I dip my mouth to hers, lifting her higher against me. She takes my tongue, lips sealing with mine, and her grip tightens around me.

"Evie—" I pant into her mouth.

"Drew, you're all I want."

I hear these words, the sweet longing in her voice. And I'm gone. My body seizes, over and over, in fits of pleasure, and I loose my seed into the falling water.

And as I do, I call her name so many times I lose count.

CHAPTER TWENTY-ONE

EVIE

I am in love with Drew Moroux.

This is my waking thought, the one filling my consciousness before I even open my eyes to the pre-dawn light.

And I smile because I know exactly where I am. From head to belly and belly to toes, I'm pressed to Drew. In fact, I'm snuggled against him like a jetpack, one arm over his middle, his legs tangled with mine. My cheek against the warm plane of his back.

And his left hand is holding my right to his chest. I can even feel his slow, even heartbeat.

Yeah, loving him feels better than anything else, but sleeping next to him is a close second.

This wasn't how we fell asleep, of course. After the shower, Drew toweled me off, squeezing as much water as he could out of my hair. He watched me braid it after we'd dressed — me in his T-shirt, and him in a pair of sleep shorts. And then he tried giving me the one pillow, even though I insisted we could share. In the end, he took the pillow, stretched out on his back, and pulled me half across him, encircling me with his arms.

It was like snuggling a floating island. I fell asleep riding the waves of his breath.

Right now, his breathing is still deep and steady, so I know I'm the only one awake. I need to get back to Janine's to let Gemini out and feed him, but I don't want to move.

Baby Aaron spent last night with James's parents so we would all officially have a night off, and I don't want Gemini to make a fuss about needing to go out or grumble to be fed and wake my friends if they can sleep until noon today.

So I bury my nose into the thick, dark waves at the back of Drew's head and inhale his warm cotton and fresh-cut lumber smell one last time.

I love this too.

Heavy with reluctance, and a bit of a tequila headache, I push myself up and scan Drew's apartment. My options for the Walk of Shame — if I don't want to wake Drew (and I don't) — are last night's dress and today's T-shirt.

Neither are great choices, but the dress clearly wins.

Drew's bed takes up one corner, and I'm on the inside. His bookcase stands at the foot, which means I'm going to need to climb over Drew to get out.

I push up into a side plank and lever one leg over him, careful not to brush against him, and plant my right foot on the outside corner of the mattress. I then lift my hips, anchoring my right hand near the futon's top corner.

I'm basically suspended above him in a wide-stance downward facing dog when Drew blinks one eye open and fixes it on me.

"Are we playing Twister?" His face is flushed and his voice gravely with sleep.

I laugh and have to brace myself to keep from collapsing on top of him. For the record, I do not recommend laughing in downward dog.

Drew rolls onto his back to study me, his sleep-stamped face morphing into a curious non-smile.

That is the only name for this expression — the one Drew makes when I think he wants to smile, in fact, is smiling on the inside but just doesn't let it show. I know this now, and I'm getting really good at pegging it.

"I'm s-s-orry," I say, cracking up, and then I brace, kick my legs up and over, and land on the floor with what I think is a decently impressive dismount. Judging by the widening of Drew's eyes, he agrees. "I didn't mean to wake you."

Drew frowns. "Did you just do a sort of handstand above me?" Disbelief is clear in his sleep-drugged voice.

I shrug. "Well, I wouldn't call it a handstand, but I can do one."

He tucks his chin and blinks twice. "You can do a handstand?"

Grinning, I nod.

"Well, damn," he mutters before stretching. His elbows go up over his head, and I get a clear view of the patches of dark hair in his armpits and his flexing triceps.

Holy moly.

His broad chest fills with a yawn, and I'm treated to the moving lines of his ribs, the bunch and pull of transverse abdominals and obliques.

Drew's pecs are smooth, but a compact inverted pyramid of dark curls covers his sternum. The patch points like an arrowhead down to the line of hair that picks back up below his navel. But the bedsheets now hide the rest of this story. Too bad.

He tucks his hands behind his head and settles once again on his pillow, but now he's wearing a real grin. No non-smile here. And I blush, because I'm pretty sure he can tell I've been checking him out.

"Like what you see?" he teases.

I go from persimmon to beet red. I *love* what I see. I'm all about honesty, but I'm not ready to tell him — or anyone else — everything I feel. And he sure as hell isn't ready to hear it. But I can still answer truthfully, even as ten trillion butterflies take wing in my insides.

"Better than pretty much anything else," I admit.

A startled laugh escapes him, and then, before my eyes, Drew blushes pink. But his smile is huge.

He reaches up with his massive, calloused, altogether awesome hand and grabs me by the wrist.

"Come back here," he says, his voice still gruff. I topple onto him, and he presses a kiss to my lips before clutching my braid and hugging me tight to him.

"Mmm," his masculine sigh caresses my neck. "You smell free."

Now it's my turn to laugh, and I do it planting kisses on his bare shoulder. "Free?"

Drew nods into my hair. "Mmm hmm. Like freedom."

Something sharp and sure snags my heart. Drew has been in prison, and I smell like freedom?

Another wave of love flushes my veins.

I draw back and look at him, but I don't recognize the expression I find.

He looks like he's processing two thoughts at once, weighing scales. I know instinctively, whatever he's thinking, I want the balance to tip on my side. I also know that since I had to talk my way into staying last night — after fighting my way into his arms — leaving now might mean losing ground, but I can't help it.

"I have to go," I say, hearing disappointment I hadn't planned on sharing. "I need to let Gem out and feed him."

Realization crosses Drew's face. "Oh, right…"

And my heart does a little soft shoe in my chest because there's disappointment in his voice too. I'm basically in a mini-cobra pose on top of him. We touch nearly everywhere. Bellies, legs, e-zones. I do not want to give this up.

I draw my lips between my teeth and brace myself. "The look you're giving me right now…"

Drew blinks, but his expression doesn't change. "Yeah? What about it?"

I smile because, right now, he's not hiding from me. "Promise me you'll look at me like that the next time I see you."

Amusement sparks in his gray eyes, but he keeps his smile in check. "And when do you think that will be?"

This question throws me. So far, I've been the only one to instigate plans, doomed though they might have been. Is this Drew's way of taking that step? With me? Nerves swirl in my stomach like a dust devil.

"I-I don't know," I stammer. "Whenever you want."

His laughter makes me bounce. And for the record, of all the ways to watch Drew laugh, lying on top of him is now my hands-down favorite.

"How about I come with you?" he asks.

"Come with me?" Did I hear him right?

Drew nods. "That's what I said."

I push myself up. "Y-yeah. That'd be great." It's frickin' amazing. I hope Janine and James really are

273

taking advantage of the chance to sleep in. Bringing Drew over before seven in the morning might be a little awkward if they're at the breakfast table having coffee.

But who cares? Drew is coming with me.

"Maybe we can get some breakfast after," I suggest, climbing out of bed. "Have you ever been to Tribe?"

Drew shakes his head and sits up, swinging his legs off the mattress. It might sound stupid and shallow, but I love that I get to see his legs. They're really great legs. He should wear shorts every day. I send up a tiny prayer of thanks to the cosmic pantheon, specifically the goddesses of love and fertility, for Drew's superior legs.

Thank you, Freya... Thank you, Venus... Thank you, Pavarti...

"Tribe?" His brows pull together. "Never heard of it."

"Well, it's really a collective of three restaurants." As I explain, he stands and plucks his jeans from the foot of the futon. I have to look down to keep from staring as he pulls them on. "Tribe Bakery, Emerge Raw Kitchen, and Reve Coffee Roasters."

Skepticism shades his eyes. *"Raw* kitchen?"

"Well, it's not all raw. They have this vegan, gluten-free strawberry cake doughnut that's like Nirvana on a plate."

One dark brow arches with a mock-serious stare. "Vegan *and* gluten-free, huh?" I can just make out the barely contained smile waiting in the wings. "Sounds frightening, Guppy."

I give him a faux scowl. "You're going to eat your words, Drew Moroux."

274

His face goes completely deadpan. "As long as I don't have to eat a vegan, gluten-free doughnut—"

I deliver a deft swat to the seat of his jeans, and Drew barks a laugh. Who knew Sunday mornings could be so much fun?

I move to retrieve my dress that's draped over the back of a kitchen chair when I feel his calloused hand close around my elbow, and I'm reeled around to face him. Standing front to front, Drew and I gaze at each other. We're both trying not to smile, both, I notice, a little breathless.

A trip to a drugstore definitely needs to be added to our agenda.

"So where is this place?"

We're talking about getting breakfast, but the electricity arcing between us is having a completely different conversation. The contrast is enough to fizz my thoughts and speed my pulse.

The sense of his question is lost in his nearness. His chest is still bare, and my hands rest against it. Drew's skin is hot and alive. Yet his flesh, though muscled and hard, still yields to my touch, reminding me how vulnerable he is. How much he's suffered. How much I want to care for him.

I'm attracted to him. No doubt about that. I've never wanted anyone like this.

But I'm also *drawn* to him. I want to be near him. Talk to him. Listen to all of his stories. Tell him all of mine. I want to celebrate his Taurus birthday. Bake him a cake. Whatever flavor he wants. I want to watch movies with him. Play silly games. Everything he missed out on while he was away.

And I want to travel with him. I don't have to ask to know Drew has never left the country. Wouldn't it be awesome to see Iceland together? Or New Zealand? Or Bali? I picture teaching him yoga on an Indonesian beach and can't help my grin.

His eyes narrow on me. "What's going on in your head, Guppy?" Despite the silly nickname, his voice is low and sensual.

"Do you like to travel?" I hear myself ask.

Drew's gaze searches mine. My question has surprised him. That's clear enough, but he also looks at me as though he's searching for something.

The hand on my elbow glides up to my shoulder and then cups my cheek. He runs his thumb along my jaw, but his expression has gone pensive. "I don't really know." His brow arches and his tone turns wry. "Haven't had many opportunities lately."

I ignore his self-deprecation. "What about when you were a kid? Did you take vacations?"

Drew's face tightens, but I'm relieved to see it doesn't shut down. "Not really. Money was tight after my dad left. We went to the beach a few times with Grandma and Grandpa." Then he frowns, but I can tell it's not a frown of distress, but one of memory. "And one year, my Uncle Nelson rented a house boat for the whole crew in Arkansas. That was a lot of fun."

His gaze shifts to the left and the lines around his mouth soften. I want to see what he's seeing, but I don't dare ask. If this is a happy memory of his family — of his brother Anthony or of his mother who now won't forgive him — I don't want to pull him from it. Instead, I keep my hands pressed to his chest and feel the easy rhythm of his heart under my right palm. His thick,

276

work-roughened fingertips against the delicate skin of my face.

Touching him is a great way to anchor into the present.

And then his focus is on me again. "You like to travel?"

"I love to travel."

He nods, a smile tugging up the corner of his mouth. "Yeah, I figured."

"Most water signs do," I say, teasing him on purpose. "We move easily. Go with the flow."

Drew rolls his dark eyes, and his low chuckle vibrates through his chest. Oh, yeah. I love touching him while he laughs.

He shakes his head at me. "Speaking of going, you never answered my question."

I blink. "What question?"

Pent up laughter crinkles the corners of his eyes. "About where this Tribe place is. And is it fancy or chill?" His scrutiny returns. "I may be a grease monkey, but I don't want to dress like one if we're going somewhere frilly."

"Frilly?" I almost splutter with laughter. First of all, I can't even *picture* Drew Moroux somewhere frilly. I shake my head. "No. No. It's on the corner of Pinhook and University."

His look is all confusion. "By the Chevron station?"

My mouth twists to the side. "Technically, it's in the same building as the Chevron station, but—"

His lids lower. "We're eating breakfast in a gas station."

It's not a question, but I feel compelled to respond. "Yes."

"Where they serve raw food."

I blink and press my lips together. "Yes."

"And menu items may or may not be vegan and/or gluten-free."

Try as I might, I can't fight the smile. "Yes."

Drew's expression is mock disapproval, and it's everything I can do not to laugh. He executes a slow nod, and I can tell he's trying pretty hard not to laugh, too. "Sure. Great. I just have one thing to say."

"What's that?"

He presses a kiss to my lips. It's not quick. It's not slow, but it is gentle and chaste. He draws back and looks down at me. "The next time we go out, I get to pick the restaurant."

Gemini leaps in gravity-defying circles when Drew and I tiptoe into the Mayfield's house.

"Okay, okay," I hiss whisper, stroking my hands down his long back as he whines his relief and excitement. "I know. I know. I was gone all night. How inconsiderate of me."

I hear Drew sniff a laugh behind me as he shuts the door.

"Come on, buddy." I turn toward the kitchen, and, elated, Gem bounds ahead, aiming for his food bowl. I'm relieved to find the kitchen empty, so I hold a finger to my lips, and Drew nods in response.

After I fill Gemini's bowl and he dives in, I grab Drew's hand, and we creep down the hall into the Mayfield's guest room. I'll admit, it's kind of a disaster.

The closet in this room is small. Smaller than my own at home, so what clothes couldn't fit there are stored in the plastic bins that line the wall.

Well, that are *supposed* to line the wall, but signs of last night's excavation in search of my dress and shoes are everywhere.

"Excuse the mess," I whisper, bending down to pick up the scattered pairs of shoes. I toss them into one of the open Rubbermaid bins, and without a word, Drew grabs two more pairs and sets them gently inside.

I glance up at him. "Thank you. I'm not a neat freak or anything," I tell him, blushing. "But I'm usually more organized than this."

Drew's brows draw together. "Why are you apologizing?" he asks softly.

I blink hard. "Because I don't want you to think I'm a slob."

"Do you think it would bother me if you were a slob?"

He stares at me. I stare back. I've been in his room twice now. His place is spartan. He doesn't have much, but what he owns is organized and clean. And I saw no sign of disarray in the garage where I found him last night. No tools haphazardly abandoned around the car. No mess from spilled oil or trashed parts.

Drew is neat and orderly. But even as I know that, I know too that he wouldn't give a damn if I were a slob.

"No," I say simply.

He gives me a slow nod, eyes glinting. "Then don't apologize to me, Guppy." His voice is low, but I know it's not just because he's trying to be quiet. "Any

279

man would be lucky as hell just to be in the same space where you lay your head."

His words pull strings inside me I didn't know were there. I feel like a pair of lace-up boots. Tall. Held-together. Kickass.

I drop the plastic lid I'm holding, stand on tiptoes, and pull him down to my mouth. His hands land at the small of my back, and he holds me close, accepting my kiss, letting me thank him for sharing thoughts that turn me inside out.

I step back but keep a hand on his cheek, brushing my fingernails lightly over his stubble. "Just give me a minute to get changed."

He nods again and then watches me as I pull a top from one bin and a pair of jeans from the closet. I move toward the bathroom and gesture to the bed, the only place to sit in the small room. "Have a seat. Make yourself comfortable."

I slip into the bathroom and close the door behind me, leaving him standing there, his breadth and height seeming to take up the whole space. I catch my smile in the mirror over the sink and stare into my own eyes.

So this is what I look like when I'm in love.

Last night's shower removed my makeup, but my cheeks still wear a flush. My lips bloom with the soft bruising of Drew's kisses. It suits me, and my smile grows.

I used Drew's mouthwash before bed and after I got up this morning, but I reach for my toothbrush like it's a long lost friend. As I brush, I think about the day that lies ahead. Tribe isn't that far. The weather, for once, is cool and dry. We could ride bikes. I've moved mine to

Janine's garage, and I know James has one I doubt he'd mind us borrowing. I don't know how much time Drew is willing to give me today, but riding bikes to breakfast would mean that much more.

Liking this plan, I unravel the rope of my braid and rake my fingers through my now zig-zagging curls. If we're going to ride bikes, I'll need tame my hair with something, but the dry air is being kind, leaving me with no frizz in sight.

I change into a three-quarter sleeve Henley. I check my reflection and decide the spruce green brings out my eyes. I pull on the jeans, and I'm still buttoning the fly when I step out of the bathroom.

"I was thinking we could ride bikes to—"

"You don't feel at home here."

We both speak at the same time, but when our eyes lock, my mouth hangs open.

"What did you say?"

I heard him. I heard him even though we both spoke quietly, mindful of the sleeping Mayfields. But his words still strike me.

He holds my gaze with his own steady one. "You don't feel at home here," he says again, but his time I hear unmistakable gentleness. It stirs something long forgotten inside me.

"What makes you say that?"

Drew's gaze flicks around the room and back to my eyes. "Your stuff's here," he says, nodding to my bins, the meditation bench, and my rolled up yoga mat in the corner. "But you haven't made this room your own."

I blink at him, wondering how he can see this so clearly. How would he know the floral print Laura

Ashley bedspread isn't mine? He's never seen my room. "What do you mean?"

He screws up his brow and turns in a slow circle until he faces me again. "I don't see *you* here. It's like you're afraid to spread out or leave your mark."

"You're right," I admit, shrugging. "But it's getting better. I mean, I don't know how long I'll be here, but I feel more comfortable than I did at first."

I'm talking, but he's not looking at me. He's frowning at the room like it offends him.

"I'm really grateful for Janine and James letting me stay," I add, though I'm not sure why.

Drew makes a noise somewhere between a grunt and a huff. *Such a Taurus.*

"Are you ready to go?"

He turns to face me, and I see him still as though he's just noticed something. "You look..." His eyes run me up and down. I watch him swallow. "You're beautiful."

Smiling, I cross the room, rise up on my toes, and kiss his scratchy cheek. "Thank you. So are you."

He makes a grunting noise, but I can tell he's amused. I turn to the dresser and pick up a hair tie. "So, are you okay if we ride bikes? You could borrow James's. It'll be fun."

Drew only hesitates for a second. "If you want to."

I stretch the tie with my fingers and shake my hair back, preparing to secure it.

"Wait." Drew stills my hand with his. "Leave it down."

I turn to face him, eyeing him like he's crazy.

"It'll be huge by the time we get there," I warn.

"Good," he says, grinning. And how can I resist that?

CHAPTER TWENTY-TWO

DREW

Who needs a car when they could ride a bike? Behind Evie.

I felt weird about borrowing her friend's bike until we actually started pedaling down the street, Evie leading the way. Now I'll just have to find a way to thank the guy.

Her ass is heart-shaped. I swear to God. A perfect, upside-down heart.

And her hair sails behind her in the breeze. The day is cool. Fall-like. I haven't been a free man enjoying the fall breeze in what feels like a lifetime.

But I remember it. I remember being a kid and feeling the rush that always came with that first cool front. How anything felt possible. How a better life was just around the corner.

God help me, but that's how I feel right now. How could I not? I'm riding bikes with a beautiful woman, and she wants to be with me.

We speed down St. Patrick Street until we get to Juliette. Evie makes the hand signal for a left turn, and I follow.

"We'll go down St. Mary and cut through UL, okay?" she calls over her shoulder.

I nod, but as soon as she turns onto the busier St. Mary, I speed up and pull alongside her, putting myself between her and the vehicle lane.

"What are you doing?" she asks, wrinkling her nose at me.

"Trying to keep up with you," I tell her. She doesn't need know it's the urge to protect her that's spurred me on.

"You weren't falling behind," she says skeptically.

I lean into the handlebars and shrug. "It's easier to talk like this."

We hear the telltale shush of an approaching car, and Evie's gaze moves from it to me.

"You're sticking out into traffic," she scolds, eyeing me with concern. "A car's coming. Move behind me."

"He'll go around," I tell her. And I'm right. The car gives us a wide berth, slowing slightly as it passes. Just as I wanted it to. There isn't much I can offer her, but I do have this. My body to place between her and any harm that might come her way.

"Taurus," she mutters under her breath, and I smirk. She can think I'm stubborn all she wants. She's safer this way.

And it gives me a purpose.

I remember our conversation last night. How important it seemed to Evie for me to have faith in her ability to take care of herself. That isn't what this is about. Of course she can take care of herself. But I know just how precious she is. How rare.

And I know how fragile life is. The best thing I could ever do with mine would be to protect hers.

We pass Olde Tyme Grocery and approach the light at Johnston Street. It's red, and a couple of cars are in front of us, so we slow. Beside me Evie makes slow zig zags left and right. I stop and set my feet on the pavement. She coasts in front of me and then circles back to pass behind me again.

"What are you doing?" I ask, watching her.

285

She keeps her gaze on her front wheel, her feet motionless on the pedals. "Trying to see if I can go without touching the ground until the light changes." The gears click ever slower as she loses momentum. She straightens her legs, toes pointing as she balances. The light is still red.

Coming up alongside me again, barely moving, Evie's face is set with a calm but determined focus. I can only imagine the core strength it takes to keep the bike balanced. With her legs raised almost even with the handlebars, it looks like she's performing a circus trick.

"You're amazing."

My words make her smile, but they don't break her concentration. The light turns green, the cars in front of us move, and only then does this incredible woman break her form and start to pedal again, never once touching the ground. The bike never even wobbled.

She takes off, and I follow.

"I want to see everything you can do," I blurt.

Ahead of me, Evie laughs. "O-okay!" she calls back.

I speed up and ride next to her as we cross the busy street and cut through campus. Evie glances left and right before turning to me, her nose wrinkled. "Did you go to college... you know... before?"

By some miracle, her question doesn't summon the gut-punch that usually hits me when I think about that time, and I realize with wonder that we passed the entrance to my old neighborhood a few blocks back, and I didn't even think about it.

"I had my head so far up my ass, college was the furthest thing from my mind." I shake my head in disgust at the stupid kid I was. "It wasn't like I'd

286

decided never to go. I just wasn't interested then in putting in the work. I thought there'd be time for that later."

I take in the red brick buildings and the oak trees dripping with moss.

"It's not too late, you know," Evie says softly.

I look back at her. She searches my face, her eyes watchful, but her expression is gentle, even. A look of pity or one of expectation might have rankled me, but I don't see traces of either, and I'm relieved.

"It's not a question of it being too late," I tell her as we pass the UL Alumni House.

Evie glances at the road ahead, prompting me to do the same, and then we look back at each other.

"Is that something you want?"

I want to give you a home.

The force of this sudden desire nearly pulls me off the bike. But it's real. And it's been waiting to pounce since I saw the guest room where she's staying. Evie needs a home of her own. Somewhere she isn't just a guest. Somewhere she isn't questioned or doubted. And I want to give it to her. To share it with her.

I picture my apartment but dismiss the idea immediately. Grandma Q would welcome Evie, I know, but Evie still wouldn't think of it as hers since it isn't truly mine. And it's too small. Too small for Evie.

I know without having to think about it that Evie needs space. Rooms of space. Not just one loft. She needs room to practice yoga. Privacy to meditate. A yard for Gemini. Evie needs a house.

And I can give one to her as a mechanic, but not until I'm full time.

As we turn onto Coolidge Street, I pledge to myself I'll ask Chip and Cody tomorrow to make me full-time. If they say no, I'll start looking for a second job.

"Should I not have asked that question?"

Evie's timid voice pulls me from my thoughts. "Huh?" I see the line of worry that's now grooved between her brows, and I remember myself. "Oh. No. No. I don't mind you asking. And, no. That's not something I want. I like working on cars. I don't need a bachelor's degree to do that."

Her smile flashes bright, and it makes her whole face shine. "I love that."

"What?" And I can't deny that hearing her say the word *love* sends the chambers of my heart into overdrive for a few seconds.

"That you like what you do. That you have that fulfillment." She looks so content, I'm humbled. How can my fulfillment, my contentment, mean so much to her?

I don't deserve her. But, God almighty, I love her.

We stop at University Avenue and have to wait for a break in the traffic before crossing. I'm glad for the delay because I need a minute to rein in my emotions. Because all I want to do is tell her how I feel, and that's just not allowed.

Traffic clears, and piping with happiness, Evie takes off. "C'mon," she calls behind her. I obey, knowing I'd ride this bike to hell itself if she told me to follow.

When we pull into the parking lot, I run my eyes over the exterior of the restaurant. Not a frill in sight. But the dreamcatcher symbol beside the restaurant's name has me beating back a laugh.

"Oh, Guppy," I mutter under my breath.

"Did you say something?" she asks, parking her bike just outside the entrance.

I shake my head not daring to speak. Evie sees me fighting laughter and narrows her eyes in a playful glare.

"Is it too much to ask for you to keep an open mind?"

I pull my bike next to hers and take the lock from her little white basket. "I have such an open mind, I'm going to let you order for both of us."

Her mouth falls open. She might even look a touch afraid. "W-what if you don't like what I order?"

I raise a brow at her. Can't she tell I don't give a shit about that? "I trust you."

I love you is what I want to say, but confessing I trust her feels pretty damn good.

Evie triple blinks. "You *do?*"

"Evie," I say, eyeing her with pretend disappointment.

She gives a little gasp of surprise before clamping her hands on my shoulders. As if to keep me still. As if I would pull alway. No chance of that.

And then she's kissing me. In the parking lot. In front of University Avenue. Across the street from the police station of all places.

I drop the bike lock and wrap her up, pulling her tight against me. It's not the first kiss we've had today, but it's the sweetest. Because she's giving it to me, demanding with the tug of her hands, the thrust of her tongue, and the arch of her spine that I give it back.

So I do.

The jangle of a bell over the door pulls us apart.

"Oh! Morning!" A young woman smiles brightly at us. Her arm is the around waist of guy who gives me a knowing grin.

Evie clears her throat. "Morning," she mutters, pink-faced.

The couple stride toward the only car in the lot, a 2018 Audi r8.

Helluva car.

The woman looks back at us over her shoulder. "Enjoy your breakfast," she calls. "Best fair trade coffee in town!"

As the couple reaches their car, Evie pulls me inside. And for a restaurant attached to a gas station, it's not bad. Not bad at all. There's only a few tables, but each sports a stained and glazed wooden surface decorated with hand-painted designs.

A young guy behind the counter waves a greeting. "Be with y'all in a minute," he says before disappearing into the kitchen. Over the sound system, a song I've heard at the garage is playing.

I like me better when I'm with you.

It's mostly just the one line, sung over and over, but every time I've heard it, I've thought of Evie.

But then again, most songs I hear these days make me think of her.

I take a look around and see immediately why she likes this place. Beside the dish return is a table that appears to be dedicated to a crystal shrine. And on the other side of the kitchen is a sitting area with bookshelves, some handmade jewelry and essential oils for sale, and a basket of yoga mats.

Evie sees me eyeing them. "They have yoga classes here in the evenings. I've only been a couple of times, but isn't that cool?" she says, sounding awed. "I mean, the whole place is dedicated to wellness."

"It's cool, Guppy."

She sniffs her annoyance at my flat tone, but I know it's not real. She's trying too hard not to smile. I take her hand and thread my fingers through hers.

"You ready to eat?" I ask, eyeing the pastry cases at the counter.

"Yeah," she steps up, tugging me with her, and plucks a laminated menu from a stand near the register. Her eyes run over it before she gives me a speculative stare.

"Do you like lattes?"

I almost choke on a laugh. "Babe, I've never had a latte."

Evie's eyes bug. "Really?"

I shrug. "Not many espresso machines on The River."

That crease appears between her brows. "On The River?"

"Angola," I say, dropping my voice. The guy still hasn't come out of the kitchen, but I don't want to embarrass Evie. "It's surrounded on three sides by the Mississippi. It's also called The Farm."

"I've heard you call it that," Evie says, looking chagrined. She shakes her head. "I'm sorry. I must sound so clueless... And spoiled—"

"Evie." I squeeze her hand. "You're neither. Right now, I'm kinda glad I've never had a latte. I get to have my first one with you."

A slow smile emerges, but she bites her lip. "You sure you really want me to order for you?"

I nod to the chalk menu on the wall. "You bet your ass. I have no idea what *Jalisco Fries* are."

Her sassy, self-assured smirk returns. "They're awesome is what they are." Her head bob is emphatic. "But that's on the lunch menu, which they don't start serving until eleven."

A low chuckle rumbles from me. "Okay, Guppy. See? You're in charge."

This, I can tell from the way her green eyes flare, pleases her immensely. And that look is addictive.

Hmm. I could be in real trouble.

The clerk returns wearing a friendly smile. "Sorry about the wait. What can I get you?"

Evie checks in with me one last time. "No allergies, right?"

"Nope."

"Okay." She hits the kid with her stellar smile, and I watch him swallow in response. "We'll have two strawberry cake doughnuts, two almond milk lattes, one sweet potato hash with sriracha on the side, and one Spanish omelette."

Evie rattles off the order, and it takes the poor guy a minute before he can shake off the effect of her smile and start tapping the items onto his iPad. I almost feel sorry for him. But I'm too busy letting the truth of it sink in.

This woman is here with me. *Me.*

The kid gives me the once over, and I imagine he's wondering the same thing. *What the hell is she thinking?*

And I'm a fool if I think this is going to last.

That thought lands like a fist to the solar plexus. If I'm being honest, it's not really a surprise. But it's the first time I've let it sink in since I've tasted her. Touched her. Slept with her in my arms.

Fallen for her…

When she goes, it's going to hurt like hell.

The sight of Evie reaching into her back pocket jerks me out of my funk. "Whoa," I say, stilling her hand that holds her debit card. "What are you doing?"

She blinks up at me in surprise. "Paying. What does it look like?"

I cough my offense. "You're not paying."

"But," Evie's curls shake with obvious affront, "you said I could order."

I screw up my brows. "I said order, not pay." I pass the guy a couple of twenties, do a double take at the total, and hand over another ten.

Shit, this hippie place is expensive. I'll need a second job to give Evie a house and a third to take her back here again.

"But you said I was in charge."

Laughter shakes from me. "And look how fast I regretted that."

Her mouth falls open and a vexed huff escapes. "But you paid at Champagne's."

"So you should be used to it by now."

Evie's eyes narrow to slits. Something like a kitten growl rises from her throat. It's as sexy as sin, but it does her no good. One day she's going to drop me like the dead weight I am, but until then, I'm going to give her everything I have.

She crosses her arms over her chest. "So, you're not only stubborn but sexist, too?"

The poor kid behind the counter hasn't picked up my bills yet. He's just watching us wide-eyed. I give him a pointed stare and tilt my gaze to the cash. He finally gets a clue and scrambles to claim it.

"Keep the change," I say and gently tug Evie by one of her crossed arms to a table. I pull out the chair for her, but she doesn't sit. She just glowers at me.

"I'm not sexist," I tell her in a low voice. "It's been a while since I dated. I'm just trying to make up for lost time."

Evie's jaw softens. Her arms drop to her side, and she sits. "Okay. Fine. You can pay for now." Her voice has softened too. "But eventually, there will need to be some give and take."

"Eventually," I say taking the seat across from her. "I'm sure you'll wear me down. You're good at that."

Her mouth twitches. I want to lean across the small table and kiss it, but I resist the urge. Being caught kissing once today is enough. Instead, I study the lettering on the table.

United we rise.

Evie's gaze follows mine. She reads the words, smiles, and reaches across the table for my hand. "Words to live by," she murmurs.

How can I tell her I have already risen?

The kid emerges from the kitchen with our coffee and donuts just as the opening tabs of a song I haven't heard in years comes through the speakers. "Like a Stone" by Audioslave. I remember that Chris Cornell is dead. That news had shocked the shit out of me last year when I heard about it inside.

I listen to him sing about death and destiny and wonder if he's found that room.

And if we're good we'll lay to rest

Anywhere we want to go.

The old words ring new. Because before I met Evie, I would have just welcomed the oblivion of the grave. A place where I didn't have to think about Anthony or Ma or all the shit I've done.

But now, I want to be wherever she is. Even if she cuts me loose in a few months. Or a few weeks.

Especially if she cuts me loose.

Who am I kidding? She'll cut me loose. She'll do it sweet. She'll be gentle, even heartbroken about it. But Evie's a smart woman. It won't take her long to realize she deserves better than me. And when she does, I'll make it easy on her. It'll be the most I can give her.

"Aren't you going to try it?"

Evie is eyeing me over her latte. I look down at the perfect leaf pattern floating atop my coffee and wonder how the hell they did that.

"You okay?" she asks, studying me with concern.

"Yeah." I shrug and pick up the cup. "Just haven't heard this song in a while."

Her brows lift. "Oh, yeah. It's sad," she says, wrinkling her nose. "It's supposed to be about heaven, but it really sounds like hell. I mean, why would you want to spend eternity waiting for someone who didn't love you?"

Breath catches in my throat. I clear it and stall my answer with a sip of coffee. The depth of its frothy top surprises me before the rich, milky coffee hits my tongue. This is nothing like Grandma Q's drip brew.

Yeah, I'm going to need to get a third job.

I swallow, closing my eyes and making a mindless grunt of approval. Then I open them to find Evie's gratified smile.

295

She is so lovely.

"I don't know." I meet her gaze, daring to answer her question. "Would it be heaven if the person you loved the most wasn't there?"

Her lips part in surprise, and I hold her stare for as long as I can without letting her see right through me. It isn't very long.

"Speaking of heaven," I say, picking up my fork and making a clean slice through the pink, sprinkle-topped cake doughnut on my plate. "You said something about this living up to Nirvana."

She beams. "Try it and tell me I'm wrong."

I do. And I can't. Because, by my own definition, I'm in heaven.

CHAPTER TWENTY-THREE

EVIE

The fact that Drew cleans his plate and then helps himself to the few surviving sweet potato curls in my bowl leaves me feeling rather smug.

My latte has gone cold, but I still sip it. I'm not ready to leave just yet. If we head back, Drew might send me home. I know exactly how I want to spend the rest of the day, and going back to Janine's isn't anywhere on my agenda.

And right now, I just want to be with him. I set down my cup, reach for his right hand, and pull it across the table.

"What are you doing?" He sounds startled — and slightly amused — but he doesn't pull away.

Instead of answering, I trace the tip of my index finger over the calluses at the top of his palm. I wonder at the rough handling it must have taken to form them. "Can you feel this?" I ask, letting my barely-there touch skim over the blunted pads, the Mount of Mercury through Jupiter.

It's barely audible over the music, but I catch his breath hitch. His voice drops to a whisper that tickles my ear. "Yes."

The sudden strain in his voice makes me feel powerful, like an enchantress. A lazy smile claims my lips as my fingertip continues its winding journey. The touch is so delicate, so secret, but the knowledge that it affects him lights me up.

"Is this all from working on cars?" I ask, forced casualness in my words. I love touching him. I could do it all day and never get enough.

"That," he says thickly, "and lifting."

My eyes flick up to his. "Lifting weights?"

He nods. "Everybody lifts inside."

This shouldn't surprise me. He's in terrific shape. Nobody has arms and shoulders like that without some kind of exercise, and it looks like he's been doing it for years. But it makes me want to show him crow, scorpion, or standing split.

"What about now? Are you still working out?"

Drew gives me a half shrug. "I don't have a gym, but I improvise. Body weight mostly, but old tires at the garage come in handy, too."

My finger ventures over the deep lines in his palm, the Linea Vitalis and the Linea Naturalis. I study the lines as I go, looking for breaks in their continuity, counting creases.

"You reading my palm, Guppy?" Drew asks, his voice laced with humor.

"Maybe," I say, feeling my cheeks heat. "Though I'm no palm reader."

His chuckle is low and rumbly. "Something tells me you're better than average."

I shoot him a look so he doesn't miss me rolling my eyes. But in truth, as much of a novice as I am, I do notice a few details I like. His lifeline — the one that seems to separate the thumb from the rest of the hand — is long, deep, and unbroken.

And he bears one marriage line.

But I don't share these facts or my reckless feeling of gratitude for them. Teasing him is much more fun. "Well, this line here," I say, stroking the line of fate and career that runs up the middle of his hand. "This is your obstinate line. It shows how stubborn a person i—"

"What?" The word is part exclamation, part suspicion.

"And as you can see, yours starts way down here." I tickle the base of his palm just above the inside of his wrist. "Which means you've been ornery ever since you were born—"

In a flash of movement, my finger disappears in his grip, and I squeal with laughter. Drew's eyes are narrowed on me, but he's fighting a losing battle against his own laugh. "Sorcerer," he mutters, making me laugh harder. But all humor dies in my throat when he tugs my finger up to his lips and kisses me reverently on the palm.

And suddenly, I'm ready to go.

"I have to work tonight," I blurt. "Baby duty, I mean. I take a shift with Janine's baby Aaron—"

Drew blinks, his gaze curious. "You stay up with the baby?"

I huff a self-conscious laugh. "Yes. It sounds weird, but it's working out for all of us. I take the middle shift so Janine and James can get a good stretch of sleep, so I can't spend—" I'm about to say *spend the night again*, but I stop myself. Who said anything about that? I blush deeply at my own flub and try to recover. "What I mean is... what are you doing for the rest of the day?"

I can't believe how needy and stupid I sound. Who shows up at a guy's house in the middle of the night half-sloshed, crashes his shower and his bed, and then claims his Sunday?

But Drew doesn't look uncomfortable. He doesn't look eager to escape. He grins at me.

"I need to check in on Grandma, but then I think you were going to show me some handstands."

299

My nerves and self-doubts vanish like soap bubbles. One minute they billow and bob and fill up my insides. The next they are just a memory.

Again, I have the keen sensation that with Drew, I am wanted for exactly who I am.

"Well, we should go then," I suggest, both relieved and satisfied with how this day is turning out.

Outside near the bikes, Drew reaches for the combination strip of the cable lock. "What's the number?" he asks.

"Six-four-one-five."

He dials in the code, but he does it wearing a puzzled frown. "Why that? What's the significance?"

"What do you mean?" I'm smiling already because I love that he assumes there must be a significance.

He arches a wry brow at me. "C'mon. Don't try to tell me six-four-one-five doesn't stand for something," he teases, unlocking the bike before winding up the lock. "And I wouldn't believe you if you said it was the last four of your social. What is it? The Age of Aquarius or something."

I burst out laughing. "N-no," I stammer, grabbing my handlebars to steady myself as I double over. "It's Gemini's mirthday."

Drew blinks. "His what, now?"

If it's possible, his confused expression makes me laugh even harder. "His *mirthday*," I try again when I'm able to speak. *"Mirth* as in *cheer* or *gladness.* I rescued Gem when he was about ten weeks old. I can only guess when his actual birthday is, so we celebrate the day I adopted him. June 4, 2015. His *mirthday.*"

"You *celebrate.*" The set of his eyes and his slight nod tell me he thinks this is totally weird.

"Of course we celebrate," I snap with mock irritation. "Clearly, you've never been to a dog mirthday party. You don't know what you're missing."

Drew quakes with laughter. "Clearly, I don't, Guppy," he says shaking his head. He stashes the bike lock in my basket. "Please enlighten me."

I mount my bike. "Believe me, darlin, I'm working hard on it." I push off and begin pedalling, feeling like I've just dropped the mike when Drew's laughter echoes after me.

As we ride back, I fill him in on Gemini's mirthday traditions. A walk through Moncus Park where he always insists on a dunk in the watering trough. A trip to Petsmart for him to pick out a new Tuffy toy and his favorite treats, salmon jerky. And, finally, I sing a rendition of "Happy Mirthday" while presenting Gemini with a homemade sweet potato oat cake in the shape of a bone.

"Party hats are optional, but we always wear them," I tell Drew as we approach the intersection of St. Mary and St. Landry. I'm watching the road, but I don't miss his deep chuckle.

"You're freakin' hilarious, Guppy."

"I'm joyful," I correct with a haughty lift to my chin. "There's a difference. People think there's not enough goodness in the world, but joy and love can be made. You just have to be serious about making and filling up your life with them."

We coast to a stop at the light. I'm waiting for him to say something in response, but when he doesn't, I

301

turn to face him. Drew is staring at me, his expression intense and unguarded.

"What?" I ask a little breathless.

If I weren't watching him so closely, I wouldn't notice the minute shake of his head. "I've never known anyone like you."

My blush is immediate, and even though his words make me shy, I love the way he's looking at me.

The light turns green, and I step on the pedal. "C'mon," I tell him and then promptly turn right, away from our neighborhood.

"Where are we going?" he calls after me.

"You'll see."

I don't want to tell him my plan because I don't want him to be all sensible and responsible and find some way of stopping me. I push hard until we approach the intersection of St. Landry and University, and then I pull into the parking lot of the Circle K.

"What's up?" Drew asks, rolling up to where I've stopped.

I pluck the lock from my basket and nod toward the convenience store. "I need something."

His brows lower with suspicion. "What do you need?"

I loop the cable of the lock around my frame before snaking it through his. "Something important."

Drew crosses his muscled arms over his chest and raises a brow. "Something important," he echoes flatly, but I'd bet everything I have that he knows exactly what I'm up to. And he's doing his best to keep me from reading just how he feels about it.

"Yep." I saunter inside the store with Drew just a few steps behind me. It takes me a moment to find the

302

personal care aisle. And then I need to make a decision. In front of me are two Trojan options. The inconspicuous three-pack and the more committed, we're-in-this-for-the-long-haul thirty-six count "Value Pack."

Three is not enough. Not nearly enough. If I'm being honest, I don't think thirty-six is enough either, but if I reach for that box — and I want to — Drew will think I'm crazy. Or horny. Or crazier and hornier than he already does.

So the three-pack it is. I pluck it off the hook, and the moment I do, Drew makes a grab for it. But I'm quick.

"Hey, now," I scold, holding the condoms away from him and putting my body between him and my hand. "These are mine. You can get your own."

His arched brow climbs even higher, but his eyes are dancing. "Get my own?" His voice is gruff with unspent laughter.

I nod. "You heard me."

Drew purses his lips and shrugs. "'Kay." And then he snatches up the "Value Pack" and takes off for the counter.

"Hey, wait a minute," I call after him. "I was going to get those, but I didn't want you to think—" I stop because how am I going to explain this?

He swings his gaze to me. "You didn't want me to think what?"

I put my hands on my hips a blow out a frustrated breath through my nose. I'm frustrated because I don't want to try to explain this in the middle of the Circle K and because I'm blushing again for the second time in five minutes.

I scowl. "You know." My answer is petulant, but that's all he's going to get.

His face is stoic, except I recognize the non-smile, and I'm about to call him on it when he closes the distance between us, hooks me by the back of the neck, and plants a hard kiss on my lips.

The shock of it makes me rock on my heels, but he's got me, so I know I'm not going down. The kiss is over in seconds, but when he pulls back, Drew is grinning.

"I wouldn't think that, Guppy." And then he turns and heads for the register. I follow again with my skimpy three-pack. But it's now become a point of honor that I buy it.

At the counter, Drew throws me a doubtful look. "You're not going to let me pay for that, are you?" he says, nodding toward the box in my hand.

"Nope."

Pressing his lips together, he nods. "'Kay. Ladies first." And then he ushers me in front of him. The clerk behind the counter, a young guy with a puff of curly hair that stands almost straight up, eyes us and our purchases with mingled respect and wariness.

"Would you like a bag for that?" he asks me.

"No thanks," I say, sliding my debit card into the chip reader. "Plastic bags are the devil."

Drew cracks up beside me. I shoot him a glare. "Well, it's true!" I punch in my PIN and then scoot to the side for him to complete his purchase.

A moment later, we are back outside — sans plastic bags — mounting the bikes again.

"So Hindu goddesses can come to your rescue, and plastic bags are the devil," Drew observes as we roll back onto St. Landry.

I slide my gaze to him to find a look of amused self-satisfaction. It's a really good look for him. In this moment, beside me on the bike, with the sun on his smiling face and the wind tousling his thick waves as we ride, he looks more at ease than I've ever seen him. I can't help but feel I might be part of the reason why. And that makes me proud.

"You're learning, Moroux," I tease, and this makes him laugh.

I love making him laugh. And I manage to do it plenty on the rest of the ride home, telling him about the time I lit some amber incense in my bedroom and set off the smoke alarm. It was in the middle of the night, and I'd woken up my whole family.

We're both laughing at this as we turn onto St. Patrick Street, and my breath halts. Because my whole family is emerging from Mom's Volvo parked in our driveway.

At my gasp, Drew's gaze moves from me to the street ahead. "Are those your parents?" he asks, sounding surprised.

And if he's surprised, I'm shocked.

Mom and Dad.

I haven't seen them since June, and for a moment, I forget everything. The secrets. The manipulations. The collusion.

They are here. Right in front of me. In real life.

The bike screeches to a halt. "Mom... Dad." Before I know it, I'm off the seat and setting the kickstand. I rush to them, and they — wide-eyed with

305

excitement and surprise — open their arms. At once, the three of us are tangled in a group hug, Mom's neroli and rosewater scent and Dad's mix of Brut and Right Guard filling my head with nostalgia. The silk of Mom's blouse and the scrape of Dad's cheek are touchstones of home and safety.

I pull back from the embrace just enough to turn to Drew, eager to beckon him forward to meet my parents. And then I remember.

And I stiffen. Because his eyes are on Tori who is standing behind us, scowling at him. And although his expression is perfectly neutral, his gaze giving nothing away, I can see past it. He's thinking about his last encounter with her, one that I still don't know the details about, but I'm sure wasn't at all pleasant.

Then the realization of exactly *why* Mom and Dad are here dawns. Gently, not wanting to hurt their feelings even now, I pull free of their arms and step backward to Drew. With intention, I reach for his hand, and to my relief, he clasps mine.

I clear my throat. "Mom and Dad, this is Drew." They don't know I'm in love with him. They don't know what's passed between us. They don't know how alive he makes me feel. How with him, I am enough. All they know is what Tori has told them and the arguments Mom and I have had when I defended him. But I want to give them a chance to let me take the lead here. And let them make the right choice.

I see the exact moment when they don't. They both stare at him for about two seconds and then their eyes cut to each other. Before they look back at me, the tacit agreement that passes between them might as well be plastered to a highway billboard it's so obvious.

"Is this your boyfriend, Evangeline?" Dad asks. My stomach drops. Dad never, *never*, uses my whole name. I'm always *Evie* or just *E* with Dad. I also note the impersonal pronoun. *This.* Is *this* your boyfriend. Not *he.* As if Drew isn't a person, but a thing.

I pull in a deep breath, marshalling my strength while also stalling for a moment. Because what am I supposed to say? *Is* Drew my boyfriend? I sure as hell want him to be, but we basically just had our first date. If brunch at Tribe even was a date. If I say that he is, will he think I'm crazy? Like some deranged octopus trying to wrap my tentacles around him when we just spent one night together? One awesome, beautiful, and groundbreaking night? And if I say he isn't, will he think I'm denying him?

The thought is like a sheetrock knife jabbed into my heart and jerked downward. Pain forces the words from me.

"We're seeing each other," I say, squeezing Drew's hand. He's silent beside me, but he squeezes back, and the relief that surges through me nearly makes my knees buckle. But I push on, wanting to make it plain how things are going to be. "Drew, this is my mom, Sondra, and my dad, Elliot."

I'm holding his left hand, and to my surprise, Drew extends his right. "Mr. and Mrs. Lalonde," he says, in greeting. "Nice to meet you."

For one terrifying moment, I'm not sure if my dad is going to accept his hand, but he does, thank God. I would have never forgiven him if he hadn't, and maybe that showed on my face. I don't know. It all happened too fast, but after Dad shakes Drew's hand, Mom pumps it twice, a tight smile on her face.

307

"My grandmother says you've always been good neighbors," Drew says, surprising me again. "But especially after my Grandpa Pete died. Thank you for that."

A tremor passes over both of my parents. Mom fast blinks and Dad shifts his weight on his feet, as if the invocation of Drew's grandparents has reminded them how unneighborly they are being now. And I want to kiss Drew. He's being polite and making an effort when my parents obviously aren't, and it's suddenly clear to me that for the first time in my life, someone is on my side.

Until a few weeks ago, I didn't know there even were sides in my family. And it was a painful and gut-wrenching realization to discover there are. Especially knowing that the two factions are so unbalanced: three to one. Even as we've stood here, Tori has stepped closer to my parents as though closing ranks with them.

But with Drew beside me, I'm no longer quite so outnumbered. And for that I love him all the more.

And I suddenly feel stronger. "What are you guys doing here?" I don't really have to ask. What's passed for family communication since I moved out has mostly revolved around my parents defending themselves, Tori continuing to blame me for upsetting them, and everyone pushing me to move back home. I know that my parents' sudden arrival is probably just an effort to take all that to the next level.

Dad attempts to answer first. "We thought it was important to come see you, given..." his focus moves to Drew and then to the front of Janine's house, "what's been going on—"

308

"What Daddy's trying to say, Evie, is that we're worried about you. Aren't we, honey?" Mom looks to my dad and then back at me before he can answer. "And we wanted to talk about plans to maybe... you know... smooth things out."

I frown. *Plans?*

I shake my head. "Look, all is forgiven. You don't need to worry about me because I'm doing fine," I tell them, meeting the gaze of Mom, Dad, and Tori in turn. "And the only thing I think needs to be smoothed out is the rotten hand you dealt Tori—"

"Evie," Mom scolds, bristling just as my Dad warns, "Hey, now," and puffs out his chest. Tori's eyes widen in surprise, and I wonder suddenly if she's felt like the lines of demarcation are also three against one, but with her on the losing side. With the way things have turned out for her, I couldn't exactly blame her.

Beside me, Drew has gone very still. I glance at him to see his signature stoic blankness, but subtle things — things only someone who has touched him, spent hours looking at him would notice — catch my eye. The slight tightness around his jaw and in the sinews of his neck. The way his nostrils flair just a little. The half-step he's taken toward — and just barely in front of — me.

And I know, the way I've known since the moment I met him, I am safe with Drew Moroux, and he will defend me. No matter what. No matter who threatens. No matter if they wield words. Or scorn. Or weapons. He will shield me. Body and soul.

I become a woman-sized sun. Love and gratitude must blaze from my every particle. I squeeze Drew's

309

hand so tight, hoping he can feel it. Feel what his allegiance means to me.

I look at my parents — at the way they are looking at him — and I know I would do the same to protect him. They are not going to insult him or diminish him. Not on my watch.

But this love, so warm and radiant, makes it easy to be patient. I don't want my family to be the enemy. They are making mistake after mistake, but I meant what I said. All is forgiven. We just need to work past this.

Oblivious to what is happening within me — and what might be happening between Drew and me — Mom grips her elbows almost protectively. She's frowning. "Clearly we have a lot to talk about. That's why we came home. To talk." Her eyes cut to Drew. "As a family."

"*Mom.*" This time, I'm the one warning. But I know there's no avoiding a sit-down with them. Hell, I don't even want to avoid it. "We'll talk, okay? Just don't be rude, please."

Relief washes over her features. "We'll talk? You mean it? You'll come home and—"

"Wait," Drew mutters almost inaudibly beside me as Mom prattles. His hand is tighter around mine.

I glance up at him and whisper back, "Wait?"

His nod is barely perceptible.

"... a chance to sort this out?" Eagerness has made Mom's voice pitch higher, as though she might float away on hope.

"Mrs. Lalonde." Drew's assertive voice, by contrast, grounds me. "Just give us a minute to put the bikes away."

Mom blinks, looking almost startled that he's spoken. And this irks me because her expression seems to suggest he has no right to speak. No part in this conversation. But from where I stand, he does. He's on my side, after all.

So I answer for her. "That's a good idea, Drew." And we move to the bikes, which we left near the curb in front of Janine's house, and we push them up the driveway and into her darkened garage. Lights are now on in the Mayfield's house, but I see no sign of my friends.

"I don't want to leave you," Drew says, and I jerk my gaze from the house to his eyes.

"W-what?" I stammer. All that registers is the possibility that he will leave me. And I rebel against this. "What do you mean?"

His dark brows are low with concern. "Evie, I know they're your parents, but I don't want to leave you with them." He shakes his head. "I can't explain it."

The tension drains away, and I want to laugh. I don't, of course. "They're not going to hurt me, Drew."

His expression doesn't change. "At Angola, you know where all the blind spots are, the places where the cameras can't see and the guards don't look. Best to avoid them, but if you can't, you sure as hell don't go there alone."

Any impulse I had to laugh dries to dust. I step closer and reach for him. My hands cup either side of his face, so beautiful it staggers me. "It's fine, Drew. These are my parents we're talking about," I say, wanting to reassure him. "They aren't bad people. They're just misguided."

311

A crease appears between his brows. "They want to control you." He seems to wince at the sound of his own words and gives a tight shake of his head. "I mean, it's obvious they love you, but, damn, Evie. They flew halfway across the planet so you'd hear them out. That's a little extreme."

My answering smile is rueful. "I see that."

He looks down at me, and the hard lines around his eyes and mouth soften. Just a little. But then the concern returns. "I'm just afraid that—"

His words catch at my heart. What could Drew possibly fear? "What?" I ask. "What are you afraid of?"

Drew watches me for a long time. He lets out a deep breath, and then his eyes drift down the length of the driveway. I follow their track to the trio who stands waiting for me in the middle of the street. Tori is the only one brazen enough to watch us in Janine and James's garage. But I can tell by their postures that Mom and Dad are tuned in, as alert and interested in us and our actions as they could possibly be without looking directly at us.

"Just that they know how to make you doubt yourself."

My breath leaves me in a rush because how can he see this so clearly? How can he see *me* so clearly?

When I speak, my voice is shaky. "Y-you're probably onto something there."

He brings his gaze back to me, but now I see the barest hint of a smile. "Don't sound so surprised, Guppy," he teases, and in spite of everything, I laugh a thready laugh.

"I'm..." I begin, shaking my head. "I'm not surprised. I feel like..."

312

Will it sound dumb if I just say it? Will he understand?

Drew's gaze sharpens on me. "Feel like what?"

I bite my lip and stare up at him. No. He's not going to reject me now. I don't know how I know this, but I do.

"I feel like you see me."

When the words are out, they do sound dumb to my ears, but Drew makes it okay when he cups the back of my neck with one expansive hand and pulls me to him. His lips are both firm and soft against mine. Sure and yet careful. The kiss feels so good. So new and promising. I want to step deeper into it, but my family is watching. And under my hands I can feel Drew's awareness that they are watching.

I edge back just enough to break the kiss, but Drew keeps his hand at my neck, holding me, anchoring me.

"You need to talk to them." He says this almost like a concession, as though it isn't a given. "You don't have to do it on their turf."

I fast blink at him. "What? Turf? Is this *West Side Story* now?"

The side of Drew's mouth quirks in a wry grin, and he rolls his eyes. "You know what I mean. Talk to them, but do it on neutral territory." He gives the back of my neck a reassuring squeeze. I could get used to this. "Let them see you as independent. In a different setting than one they've always controlled."

It's good advice. In fact, it's a plan.

I nod. "That helps. Thank you."

"I wish I could stay with you," he says, shifting his eyes toward the street where my family still waits.

313

Pretending they aren't watching us. "But I don't think my presence would help."

A sudden urgency makes me grip the front of his shirt. "They'll come around, you know," I tell him, hoping with all I have he doesn't decide I'm a lost cause. "They're good people. I swear. You just need to give them time."

He looks back at me, those eyes impassive, but I can see he's not convinced. "Time's precious, Guppy." When he says this, my stomach absolutely plummets. But then that lazy grin returns. "I'd rather give it to you."

I let go the breath I've been holding and practically sink into him. He drops his hand from my neck, fumbles around in his pocket, and pulls out a phone.

"Finally got one of these," he says with a nod.

My smile is immediate. As is the desire to tease him. "Oh? And how many contacts do you have in it?"

Drew frowns at the phone as if in silent contemplation. "Five. Grandma Q, my Aunt Josie, my Aunt Shelly, my sister Annie, and the garage." When he looks back at me, the corners of his eyes are crinkled with mischief. "I'm hoping to add a sixth one today."

"Wow. Six whole contacts," I muse, affecting awe. Then I tip open my hand. "May I?"

He places the phone on my palm. "Be my guest."

I open his contacts, tap in my number, and then pass the phone to him. "Text me so I have your number."

His unguarded look as he takes the phone should be all the clue I need, but when my phone chirps with his text, I still lose it.

314

I do see you.

CHAPTER TWENTY-FOUR

DREW

I don't want to leave her.

And my fear that her parents will convince her to drop kick me out of her life is only part of the why. These people may be her family, and I'm sure she's right that they are good people — honestly, how could the people who made Evie be anything else? — but the way they looked at her when she introduced me...

They just don't take her seriously.

They love her. That's obvious. Who couldn't love Evie? But I can't shake the feeling that although they adore her, she is still the butt of some family joke. As though she's the one who makes them throw up their hands and roll their eyes.

As though they don't see the way she touches the world. She can summon the pantheon of every culture — and likely make them do her bidding. She can heal with a word. Her smile alone can save a man.

Even one as damned as me.

How can they not see that?

I don't want to leave her, but I know staying won't help. The Lalondes want me to go, to be a memory. And I can see that puts Evie on edge. She doesn't want them hurting my feelings.

It wouldn't. They couldn't say anything about me I haven't thought already. We all agree Evie deserves to be with someone better. They just don't know that I can't make myself stay away. Not anymore.

Evie blinks as she reads my text, and then her eyes dart to mine as green and as wide as I've ever seen them. Now full of the most innocent of hopes. I didn't even debate telling her. Didn't hesitate.

Because what if no one else sees her? It seemed impossible twenty minutes ago. Before I met her parents. I mean, who could be so blind and miss out on everything she is? But if they can't see it, the very people who've raised her, then who else in her life has missed it? Her sister cleary has. And surely that Drake asshole.

What if I'm the only one? If I am, she needs to hear it.

"I see you, Evie," I say aloud. "And I'm damn lucky."

With all the force it takes to clear a fence or pop into a handstand, she flings herself against me. My breath goes for a second, and I have to fight to inhale as I wrap my arms around her. Evie's family is still watching us, but I bend down and kiss her anyway.

No tongue or raunchiness or anything. Just a firm, promising kiss. And let them watch. Maybe it'll give them a clue.

"Drew... You have no idea..." She's muttering little snatches of phrases against my lips as I continue to stamp hers with kisses. "No one's ever come close... *Tuatha de Danann...* "

I have no idea what this means, but I'm sure it's something that would make me laugh, so stifling my humor, I force myself to let her go. She needs to deal with her family, and I need to let her. But...

"Call me. If you need something, call me."

She's quick about it, but she brushes her eyes with the backs of her hands, and it's only then I realize just what my testimony means to her.

Yeah, telling her was the right thing to do.

With my thumb, I catch one glinting tear on her lower lashes. "You good, Guppy?"

Evie nods, visibly swallowing.

I want to wrap her in my arms again. Shield her from whatever others might aim at her. I want to tell her how rare she is. I want to take her to bed and worship her.

And for the second time today, I want to give her a home.

I glance back at the three members of her family. Each one of them now stares openly at us. Judgement is written all over their faces. Maybe it's just their judgement of me, and for that I'm sorry. But even if I weren't in the picture, I can see Evie can't be herself and live with them again.

She needs a home.

I stroke her cheek once more, drop my hand to hers and squeeze her fingers, and then I make myself move. Walking away from her is one of the hardest things I've ever done.

At the end of the driveway, I nod to her parents and Tori. Maybe there are courteous words I should say, but I can't find them. They wouldn't want to hear them anyway. I'm at the corner of St. Patrick and Souvenir Gate before I remember the giant box of condoms that's still sitting in Evie's bike basket, and a laugh nearly escapes me.

They couldn't have seen it. We parked the bikes too far away. And if they had seen it, I can only imagine Evie's father would have attacked me in the street. I wouldn't have blamed him for that either.

I turn the corner and make my way back to Grandma Q's. I need to check on her, and I'm grateful to have something to do. Otherwise, memories of last night and worries over how Evie is managing with her family would tangle me up.

It's nearly eleven when I step into Grandma's kitchen and find her at the table, paying bills with her checkbook and an old fashioned ticker-tape adding machine. And I should totally be prepared for it. I'm really a fool not to see it coming. But my mind and heart are just too full, so it takes me be surprise.

"You finally came to your senses, I see," Grandma says, eyeing me over her bifocals as soon as I shut the kitchen door.

I stand, stunned silent for a moment, wondering just how she knows. Does she watch the apartment stairs twenty-four-seven? Is there a hidden camera I don't know about? Or does she just consult a crystal ball?

"I guess that means you don't disapprove of overnight guests in the apartment," I say dryly.

Grandma snorts. "I wouldn't say that. I came of age before Vatican II," she says, raising her eyes to the crucifix over the door before crossing herself. "But I do approve of Evie."

This isn't a surprise, but it makes me grin anyway.

"Besides—" Grandma coughs once, clears her throat, drops her gaze back to the papers in front of her. "I could see you settling down with her — sooner rather than later if my guess is right. And then I wouldn't have to worry over you."

So many parts of this statement bounce against my brain I have to shake my head to clear it.

"Don't get ahead of yourself, Grandma." My voice is calm, but my heart thumps hard in my chest.

319

She's just spoken a hope I haven't even let myself examine too closely.

But it's there. Smoldering. And I know better than to give it any air. Because even though that is what I want, it'll never really happen. Not if Evie is as smart as I think she is.

"At my age, I can't get very far ahead of myself before I find myself in the ground," Grandma Q mutters, and then, as though to punctuate this morbid statement, she coughs again.

I frown. "You feeling okay today, Grandma?"

She waves me away without meeting my gaze. "Happens every year when they burn the cane. It's just a tickle in my throat."

I'm tempted to point out that it sounded like more than a tickle, but that would just annoy her.

I take a seat across the table. "You need any help with that stuff?"

She eyeballs me over her glasses. "Does it look like I need help paying the same bills I've been paying for the last fifty-odd years?"

I swallow a laugh. "Is there anything I can do for you today?"

Grandma Q makes a huffing sound. "You can fix that car that's taking up all the space in my garage."

Well, okay then.

"I'll get right on that, Grandma," I say, biting back my grin and getting to my feet. But I press a kiss to the top of her head before moving to the door.

"I'm making smothered pork chops for dinner—" Grandma says with a strange lilt in her voice, "if you'd like to ask Evie to join us.

I pause with my hand on the doorknob and glance back at her. "I'll see if she's free."

I walk out watching my grandmother trying to swallow her own smile before I close the door behind me. But then as soon as I do, I hear her coughing again.

Might need to get that checked out.

I cross the yard and step into the garage, and although everything is exactly where I left it last night when I led Evie upstairs, the place is completely transformed.

At least, it feels nothing like it did before.

The Supra is still here. And it's still Anthony's. And there's still that ache of familiarity and longing for him when I look at it, as though he might be behind the wheel or checking under the hood if I just walked in at the right time.

But the wrecking ball of despair that would hit me at the sight of it —the one that would make it almost impossible just to touch the car at first — is nowhere in sight.

Maybe it's just waiting. Biding its time for an opportunity when I'm not so distracted. But I welcome the difference. Even if it's only short-lived.

Yet I don't think it's temporary. Evie has been here. I kissed her for the first time right here. I made her come on the hood of that car. Her cries of desire filled this space. She's blessed this place.

Before meeting Evie, I would have laughed at the idea of anyone having the power to change the energy in a place. Or banish ghosts. But if Evie's climax wasn't a kind of magic, then I don't know what is.

And that wasn't the first time she has transformed the world around me. Her presence had the same effect on my apartment. What's the point in doubting her powers? The woman is a sorceress. And she's mine.

For now, anyway.

She's stronger than her family gives her credit for. Than even I gave her credit for. I have no doubt her parents and her sister will do anything they can to convince her to stop seeing me. She won't do it just to please them. Yet their points against me might be enough to seed doubts.

And as much as I know she should have doubts and she should listen to them, the thought of losing her now summons a new kind of pain.

The pain I carry for Anthony and all I've done and all those I've hurt — that pain is worn smooth. Sanded down by time and familiarity. It still hurts like hell, and I still suffer. But it has become a part of me, walking every step with me for what seems like a lifetime. And I earned it. Welcomed it. Almost like an old friend. I can't imagine myself without it.

But this? Having Evie only to lose her?

The thought alone is sharp. Jagged. Lethal. I have no defenses against it. And if it comes, I will have no refuge. I know with every cell in my body I will long for her until I die.

The temptation to leave in search of her now is so potent, my groan fills the empty garage.

I'm undone. At loose ends. I should dive into the repairs and lose myself in cylinders and gaskets, but instead, I dig out my phone.

Me: How's it going?

It's only been about thirty minutes since I left her, but I need to hear from her. It's crazy and stupid and weak. But I need her.

And to my relief, her response is immediate.

Evie: S'ok. M&D wanted to talk now @ home. I nixed that. Having dinner @ Masala's tonight.

I grin at her shorthand and her triumph.

Me: Good. Guess you can't make it for pork chops. Grandma Q will be bummed.

She sends me a tearful emoji.

Evie: Can I come by after? I need the afternoon to yoga & meditate. Kind of nervous.

My brows draw together. I wish I could go with her. Just for moral support.

Me: You got this. And if things go south, just call for Collie.

Laughing emojis fill my screen.

Evie: KALI! And why do you think I chose an Indian restaurant?

My own laughter bounces through the garage. God, I love her.

Me: Ah. Got it. And yes. Please come over after.

I will see her in a few hours. The worry of moments ago eases.

Evie: I like you texting me.

She doesn't need to know I couldn't help myself.

Me: Good. I'm out of practice, but it's fun.

"You can't tell me that's from burning cane."

Grandma can't speak yet, coughing viciously for the third time since we sat down to dinner, but she's eyeing me with menace.

"I'll be the one," she rasps and then covers the cough with her napkin. "to say what it is."

I narrow my gaze at her. "When did that start?"

She shakes her head, frowning, and points a gnarled finger at my plate. "Eat your pork chop." Grandma Q clears her throat, and her voice comes out a little stronger. "It's getting cold."

My plate is a southern feast. Smothered pork chops in gravy. Rice. White beans. Cinnamon apples. My favorite meal of all time.

One glance at Grandma's plate shows a stark contrast. She's served herself a few morsels of meat, not even a whole chop, a little mound of rice and gravy, maybe a forkful of beans, and two apple slices.

"Aren't you hungry?"

She shrugs like it's nothing. "I tasted this and that too much while cooking to make sure everything was done just so," she says, pushing her fork around on her plate. "Ate half my dinner standing at the stove."

I've heard her complain of spoiling her appetite this way before, so I take another bite, wanting to appease her. She went to all this trouble for me, after all.

"Well, it's great," I say, and that's the truth. It's the second time she's made pork chops for me since I've been back. The first time, I realize, was the night I met Evie. Here in this kitchen.

My praise lifts creases around her eyes. But a closer look at her face has me wondering about her color.

She coughs again.

"I think you need to see a doctor."

Grandma Q rolls her eyes at the ceiling. "And when he tells me it's just a cough from the cane burning, what'll you give me for the two hours I'll lose in his office?"

She may be getting sick again, but it can't be too bad if she's still sassy. "I don't know, Grandma. What do you want?"

She makes a noise of impatience. "I told you already. I want you to bring Evie for dinner."

A grin splits my face. "Sorry, Grandma. Her parents are in town, and she's out with them tonight." But this is something I can offer. "I'll see if she can come tomorrow night."

She gives me a scandalized look. "Tomorrow's leftover chops. Better make it Tuesday. Tuesday is shrimp creole."

After dinner, I clean up and send Grandma to bed. I know she won't go to sleep yet, but she will take a bath and watch TV in her room, and that's about as close as she gets to letting herself rest.

When I hear the water running, I call Aunt Josie and tell her about the cough. Her guess is it's probably nothing but promises to call Grandma's GP in the morning. Which is a good thing because if she didn't, I would, and I'd take off at the garage to make sure Grandma Quincy saw someone.

I knew — before my release — some things about life on the outside would be challenging. I never imagined worrying about other people would be one of them. This is twice in one day, and I'm not a fan.

325

But Evie and Grandma Q. Where would I be without them?

I turn out the lights in the kitchen, lock up, and head to my apartment with one thought in mind. If I have to worry about people, at least I picked good ones.

I try to pass the time by tidying up my small space and pricing replacement parts for the Supra on my phone, but I can't help wondering how it's going for Evie. So when she texts me just before nine o'clock, my shoulders finally loosen.

> *Evie: Sorry so late. You home?*
> *Me: Yes. Come over.*

I wait for her reply.

And wait.

I've almost convinced myself that her parents have talked her into dumping me when she responds.

> *Evie: Can I bring Gem?*

Tension leaves me in a rush of breath.

> *Me: Yes. Anytime.*
> *Evie: :) We'll walk down.*
> *Me: I'll meet you halfway.*

I glance around the apartment one more time. It's clean. The floor is swept. My bed is made up with fresh linens. I have no expectations of what might happen with Evie, and I know she can't stay late, but I want her to feel at home here. To feel comfortable. And if she can tell I made an effort, so much the better.

She deserves someone who makes an effort.

I'm at the corner of St. Patrick and Souvenir before I spot her just leaving her friend Janine's house. She has Gemini harnessed and leashed and a backpack dangling from one shoulder. Under the light of the streetlamp, I see Evie has traded the jeans and green shirt for flowing yoga pants and a long-sleeve tunic.

She looks comfortable. And damn touchable.

But I check my itching palms when I close the distance between us and take in her face. She's exhausted.

I reach for her. "You okay?"

She slams against me, hugging me tight. She doesn't say a word. It doesn't take me long to figure out it's because she can't.

And as my arms close around her, I have no doubts about my purpose. The one job I have right now is to make it better.

CHAPTER TWENTY-FIVE

EVIE

I bury my nose into the clean cotton of Drew's shirt. It radiates his warmth, and I let myself hide in it.

It feels like my skull is a cannon that's just been fired. A thousand times.

"My head is killing me."

His arms, snug around me, shift until his hands cradle my head. "Yeah?"

His big palms shielding my head feel good. Like he might be able to keep it from exploding. I manage a nod. "It happens when I get really stressed."

Drew makes a disapproving grunt. I hear it rumble through his chest. "Didn't go so well, did it?"

I inhale through my nose and sigh out the exhale. "Not really, no."

We're quiet for a minute. It's fine by me. My eyes are closed. The softness of his shirt presses against my forehead, and his hands hold my head. I'm good right here until the throbbing stops.

"You don't have to come over if it's too much." His voice is low, sturdy, but I can hear resignation in it. Like he's disappointed but doesn't want to let it show. I lift my gaze and take him in. Even in the dim light of the streetlamp, I can see he's frowning down at me, concern deep in his dark eyes.

"I want to come over. I don't want to be anywhere else." The tightness in my throat threatens to swallow my words, but they're so true. Despite my parents' pleas, I can't go home, and while Janine's house is welcoming enough, the circle of Drew's arms is the only place that feels right. "Janine gave me the night off. Can I sleep over again?"

The side of Drew's mouth quirks. "You really have to ask?"

For the first time in hours, my smile is easy. "Let's go."

Always excited for a walk, Gemini goes manic when we peel off the road and head up the drive toward Drew's apartment.

Drew leads me to the stairs where Gem's claws make an unholy racket. It's enough to make us both laugh.

"Oh, God, I'm sorry," I try to whisper above the noise. "I hope he doesn't wake Mrs. Vivian."

Drew grunts again as we reach the top. He pushes the door open and Gemini scrambles inside, tail whipping with excitement.

"We didn't wake her. Don't ask me how she does it, but she seems to know everything that happens around here."

I think about the box of condoms in my backpack and bite my lip. "Really?"

His gaze meets mine, a glint in his eye. "Don't worry," he teases, "I've already done a sweep for cameras."

His joke catches me off guard, and I laugh again. I've been with him less than ten minutes, and already I feel so much better.

"Here, let me take that," he says, reaching for my bag and my mat carrier. I slide it off my shoulder and hand it over. He sets it down beside the armoire and then looks around his apartment with deliberate scrutiny. "I wish I had somewhere for you to sit that wasn't a kitchen chair or the bed."

I offer him a one shoulder shrug. "I can sit anywhere. The floor is fine."

I'm about to drop into a lotus sit when he grabs my elbow. "You're not sitting on the floor," he says, a wry arch to his brow. Then he points to the futon. "Sit on the bed."

And before I can respond, he's plucked one of the kitchen chairs from the table. Drew places it facing the foot of the bed and sits on it. He eyes me with a patient stare, clearly waiting for me to take a seat. I sink onto the futon and curl up in easy pose, legs crossed and back straight.

Wagging, and still taut with the excitement of being somewhere new, Gemini approaches the bed and bats a paw against the frame, asking permission to jump on.

"Get up there boy," Drew says, slapping the mattress. Gem doesn't need to be told twice. He hops up, turns around a couple of times, and curls up beside me, his ridged back pressing against my thigh.

Drew and I eye each other in silent amusement before I find myself looking away, feeling a sudden shyness.

"You don't have to tell me what happened," Drew says after a minute, "but I'm ready to listen if you want to."

"I do want to tell you," I confess, but I'm torn. I gave Janine the short version, and she cautioned me against sharing the worst of it with Drew.

His patient expression doesn't change. "You don't sound too sure of yourself, Guppy."

"I want to tell you," I say again, and I force myself to hold his gaze. "It's just embarrassing."

A flicker of surprise flashes in his eyes. "Embarrassing?" Concern now overtakes the surprise. "Did they do something to embarrass you at dinner?"

Drew's protective streak is showing, and I realize at once why I want to tell him everything. It's because he makes me feel so safe. And I know when I do tell him, this feeling of being adrift and alone will ease.

"It wasn't like that," I explain, shaking my head. "Nobody made a scene or anything."

He leans forward and rests his elbows on his knees, his strong, weathered hands clasping each other between them. "Then what embarrassed you, Evie?"

I hesitate. Not because I don't want him to know, but because saying it aloud will make it more real. And then I'll have to believe it. And I don't want to.

Drew watches me for a moment before his gaze shifts to his right. His expression hardens, as though he's just made up his mind about something, and he looks back at me.

"You want to see something embarrassing?"

I blink. "Um…" I stall, curious but cautious. "I don't feel like there's a right answer to that question."

His mouth pulls to the side, humor dancing in his eyes. "Well, too bad. You're seeing it." He gets to his feet and moves across the room, stopping by the yellow dust cover.

"Do you have any idea what this is?" He's studying my face, but his own is as stony as ever. It's impossible to tell what he's thinking.

I shake my head. "Something of your grandfather's?" I guess, but even as I do, a tightness in my gut tells me it's nothing innocent or nostalgic.

"No," Drew says, his voice so low it's almost inaudible. He leans down and takes the corner of the yellow sheet between his fingers, almost as if he's unwilling to touch it.

When he peels the sheet back, I see a flat screen Samsung TV, probably about forty inches, a PlayStation 3, and two picture frames lying face down on a shelf. I have no idea what to make of this.

"Do you game?" I ask frowning. Of course he doesn't. The PlayStation is a relic, and none of it is connected. Plus, all of this has been under a sheet every time I've been here.

The hint of a smile pulls at his mouth, but it doesn't come close to his eyes. "No, Guppy. I don't game. Not anymore."

I look between him and the electronics and back to him again. Not anymore. He used to. And my guess is, since there are two remotes, he used to play with Anthony.

"Is this about your brother?" I ask, my voice just above a whisper. If it is, why is he embarrassed?

Drew nods. "This is proof I'm a criminal."

The words send a jolt through me. I know what he's done. It's the harshness in his tone that hits me.

"Do you think that bothers me?" I ask, hoping this isn't a new tack to push me away. I'd hoped we were passed that. And after the disillusioning night I've had, I don't think I could handle it.

Drew drops the sheet to the floor and comes to sit beside me on the futon. "No," he says firmly. "I know you don't. But I stole this shit. With Anthony. And when Annie and Grandma moved my stuff in here, they brought this too."

He glances back at the TV and company. "It was here when I moved in. That and the pictures of me and Anthony. This big, ugly reminder of how instead of having my brother, I have this stuff." He waves a hand at the pile in disgust. "That, Guppy? That's some embarrassing shit."

I swallow. "It's h-heartbreaking." My voice washes out on the word. I clear my throat. "Not embarrassing."

He leans back on his hands and raises a brow at me. "The reminder of it is heartbreaking. Awful, yes." The way he's looking at me is so open. So raw. "What's embarrassing is how it holds me hostage. This stuff. What it means. I can't get rid of it. And I can't look at it."

He blinks a slow blink. "That's embarrassing."

I lay a hand on top of his. "I think it's human. How else could you possibly feel?" I want to comfort him, and at the same time, I'm so moved he trusted me enough to tell me all this.

Drew's brow arches in a perfect slope. "I told you that to make you feel better," he says, giving me a half smile, turning his hand over so mine rests in his hold. "Not for you to try to make me feel better."

I bite my lip. "I—"

"I know, Guppy," he says, his eyes glinting again. "You're just doing what you do. Always trying to give someone your light. I get it. And it helps."

My eyes bug. "It does?"

He sniffs a laugh. "Of course it does. Even taking that damn sheet off that stuff makes it easier. Takes away its power, maybe."

If he tells me more, will it give him even more peace? I want that for him. I'd do anything to give that to him.

"Tell me about Anthony."

I watch his chest rise and fall, and his gaze lowers, but his non-smile is in place, so I don't think he minds me asking. He rises, crosses the room again, grabs the picture frames, and comes back to me, sitting beside me again. He hands me the frames, and I come face to face with a younger Drew.

In one picture he's standing with a guy who could only be his brother. Drew's hair is shagging, falling into his eyes, but he's smiling. His brother is looking at him, one arm slung over Drew's shoulders. I can see love in his eyes. Anthony loved his little brother.

In the other, Drew, Anthony, and their little sister Annie sit on the edge of what looks like houseboat, all of their legs dangling in the water. None of them look into the camera. Instead, each is laughing, Annie covering her mouth, but her brothers laugh with open mouths, eyes squeezed shut. The pictures make me smile, but I get how painful they must be for Drew.

When I lift my gaze to his, his eyes are full of meaning. "He was the best, but he wasn't perfect." He says this as though it's crucial I understand.

"Of course he wasn't perfect," I say, and I'm glad I do because some of the intensity I read in his eyes eases. "What made him so human?"

His breath comes out in an amused huff. "He put up with my shit way too much."

It feels safe to, so I tease him. "I think that would make him superhuman."

He puts on a withering look, but he's trying not to laugh. "You know, Guppy, my brother would have really liked you."

"Well, of course he would have," I say coyly, but the thought makes me sad. For Drew. For Anthony. For me. I look down at the young man in the pictures and wish I'd had the chance to know him. "I'm sorry. You were trying to say something important. What do you mean he put up with too much shit?"

Drew watches me for a moment, and I can't tell what he's thinking. He takes one of the curls that has fallen over my shoulder in his grip and gently tugs it straight and long. He releases it, and it springs back in place. He captures it again and rubs it between his thumb and forefinger. Slowly. Lovingly.

If he needs more time to tell me all this, he can have it.

"He let me get away with everything," he says, still looking at the curl he's holding. "He should have beat my ass the first time I stole anything."

"How old were you the first time?" I ask.

His look goes grim. "Fourteen." He's searching my face for shock. Or disgust. But he won't find either. "I broke into a neighbor's car. The guy had left his wallet in the center console. I stole $200 and his Usher CD."

I can't help it. I smile and he smiles back. "I know, right? Driven to a life of crime by 'Yeah!'"

"Hey, nobody can listen to that song without moving," I defend.

Drew rolls his eyes, but his grin stretches. "When I told him, Anthony said to take it back." He shakes his head and looks away. "I would've done it, but I was more afraid of getting caught on the return trip. So I

335

offered him half the cash, and I guess that was too tempting because he took it."

"And that's how it started? You sharing what you… took?"

"The first time," he says with a nod. "But what really got me was the rush I'd feel. The hit of adrenaline. The euphoria of being where I knew I shouldn't be… And just doing what I wanted."

His eyes lock with mine as he says this, and I stay quiet, wanting him to feel safe to tell it all.

"I told Anthony about that. The feeling. And he wanted to try with me." Drew swallows, guilt etching his every feature.

"Did he feel it? That rush?"

His nostrils flare as he pulls in a slow breath. "I think he felt it, but I don't think it hooked him the way it hooked me." He puts a hand to his head, spanning his forehead between his thumb and middle finger, the muscles and tendons in his hand standing out with strain. "He came along with me to try to keep me out of trouble."

He drops his hand and drags his gaze to mine, and I see the war he's fighting. Regret and shame hang on him like weights. It looks like he's using all his strength to meet my eyes.

"That's why he's gone. He was looking after me, and I put him in danger."

I lean forward and set down the pictures on his little kitchen table before laying my hand on his knee. I'd like to tell him it's okay, but we both know it isn't. And when there's nothing else, sometimes honesty is a gift. "It's a lot to live with," I murmur.

Drew's breath leaves him in a rush. "Yeah. That's the truth." He's watching me so closely now. "A life sentence."

I nod because I know he'll have to live with this forever, but... "A *life* sentence," I tell him. "Not a death sentence. You're still allowed to live your life."

He blinks his eyes wide.

"And what you make of your life matters."

It's as though the words give him the permission he needs after sharing this story. He hooks an arm around my back and pulls me against him. Our lips meet for the first time since we kissed in front of my family, and I feel the pent-up power of reunion. We both need this. What we have — what we are making right here — is critical for each of us.

I cup my hand to his face and pull back. He may not need me to say it, but I want to make sure. "What you make of your life matters to me."

Drew's eyes flame. "The car is his," he says, and it takes me a moment to figure out what he means.

"The one in the garage?"

He nods. "He loved that car. Grandma kept it for me."

A smile as Mrs. Vivian's genius runs away with me. "And you're restoring it."

His brows lift a little as he shrugs. "We'll see. I'm trying, anyway."

My smile grows. "I'm glad."

He leans in and tastes my lips once... twice... three times. And then he pulls back and locks his eyes with mine. "You know all of my secrets now. Everything worth hiding or worth hiding from," Drew says, his gaze moving between my eyes. The look I read in his and the words on his tongue make me go a little breathless.

He seems to be waiting for something. And maybe now is the moment to tell him I love him. Because I absolutely do. And would he share all of this with me if there wasn't love, or at least trust, on his part? Maybe I should —

"So if you feel like telling me what embarrassed you tonight, I'm all ears, Guppy."

My mouth falls open, and I swear, my heart must stop. It has to stop at least for moment. One little organ can only handle so much love.

Drew gave me all of that, his shame and his shadows, to make me feel safe. Safe enough to tell him anything.

"Oh my God," I mutter, completely awed. I grab a handful of his shirt and pull him to me, suddenly desperate to kiss him. And not as a gentle reunion. When I crush my lips to his, it's a force of nature. A chemical reaction. A law of physics. It is a *must*.

I must have him.

Drew opens for me, and my tongue sweeps his mouth. He is heat and home. His tongue catches mine and answers it stroke for stroke. A low hum of satisfaction comes from deep in his throat, and it's a sound I'd sell my soul for.

I. Love. Him.

I push against him, pressing my hands to his pecs in supplication. Because this isn't happening unless Drew allows it. I know that much. But it's got to happen.

And when he leans back on the mattress, taking me with him, it's like the Fourth of July. The heat and starburst of a thousand fireworks. Our movement wakes

338

Gemini, and he jumps from the mattress. I'm only dimly aware of him curling up under the table as my hands slide under Drew's T-shirt just as his slip beneath my top.

Drew hisses a surprised breath when his palms move over my bare back. It seems my decision to go braless is appreciated. He growls with lust a moment later when those hands move to my breasts, free under the tunic.

"You brought them?" he rasps between kisses. "Please tell me you brought them."

I don't even have to ask. "Backpack," I pant against his lips.

Kiss. Bite. "Thank Christ."

And then I'm on my back, and Drew is gone. I prop myself on elbows to find him yanking open my bag. He tosses the box of Trojans onto the bed in easy reach, and then he's on top of me. Kissing me. Holding me like we'll both die if he lets go.

And we just might.

His mouth moves to my neck, and I moan at the pleasure.

"Evie." He says my name like a prayer. Like he's saying *Amen.* "So sweet. My God, you're all the sweetness in the world."

"Drew..." I close my mouth because the words are right there, overflowing from my heart, filling my eyes with tears. The weight of him — between my legs, against my front — is the anchor I've wanted my whole life.

His hands move over me in long, exploring strokes, leading heat and desire to my already throbbing sex. One hand cups my right breast and his thumb

339

brushes over my nipple. I gasp, and his other slips beneath fabric to grab my ass.

We both have on way too much clothing.

I clutch the hem of his T-shirt but then quickly give up when it's clear he's not letting go of me, so then I grab the bottom of my own shirt and meet no resistance when I tug it off.

Drew's grunts before his mouth closes over my left breast.

"Drew... my God... *Tuatha de Danann...*" My voice is nothing but a hoarse whisper.

"What's that, baby?" he asks between suckles.

I glance down at the sinfully erotic sight of him at my breast and try to parse out his question. I close my eyes instead.

"Thoo-a-day-do-nun... You said that this afternoon... What are you calling me, Guppy?" Drew's voice is low, laced with both humor and lust. The tip of his tongue draws spirals around my nipple. "Need to know so I can live up to it... Open your eyes, baby."

I obey, blinking at him in an aroused daze, and somehow find the words. "The last race of gods to walk the earth," I pant, grinding my pelvis against his hardness. "from Irish lore. Lovers... warriors... protectors... *beautiful.*"

And then he's hovering above me, his gorgeous face just inches from mine. His eyes blaze behind a mystified frown. He brands me with a searing kiss, one that stretches on and on, our bodies pressing ever tighter together. I ache with desire. I need him inside me.

I tug on his shirt again, and, between kisses, he finally lets me take it. My hands skate over the smooth skin of his muscled back. He feels glorious.

340

"Make love to me." I whisper into his ear.

Drew cocks back his head to stare down at me. "Are you sure, Evie?"

I blink up at him, disbelieving. "Yes. God, yes."

The calloused fingers of his right hand graze down my cheek, the rough touch surprisingly tender. His gray eyes are filled with concern. He opens his mouth. Closes it. Then scowls. "Your safety is everything."

Love. So much love.

I bring one hand up and let my fingers mirror against his cheek the motions of his touch on mine. "I've never felt safer, Drew."

And then because I know he's barely keeping his doubts at bay, I grasp for the box with my free hand.

341

CHAPTER TWENTY-SIX

DREW

Make love to me.

She wants me to make love to her. Does she know I've never made love? Not really.

I've had sex, sure. Not love.

But with Evie that's what it is. And lovemaking is something completely different. And I'm not about to let it be anything less.

Not rushed. Or careless.

The feel of Evie, bare-breasted beneath me, is enough to tempt me to yank down her pants, unzip my jeans, and take her here. Now. With urgency.

But that would only satisfy the desire for her. Not the love.

I push myself up, drawing my groin out of the cradle of her body, and plank above her. Her eyes watch me, curious for a moment, and then Evie's hands fall to my fly.

Stopping her is critical. I shift to the side and come to my knees. "Not yet," I say, grasping her wrists just as she undoes the button.

A line forms between her two delicate brows. I take her arms and loop them around my neck.

"What are you doing?" she asks, her frown etching deeper.

"Making love to you." I straighten, taking her with me. And then, gathering her in my arms — one under her knees, the other tucked around her bare back — I rise.

"Where are we going?" Her eyes, a touch wide, make a quick sweep over the tiny apartment.

"Not far." And I lower her back down, but this time centering her on the bed with her head on the pillow as it should be. Not in the middle of the mattress as if joining with her were an accident.

This is purposeful. Intentional.

She gives a startled *Oh,* as she settles against the pillow, still looking at me with confusion. I lean over her and press my lips to hers, letting our mouths fuse, melt open, tongues slide and grip.

But just for a moment.

Then I pull back and stand again. This time alone.

Evie's cheeks are flushed. Maybe from the kiss. Maybe from the carrying. She's watching me with rapt attention, and the blush on her skin, the anticipation bright in her eyes — all that is Evie nearly steals my breath.

"You're so damn beautiful."

My voice sounds foreign to my ears. Deeper. More animal. But for now, I've harnessed the beast that wants to run wild with her. Gentling him with a promise of grazing. Of years, not seconds.

"Come back," she says, her voice trembling. With desire? With nerves? I can't tell, but the urge to return and cover her with my body is almost maddening.

"Soon." And I reach for my fly and finish the job she started. What comes next will be torturously slow. Deliberate. Expansive. And I want both of us to be completely bare so every inch of skin, every nerve ending can bear witness.

Evie's eyes widen as I drop jeans and briefs to the floor.

"You're beautiful," she whispers, her gaze sweeping over me. The same word that captures her can't possible describe someone like me. Ex-con auto mechanic? No way. But if she likes what she sees, I'm not gonna argue.

I sit beside her, and when she reaches a hand to me, I catch it in my own, bring it to my lips, and kiss her knuckles.

"Just wait."

Her brows dip. "But I want to touch you."

"You will touch me." Even saying the words makes my already straining cock leap. And if she touches me now, my control might slip. "Just let me touch you first."

I see by the way her lashes flutter that she doesn't have any real objections to this. Indeed, when I clasp the waistband of her yoga pants, she lifts her hips so the pants and a pair of pale pink panties slip right off. For the third time in less than twenty-four hours, I'm treated to the sight of the tiny triangle of curls hiding her sex. In the garage when I had no more control than a falling boulder. In the steam of the shower where Evie held the reins. And now, here in the quiet of my room, where I can look all I want.

She is grace. From head to toe.

Pardon and innocence and forgiveness all at once. A clean conscience and a cleaner soul.

Everything I want. As close as I'll ever come.

I long to touch her most sensitive spots. Roll her nipples between thumb and forefinger. Lap again at the crest of her cleft. Shape her perfect behind with both hands.

344

But that can wait. Instead, I glide fingers down both sides of her waist, making her suck in a surprised breath.

"Turn over," I coax. And Evie, curious as always, narrows her eyes in scrutiny for a long moment. But then, game and fluid as always, she rolls onto her stomach, giving me the mesmerizing view of her backside.

The artful line of her spine... the angles of scapula and sacrum... the taut roundness of her bottom all conspire to strangle me.

I stifle a groan because I can't kiss and stroke and worship everything at once. Instead, I touch my fingertips to the middle of her back and sweep upward, letting my short nails graze lightly over the sweet expanse of skin.

"*Mmmm...*" Her pillow-muffled moan is my reward. And also my guide. I move up, down, along her shoulders, above her buttocks. Lightly raking my nails over every inch. Evie gradually sinks further into the bed, her breath coming in full, sweeping sighs.

"Oh my God... I love this." Her words pour out slow like honey. I chuckle at her obvious pleasure, lean over, and plant an open-mouth kiss on her spine. Evie hums again. And then I trade fingernails for thumbs and start working them into her muscles.

Her next moan is deeper. And deeply gratifying.

"That's... just... *amazing.*"

With firm pressure, I move my hands a couple of inches lower, fanning outward from her spine to her sides.

"Do you know…" she says before pausing for a long exhale, "that massage has been a healing art for more than five thousand years?"

I didn't know this, but, of course, Evie does. "You don't say." My touch moves lower, reaching the two dimples at the small of her back above her bottom. Evie has her head turned to the right, resting on her left cheek. Her eyes are closed, but her lashes flutter when my fingertips sweep the top of her buttocks. "Tell me more."

"China… Egypt… and later I-India," Evie stammers when I gently squeeze each globe of her magnificent, heart-shaped behind. The flesh, firm though it is, yields to my hands with ball-tightening satisfaction.

"India?" I prompt after several seconds of silence — seconds I have used to massage the creases above her thighs.

"*Mmm*… Yes…" Evie draws in a deep breath, but she doesn't open her eyes. "Like yoga," she says, speaking slowly, "its arrival in the west is fairly recent…"

I grip and release the back of her thighs, my thumbs swirling against the softest skin on the insides of her legs. When she squirms just a little, rubbing her pelvis into the mattress, I don't miss it.

I flatten myself against the bed beside her and kiss her, open-mouthed again, behind one knee.

Her gasp tears through the room. "Drew. *Oh my God.*" When I move and repeat the motion on the other leg, she turns her face into the pillow and smothers her moan. It looks as though she's fighting to keep herself still.

I grin at her struggle and bare my teeth.

"Drew!" she squeals, and I swear, the sound of my name has never made me so happy. She feels my laughter along her limbs and kicks like a swimmer. "I'm ready to turn over."

I gently squeeze her calves and dot the backs of her thighs with soft kisses. "Not yet," I whisper. When I nudge her legs apart, she stills at once.

"But I want to touch you now." There's a plea in her voice, and it moves me. Outside and in. But I'm not stopping yet.

"You're just going to have to wait your turn," I gently scold.

She sighs, but since I've inched my hands a little higher between her legs, I don't think it's out of frustration. I move higher still.

"But I want to give all this to you," she protests.

Okay, maybe there's a little frustration. She wants to give. But she's always giving.

"Evie, why don't you just take for a little while?" My hands rise ever so slowly.

"Because... Because—" She gasps when my thumbs part her.

When I touch the slickness of her petals, I'm the one who moans. She's so wet. So ready. How can this be for me?

The urge to taste her again sweeps aside all my careful plans. With a barely restrained force, I flip her over and catch the startled look on her face before I bury mine between her legs.

The scent and taste of her arousal drive me mad. I fill my hands with her ass and strain against her, my

347

tongue chasing and dancing with her swollen clit. Evie calls my name.

At first, she stretches the word out, cooing it with something like praise. But then urgency cuts the sound short. I hear this — the rising desperation in her voice — but it seems to happen a long way off. Not in the immediate realm of her slick flesh, the tightening of her thighs, and the tiny quivers I can almost taste.

It's when she threads her finger into my hair and tugs hard that I finally hear what she says.

"Drew, *now*. Make love to me *now!*"

I raise my eyes to find her face flushed, her upper lip dotted with sweat. It's the look of erotic anguish that launches me. I move up her body, grab at the ridiculous box of Trojans, and tear one away in mere seconds.

"Yes… Oh thank God…" Evie pants as I roll the thing down over my straining cock. She reaches for me, and her hand closes around me. I cover her grip with mine and guide myself to her opening. The very tip of my sex touches the very edge of hers.

And I stop.

Our eyes lock.

I'm not sure what I expect to see in the green depths of her eyes. Desire? Need? Those are there, but what I see — what makes me want to freeze this moment and live in it for all of time — arrests me like the law never could.

Evie stares into my eyes as if she's seeing the answer to every question. In me.

"Drew," she says my name again, but it's different this time. Centered. Sure. And I know exactly what she's about to say. She's going to give me her heart.

And I have to stop her. Not for good. Just long enough to give her mine first. She's always the one giving. And what more do I have to offer? At least I can take the plunge first. Make it safe for her.

I cover her mouth with mine and drive my hard flesh into her softness. Evie cries out as I fill her, and I catch each sound with teeth and tongue. They are mine now.

When her body clamps around me, my plan to offer her everything I have goes fuzzy at the edges. Her hips lift to take me all the way, and my mind nearly empties. For a moment, I'm aware of nothing but my joining with her. The pull to be deeper inside the sweetest, purest love I've ever known.

Evie's.

But also mine.

What I have for her is the best I've ever had. The best I've ever been. Here. Now.

I draw back and plant myself deep again, the full-body pleasure of it curling my spine, blowing my mind.

I break our kiss, inhale, exhale, and sense returns. And once again, I find myself wrestling for control. Somehow, I must manage three things at once: Hold back the tide of my own desire, even as Evie mirrors my movements thrust for thrust. Bring her to her pleasure before I surrender to my own. And tell her I love her.

But surely Evie deserves more than those three words.

How do I say it? She has freed me and captured me at the same time. Because of her, I can see a future where only shadows lurked before. Loving her makes me better. Better than the man I was.

The truths of loving her tangle themselves up with the sensation of making love to her. Her breasts against my bare chest, our hearts beating above and below each other. Her eyes locked with mine, silently witnessing as past and future surrender to now. The rhythm of our joining that grows more powerful, more blinding with each thrust.

I grasp for the words, but tongue and brain have both ditched language for other interests.

And then failure threatens on every front.

"Drew, my darling," Evie begins, and it's the claim that tips me over the edge. Nerves light up all down my spine, tightening my balls, and firing my glutes. "I—"

I'm going to come. Like never before. And Evie's not there yet.

The words — as feeble and insufficient as they are — spill from me. "I love you... I love you, Evie." And even as my control fractures, I angle my hips and drive into her, gripping her ass and heaving her into me. Hoping, praying that the pressure is enough. The friction is enough.

That I am enough to give her what she needs.

And by some miracle, her brow creases. Evie turns her head to the side, biting her lip and wearing the look of exquisite agony, as we both break. Our bodies crash and crash and crash against each other, and I'm pretty damn sure my heart explodes.

But, after a moment of white-hot oblivion, I feel it beating again, slowing in its race to my death, taking cues from Evie's heart, already easing to recovery.

I try to listen for the sound of hers, but all I get is a small giggle.

350

And then another.

Evie is laughing. I lift my head from the crook of her neck and peer down at her in confusion. This just makes her giggle harder. Then, to my great amusement, she snorts. And I collapse on top of her, sacked by my own laughter.

Laughing at God knows what, gasping for breath, and probably suffocating Evie, I struggle to understand. "Wha... What's so funny?"

But she just laughs, and I'm only half-joking when I ask her, "I-is this a thing? Should I pr-prepare myself... for this... every time?"

And at this she laughs so hard, she stops making noise. I find the strength to push into a half-plank to give her lungs room because how can she be breathing? But she must be breathing because her face is flushed with joy, even as her eyes run.

She is beautiful. She is everything beautiful.

Evie shakes her head and wipes her eyes. "No," she manages on a gasp. And, I have to admit, a small part of me is disappointed. If she really did dissolve into laughter after every time we make love, I wouldn't mind.

"It's just that..." She inhales and sighs, looking up at me with wide-eyed wonder. "You beat me to it."

I blink and feel my face flame. "Sorry about that. It's been a long ti—"

"No, silly." She gives me a playful scowl and drapes her wrists around my neck. "Not that. We tied there... I mean... W-what... you said," she stammers, looking suddenly shy.

Forgetting my own embarrassment, I arch a brow. "When I said I love you?"

Evie bites her bottom lip and nods.

I did beat her to it. But just barely. Thank God.

"I needed to say it first. So you'd have no doubt I meant it."

She gazes up at me, her face softening. "I love you, Drew. I love you, too."

I knew she'd say the words. But I had no idea they'd feel like this. Like a divine rain that washes the soul clean.

I lower again and kiss her. Kiss her with all I have.

Evie has come prepared.

In addition to tooth brush and pajamas, she has brought her yoga mat. And after leaving my arms, protesting that she needed to get ready for bed, Evie, brushed and changed, rolls out the mat alongside my bed.

"So there's a nighttime yoga routine?" I ask, watching her line up the edges of her mat with the wood planks of the floor."

"There's several, actually." She lowers down onto the mat on hands and knees. From my spot on the bed, her pjs, a baby blue tank top and blue and white striped shorts, look both innocent and sinful.

"Several?"

Evie sways her lower back and points her chin to the ceiling, drawing back her shoulders. Then she drops her chin and reverses the curve of her spine.

"Yep," she says, exhaling. "Tonight'll be a short one. I'm exhausted." Spreading her knees, she sits back on her heels, hinges at the waist, and folds like a clamshell, her hands stretching out in front of her.

I roll onto my side to keep my eyes on her. "What's that called?"

When Evie answers, her voice echoes from under her arms. "Extended child's pose. Super relaxing." And she does sound pretty relaxed. "It helps you get to sleep."

I picture our activities for the last hour. "You think you'll have trouble sleeping?" There might be a hint of self-congratulation in my voice. I know she hears it when her shoulders shake in silent humor.

Evie turns her face to me, peering at me over her outstretched arm. "Any other day, honey, and I'd be asleep already."

I do my best to keep my grin wry. *Honey.* Warmth marks my insides like I've swallowed whiskey. Sometimes, Evie makes it damn hard to be stoic.

But after the feeling sinks in, I catch her words and sharpen my focus.

"You still worked up about your parents?"

She shrugs, her arms still outstretched. Evie's young, but the motion makes her look younger. Almost childlike. She may be strong and stubborn and magical and amazing.

But she's vulnerable too.

"Would telling me what happened help?" Again, I don't want to push her, but I also don't want her to take her worries to bed if I can offload some of them.

Evie rises and then swings her legs out in front of her, making her body an "L". "I don't know. Maybe," she says, sounding doubtful. Before my eyes, Evie folds over, sandwiching her torso over her legs.

My eyes bug at the sight of her.

"What?" she asks, resting her cheek atop her right shin and watching me from this unnatural position.

"My hamstrings are screaming just looking at you."

I think it's my horrified tone that makes her laugh. *"Paschimottanasana.* Seated forward fold. Great for stretching the posterior chain and lower back. It helps get the body ready for hours lying down."

"I'll take your word for it."

She giggles again and sits up before sprawling onto her back and raising her knees. "And this one is Bridge Pose. Whenever I have insomnia, this is my go-to." Her feet stay planted on her mat as she lifts her hips. Then she clasps her hands beneath her, tucking her shoulders under her. She tilts her chin toward the ceiling, and her spine seems to follow, as though she's doing an abbreviated back bend.

The hem of her tank rides up, exposing the pale skin of her taut abdomen. Every line of her is lean and strong. But still somehow soft. Inviting. I'd love to run a hand all the way up her body and back down again.

Maybe she'll let me do that when she comes to bed. For now, she looks pretty focused. And who am I to mess with her concentration?

"Do you have insomnia a lot?"

Without turning to look at me, she speaks to the ceiling. "Sometimes. I try not to get stressed out, but I can't sleep when I do." Evie releases her hands and lowers herself to the mat, from neck to hips. Then she turns to face me. "If I weren't with you tonight, I'd definitely be stressing."

354

She's been hinting about the dinner with her parents all night, but not telling me straight out. "Tell me what happened."

Evie crosses her ankles, grabs one in each hand and rocks herself one... two... three times and is then standing at the foot of her mat. As usual, I'm impressed, but I stay quiet, wanting her to know I'm listening.

She does a little pirouette, bends over, and starts rolling up her mat. "It's not so much what happened as what it means," she says cryptically.

I scoot over, making sure she has room to come to bed. Again, I say nothing. She wants to tell me. That much is clear. But something is holding her back. Without looking at me, she stuffs her yoga mat back into its sling.

She totes it to the corner by the bathroom where she's left her backpack and returns to me. I reach for her as she climbs into bed, claiming her. Already needing to touch her again.

Evie lets me tuck her against me.

And it feels so fucking good.

She snuggles into me and gives a contented sigh that tells me she agrees. And I realize she's the first woman I've slept with. Like this. Curled up in bed with her secure in my embrace.

I might have passed out beside a girl I was making out with at a party, both of us drunk and senseless. But I wouldn't have needed to press her against my heart in the most fundamental of claims. The pleasure — the power of it — is shocking.

Humbling.

Because the way she's hitched up against me, folded into my embrace with her legs tangled through mine, she's claiming me too.

Really, it all comes down to that.

She's here because she wants to be. She wants to be with me. I can't imagine why, but I'm so goddamned grateful I could die of it.

"Mmmm," she moans softly, nuzzling my neck. "I wish I could stay right here for about a year."

I press a kiss to her cheek. "I'm game, but I don't think you can stay still that long," I tease.

The left side of her mouth comes up, but though she's grinning, it doesn't meet her eyes. "Maybe just a few weeks then," she says, her tone a little rueful. "At least until my parents go back to Abuja."

"Spill it, Guppy." It's so obvious now. She's nervous about telling me what happened. I ignore the flash of tension that streaks through my middle. My job is to comfort *her*.

She tilts her head back against my bicep and stares at the ceiling. "I guess I'm in denial."

"About what?" If she says me — if they're trying to make her see reason — I won't put up a fight.

"About who they revealed themselves to be tonight." She flicks her gaze to mine. "My parents, I mean."

I frown. "What do you mean?"

Her lashes lower, and I can tell by the line that appears between her brows she's lost in thought, in her memories of the evening. Then she looks back at me. "You know how when you're little, you think your parents can do anything? That they never make a mistake?"

I bunch my lips, weighing my own words. "It's been a long time since I thought that." My old man used to hang the moon as far as Anthony and I were concerned. Then he left. "But, yeah, I know what you mean."

"It's been a long time for me too. Probably around twelve or thirteen—"

I bite down on my grin because that's about five years later than I came to the conclusion that my parents didn't have all the answers.

"And, trust me, even though I loved them, in high school, I thought they were wrong about nearly everything," she says, and the look in her eye has me picturing a rebellious teenaged Evie. The image I come up with is adorable, but to keep her talking, I hold my tongue.

"But it's only been recently that I've really questioned their decisions. Their beliefs." Her green eyes are clouded with doubt. "It makes me wonder if I really knew them... and it's like the rug has been pulled out from under my feet."

She casts her eyes down, and I wait for her to continue, but as I do, I just watch as her frown deepens, and she looks more and more upset.

"Tell me, Evie." I give her a squeeze.

Her mouth twists to the side, and she blinks at me. "Maybe it's really not that big of a deal."

"Tell me."

She huffs a sigh. "They offered to send me to Europe for six months."

If I weren't holding Evie's warm body against me, I would swear someone has splashed me with ice water. Because I know how much she wants to travel.

A sinister fear uncoils in my belly. Whatever I do, I must keep it in check. If this is the way she leaves me, I have to make it easy.

But then my mind starts going. Maybe this is why she found it so hard to tell me. What if she chose to wait until after we made love to break the news?

I don't know how I feel about that. Right now, there's too much to feel. A whirlwind of emotions begins to take shape in me, around me. Would I have done it? Made love to her? If I knew she'd go now? Tomorrow?

Yes. God, yes.

Would I have told her I love her?

The question stops me cold.

I'm not going to lie to myself. The answer to that is no. Just no. But I can't bring myself to regret saying it. I've never come close to saying it before. Never felt it before. So who knows if I'd ever feel it again. So, yeah, I'm glad I had the chance to feel that. The abandon to give her my all.

No matter what, I'll always have that.

I swallow, hoping my voice comes out even. "You gonna go?"

I feel the shock that jolts through her body. Evie gapes at me. "Are you kidding?" She looks disgusted. And maybe even a little offended. I mask my relief.

"I know you've always wanted to go," I say evenly.

She glares. "Drew, they're just trying to buy me." Her green eyes practically spark with ire. "Using money to make me do what they want. Of course I'm not going."

Of course she's not going. This is Evie. The incredible woman I love.

"I was stupid to ask," I say by way of apology.

She stares at me a minute, the glare fading by degrees. "Yeah," she says with just a hint of sourness. "You were."

I can't help my chuckle. "I'm sorry," I say, apologizing for doubting her and now for laughing.

She narrows her eyes at me, but her own smile is undeniable. "You're forgiven." But she watches me, and I see thoughts pass behind her eyes. Her hand comes to my chest as worry cinches her mouth. "Did you want me to go?"

"God, no." My hand clutches hers to my heart, a reflex to keep her near me. My answer came out too fast, too uncontrolled. I pull in a breath, let it out and try again, forcing myself to ease the pressure against her hand. Still, I can't make myself let go. "I mean, if you wanted to go, I'd be happy for you."

I'm relieved to find it's not a lie. I'd be devastated for me. I'd be shucked like an oyster. But I'd treasure her happiness. Cede to it.

She scrutinizes me for a long moment, and I feel like she's trying to see into my head. Witness this battle that wages inside me. Evie bites her lip, and suddenly she looks so vulnerable, so lost.

"I feel like I don't know anyone. What I thought of my parents was really just an illusion. A projection of what I wanted to see... I still love them, but the illusion is gone now." she says, looking anguished. Her green eyes, now pooling, flick between each of mine. "It's frightening."

I wrap my arm around her again. "Evie—"

"Let me finish," she rasps.

I close my mouth and lock my gaze with hers. "I'm listening."

She blinks back her tears, and I see the effort she makes to master her emotions. She's trying so hard to be strong. Watching her yanks at something inside me. I want her to know that here, in my arms, she doesn't have to be strong.

Evie takes a deep breath, and I watch her resolve harden like iron. "I don't want any illusions between us. I need to know that the person I'm with is real. No fronts. No hidden agendas." I watch her swallow, and then my beautiful Evie looks at me with real fear in her eyes. "Can you give me that?"

I don't stand a chance. Whatever I have is already hers, and if this is what she wants, who am I to deny her?

"You want real?" I ask, my voice coming out hoarse.

She bites her lower lip but nods. "Yes."

As we stare at each other, the room goes so quiet, I'm sure neither of us is breathing. I'm about to give her all the power, leaving nothing for myself.

But maybe that's love, right?

"Evie, I love you so fucking much it's tearing me in two. I want to be with you, touch you, kiss you, know everything about you, and give you all the nothing I have," I tell her, sounding just as unstable as I feel. "And at the same time, I want you to hurry up and come to the conclusion that anyone else would have already landed on. And that's the fact that I am not even half the man you deserve."

She scowls. "Drew—"

"No." I shake my head. "You asked for real. Now you let *me* finish."

She blinks, taken aback. "Okay," she says a little curtly but nodding. *"I'm* listening."

Evie's still cradled in my left arm, but I'm leaning over her, staring down into the bottomless wells of her eyes. I let go and fall in.

"I know it'll happen. You'll figure it out, and you'll go. I know it, and at the same time, I dread it like death." I feel my own brow lift. "Worse than death, if I'm being honest. If you take your parents offer and hop on a plane, I'll drop to my knees. Because I won't be able to stand it. And because I know you'll be better off."

My heart is pounding so hard, I'm sure she can feel it, pressed against her as I am. And my throat is so tight it sounds like I'm growling, but I've put it all out there.

"Now there's nothing you don't know about what I think and how I feel." I want it to sound like a dare, but in all honesty, my voice softens with relief.

Unable to resist, I cup her cheek. She's so lovely. I clench my teeth against desire, against this aching knowledge that I'm screwed. Defying all sense, confessing I want her to go has made me hard again.

"You finished?" she asks, her voice almost a whisper.

Breath leaves me in a rush, something between laughter and surrender. But I've already surrendered, so it must be gallows humor.

"Yeah, Guppy."

My breathing slows as I gaze at her. And as I calm down, I realize she's glowing. Her face is shining even before she really smiles. When she does smile, it's slowly, and then it's huge.

"What are you grinning at?"

Did I just feel her wriggle her thigh against my cock?

Yeah. Yeah, I did.

She shrugs innocently. "I'm happy."

This time my burst of breath is much closer to a laugh. "Why? I just told you I think we're doomed."

"You told me," she begins, beaming as brightly as ever, "everything I thought you would."

I screw my face up in confusion. "And the fact that I think we're doomed makes you happy."

Evie shakes her head, giggling deliciously. How can she look so sexy, laughing at our inevitable demise?

"No, you bull-headed Taurus." Her hand at my chest becomes a fist and she bops me with it. "I'm happy because I knew all of that already. How conflicted you are about us. How you think you don't deserve this... And how you love me..."

She pauses, and her eyes widen as though she's surprised herself by saying this aloud.

"I knew. I knew all of what you felt. And that means I really do know you. Not an illusion. I can trust you." And then her smile re-doubles. "Better yet, I can trust myself with you."

Evie reaches up, grabs me by the back of the neck, and tugs me down. She kisses me hard. I lose myself in her kiss like a man with a fever. But even lost in its power, I feel her other hand glide down my torso, down below my abdomen, where she grips me. Then she wrenches her mouth from mine, panting.

"And I fucking love you too."

362

CHAPTER TWENTY-SEVEN

EVIE

I awake to the arresting sight of Drew's muscled legs disappearing into a pair of jeans. He catches me watching as he tucks himself into the fly and grins.

"Go back to sleep, Guppy. I'm gonna walk Gem and then check on Grandma." He bends down, still shirtless and kisses me on the forehead. Even in the soft dawn light that just barely tints the apartment, he's breathtaking.

Did he just say he'd walk Gem? And I get to stay in bed? I stretch my limbs luxuriously. My body feels deliciously heavy and pleasantly sore in a few places. Another half-hour of sleep would be wonderful.

"Thank you." I stifle a yawn and roll onto my side.

Clearly, he finds my sleepy-headedness amusing because his grin has grown. It's probably because of my frizzed out curls. I resist the urge to pull the covers over my head. I close my eyes instead.

"Don't laugh at me," I mutter, feebly swatting a hand in his direction. Of course at this, he laughs.

"I'll be back." He chuckles. But without opening my eyes, I just nod. I think I hear the jingle of Gemini's leash and the excited *click-clack* of his dancing paws on the wood floor, but after that sleep pulls me under.

I open my eyes to full sun and Gem's warm body curled against the curve of my legs. I blink at the startling brightness, but it's obvious that Drew's not here. I push myself up and scan the floor at the head of the futon for my phone. It's right where I left it, and a press of the home button reveals that it's 7:52 a.m. My alarm will go off in eight minutes, but I don't have class until noon.

I flop back against the pillow. Where is Drew? It has to be at least an hour since he walked Gem. The sun wasn't even fully up then.

I frown. Doesn't he have work?

Did he leave for work without waking me?

I press my phone again and squint at the screen. I have three messages. Two from Mom. One from Tori. None from Drew. My sister's text is from last night around eleven o'clock.

Tori: You're a fool if you don't take M&D's offer. I had to put my life on hold for 3 years for that kind of payday. All you have to do is drop that loser.

A high-pitched snarl leaves my throat, and Gemini pops his head up at the sound, looking around the apartment for invaders or wild animals.

"Sorry, Gem," I croak, deleting the text. "Definitely too early for that."

I debate not reading the messages from Mom, but I decide that no matter what, I need to meditate for a little while, so I might as well get all of the potential stressors out of the way and then give myself time to clear my head.

Mom: Your father and I didn't mean to upset you last night. We just want you to know you have options. Maybe the two of us could talk today. What about lunch?

Mom: Are you awake?

The first message is time stamped at seven a.m. on the dot. The second from five minutes ago. I'll bet it was the buzz on my phone that woke me. I close my eyes and breathe in and out slowly three times.

It does me no good. The tension. The disappointment. The pain from last night are all still right there. Taking up space in my emotional body. I throw the covers aside and climb out of Drew's bed.

Drew's absence, I admit to myself, is another thing that's gnawing at me. Why didn't he wake me before he left?

I shoot him a text.

Me: Hey, did you leave already?

He might still be in Mrs. Vivian's house, but I'm not about to go down there and check. I put down my phone and make up the bed. I head to the bathroom, wash my face, and brush my teeth, trying to stay as present as possible.

The morning routine is enough to cleanse some of my tension, so I decide to try to sit in meditation. I put off getting dressed, knowing that my pjs are more conducive to a lotus pose than my jeans, and I crawl back onto Drew's futon to settle in. I silence my phone in case Mom decides to text a third time or, worse, call me.

I close my eyes, breathe, and let my body sink into stillness.

I follow my breath, the only sound in the room besides Gem's almost imperceptible snoring, and try to simply be.

But thoughts from last night just won't let me. And I relive the worst of them.

As though the dinner was scripted, my parents waited to address their "concerns" until after we'd ordered, chatting instead — Mom mostly — of life in Abuja and the aardvark that had decimated her flower beds in just one night.

365

But as soon as the vegetable pakoras arrived, their conversation became tactical.

Mom with her *"We're here because we care. You've got us worried these days…"*

And Dad's almost jokey delivery, smiling wide as he listed my crimes, *"You've got to admit, E, you haven't got the best track record when it comes to decisions with consequences… You quit school almost overnight. Not a word to any of us… And what about the time you found Gemini? Spotted him at the pet adoption outside Petco, when you were what? Supposed to be getting coffee for your boss? And when they wouldn't let you keep him in the office that afternoon, you quit. Remember that? Don't get me wrong, honey. We all love the little guy, but who do you think paid to get him de-wormed and vaccinated? And now this shady character you're seeing? My goodness, Evangeline…"*

My stomach burns right below my xiphoid process. Just like it did last night when I had to listen and defend, try to make them see that none of those decisions, quick though they were and life-changing as they might have been, were wrong for me.

Least of all Drew.

But it was like trying to start a campfire with wet matches. A lot of effort and mess and falling darkness. No warmth in sight.

And they couldn't understand why I was so offended when they tried to bribe me to leave.

Mom: *"Why can't you see this as an opportunity? You're young. You're free. No school schedule holding you down. No real responsibilities…"* As if my job means nothing. As if I can just walk away from Gemini.

Dad: *"Take six months. You know what I'd give for six months just to travel and see the world? This guy just got*

*out of prison, E. Pri-son. Let him get his life together. If he's
still on the straight and narrow when you get back, what have
you lost? If he's not, you've dodged a bullet, honey."*

And that was when I asked for the check. My dad
practically fell over himself in his attempt to grab the
thing from the server, but I took the little plastic-covered
book, stuffed a twenty and a five in, handed it back to
the guy, and left, angrier than I'd ever been in my life.

And, yes, I was angry on Drew's behalf. *Straight
and narrow.* My God. The man lives with his
grandmother. He pickles her okra. He tends her garden.
He takes care of her when she's sick.

He grieves his brother and wears his guilt like a
stone around his neck.

And still he has room in his heart to love me.

I breathe in and out. I didn't stick around to say
those things to my parents. Perhaps I should have.
Maybe I'd feel better now.

Now.

The thought comes as a much needed reminder. I
am not back there. I am here. Here in Drew's space. I
inhale and feel the slight scratch of the coarse cotton
bedspread beneath my bare legs. I exhale and hear the
whine of a siren in the distance. The sounds of Monday
morning. Inhaling again, I scan my attention over my
body, starting at the soles of my feet and moving up.

I note again the sweet soreness of my inner
thighs where I cradled Drew's weight more than once.
My hip joints, too, feel newly stretched and pleasantly
aware. The burn in my belly, my body's reflex to last
night's dinner, has cooled some, but I can still feel its
nagging.

367

I think I know what it means. The belly chakra is the seat of power. But am I struggling for power I don't need? Trying to control an outcome when l should just accept?

Or do I need to claim the power that is truly mine?

The distant siren has grown closer as though affirming for me that this is the answer I must hear. Opening my eyes, I give up on the sit. My mind is working too hard to allow simple awareness and observation any space.

But the burning knot in my gut is still there, and it feels so familiar. As if —

The siren wails, shrill and insistent. It can't be all the way on Congress Street. It's too loud. I push myself off the futon in time to look out the streetside window and see an ambulance on St. Joseph Street. But instead of racing past, it slows...

And pulls into Mrs. Vivian's driveway.

"Oh my God!"

I lunge for the door before skidding to a halt. I'm still in my pajamas — shorts that cover only a little more than panties and a tank top with no bra. I grab last night's yoga pants and kick my way into them, pulling them over my bottoms before doing the same with my cast-off tunic. I still don't have a bra, but oh well.

Gemini, smelling urgency and distress, whimpers and claws at the door.

"Stay, buddy," I say, wedging him aside and slipping out the door. I hear him bark as I shut it behind me, and I send up a silent apology as I take the stairs barefoot. Mrs. Vivian's back door is unlocked, and I don't even knock.

"Drew?" I enter calling his name because the kitchen is empty. I scan the dining room and the living room, but there's no sign of him or his grandmother. And it's then that a knock sounds against the front door.

"Drew!" By some miracle the deadbolt flips easily under my shaking fingers, and I pull the door open for the EMTs. "What's wrong? What's happened?"

Wearing a look of shock, the guy pulling the stretcher opens his mouth to answer, but I hear Drew.

"Evie, back here!"

I've never passed Mrs. Vivian's living room before, but I take off toward the direction of his voice, one of the medics at my heels. Family pictures, stitch samplers, and a crucifix blur in the periphery as I tear down the hall. I hear coughing and rush to the bedroom at the far end.

Drew is there, leaning over Mrs. Vivian who slouches against the headboard. Her lips are blue and her face misted in sweat.

She looks ancient.

I quickly step aside to let the medics push through, bringing with them the stretcher and an explosion of questions.

"When did the shortness of breath start?... Are you on any medication?... Are you having any chest pains?"

Mrs. Vivian struggles to answer them, panting her voice barely audible. She coughs again, but it sounds dry and feeble.

"She's recovering from shingles," Drew says when one of the medics asks if Mrs. Vivian has been ill recently. It's when he speaks that I see he's shaken, his own color washed out. The urge to go to him is primal,

369

but the room is crowded with five people and a stretcher, and Mrs. Vivian's bed separates us.

So instead of going to comfort him, I concentrate on exuding calm from where I stand pressed against the far wall. Help is here. In fact, the two paramedics, a young African American woman, and a short, stocky redheaded guy, minister to Mrs. Vivian with swift and sure motions, the woman fitting an oxygen mask over her mouth and nose, draping the tank on the bed beside her, while the man checks her blood pressure.

"BP is 182/118," he says. "Mrs. Quincy, have you taken your blood pressure medicine today?"

Drew's grandmother shakes her head, her eyelids looking heavy. The medic glances over his shoulder at Drew.

"Do you know where it is? Last thing we want now is a stroke."

Drew turns to the door. "I'll get it."

But I leap ahead of him. "I'll get it. Just tell me where to find it."

Our eyes meet for the first time since I rushed in ahead of the paramedics, and I see something pass over Drew's face. Gratitude? Relief? Whatever it is, he looks glad to see me.

"On the counter by the coffee pot. The Nadalol," he says.

I nod, give him a bracing smile, and dash out. The medicine bottle is exactly where he said it would be. Right next to the coffee pot, which is full and smells fresh. I hadn't noticed in my mad dash through the house, but there's also a pan of biscuits on the stove.

Mrs. Vivian couldn't have made these. Drew must have.

I fill a glass of water and race back to Mrs. Vivian's bedroom, but I do it loving Drew Moroux just a little more.

When I return, Mrs. Vivian's color looks a little better, thanks, I'm sure, to the oxygen. This time I aim for Drew's side, and as soon as I hand the medicine and water off to the paramedic, I lay a supportive hand on Drew's back.

He glances down at me, eyes soft.

"They think it's pneumonia," he says quietly. "They're taking her in."

The female EMT is making adjustments to the stretcher, lowering it even with Mrs. Vivian's bed before wheeling it around to the side.

"People my age... go to the hospital," Mrs. Vivian pants, the words muffled by the plastic mask, "and never come out."

I glance at Drew to see his jaw tighten. "You have to go, Grandma. And I don't want to hear any more talk about dying."

His grandmother shrugs, looking petulant. "Might just be my time."

Under my hand, I feel his back stiffen. "Grandma—"

"You're a beautiful girl," Mrs. Vivian says to me, talking over Drew, but pausing to cough dryly behind the mask. "Just right for him...You'll take good care of him... Knew it the day you met."

I don't know what to say to this, but I lean into Drew's side, and as if by instinct, he clutches me to him.

"Enough of the drama, Grandma," Drew scolds. His tone may be light, but I don't miss the fear in it.

"Don't commend me to Evie's care like you're settling your affairs."

The old woman's eyes smile. "My affairs are already settled, Andrew."

Drew gives a low grumble of frustration, but Mrs. Vivian just bats a withered hand at him. "Don't upset yourself." She coughs again and takes a few gulps of air. "I've done everything... I wanted to do... And I don't plan on that stopping... anytime soon."

When Drew's shoulders relax, I feel it down the length of my body. I squeeze him around the middle.

"Good. Aunt Josie, Aunt Shelly, and Annie are going to meet us at the hospital." He makes it sound like a warning. "And they're not gonna want to hear any of that talk either."

"Alright, Mrs. Quincy," the female paramedic says, reaching across the bed to her. "We're just going to get you onto the gurney, nice and easy."

I look up at Drew and whisper, "What can I do?"

His eyes run over me and then narrow as though he's calculating. "You have class today."

I do, but that doesn't matter at the moment. "You have work too, don't you?"

The corner of his mouth turns up just a little, but regret quickly swallows the grin. "I called my cousin to see if I could come in late. I made breakfast. I wanted to drive you to work."

My heart thumps a clumsy beat in my chest, and warmth floats like a veil over my skin. This is what it feels like to know Drew's love.

I swear, there's nothing better.

But I want him to feel the same from me. I want to give him whatever he needs.

"You need to ride with Mrs. Vivian. My morning's free. I'll pack a bag for her and bring it to you at the hospital."

The way he blinks tells me he hasn't thought this far. But if Mrs. Vivian has pneumonia — if she's on oxygen as we speak — she's not coming home tonight. And the look of dread as Drew comes to this conclusion squeezes my heart.

The medics have Mrs. Vivian strapped onto the stretcher. They raise it, make a few adjustments, and then begin to negotiate her through the bedroom.

Drew nods. "Okay. Yeah." But then he reaches into his pocket and pulls out a set of keys. "But take Grandma's car. Meet me at the hospital — General — and I'll drive you to work. I'll need a way to get home anyway."

I don't understand why driving me to work is important to him, but I see it is. Who am I to argue? I take the keys from him.

"Okay. I can find a ride home after."

He shakes his head. "I'll come get you."

I frown at him and let my eyes follow the medics as they move the stretcher through the bedroom door. "But you'll have your hands full. I—"

"I'll come get you," he says again, moving toward the door. "I won't be going to the garage today. Just let me know what time."

I follow. "I finish at four." And then I frown. "I wish I could stay with you. Help whatever way I could."

Drew stops at the door. Then he's standing right in front of me. Pulling me into a tight embrace, He plants a quick kiss on my lips. "You are helping. See you at the

373

hospital." He releases me and then is out the door. But from the hallway, I hear him call. "I love you!"

"I love you, too!"

The front door closes, and I stand in Mrs. Vivian's bedroom, a little lost for a moment. My life has tilted on its axis a few times since I met Drew. It tilts now. A heady wave of awareness washes over me. A moment of clarity that is present, past, and future all at once.

It is as though future me is seeing the present me standing at the foot of Mrs. Vivian's bed and recognizes this moment — outside of time — as the turning point. The one that separates my life from who I was and who I will be.

The sensation makes me shiver, and as soon as I do, it's gone. I blink and make myself move. *Pack some things for Drew's grandmother,* I tell myself. Using her bed as a staging area, I gather her reading glasses and the copy of *Garden Gate* magazine from her bedside table. Her robe and slippers, a clean nightgown and underwear make the pile. I take everything that seems to orbit her bathroom sink: hairbrush, toothbrush, face cream, and bobby pins.

I find a small, leather valise in Mrs. Vivian's closet. It's mauve and it looks like something from *TV Land.* And I can't help but wonder when was the last time Mrs. Vivian went on a trip. I open the clamshell lid and find it empty, with the exception of the quilted lining of the interior and the air that likely has been trapped in there since 1975. I quickly pack her clothes and toiletries, lock the front door and go out again through the back.

With her case in one hand and Drew's keys in the other, I stare at the steps that lead up to his apartment and try to make a decision.

Gemini. I need to let him out again before I leave and am gone until four. Do I take him back to Janine's. Would Drew mind if he stayed in the apartment all day? Would Gem freak out?

"Evie?"

I whip my head in the direction of my old house to see both of my parents hurrying off our back porch toward the fence.

"We heard sirens—"

"What's going on?"

Mom and Dad talk over each other, advancing with identical looks of worry.

"Are you alright?"

"Did he hurt you?"

My jaw sets. I place the valise on the bottom stair and slowly, mindfully cross Mrs. Vivian's back yard. My parents need to be set straight, but I know my knee-jerk anger at their assumptions and prejudices against Drew won't help me.

I reach the fence, and before I can say anything, each of my parents grabs one of my hands — as though if they just hold on tight enough, they can keep me from every harm.

"The sirens were from an ambulance," I say evenly and watch as their eyes bug and their mouths fall open.

"What—"

"Is—"

"Mrs. Vivian was having trouble breathing. They think it's pneumonia." Mom's hand flies to her mouth,

375

and Dad's brow creases in concern. "Drew left with her in the ambulance, and I'm headed to the hospital to bring her a few things."

"Is there anything we can do?" Mom asks, and while I'm grateful for the offer, I can't let her or Dad off the hook. I free my hands from theirs and stand up straight.

"Drew would never hurt me. Why would either of you jump to that conclusion?"

My parents glance at each other. I don't miss the hint of guilt in either of their faces. Mom speaks up.

"Well, you weren't returning my calls, and Janine said you stayed here last night—"

"You called Janine?" My voice pitches higher all by itself.

My mother lowers her gaze as well as her voice. "Your father actually went over there."

I glare at him. "What the hell, Dad? It's not even nine in the morning."

"Honey, we're only in town for another week," Dad says, going straight for the guilt. "We want to see you, and we want to work things out."

I nod, acknowledging the truth in this. But that burning triangle in my middle is starting to glow yellow again. I hate being at odds with them. But I also hate the expectations they have for me.

"Everything will be worked out when you guys realize that I'm an adult, and I will lead my own life."

This time Mom frowns. "Evie, you have to know that's exactly what we want for you. For you to be ready to lead your own life. We—"

I put up a hand to stop her. "No...No." The edge in my voice is made of stone. I don't think I've ever heard it before. "Do you hear yourself? Because I do. You are saying that you *want me to be ready*. I'm saying I *am ready*. And even if I'm not, Mom, even if I have to plow headlong through years of mistakes, they are mine to make."

Dad wraps his arm around Mom's waist and pulls her closer. They look united. Indivisible. "Evie, one day, I hope, you'll be a parent, and then you'll understand. The hardest thing in the world is watching your child *plow headlong through years of mistakes*," he says, echoing my words with an uncomfortable emphasis. "If you'd only just let us help you, we could save us all a lot of misery."

I sigh. This is getting us nowhere. And Drew is waiting for me.

"You want to help me? Right now?" I ask, moving my gaze back and forth between them.

"Yes, of course," Mom says.

"You know we do, E," Dad says.

I nod tightly. "Good. Stay right here." Without giving them a chance to respond, I turn and sprint across the yard before taking Drew's stairs two at a time. I open his apartment door and find Gem already standing behind it, pacing with excitement. "Guess what, Gemini? You're going to spend some quality time with Grandma and Grandpa today."

I work his squirming body into the harness and clip on his leash. "Let's go." His descent down the wrought iron stairs makes just as much noise as his climb did last night, but when he sees my parents at the back fence, Gem pulls so hard he nearly dislocates my shoulder.

Barking with joy, Gemini bounds up to the fence and slaps the top of it with his paws.

"Gem!" Mom squeals as he licks her face, but she doesn't push him away. My dad just laughs when he gets the same treatment. The reunion is so happy and uncomplicated I find myself smiling too.

Thank God for dogs.

Dad scrubs Gemini's head with rough affection. "So... uh... he stayed with you last night?" he asks, keeping his eyes on my dog.

"Yeah, Dad. Drew says he's welcome."

Tight-lipped, Dad nods. He presses his mouth to the gold flap of Gem's ear." Good boy," he whispers.

I roll my eyes. "Gem really loves Drew." I bite down on the urge to confess that I do too. "He's a great judge of character. Maybe you should give Drew a chance."

An uncomfortable silence settles over the three of us. Fine. We're done talking if we can't talk about this.

"Look, I have to go. Gem can stay in Drew's apartment or he can go back to Janine's but if—"

"We'll look after him," Mom chimes in eagerness brightening her eyes. "We'd love to. Wouldn't we, Elliot?"

Dad scratches Gemini under his chin, one of his favorite spots. Gem's lips pull into a canine smile. My dad chuckles. "I sure have missed this face," he mutters. Then he looks up at me. "I know you're asserting your independence and all that, but are you okay for money? Dog food and heartworm prevention and flea medicine is expensive. I wouldn't want him to miss a dose because you were short."

I raise a brow at him. "I'm not short, Dad." But he's right. Those things are expensive, and even though I need to make sure Gem's covered, I haven't really had a chance to sit down and iron out my budget. It is about time for his monthly flea treatment...

But Mom and Dad don't need to know that.

"We just don't want to see you struggle when you don't have to," Mom says, her voice gentle.

I shake my head. "I'm not struggling. Really, I'm fine."

"Evie, we know how much things cost," Dad says. His voice is even, but the subtext leaves little room for misinterpretation. Either I don't know how much things cost or I know and I'm simply in denial about being able to support myself.

"Good thing I have two jobs, Dad. And I have things to do before I go to the first one. Here." I tug Gemini away from the fence so he's back on all fours again, and then I brace my knees and scoop him up, one arm around his chest, the other under his rump.

"What are you doing?"

"Evie, my goodness—"

Gem protests in his own way, bucking as his tail spirals, but I hoist him over the fence and into Dad's arms.

"Good heavens. He weighs a ton." My dad grunts and sets Gem to the ground in my old yard. I can't resist.

"Yeah," I say, panting. "I'm stronger than I look."

The waiting area in the LGMC ER is crowded and loud. I don't see Drew anywhere. I didn't text him to let him know I was here because I don't want him feeling rushed on my account. I still have more than an hour before I need to be at the studio, and if he can't leave, I have plenty of time to get a ride.

I scan the room again and spot a cluster of women at the nurse's station. It's been years since I've seen her up close, but I swear one of them is Annie Moroux. She's with two women I think I recognize as Drew's aunts, and they are talking to a nurse.

I make my way to them, and Annie raises her gaze to mine as I approach.

"Evie," she says with recognition. And is that relief in her eyes? She breaks away from the group of women, but I notice they all turn to look at me. Even the nurse — who is wearing a particularly ugly scowl.

"Hello," I say, nervously. "I'm sorry to interrupt. I'm looking for Drew—"

Annie grips me by the arm. "Come on." She spins me around and drags me in the opposite direction.

"Is everything okay?" My gut tightens with worry. "Mrs. Vivian? Is it bad?"

Annie glances back over her shoulder. "That nurse is my mom."

For an instant I'm just dumbstruck, and then it hits me. Annie's mom. Drew's mom. The one person who won't forgive him.

"Oh… I'm guessing that's not good."

Annie looks back at me, shaking her head. "It's not." But then she forces a smile. "But it's good to see you, and I'm glad you're here."

She leads me away, and before I know it, we're walking past the hospital cafe and through the side exit that opens onto Hospital Drive. As soon as we're out on

380

the elevated walkway, I see him. He's sitting on the steps with his back to us.

Alone.

"Look who I found?" Annie announces, sounding far too cheery. Drew turns, but before his eyes even land on me, I see his devastation. He's quick to hide it, wiping his expression clean, but I know he's hurting, and my guess is Annie knows too.

But she keeps talking, and it's so over-the-top cheerful, it's almost grating. "Guess I was right, about you two. Wasn't I, big brother?"

Drew blinks at Annie and gives her a weak imitation of a smile. "You were right." He's so miserable. I just want to hold him.

I give Annie a quick tap on the elbow. "Thanks for helping me find him." Our eyes meet, and I see the moment she reads my *I got this* look.

"Okay, well, I'm going to head back inside and see if there's any news on Grandma," she says, brightly. "I'll text you, Drew, if I hear anything."

Drew nods and watches his sister disappear inside. I walk over to the steps and drop down on the step above his, but he doesn't look at me. He's staring at his shoes, his profile perfectly blank.

"It's okay." I lay a hand on his back and rub in a slow circle. "You don't have to pretend you're alright with me."

The only change I notice is in the muscles of his jaw. They stand out as he wages whatever war he's fighting.

"It's okay," I say again. And then something in him snaps, and he turns to me with heartbreak in his eyes.

"Do you know what she said? When she saw me?"

He looks so raw, my throat threatens to close. I manage to shake my head.

Drew swallows. "Ma—" He breaks off and gives a violent shake of his head. "No. *Lottie...* Lottie took one look at me and said, 'You trying to kill my mama too?'"

A sound escapes me like I've been punched. Torn open. And I know this can't touch what he felt. What he's feeling now.

I grab his shoulders and haul him into me, cradling his head to my heart. For a moment, he doesn't move, and I'm afraid he's putting up his wall again, but then his arms slip under mine and wrap around my back, and his whole body sags.

And I feel it. His weight against me is love. It is trust. I know with a kind of heart-bursting certainty that he would give this to no one else. I run my fingers through his hair and hold him against my bursting heart.

We stay like this for a long time. Cars pass us. Hospital staff clop up and down the walkway, pretending they don't see. And maybe they don't. People must cling to each other all the time just outside of hospital doors.

I hope he doesn't need me to, but I say it just in case. I lower my lips to his soft hair. "You know it's not your fault Mrs. Vivian is sick, right?"

He makes a noise, and I can't tell if it's dispute or dispair. Drew shakes his head against me. "I don't know," he says, his words barely audible. "She's been coughing."

"Ah, well, that's different," I say, gently teasing. "Clearly, that's your fault."

His back shakes with the ghost of a laugh, and I stroke his head. When he looks up at me with that wry expression of his, I know he's okay. Hurt and upset. And scared. But okay.

I hold his gaze for a long time. "I don't think either of our parents have made great first impressions."

Drew frowns. "What did she say to you?"

"Nothing. She just gave me a dirty look when I asked for you."

His eyes narrow. Any trace of despair is gone. The man I love simply looks pissed.

I raise a finger and point at him. "See? That right there is how I feel when I think about what she said to you," I tell him, narrowing my own eyes. "I mean, how dare she?"

Drew's eyes brighten. "You gonna get in her face, Guppy?"

He's teasing me now, but I'll take it. Anything is better than how I found him.

"Don't think I won't. I'm tougher than I look."

He sniffs a laugh. "Don't I know it." Then he pushes himself to his feet and reaches down a hand to me. "C'mon. We gotta get you to work."

He tugs, and I pop up like a spring and land against him, trying not to giggle. Inspiration strikes.

"You know, I'm strong…"

"Yeah?" Drew squeezes my hand, and he starts walking, but instead of heading back inside, we take the sidewalk.

"But you're a hell of a lot stronger. With a little practice, we could do some amazing couples yoga poses."

383

"Oh, God, Guppy," he mumbles under his breath, but the line of his mouth twists with amusement.

"Have you ever seen any pictures of that? They're really beautiful... Sensual."

He arches a wicked brow at me. "Sensual, huh?"

I nod and bat my eyelashes at him. As we walk, I tell him some of the names. Supported Scorpion... Lifted Locust... Folded Leaf. I'd love to try some flying poses with him.

When we reach Mrs. Vivian's car, I hand over the keys.

"Are you going to come back here after you drop me off?"

Drew doesn't meet my gaze as he puts on his seatbelt. "Yes. I don't feel welcome, but I'm not there for anyone else but Grandma Q."

"Good," I tell him. "And for the record, I don't think you're unwelcome. Judging by the body language of Annie and your aunts, I think your mom's attitude makes them uncomfortable. If anyone's unwelcome, it's her."

It's not evolved to take a little pleasure in this. I should forgive Lottie Moroux for her misplaced anger and grief. And if I really think about it, I do. Sort of. But she's hurt Drew. For years. And I can't help the flush of hostility that inspires.

Drew starts the car and navigates it through the parking lot.

I can't explain it, but thinking about Lottie Moroux's rejection of her son makes my parents' acceptance of him that much more important to me. I want him to feel welcome. To feel he has a place to belong.

A family.

Without even having to think about it, I know that I'll only be spending Christmas with my family if Drew is welcome there too. I meant what I said to my parents. They need to give Drew a chance. Get to know him.

If they would just replace the scary picture they have of him with the real Drew, I know they would grow to love him. Who wouldn't?

He's soulful, yet silly. He's strong, yet so vulnerable. He's loyal.

If they had any idea how protective he is of me, they'd at least have to respect the man.

I glance over at him and know with certainty he isn't thinking about his mom or my parents. He's worried about Mrs. Vivian.

I wish there was something —

The car in front of us screeches to a halt, and Drew hits the brakes, reaching out his right arm to stop me from flying forward.

"What the hell?"

The car in front of us moves again as I see it, and my heart leaps into my throat.

"Oh, my God! It's a dog!"

A little black and gray scruff ball streaks across the sidewalk headed to the parking lot of South College Condominiums.

"He could have been killed." I plant my hands against my chest, trying to steady the painful pounding inside. If I were alone, I'd pull over. No doubt about it. I'd check for a tag and try to get in touch with owner.

"Can we—" I start to ask but stop myself. Drew is giving me a ride to work, and then he's going back to

385

the hospital to be with his sick grandmother. I can't ask him to go on a canine rescue mission with me.

"What?" Drew asks.

I swallow the words. "It's nothing."

We pass the complex, but I can't help but crane my neck to follow the little dog as he trots through the lot, heedless of cars that could turn off South College almost without slowing.

I'm squinting, but before he drops out of sight, I make myself accept that he doesn't seem to have a collar. That and his scraggly fur suggest no one is going to be coming home from work tonight and looking frantically for the little guy.

Not like I would.

I want to beg Drew to turn the car around so I can go find the little scruffy dog, take him home, and get him cleaned up. Gemini would love a buddy, and I—

I realize with a grimace that this is exactly the kind of impulse that drives my parents crazy.

Giving Drew a sidelong glance, I wonder with a knot in my gut if it's something that will eventually drive him crazy too.

CHAPTER TWENTY-EIGHT

DREW

ANNIE: They   admitted   Grandma   to geriatrics. Running tests now.

I make a noise in the back of my throat as I read my sister's text at the stop light. Evie's eyes snap to me. She's been quiet the last few minutes, but she's on high alert now.

"Bad news?" she asks, worry tightening her voice.

I shrug, put down the phone, and focus on traffic. "Not bad. Just… real." The hollow feeling in the pit of my stomach hasn't faded at all since I walked into Grandma Quincy's room and saw her like that.

And I should have known. When she wasn't in the kitchen with her coffee when I came in. I knew how bad she'd been coughing. I should have checked on her right then instead of telling myself to let her sleep while I made coffee and breakfast.

But I'd wanted to surprise her. Her and Evie.

I'm gripping the steering wheel hard, and Evie lays a hand on my elbow. "You're worried."

I glance at her and make the turn onto Johnston. "Of course, I'm worried. Grandma's eighty-three."

She's quiet for a moment, and then, "I hate worrying. I usually try to figure out what's underneath the worry, and then I feel that instead."

I can't help it. I look at her like she's crazy. Like she's my one and only Guppy.

She nods and drops her hand to my knee, smoothing it over my jeans. The touch isn't sexual. It's loving. If I could lean into it, press back, I would.

"What's underneath your worry, Drew?" Her voice is so gentle. It's like the pull of the tide on a calm day at the beach. I feel like I'm being tugged along with it. I turn into the lot of the Yoga Garden, park the car, and kill the ignition. I already know we're going to be here for a few minutes.

"I don't really get your question," I tell her, and I mean it. I'm not trying to be stubborn and block-headed. "I mean, isn't it obvious?"

Evie gives me a soft smile, but I can see a wisdom in her eyes that... well... I've never noticed in someone so young. I sure as hell didn't have it at twenty-one. "What's obvious?"

"Why I'm worried. I mean, Grandma's old. She's sick, and it's serious."

She watches me for a moment, but she's not searching my face. I think she's waiting. Waiting for me to take it a step further. But she can just keep on waiting because I'm not going to say that out loud.

Okay, maybe now I am being stubborn.

"Is it her death you're worried about?"

My breath escapes me like I've been punched in the gut. "Don't say that."

Her green eyes soften with compassion and what I now recognize as love, and she grips my hand. "I'm sorry. I didn't mean to upset you. It's just—" She stops, frowning a little as she presses her lips together.

"What?"

Evie shakes her head. "No. I'm not going to push. If you're not ready to talk about this, I don't want to make you."

But the initial shock — the instinctive recoil from the idea of death, the way someone jumps back when

388

they see a snake — has faded. And now, I'll be damned if I'll let her walk away without hearing what she has to say.

"No. I'm alright," I insist. "Tell me."

She looks at me now, and this time she is searching. Assessing. Making sure I can handle whatever she's about to give me. And the truth of it hits me like a falling oak.

"I want whatever you have for me, Evie. Hard truths. Yoga poses. Lessons in Chinese mysticism. Whatever," I tell her, completely serious. "Spill it."

Her slow smile has become one of my best friends. I want to know it for the rest of my life.

"Okay." She nods, still smiling, but her eyes have an intent kind of seriousness. "So, I think we've established that you're worried about your grandma dying."

This time, it's not a shock, but the thought still makes my stomach ball up. "Yes. I am."

Her hand squeezes mine. "Why?"

My eyes bug. "Why? Because I love her? Because I don't want to lose her?" The words spill out of me almost without my consent. "Because she and Annie are the only members of my family who've never given up on me—"

I have to stop here and swallow hard. She waits, her face open and patient while I clear my throat.

"Because she has done nothing but love me. Me. Of all people."

Evie's smile stretches wider. "It's not so hard to do, you know," she says gently.

I look at her askance. "You realize you've just met my mother, right?"

She huffs a laugh, but she quickly dismisses it. "Okay. How do you feel right now? After telling me that?"

Frowning, I stare at her. I take a breath, filling my lungs and turning inward. How do I feel?

My throat's still a little tight from trying to keep my emotions in check. But—

"I'll be damned," I swear, looking at Evie like she's a twenty-first century witch. There is sadness, but more than anything else, what I feel right now for Grandma Quincy is love and gratitude. "If I think about it… if I turn to it…"

Evie's head bobs in understanding. "The worry is still there if you reach for it, but—" she says lifting the hand that isn't gripping mine, turning her palm up, and letting it rise through the air, "if you let it go and feel what's underneath the worry — the love, the grief, whatever — that's authentic. That, to me, is being more present. More alive."

I blink at her, a calmness coursing through me. An awed sense of feeling… *blessed*. "You are fucking amazing."

Evie leans into me, her smile shining like a beacon, and I wrap my arms around her. Why is this woman with me? She just has to open her mouth, and my life changes for the better. What can I possibly offer her?

She presses a kiss to my cheek and draws back. "I need to go in and get ready, but—" She stops and looks at me, indecision playing on her face.

"What?"

Evie stares at me for a minute before shaking her head. "Never mind."

My left brow arches. She did this in the car a few minutes ago. "What's bothering you?"

She blows out a breath. "I talked to my parents today." As she speaks, her light dims. Just a little. I hate that. "They heard the ambulance this morning and were worried."

Something passes over her face, and I know without needing to hear it. They were worried about her. It's like a punch to the jaw. But can I really blame them? If I had a daughter who was sleeping with a guy who just got out of Angola?

Shit, I'd lose my fucking mind if I heard sirens pulling up at his place.

What the hell is she doing with me?

"I do things that drive my parents crazy," she says with a little wince. But her eyes are trained on me watching me so closely. "Do you think…"

Out of nowhere, I get the feeling this is some kind of test, and I've missed the lesson.

Or have I? Whatever's going on in her head is making her uncomfortable.

Worried.

I turn the tables on her. "You're worried."

She blinks at me, surprised. "What?"

I lower my brows and duck my head toward her. "You. Are. Worried. What are you worried about?" I ask, and then grin because I can't help it. "And what's underneath the worry?"

Her smile is back along with the sweetest of blushes painting her cheeks. "You learn fast," she says softly. Then she clears her throat, looks down for a moment, and meets my eye. "I'm worried that… the way

391

I am… will start to annoy you. Like it annoys my family."

The way I am.

An ache deep, deep inside of me stirs at her words. I'm not even sure what she means — what exactly she's talking about — but those four words seem to capture everything about her. And that everything — that rare, bewitching, brilliant everything — has been rejected.

The way she is is the reason my life may not be a total waste after all. Maybe. Just maybe. If I can make her happy.

Then again, Evie's always happy. I love that about her. So I guess my life won't be a total waste if she can be happy with me.

My arms are still around her, and I rub down her spine and bring a hand to the back of her neck so she feels me.

"*The way you are,*" I stress the words so they capture the whole of her, "is what I'd die to protect."

I feel a shock run through her. "*Drew.*" Her hands raise to my face. She's frowning at me. Startled. Confused. She licks her lips and shakes her head, her eyes shining. "How am I supposed to go to work now?"

I give the back of her neck a little squeeze. "Knowing that your worry — and whatever is behind the worry — could never apply to me." If I wouldn't come off sounding like more of a lovesick fool than I already do, I'd tell her now that loving her is the ladder that lets me climb out of hell. And who she is is the water that stops the burning. "I'm not your parents, or your sister — thank God—"

This earns me a snicker, and Evie brushes her sweet lips against mine. I keep going. Just like I did yesterday. Because this is something I can give her.

"Their mistake, as good and loveable as they might be, is that they don't see how the way you are makes everything better." Her eyes go wide, and she opens her mouth to say something, but I'm not finished. "I'll make my own mistakes, Evie. Plenty of them. But I won't make that one."

Her bottom lip trembles before she bites down on it. In fact, her whole body is trembling. I feel it, so I tighten my hold on her.

"That's... Drew, that's the nicest—" Evie shakes her head and seems to scold herself. "No, nice is so dumb. It doesn't come anywhere close... It's the most precious thing anyone's ever told me. I'll never, never forget it."

Triumph leaves me weightless. Her lips touch mine again, but this time she's demanding more than a gentle caress. I give her what she wants.

I will always give her what she wants.

We kiss until the sound of scattering gravel reaches our ears, and we break apart to see a car pulling into the space beside us.

Evie eyes me sheepishly. "That's one of my students."

I glance over my shoulder, hoping like hell it isn't that asshole Drake. But to my relief, an older woman with white hair and glasses gives Evie an amused look.

"Mrs. Guillory is going to have a field day with this," she says dryly. I turn back to her and run my eyes along her body.

"I think you can take Mrs. Guillory."

393

Evie's laughter fills the cab of Grandma Q's Buick. She reaches into the footwell and grabs her bag.

"I'll pick you up at four."

She nods, her eyes on me. Evie seems to take me in. "I love you."

God, I'm the luckiest ex-con alive.

"I love you, Guppy."

She opens the door and climbs out, but as soon as she does, she ducks her head back in. "Would you do me a favor?" she asks, looking only a little timid.

"Name it."

One side of her mouth quirks up, but she seems to hesitate for a moment.

"Name it, Guppy. It won't annoy me."

The other side lifts up. "When you're on South College, could you keep your eyes open for that little dog the car in front of us almost hit? If you see him, I'll ask Janine if I can borrow her car this afternoon and try to find him," she says as though she's already worked out a plan in her mind. "He'd have a much better chance in a shelter than beside a four-lane road."

It hits me then that this is what she was talking about. This is what annoys her parents. That her heart is so big and boundless, that she's still fretting over a stray dog she saw on the street.

I swear to God, I'll never want to change the way she is.

"Sure thing, baby. I'll keep my eyes peeled."

And I do, but there's no sign of the little mutt who darted through traffic to catch Evie's eye. At least looking for it keeps me from dreading my return to the hospital where what stands between me and the person in my family who loves me the most is the one who hates me the most.

But I walk through the main entrance of the hospital without seeing Ma... I mean Lottie. (I can't really call the woman *Ma* if she's disowned me.)

I figure out that the geriatric wing is on the sixth floor, and I take the elevator. My phone has no signal on the ride up, so I can't ask Annie for Grandma Q's room number, but it turns out I don't need to. The nurse's station is right in front of the elevators.

When I reach her room, my eye falls at once to Grandma Q. Clear tubes cross her face, pumping oxygen into her nose. She looks impossibly small and lies as still as death on the hospital bed. The sight is like stepping through ice into freezing water. Shocking. Paralyzing.

Annie's in the chair on the other side of the bed, her laptop balanced on her knees. My sister watches me with sympathy in her eyes.

"Where is everyone?" I whisper.

She rises, puts down her computer, and tiptoes over to me. "Ma's on duty downstairs. Josie has to watch the boys this afternoon, and Aunt Shelly went to get us some lunch," she says, giving me a rueful smile. "I hope you like Schlotzsky's."

I haven't had time to think about food, but at the mention of lunch, my stomach complains loudly about missing breakfast. It feels like ages since I woke up, but it's only a little after eleven. "I'll eat anything right now." My gaze flicks to Grandma. "How is she?"

Annie's mouth presses into a thin line. "Definitely pneumonia, but they're doing some blood work," she says, her voice dropping. What good it will do, I don't know, since Grandma can hear everything.

At least, I hope she still can.

"The doctors are worried about a secondary infection." Annie's eyes lock with mine. "It's not good, Drew."

A rasping, rattling sound comes from the bed, and we both turn to see Grandma blinking at us. "Don't scare the boy, Anne Marie."

Grandma's voice sounds thready and tired, but at least she has it in her to scold Annie. I take that as a good sign and approach the bed. "She's not scaring me, Grandma. You are."

Her gaze, which looks just a little unfocused moves to Annie. "Sweet girl, give me and your brother a few minutes."

Even as weak as Grandma sounds, Annie wouldn't dream of disobeying her. None of us would.

"Yes, ma'am. I'll... I'll run downstairs for a newspaper." And she scurries out before either of us can respond.

Grandma Q pats the mattress on her left side, near the now-empty chair, her eyes closing. "Come sit by me, Andrew."

My feet feel like their chained to cinder blocks. My gut protests. Whatever she wants to tell me, I'm pretty sure I don't want to hear it. But I move. This is Grandma Quincy. Whatever she wants, she gets.

When I sit beside her, I cover her hand with mine so she knows I'm here. Her hand is warm and dry, but when she turns it over to clasp mine, it feels so weak.

Grandma Quincy tilts her face in my direction and peels her eyes open. "You know what I want to say to you, Andrew?"

396

The sound of my exhale fills the room. "No," I deny, but I'm thinking about her words from this morning when the EMTs arrived. Words about it being her time.

She closes her eyes but her brow arches. "I'm ready, Andrew."

I'm shaking my head even though she can't see me. "I'm not, Grandma."

My grandmother has the nerve to laugh. At least she makes a noise that starts off sounding like a laugh, but trips head first into a spluttering, wheezing cough that goes on and on. I'm on my feet, looking for the buzzer to call the goddamn nurse when she raises her hand to stop me.

"Not going... right this minute," she rasps, watching me through slitted eyes. I sit again, but my stomach feels like it's caught in a bear trap.

"Since when do you talk about giving up?" I keep my voice low, but I can hear anger in it all the same. The peace I felt while talking to Evie just a little while ago is long gone. "You're too strong to talk like that."

Slowly, very slowly, my grandma nods. "I've been strong. All my life. I've done everything I've needed to do...including making sure you got back on your feet after." She fixes me with a hard stare that makes me feel a little ashamed. "I'm tired. I'm ready for my rest."

Is it selfish to want her to be around for years and years? Hell, I don't care if it is.

"But I'm here now. I can take care of you," I promise. "I can take care of the house, the yard, your vegetables..." I trail off because she's eyeing me like I'm a fool.

"Meanwhile, I'd be doing what? If I'm gonna turn to dust, I'd rather do it in the ground beside your grandfather."

She closes her eyes, and I let myself relax a little. If she can argue like this, she'll rally still. No one really chooses when they're gonna go, right?

Of course, if anyone could get death to do her bidding, it's Vivian Quincy.

"I miss him, Andrew." Her words come out so low, I almost don't make them out. Her eyes are shut, her face sagging with fatigue. But beneath the oxygen tubes, I see the faint line of a smile at the corners of her wrinkled mouth. "I been... dreaming of him again..."

She sighs, and I hear her breath rattle before she coughs again, but this time it doesn't scare the hell out of me. I'm sure she's fallen asleep, and I'm about to text Annie to come back, but then she stirs again.

"He likes... your girl..." she slurs. "Laughed when she... jumped right over the fence..."

My spine goes rigid. "What'd you say?"

Silence.

"Grandma, what did you say about Grandpa?"

Is she asleep? I run my hand along the back of my neck, smoothing down the tiny hairs that now stand on end. Her breath deepens, but then she frowns.

"Mad at your mama..."

"Who is?" Me? Her? Evie?... *Grandpa Pete?*

The thought gives me another shiver, and I shake my head to clear it.

"Why, Anthony, of course."

I leap out of my chair like it's on fire. Annie choses that moment to walk back in, finding me practically pressed against the wall. Her eyes bug.

"What's wrong?" she hisses.

I look from her to Grandma and back again. "Was she— When you—" I stop. Swallow. Blink at her. "While you were here with her, was she talking about... about Grandpa Pete... a-and Anthony?"

Annie's brows rise as one. "Um... no?" Eyes wide, Annie looks around the room and hisses. "Are they *here?*"

This time, instead of shuddering, I get pissed. "If they are, they're gonna have to get through me before they can have her."

"Drew." Annie cocks her head at me, half-pitying and half-amused. "Maybe... maybe we need to prepare—" Then my sister looks at Grandma Quincy, her expression collapses as she seems to hear herself, and before I know it, she's clutching me in a hug.

Stunned silent, I lift my arms like a robot and hug her back. She sobs against me, making little squeaks as she cries, giving me all her weight. I let myself relax as I take it. Whatever happens, no matter how shitty I feel at the thought of losing Grandma, I'm not the only one.

I'm not alone.

I squeeze Annie tighter, thinking about how many years Grandma has been the bridge that connected her to me. Before my sister could drive to see me on her own — and even after — Grandma Q would take her. My mother sure as hell wasn't going to.

It was those Sunday afternoon visits every other month that shored up what we have.

Resting my chin on Annie's head as she weeps, I look over at our grandmother and silently thank her for my sister. We'd probably never be this close now if it hadn't been for her.

A new brand of guilt marks me.

Grandma Q has given me so much. Who am I to ask for more?

CHAPTER TWENTY-NINE

EVIE

"How's Mrs. Vivian?" Mom asks before blowing across her tea. She insisted on coming to my Level I class this morning, and judging by the way Tori scowled the whole time, Mom must have twisted her arm to come along. So now we're sipping oolong in the tea room at the Yoga Garden, killing time before meeting Dad for lunch.

One happy family.

"They moved her to the ICU yesterday," I say and watch Mom's mouth form a startled *O*. Even Tori winces. It's Saturday. I haven't seen Drew since Thursday, but he looked like hell then. He's spent almost every night this week at the hospital after working at the garage all day. I've tried to meet up with him when I could, bringing him the occasional sandwich or latte, but between classes, baby duty, and my parents visiting, it hasn't been easy.

Mom *tsks*. "Well, I'm sure that's very hard on your friend," she concedes, her eyes sympathetic.

I should be grateful for the sentiment. At least it's a sign she's *trying* to have compassion for Drew, but since she's made an attempt every day this week to get me to take my *dream trip* or keep my *options open,* I can't really bring myself to feel too excited about it.

"It *is* hard for him," I say, feeling the now familiar surge of protectiveness for Drew. "He's very close with her." I think about the last time I visited the hospital, before they moved her to ICU. Drew was trying to get her to eat some mashed potatoes and gravy, but Mrs. Vivian kept turning up her nose even though she was barely conscious.

"Tastes like instant," she kept complaining. So Drew would wipe her mouth as if she were a baby and try again a minute or two later when he hoped she'd forgotten her protest.

She hadn't.

Seeing them like that had squeezed my heart and brought tears to my eyes. "He's really sweet with her," I say, my nose stinging. "Losing her is going to devastate him."

Mom's manicured brows lift in shock. "Don't say that, Evie," she scolds lightly, scandalized. "You don't know what's going to happen. Mrs. Vivian's a strong woman. More active than any senior citizen I know. She could pull through."

I don't tell her that Mrs. Vivian is already in another energy plane, having end-of-life experiences with those who have moved on. This feels too precious to tell. I was honored when Drew shared it with me — as well as his fear and wonder. It freaked him out a little, but I think talking helped. Keeping all of this sacred feels like the best way to honor him as he goes through this.

But more than anything else, I think Mom would just dismiss it. I guess I'm glad she and Tori came to my class. Maybe they are making an effort to get to know who I really am and what I value, but I didn't miss how stiff Mom got when I opened class with my singing bowl and a few chants.

Though, I have to admit, her body looks more relaxed now as she sips her tea. And her eyes are a little softer. Maybe she got a taste of just how awesome yoga is. If so, I'm grateful.

So I go with that instead of talking about Mrs. Vivian. "I'm glad y'all came today," I tell them, meeting both their gazes in turn.

Holding her cobalt blue teacup between the fingers of both hands, Mom casts her focus around the studio. She's smiling.

"It really is a lovely place." Her tone is warm, appreciative. "I wonder how the owners do." Her brow creases as she seems to be calculating in her head. "Do you know if this is their sole income?"

I squelch a sigh with a sip of tea. I can already tell where she's going with this. "I've never asked." This is true. Technically. But not completely. And the guilt of knowing that I'm willfully deceiving her makes me speak up. "But I think the owner started in marketing."

Mom purses her lips, considering. "Well, small businesses are risky." She looks around, taking in the whole boutique, tea shop, and reception area. She slips off her stool, moves to one of the display mannequins, and reaches for the price tag on its shirt. Her brows lift in approval. "But a business degree sure comes with a lot of options."

I finish my tea and set my cup in the saucer instead of telling her I don't want a business degree. I glance at Tori who is smiling like this is Christmas morning. Mom comes back to the table.

"If you went back to school in business, by the time you got out, Daddy would be retired. We wouldn't have the house note," she says with a shrug. "We could help you open a place like this if the market was right at the time."

The thought of having my own studio holds some appeal, but I know I can't go there with Mom. Not

403

right now, anyway. "I really just want to teach yoga, Mom. I'm happy right where I am."

She winces. "But you're not even full-time. What about things like insurance and benefits? You can't stay on our plan forever, you know."

I resist the urge to roll my eyes. "I do know, Mom. But I have five years to figure out the insurance. A lot can happen in five years."

Mom nods curtly. "Yeah, like earning a bachelor's in business."

And it's as if her words cast black magic. Because as soon as she speaks them, the bells over the door jangle, and in walks Drake Jordan. His head whips around to us, and I read both surprise and satisfaction on his face.

His gaze moves to me and his eyes narrow, giving him a look of mischief. "Who's earning a bachelor's in business?"

Mom and Tori both turn to look at him, and I silently curse. Drake doesn't miss the opportunity. Walking over with his hand extended, he smears on his most charming smile as he approaches my mother. "Hi. I'm Drake. Evie and I are friends." His gaze flicks around the three of us. "Am I wrong, or do I see a family resemblance?"

Mom smiles, but Tori, true to form, just gives him a suspicious stare. Mom takes his hand. "Sondra Lalonde. Nice to meet you, Drake." She releases his hand and gestures toward Tori. "This is my daughter, Victoria, Evie's sister."

Drake offers her his hand, and she takes it, still unsmiling, but watchful. "Tori," she says, but it's not unfriendly. I narrow my eyes at her as Drake presses his palm against hers. Tori blinks. Twice.

On someone else, it would count as batting her eyelashes.

I may vomit.

"I apologize for intruding," Drake says before releasing Tori's hand. "I just heard you talking about business degrees. I'm getting my MBA."

Yep, vomiting is a very real possibility.

"Oh!" Mom turns to me wide-eyed. "Well, honey, I bet your friend Drake here could tell you everything you'd want to know about majoring in business."

Yep, she's right about that. Drake could tell me everything I'd want to know, which is zilch, and plenty I don't. And then some. But doesn't she remember me talking about him? The guy I was going on a date with but didn't really want to see?

A quick glance at Tori lets me know *she* remembers. She's leering, her eyes practically shining with enjoyment.

We'll never be close. I've probably known it deep down all my life, but the realization is now crystal clear to me. She's my sister. My only sibling. And we are never going to be tight. We're never going to turn to each other for help. Or share holidays together when Mom and Dad are gone. Or have each other's kids over for sleepovers.

And that realization makes me sad, but I can't say it's really much of a surprise.

I get why she's been so angry for so long. She sees me as her nemesis. One she can't fight outright. She wants to believe the worst about me because I give her misery meaning. We're never going to get past this.

Great.

Drake turns back to me. "Are you teaching the eleven o'clock vinyasa class?"

I shake my head. "I switched with Allison so we could spend the day together," I say, gesturing to my family. Dad's going to meet us at The Blue Dog for lunch, but after that I want to find Drew.

Just the thought of him centers me in the midst of this awkward moment with Drake, Mom, and Tori.

Drake gives a disappointed moue. The expression looks ridiculous on him. "Darn. The schedule had your name on it. I was hoping I could talk you into getting a bite with me after class."

To my horror, Mom looks genuinely sorry. "Oh, I wish she could, Drake, but we're having a family lunch today. Maybe—"

"Mom," I cut in, determined to stop her from making any plans for me with Drake Jordan. She eyes me, clearly surprised at the sharpness of my tone. I ignore her and face Drake, squaring my shoulders. "Thanks for the invite, but I'm seeing someone."

It's almost impossible to believe, but all three of them — Mom, Tori, and Drake — have the exact same response. They all look like they've been slapped with a dead fish.

Drake's face screws into a frown. "Not that criminal who threatened me on your doorstep," he says with disgust.

"Oh my God." Mom gasps, whipping her gaze to me.

406

"Wait, what?" Wide-eyed, Tori ping pongs her focus between Drake and me.

I'm shaking my head. "He didn't threaten anyone."

"Evie," Mom scolds. "When was this?"

"Drew didn't threaten anyone, Mom. I swear." I turn back to Drake. "Drake, be serious. Tell them what really happened."

He sniffs derisively. "You mean when I was walking you to your door, and he jumped out of the bushes, got in my face, and told me he'd just gotten out of prison?"

I open my mouth to protest, but then I realize what he's saying is true. Mostly. It's just the way he's saying it sounds bad. Really bad.

Shit.

I face my mother, who looks traumatized. "He wasn't in the bushes. Drew was going for a walk."

She's not listening. It's written all over her face. Her eyes are on me, but she's not even seeing me. She's picturing a headline or a crime scene photo. One involving me. "Mom, listen to me. Drew was just walking by while Drake and I were talking. He heard some things he didn't like, and he came to make sure I was okay. That's all. That's all, Mom."

Drake doesn't even have the decency to pretend to feel guilty. But he remembers exactly what was going on that night. I know he does. And if Tori looked like it was Christmas morning a few minutes ago, now it's like she's won the frickin' lottery.

"I told you he sounded violent," Tori says with a practiced lack of malice in her tone. She sounds so calm, so reasonable, so unlike Tori, I almost snap.

"He was looking out for me," I defend, feeling that all to familiar flush of protectiveness for Drew. "It's what he always does."

Mom closes her eyes, lifts her brows, and shakes her head, looking just as exasperated as she did when Tori and I used to fight as kids. "Let's not talk about this now, Evie." Then she blinks at Drake with a ready smile and slips off her stool. "We need to get going, but it was so nice meeting you, Drake." She offers him her hand again, and Drake, that... that... that...

Hamflower.

I hear the insult in Drew's voice, and I swear, I almost laugh.

Drake shakes Tori's hand, and then he has the nerve to touch my elbow before leaning in and pressing a kiss to my cheek. I turn to stone beneath his touch, but the urge to strike him is almost overpowering. My parents haven't exactly softened toward Drew in the last few days, but at least they have some compassion for what he's going through with Mrs. Vivian. I already know Drake's comments aren't going to help.

Drake waves as he disappears into Studio A, and the three of us grab our bags and head out the front door. Mom waits until we're safely on the front porch before she speaks.

"How. Embarrassing," she says, making each word its own sentence.

My brows bunch together. "What? Why are you embarrassed?"

She pulls the keys to the Volvo from her purse and jingles them in agitation. "Because, Evie. The person you are seeing, a hardened criminal, harassed that young man on my property."

I think my jaw actually comes unhinged. *I'm* about to come unhinged. I jab my finger toward the studio. "Mom, that's the guy you told me not to go out with. Because I didn't like him, remember?" We reach the car, but I put my body between hers and the driver's side door. "I should have listened to you on that one, but I didn't, and when he took me home, he kept trying to get inside even though I was trying to tell him no."

Mom stiffens at this before a crease forms between her brows. "But why was that Moroux boy out there at night. Was he waiting for you to come home?"

I can't help it. My eyes roll like a tiny white ball on a roulette wheel. "Mom, no. He was out for a walk. He heard us on the porch and stepped in." I pin her with a glare. "I was grateful."

I was also irritated with him that night, but I don't need to tell her that.

And though I'm irritated right now, the thought of Drew centers me. Fills me with warmth. He's looked out for me from the moment we met. I want more than anything to do the same for him. Protect him. Let no one abuse him.

The thought rises from within me like a prayer.

Let no one abuse him.

Mom just shakes her head. "I don't know, Evie. That young man seemed very taken with you," she says, sounding uncertain. "And he's getting an MBA. On the face of it, he sounds like he's a lot better for you than—"

I raise my hand, palm out. "Stop. Mom, stop right there," I warn. "There is absolutely nothing Drake Jordan can give me that I want. That date he took me on? It was miserable because he never once respected my wishes. Not with what I wanted to eat or drink and certainly not when I wanted to end the evening."

Again, Mom looks startled, and she opens her mouth to speak, but I don't give her a chance.

"Drew sees exactly who I am, and not only does he *accept* who I am," I say, stressing the word, "he *likes* who I am. Knowing him has made me realize just how rare that is."

Mom's lips part. She looks stunned. "Are you saying that you think we don't *like* you?"

The hurt in her eyes squeezes my heart, and I let go a sigh. "Mom, I know you and Dad love me..." I can't seem to bring myself to add Tori to the list. I don't even let my eyes land on her, but I feel her presence beside me, and it's definitely not loving. I shake my head, bringing my focus back to my mother. "I know you love me. I just don't think you are crazy about who I am."

Looking crushed, she almost stumbles forward and grips me by the shoulders. "Evangeline, my goodness, what a thing to say." She shakes her head. "Of course we're crazy about you. Why would we fly halfway around the world to see about you if we weren't crazy about you?"

"Mom." Frustration draws out the word. I put my hands over hers as they clutch my shoulders. "That's not what I mean."

She expels a gust of air. "Well, thank goodness." She shakes her head and glances down at her wristwatch. "Look, let's talk more about this over lunch. Your father is going to be waiting for us."

Wordlessly, I agree and climb into the back seat of the Volvo. Tori rides up front with mom, but more than once, I catch her staring at me as we drive.

410

At the Blue Dog Cafe, I order the crab corn bisque and a Perrier.

My dad frowns. "That's all your getting?"

"Dad, it's lunch. And everything else looks enormous." I eye the menu again. I'm sure the Crawfish Enchiladas and Blue Crab Spaghetti are delicious, but it seems like a lot of food for eleven-thirty in the morning.

My dad makes a noise of disapproval before turning to Tori. "What about you, T. What'll it be?"

Tori scrutinizes the menu. "I'll have the Chicken & Sausage Gumbo and the Devilled Eggs."

"Another soup," Dad scoffs. "Well, I don't care what time it is, I'm getting the Cracklin' Crusted Gulf Catch."

Mom gets the BBQ Shrimp & Grits, and Dad seems satisfied with this. We're sitting at a table for four with Tori and I across from each other and our parents on either side. As soon as the server leaves after taking our order, Tori leans back in her seat, eyeing me with a predatory smile.

"So, Evie, is Drew on probation?"

The question sends a shock through me, electricity zinging in my spine and fingertips. I'm aware of my parents stiffening as they turn to me in almost synchronized moves and await the answer.

The truth is my friend, I remind myself, and I nod. "Yes." But I don't give her any more than this.

Her expression doesn't change. The answer doesn't seem to surprise her at all, so I immediately know the question is not out of innocent curiosity or even the impulse to rile me.

"So he has a probation officer and, like, rules he has to follow?"

411

I narrow my eyes on her. I don't know what she's up to, but I know I don't like it. "Yes."

She takes a sip of her iced tea and smiles at me. "Like what?"

I think about the terms that I know about — what Drew and I have talked about briefly — and I realize none if it would harm him if I told them, and it may even help my parents see things differently.

I count off a few of the terms on my fingers. "Well, he has to have a place to live and a job. He gets drug tested every three weeks." I move my gaze between my parents to make sure they are listening. "Of course, he's passed those. He can't associate with criminals, but since he spends most of his time at work, with his Grandma, and with me, I don't think there's much of a chance of that."

Mom blinks, and I think for a minute that what I'm saying about him — about how simple and pure Drew's life is — may be sinking in.

"You said he works in automotive repair?" Mom asks tentatively.

I nod, proud to talk about Drew, finally. Talk about him instead of just defending him. "His cousin owns C&C on Johnston Street. He's also restoring a car at Mrs. Vivian's." I don't mention it's his brother's car.

"What kind?" My dad asks, seeming interested in listening for the first time. It doesn't escape my notice that Tori scowls at his question.

"It's a Toyota Supra," I say. "I'm not sure of the year, but it's from the 90s. Right now, he's working on saving the engine and replacing the wiring."

Dad's mouth bunches in such a way I know he's impressed in spite of himself. Tori's eyes blaze and her top lip curls.

"So what would happen if he, you know, violated his parole?" The question is so jarring, my parents join me in staring openly at her.

"I…" I shake my head, wondering why my sister has to be so difficult. "I really don't know."

Dad picks up his Diet Coke. "He'd be arrested," he says, as though it's nothing. As though he's not talking about the man I love.

I press my feet into the floor and remind myself I'm connected to the earth. I remind myself that I am one with the source of all things, and that the universe is a loving and supportive universe. I breathe in love and breathe out love before meeting my sister's gaze again.

"He's not going to violate his parole, Tori. Drew is past all that."

The server chooses that moment to approach the table. "Your bisque, ma'am." He says, placing the bowl in front of me. My dad frowns.

"A cup? You got a cup of soup?"

"It's a bowl, Dad."

He looks at me like I've grown two heads. "Get something else, Evie, please. You can eat it later if you have to."

I give the server a pleading look. "What's good leftover?"

He offers me a kind smile. "Almost everything, ma'am, but might I suggest the Blue Dog Burger."

I nod, smiling back. Drew is going to have a burger for lunch. He'll love it. "Bring me one of those."

"Her body is shutting down. It's really just a matter of time now." Drew stares at the takeout box I've handed him as though it just materialized in his hands. He opens the lid, blinks, and closes it again, giving me a tired smile. "Thank you. That looks good."

But I can tell by the look in his bloodshot eyes he has no appetite. "You need to eat something." We're standing in the side parking lot of C&C garage next to Janine's car. She let me borrow it to come see him, and now that I have I don't want to leave.

"I will," Drew says, but I'm not convinced.

"When?"

My insistent tone seems to wake him out of his stupor, at least for a moment. His smile lifts just a little higher. "Easy, Guppy." His voice is a gentle rumble, and the words let me know he's okay. He's tired. He's hurting. But he's okay.

As if to drive this fact home, he sets the takeout on top of the car, grabs me by the wrists, and wraps my arms around his sturdy waist before he closes his arms around me. He's big. Warm. Wonderful.

Drew's lips are against my hair, and I hear and feel him hum. The sound is relief and gratitude and satisfaction all in one. At least, that's exactly what I feel.

"I'm glad I have Annie, and I'm fucking grateful I have this job, but Evie," he says, his words low and meant for me only. "You — having you — that's what makes me feel like I can handle what's coming."

I draw back just enough to meet his eyes. He's letting me see all the way in, and I witness sadness and pain. I don't miss the fear either, but he's also looking at me. Looking at me like I'm his cosmic reward.

My heart might be able to lift me off the ground. Because he's my cosmic reward. If I've succeeded in being good and loving and conscious, he's the boon for all of that and more.

"Like a promise?" I say, gazing up at him as though he were the covenant of all the gods.

Confusion forms a line between his brows. "Like a reason," he says.

"A reason?" Now I'm the one wearing the confused frown.

Drew shuts his eyes for a moment, shaking his head. "Never mind. Don't listen to me. I'm too tired to make sense."

But I bring a hand up to his chest and place it, instinctively, over his heart. "No, tell me. What do you mean?"

He watches me for a while, and I see the moment when he relents. I don't think anyone else would notice the subtlest shift. The muscles in his face. The easing around his eyes. The way his shoulders lower just a touch.

I've learned him by heart.

"I matter to you." He says the words slowly, and they still almost knock me over.

"Well, of course you do. You mean the world to me." A sudden flame of indignance licks up my spine.

The left side of his mouth hitches up. "And you let me know it. It's just—" He shakes his head again. "Families are weird."

I snort. "Tell me about it."

415

This brings a half-chuckle from him, and he squeezes me tighter. "Yeah? Well, with mine, I don't know how things will fall out without Grandma around." He frowns down at me. "I have my job here because Grandma browbeat my cousin into giving me one."

I bite my lip. "You don't think he'd fire you after..." I can't bring myself to say it. Drew's cousin wouldn't do that. Would he?

A wince passes over his face. "I hope not." Drew shrugs. "He doesn't avoid me like he did when I first started. He seems to like my work, but..."

"But you aren't sure," I say, thinking of the terms of his parole. But then I get ahold of myself. "Scarcity is an illusion."

Drew narrows his gaze, but his non-smile is open for business. "What?"

"The universe is a place of abundance, so fearing the loss of something you have like a job or a car is really foolish," I explain. "Everything you need already exists. If you lose this job, there will be another one to take its place, and you will learn something from both the leaving and the taking."

"You see, Guppy," Drew says, cocking a brow in amusement, "This is why I'm such a lucky bastard. If everyone in my family but Annie turns their backs on me, I still have you to teach me all this cosmic truth shit."

I swat him lightly on the chest, and he laughs.

"It's not shit," I defend, but this only makes him laugh harder.

"I know it's not shit. I just like getting you worked up."

I *humph,* and I can feel his body fighting to keep from losing it. He leans down, and still snickering, presses a kiss to my lips. He holds his mouth there until my pout softens to welcome him. And our lips take slow sips of each other.

"I love you," I whisper against him.

His exhale is audible between us. "My God, Evie, I love you so fucking much."

I kiss him again, but I keep it chaste. He's at work, after all. The universe may have plenty of jobs, but that's no reason to get him fired for PDA.

I bring my hands to his biceps when I pull back. "Are you going to the hospital tonight? I can stay with you until ten or so."

Drew shakes his head, his lips pressing together. "No. Apparently, Lottie gets off at six, and she has the day off tomorrow, so she wants to stay with Grandma." Bitterness sharpens the gray of his eyes. "So that means I'm banned."

This hurts him. I feel it. And I hate it. "Does Mrs. Vivian know? Is she…"

"She's in and out," he says. Then shrugs. "Out mostly. But she still comes around to fuss at us every few hours."

I can't help it. I laugh. "Fuss at you?"

Smiling a weary smile, Drew nods. "Yeah, last night, Annie was with me, and she must have heard her sniffling because she told us to stop crying."

My eyes go wide. "She did?"

A low laugh shakes from him. "She did. She told us to save it for the funeral or else we'd run dry."

I laugh. Even though it's gallows humor, Mrs. Vivian is still giving Drew and his family the gift of herself. I have no doubt he'll be telling this story for the rest of his life.

"She's something else."

Drew's eyes come to mine, and he nods. But I watch him swallow, the grief already back. He holds my gaze. "Can I come get you tonight after your shift with Aaron?"

I blink. "I can come to you. I'll be up and it'll be late—"

But he's already shaking his head.

"I don't want you walking by yourself at night."

I arch a brow. "I'll bring Gemini."

He keeps shaking his head. "Now that I know what a wus Gem is, no way."

I splutter a laugh. "He is not a wus."

Drew's brows lift as he regards me skeptically. "I sneezed the other day, and I thought he was going to hide under the bed."

This is true.

"Okay, fine. I'll text you when Aaron's back down."

He nods. "And I'll come get you and Gem."

CHAPTER THIRTY

DREW

I leave the garage at five and drive straight to the hospital. Running into Lottie is something I've tried to avoid all week, but I want to see Grandma.

When I get to the ICU, I find Aunt Josie there with a novel propped on her lap and her cheaters at the end of her nose. She looks up and smiles as I enter. Grandma Quincy looks small and sunken on the bed.

I nod toward her and whisper. "How was her day?"

Aunt Josie's brows lift high, making lines snake across her forehead. "Oh, she's been talking," she says meaningfully. "Though not to anyone in here."

Evie may say it's normal, but all that stuff about the veil lifting between worlds just gives me the heebie-jeebies. I smooth down the hair on the back of my neck and make myself sit in the empty chair next to Josie.

"Did the doctor come by?"

My aunt nods and lets out a sigh, and her face suddenly looks older. "They'd like to talk to us about the option of moving her into a hospice room."

"What does that mean?" Logically, I know what it means. I'm still not ready for it.

"It means," Josie closes the book on her lap and turns toward me, "they'll move her into a private room, and make her as comfortable as they can, but they won't be giving her anything to make her well. No more antibiotics. No more steroids."

The first year I was in Angola, another piece of fresh meat thought he had something to prove. Being the newest white guy, I was easy to spot. He waited for me outside the mess hall, just a few feet out of sight of one of the guards. Before I knew it, his knee was in my middle, and my breath was gone. Just gone. With no sign of returning.

That's what this feels like.

The guy got away with it for all of twelve hours. The next morning, I tripped him on his way out of the shower and got one good kick with my steel-toed boot before a couple of trustees grabbed me by the collar and marched me out before the guards could come.

But today, there's no one to lay in wait for. No one against whom I can deliver revenge.

I look over at Grandma and let out a breath. Hell, she looks so weak and wasted away, I can't blame her for not fighting. If a nice room and a painless end is the best we can offer her, I want her to have it.

I look back at Aunt Josie. "Who needs to be the one to decide?"

She rolls her eyes. "Mom put Nelson in charge of her medical power of attorney years ago. She said us girls were too sentimental to be expected to make a decision like that." She says this like it's a joke, but I think I can see the relief in her eyes that this choice isn't one that'll land squarely on her shoulders.

I sure as hell wouldn't want it.

"Does Uncle Nelson know what the doctor said?"

Josie nods. "Nelson, Lottie, and I are going to meet with the him tomorrow morning." She tilts her head to the side and gives me a wistful smile. "And then we'll probably meet with the hospice staff."

I swallow against the sudden stone in my throat and nod.

As if chiming in on the conversation, Grandma Quincy takes a long, ragged inhale. The sound of it, so

420

hollow and whistling, is unearthly. As though over my grandmother, life and death are clasping hands, sealing a bargain.

Grandma exhales, and I can't shake the sense that her breaths are numbered. But so are mine. So are everyone's. I close my eyes and try to calm the fuck down.

Evie.

I reach for her in my mind. I want her with me, pressed against me. Not just because being with her quiets me, though it does. Like nothing else, she conquers the guilt. The fear. The meaninglessness.

But more than that, I want her with me right now because if my breaths and days are numbered, I don't want to waste any more time. I've lost enough already.

I want her and I need her.

It's at this moment, Grandma Quincy smiles wide, her eyes still closed. "I know," she says.

I glance over at Aunt Josie who just shrugs.

"He'll be alright," she says, still smiling. "It's all taken care of."

I suppress a shudder because I'm pretty sure she's not talking to me or Josie. We watch her smile vanishes, and an angry frown takes its place.

"She better not!"

Beside me, Aunt Josie snickers. "Who you talking to, Mama?" When Grandma doesn't respond, Josie raises her voice and asks again.

Grandma flinches against the noise and looks almost annoyed, although her eyes remain shut. "You're father, of course!" she snaps.

"Oh!" Josie says, breaking into a giggle. "Hi, Daddy!"

421

I'm ready to jump out of my skin, and I rake my hands through my hair just to keep myself in the chair. I grind my teeth together and try to remember what Evie told me about square breathing, but I can't. I reach for my phone instead.

Me: Freaking out a little.

I watch the screen and feel a measure of relief as soon as the read receipt appears.

Evie: What's wrong?

"There you are, Anthony," Grandma coos. I freeze in my seat, and the hair on my arms stands straight up. My thumb hovers over the keypad, and then I just admit it.

Me: Apparently, I'm afraid of ghosts.

Evie: You at the hospital?

Me: Yep.

I'd be lying if I said I'm not about to lose my shit, but talking to Evie grounds me just a little.

Evie: Who's there?

Me: Besides Aunt Josie & Grandma? Pretty sure my grandpa and brother.

I follow this with a scream emoji, and she sends me a line of laughing/crying faces.

Me: So glad you find this amusing.

Despite my sarcasm, the thought of her laughing about this helps me breathe a little deeper.

Evie: I'm sorry. I'm not laughing at you, my love.

Seeing the words, the way she has claimed me as *her* love hits me like a shot of morphine. An intoxicating warmth rolls over me, and I almost moan in relief.

Evie loves me. What is there to fear?

Adrenaline begins to drain away, leaving me so tired. I'm so fucking tired. I just want to crawl into bed with her and sleep for days.

Evie: Do you want to say anything to them?

I blink at the screen, alert again.

Evie: They can probably hear you.

"Shit," I say aloud, the morphine feeling unfortunately gone.

Josie frowns at me. "What's wrong?"

Unable to explain this to her, I just shake my head.

Evie: The universe is giving you an opportunity. Take it.

I narrow my eyes at the screen as a low rumble escapes me. Not that she can hear it.

Evie: Don't be stubborn.

Okay, maybe she can hear it.

Me: I swear, I'm in love with a witch.

Another string of laughing emojis pops up.

Evie: Talk to them. You'll feel better.

I roll my eyes.

Me: I can't. Josie's here.

Evie: Ask her to give you a minute.

I scoff at the phone.

Me: Hell no.

She's quiet for a moment, and I grow antsy that I've offended her.

Evie: Then write it here. Just put it out there.

I lean back in the chair and frown at my phone. What would Evie think of me if she knew what I had to say to my brother?

And in her weird, spooky, Evie way, she seems to read my mind.

423

Evie: You can say anything in front of me. I will always love you.

Damn.

I clear my throat against the sudden tightening.

"I won't interrupt, Peter," Grandma says, sounding defensive.

"Jesus Christ," I mutter, my guts turning to ice water.

Beside me, Aunt Josie just laughs and shakes her head. "Strange, isn't it?" She doesn't seem freaked out at all. In fact, I think she's enjoying it.

Evie: Go for it.

I scowl at the phone but give in.

Me: Fine.

I inhale. Exhale. Settle deeper into the chair.

Evie: Pretend like I'm not even here.

Me: That'd be easier if you'd be quiet.

She sends me an emoji of a monkey covering its mouth.

I close my eyes and try to get still. Evie meditates all the time. I don't know how the hell she does it. If I'm not working with my hands, my head is like a three-ring circus.

I push the thoughts of monkeys and trapeze artists from my mind and try to picture my brother standing over Grandma's hospital bed. The image of him with blood spurting from his neck is the first to appear, and I open my eyes.

Fuck.

Shaking with nerves, my thumb hovers over the screen, and I make myself type his name.

Me: Anthony

I press send, and I see his name join my conversation with Evie. She sees it too, and knowing this knocks down every wall. His name blurs as my eyes fill.

Me: I'm so fucking sorry.

My face is on fire, but the first tear that streaks down my cheek is hotter still.

Me: Miss you every fucking day.

Me: Why didn't I listen to you? So stupid.

A mortifying sound breaks from me, and I squeeze my eyes shut, unable to face Aunt Josie. But I hear her rise, and then her hand is on my shoulder.

"Sweetheart, I'll just be downstairs if you need me," she whispers.

I don't even hear her leave because I'm crying like a fucking baby.

I clear my throat but keep my eyes closed. What the hell else do I have to lose?

"How many times did you try to warn me?" I say aloud. There's no response to my shameful words, just the shallow sound of Grandma Quincy's breathing. "Anthony, I'd do anything... *anything*... to take back that night. If there was anything I could do to make it right, I'd do it." My voice is strangled. It doesn't even sound like me. But then this feeling as though my whole body is being wrung out like a dirty rag is one I've never had. And one I never want to repeat.

"Ma hates me. I'm sure you hate me too." I say this and break down all over again, imagining he can hear me. Imagining this is how he feels. "I don't deserve it, brother, but I ask your forgiveness."

A rattling, rasping pull of breath has me opening my eyes. I quickly swipe them with my fists, and get to

425

my feet. Grandma's eyes are still closed, but she looks fitful now, frowning hard, her eyes twitching.

Probably my fault. I should have kept quiet.

I clear my throat again. "Sorry, Grandma," I mutter. I wonder if she's in pain. If I should call the nurse.

She takes another rattling breath and speaks on a tired exhale. "He can't... hear you."

I let go a sigh, feeling ridiculous. Of course my brother can't hear me. He's dead.

"He can't hear you, Anthony," she says, the words just above a whisper. But then a smile spreads across her face, as though she's illuminated from the inside. A rush of chills falls down my spine. "He doesn't know we're... having such a wonderful time."

"*What?*" My voice cracks on the word in a way it hasn't since I was thirteen. "What'd you say, Grandma?"

She just keeps smiling in that uncanny way as if she can't hear me either.

"Grandma, what did you say?" I ask again, so fixed on her I don't hear the footsteps that halt in the doorway.

"What the hell are you doing here?"

I jump at the sound of Ma's voice. As if she's caught me red-handed. As if I'm guilty.

Which, of course, I am.

I swallow and force myself to hold her ice cold stare. "I was just leaving." And I would, but she's glaring at me, standing like a monument of disdain in the middle of the doorway.

Her eyes rake my face, and I know she sees the evidence of my weeping. Hell, my lashes are still wet. She scowls.

"Save your crocodile tears for someone else," she hisses, crossing her arms over her chest. "And if you think you're stealing that house from under us, you're out of your goddamn mind."

It's like a punch aimed right at my chin. My head snaps back almost as far. *"What?"*

She takes three steps toward me, and I'd bet money she's about to slap me across the face. And I'm going to let her. "Don't think I don't see you for the thieving bastard you are."

"Ma—"

"Don't call me that." She speaks through gritted teeth, but now that she's right in front of me, I see something else in her eyes. She hates me. That's clear. But there's heartbreak too. Calling her *Ma* doesn't make her angry. It hurts her.

"I'm sorry, Lottie," I whisper. "It won't happen again."

Her face pinches into a grotesque mask of loathing, but her eyes fill. All at once, instead of being afraid of her, wanting to hide from her anger and my guilt, I want to embrace her. Comfort her.

But that's not allowed.

"I'm sorry for everything." And then I step around her and aim for the door.

"He wants you to forgive him," Grandma mumbles.

I don't pause when I hear Lottie scoff, and I'm in the doorway when my grandmother repeats herself, louder this time. *"Anthony* wants you to forgive him."

427

I drive home in a fog, raw and empty, with just one thought in mind.

Evie.

She'll come over tonight. I'll take her to bed, love her, and wake up beside her in the morning. And then maybe I'll be able to face whatever tomorrow will bring.

But when I climb the stairs to the apartment, I hear the scratching and clicking of canine toes on wood. And before I reach the top step, she is there, saying my name.

Thank God.

Evie crashes into my arms, and Gemini jumps on my legs, and everything that felt empty and raw a moment ago now is full and soothed. I'll be damned if I will cry again today, so I laugh instead. And laughing, I scoop this beautiful, bewitching woman into my embrace, and as if on instinct, she wraps her legs around my waist before I carry her inside.

That's when I smell the most tempting aroma of marinara and oregano. I am suddenly starving.

"God in heaven. What is that?" I ask spinning her around to find a cardboard box bearing the Pizza Village logo on my table.

"It's just pizza," Evie says, shrugging, her voice soft and humble.

"Just pizza," I echo dumbly. I look back at her as though I've just caught her levitating. Honestly, at this point, that may not even faze me. "You are an angel. A fairy. A goddess."

She tips her head back, laughing. The flesh of her fair throat tempts me, and it's too much. I dive in for a taste. I let the tip of my tongue graze her flawless skin and ride the length of her neck up to her ear.

428

Her laughter turns breathy, and I let my lips hover over her ear's dainty shell. "You bury me," I tell her. "I'm completely gone. You give me what I need before I know I need it."

Though I'm damn grateful for pizza, she's got to know I mean more than that. For what just happened at the hospital. And a million other things.

I'm not really ready to examine what just happened at the hospital, but I know it wouldn't have happened without her.

I've never loved anyone, anything, like this.

I've never felt loved like this.

I kiss Evie. She's still clinging to me, and I'm pretty sure I could hold her and kiss her like this for years. At least eight. I don't even think my arms would get tired.

"You bury me," I say again after freeing her mouth.

Evie shakes her head, brushing plump lips against mine. "I don't want to bury you. I want to feed you." Then she wriggles in my grip. "Put me down, love."

I ease her to her feet. "I don't have any plates. Just napkins."

Evie shrugs. "We'll eat over the box."

Yeah. I want to marry her.

"Cheese and pepperoni seemed like a safe bet," she says, lifting the box lid.

The mouth-watering scent of hot pizza has me moaning. "Mmm. God, pizza." It's one of the things I still haven't had since getting out. I grab a slice, remember my manners just in time, and offer it to Evie.

She accepts it with a smile, and then I dive in, scoop up a giant slice, and take the world's biggest bite.

And it's mind-blowing.

"Iwillloveyouforever," I vow around a mouthful of awesome.

Evie giggles as she takes a bite and cheese stretches from her slice. "You're so easy to please."

I grunt in agreement as I close my mouth around the next bite. What else do I need other than what I have right here?

Evie gives me a rueful smile. "It's refreshing." She says this almost under her breath, but I don't miss her meaning.

I swallow and watch her more closely. "Tough day with your family?"

She shrugs and tilts her head from side to side. "No more than usual."

I grunt again, but this time it's not because the pizza is so damn good, though it is. "Did they hassle you about me?"

It's an issue. And I know it bothers her. It bothers me too, but I'm caught. The Lalondes could hate me for the rest of their lives, and I wouldn't go anywhere.

Evie picks up another slice. "For the most part, it was about work." She sends me a grim smile. "And going back to school."

Then she watches me for a while, seems to debate something and sits up straight, looking decisive.

"I hate dishonesty. Even lies of omission," she says, and I go still, already knowing I won't like what she's about to say. Then Evie wrinkles her nose. "Drake was there."

At first my stomach pitches. "At lunch?"

430

A shocked laugh bursts from her. "No, oh God, no." She leans in and grips my knee with the easy affection that I've come to rely on as much as blood in my veins. "At the yoga studio. He tried to schmooze Mom and Tori."

The fuckwad.

Evie rolls her eyes. "He asked me out in front of them, and when I told him I was seeing someone, he guessed it was you and made a big stink."

My eyes become slits. I can't touch him, but I want to kill him. Evie doesn't miss any of this.

She squeezes my knee again. "I'm sorry if that upsets you, but I couldn't keep it from you." The soft sincerity in her eyes holds mine. "That would dishonor who you are to me."

And with that, the urge to commit murder one disappears. Fuckwads will always be fuckwads. This one won't have Evie. She's mine.

All I really need to worry about is a worthy man stepping into her path. And if she can be honest, so can I.

"Is it wrong of me to hope that the only men who ever hit on you are cock-faced douchebags?" I say this right as she's taking another bite of pizza. Her eyes bug, she chokes, and she's caught between laughing and coughing for the next minute and a half. I pat her on the back, but it only makes her laugh harder.

When she catches her breath, Evie shakes her head at me. "You're terrible."

I quirk a grin. "Why? Because I said *cock-faced douchebag* or because I hope that's my only competition."

Her left brow becomes a sharp peak. "Both." She picks up her abandoned pizza slice and takes a hearty

431

bite. "But I love you anyway," she says around a mouthful.

I open my mouth to tell her the same, but she raises a hand to stop me.

"You," she stresses. "No one else."

Not touching her isn't an option. She's wearing a dark orange blouse with a drooping bow at the neckline, and I reach over and tug the bow open. I drag my gaze to hers and find amusement with just a hint of shyness.

But nothing that tells me I should stop.

The bow was hiding two small buttons at her collar. I shift my body toward her, knees zippering with hers. With my left hand, I palm her thigh, and with the right, I attend to those buttons. When her collar falls open, I meet her eyes again.

Her smile is bright now. She drops her pizza crust into the box and brushes her fingers with the napkin before going still and watching me again.

I peel back her collar, lean in, and press my lips to the delicate dip at the base of her throat. She tastes warm and sweet with just a zing of salt I find when I let my tongue trace the groove. The moment I do, her breath catches, and the next thing I know, her hand is at the back of my neck, fingers rooting into my hair.

The thoughts I'm having are too pathetic to share. I can't pledge her my life, my body, and my soul over a box of pizza. But they are hers.

And if I can't tell her all of that without words, I can make her feel good.

Buttons surrender one by one, and when I've slipped the gauzy blouse off her shoulders, and she's watching me with half-lidded eyes in her bra and blue jeans, I can't speak at all.

So I stand, pluck her off the kitchen chair, and her legs wrap around me again. We travel the short distance to my bed where I lay her down. And because kissing her must happen now — right now — I lay on top of her fully clothed.

I know how strong she is, but, now, beneath me, she is all yielding softness. Her body cradles mine like I belong right here. There's just enough room for the two of us. None for ghosts. Nor fear. Nor shame.

CHAPTER THIRTY-ONE

EVIE

On Monday afternoon, Tori and I drop Mom and Dad off at the airport.

We spent almost all of Sunday together as a family, and it was the first time during their visit that no one gave me grief about my job, my abandoned degree, or my boyfriend.

Thank you, St. Monica, oh patron of disappointing daughters.

In fact, Drew told me my parents had gone by the hospital early Sunday morning. He ran into them on their way out, but his Aunt Shelly said they went by Mrs. Vivian's hospice room and told stories about Drew's grandma for about twenty minutes.

At first, I'd been peeved they hadn't asked me to join them, but now I'm really glad they didn't. The visit had been their idea. A gesture of neighborly respect for Mrs. Vivian and her family. And for Drew.

He'd said when he saw them they'd both greeted him politely, shaking his hand in the hospital lobby. I would rather them be warm instead of just polite, but it's better than nothing. Right?

Time will help. Mom and Dad are still coming back for Christmas. I'll make a point to talk about him in our Skype's and texts, and they'll see they have nothing to worry about. They might even start to realize how wonderful he his. How well he treats me. It may take a little while, but they'll accept him.

I hope so, anyway. I hope they'll accept me enough to accept him.

These are my thoughts as Tori and I leave the airport and make our way to University Avenue. She's said nothing since we hugged Mom and Dad goodbye, and that's fine with me. I know from Mom that she is putting together applications for pharmacy school in the hopes of starting next semester.

I'm happy for her.

It also means, no matter what, she'll be moving away. And I can't say I'm unhappy about that. Mom and Dad tried to talk me into moving back into the house, saying that when she goes, they'll needs someone to live in it.

I have to admit, the offer is tempting. Without Tori there, it isn't like anyone would be "keeping an eye" on me. I'd have the place to myself, and I would feel more comfortable than I do at Janine's.

But I wasn't ready to say yes. Instead, I put them off, telling them we could talk about it in a month or two. We'll see how things go until then. How they treat me. If Tori gets accepted into a program.

No matter what, it's still hard to tell them no, so when Mom asked me to keep driving the Volvo so it doesn't die on her next time she's in town, I gave in. And I'll admit, this will be easier on me too.

Tori and I pass by Tribe, and a smile drifts over my face. I'm off tonight, and Drew stayed with Mrs. Vivian last night, so he'll be home. We'll be together.

When we turn onto St. Landry, Tori starts talking. "I applied to UT's pharma program last night."

I glance over at her, and she's wearing a glib smile. Good for her.

"University of Texas? Wow. That's great, Tori."

She never shares much, but if she's telling me this, it must be important to her.

435

She doesn't look at me, but she nods a slow nod. Up and down. Up and down.

We ride in silence.

At the turn on St. Mary, she breaks it. "Well, aren't you going to ask me why UT instead of UL-Monroe or Ole Miss?"

I can tell by her profile that her expression has soured. Obviously, I was supposed to ask. Silly me for not asking.

"Sorry, Tori. Why UT?" I parrot.

The glib smile returns, but she says nothing.

"Tori?"

She makes the turn onto Souvenir Gate, and I give up, let go a sigh, and look out the window. I don't know what game she's playing, but I don't have to be a contestant.

When we pull onto St. Patrick Street, Tori makes the smacking noise of someone who has just heard disappointing news.

"I think you should come in for a little while, so we can talk, Evie."

I turn to her with a frown. "What? Right now?"

She presses her lips into what's supposed to pass for a regretful simper, and nods. "Yes, right now. I'm afraid I have some bad news."

Alarm tingles down my spine. Whatever this is about, it isn't good. I hesitate. "Can we get together later? I have a class in the park and—"

"Oh, no," she says, shaking her head. I swear, she sounds like a Disney villain. "I don't think you'd want to wait to hear this."

Shit.

I swallow a cold knot in my throat. What the hell is she up to?

She pulls into the driveway and kills the engine. Tori turns to me with a frightening smile. "Well, are you going to come in?"

I can taste my heartbeat, metallic with fear. "What's this about, Tori?"

Tori tilts her head to the side, giving me an almost pitying smile. "Oh, I think you know."

And I do know. Somehow, without her saying anything else, I know this is about Drew. And whatever it is, it's bad.

"Let's go inside, shall we?" She's out of the car before I can reply. I have to make my limbs move. My hands and feet prickle with pins and needles, and my mouth is completely dry. My tongue seems to have swollen in mere seconds.

I try to swallow as I slip out of the car. Panic tells me to run. Run for help. But I don't even know what I'd be running from. I force myself to breathe the way I teach my students to. To clear my head. To figure out what's going on so I can take action.

Like a zombie, I follow my sister inside our parents' house. She closes the door behind me and takes her time hanging up her jacket and purse. Removing mine is out of the question. I need whatever protection I can get.

Tori leaves the foyer for the living room, and I follow. She gestures toward Mom's pristine, cream white Bridgewater sofa, and, mechanically, I perch on one of its stiff cushions. My hands are shaking, so I rest them on my knees.

Taking a seat at the other end of the sofa, Tori regards me with a smug smile. "You're going to break up with Drew Moroux."

Her words knock the fear right out of me. How ridiculous. "No. I'm not."

She bats her eyelashes, her smile never wavering. "I think you will."

"Never." I shake my head. "I love him."

Her lips stay stretched across her face, but at my words, something in her expression hardens. She may be smiling at me, but I see hatred in her eyes.

"I'm sorry you think you're in love with a criminal," she says, her nostrils flaring. "That will make hearing what I have to say that much more upsetting, but you'll thank me in the long run."

I shake my head. "Tori, there's nothing you could tell me about Drew that would upset me. I know the man he is. We love each other, and you're just going to have to accept th—"

Tori springs to her feet, hands balled into fists. "I will *not* accept my sister dating someone who has broken into this house and stolen from me!"

Her words ring in my ears, but I can't process them.

"What? No, To—"

"Yes. He broke in and took things. From me." Her nostrils flare as she practically yells in my face. I lean away.

"Tori, don't be ridiculous. Drew never stole from us."

Her mouth pulls to the side in a sneer. "Not us. *Me.*"

438

I get to my feet. I've had enough. Staying any longer is just going to drive an irreparable rift between us. "I don't know what you're doing, Tori, but I'm not interested in—"

Slowly, Tori sits again and gives me that chilling, all-knowing smile. "Oh, I'm sure the police will be interested."

Time stops, and it takes my breath and blood with it.

And the moment I understand what she's done — what she's planning to do — breath and blood resume at racing speed.

"W-what have you done?"

She gives me that awful, phony smile of pity. "Oh, dear Evie. It's not what I've done. It's what your boyfriend has done," she says softly, her lips vanishing as pretend regret draws down her mouth. "He's committed burglary again. While on parole. I don't think they'll go easy on him."

I shake my head, fear leaving me mute. After a long moment, I force the words out in a rasp. "You can't do this."

She shakes her head. "Believe me, I don't want to." But anyone looking at her could see that she wants this. She wants to hurt me anyway she can. And hurting Drew is the surest way.

"Tori, y-you're talking about making a false accusation against an innocent man." My voice shakes, and I'm sure she can hear the fear in it. But she only gives me a doubtful look.

"Oh, no. Not innocent." Tori shakes her head. "I'm sure the police will find plenty of evidence, both here and on Mr. Moroux's property, for a conviction."

439

Horror washes over me. Threatens to drown me. Drew's apartment. Ever since Mrs. Vivian has been in the hospital, he's left it unlocked for me, so I could wait for him or join him in the middle of the night.

Oh God.

"What did you do, Tori? What did you plant there?" Her color is high. Her eyes bright. She's loving this. Why does she want to hurt us this way? "Tori, why would you do this?"

She reaches forward and clamps her hand around my wrist, eyes locking with mine. "Evie, I'm the victim here. Something has been taken from me, and I can't let that go unanswered."

Her grip on my wrist is tight, almost painful. "Tori," My voice breaks on her name. "Drew has taken nothing from you."

She stares at me with unblinking focus, and her eyes say it all. Drew hasn't taken anything from her. I have. And this is my punishment.

"Don't do this to him," I beg, shaking my head. "Whatever reasons you have to hate me, don't hurt Drew."

"Hate you?" The reptilian smile returns, and her grip becomes vice-like. "How could I hate my perfect baby sister who's always had her way? How could I hate someone who I've made so many sacrifices for?"

My eyes well with tears because the person in front of me can't be my sister. We've never been close. It's been difficult between us for years. But I've loved her. I've loved Tori, and it's clear to me now that she's only hated me in return.

440

"Please, Tori. If you do this, Drew will go back to jail." I shake my head. "He's lost so much already. You can't."

Her mouth pulls to the side as though she's considering, but it's all bullshit. "Hmmm. Yeah, he would go back to prison. I mean, there's probably a lot of evidence the police would find against him." She nods as she says this as though it's a shame. "I know from my one forensic chemistry class that things like clothing fibers, hair, even shoe prints can really be damning in a case like this."

"My God, Tori!" I yank free from her grip. The notion seems impossible, but looking at her, I don't doubt it for a second. She's planted all of this. She's been in Drew's apartment, taken whatever she wanted, left something of hers behind, and then hidden "evidence" here. And where that would be — which window sill or door, which room or floor I have no idea. The back of the house is all windows. On the bottom floor alone, there must be twenty at least.

I'll clean them all. Clean the whole fucking house.

She narrows her eyes at me, and I know she's followed my thoughts. "Of course, I couldn't really be sure *when* this happened," she says with meaning. "Or when it might happen again."

I understand what she means. She has more — more hair, more clothing fibers — she could hide later. Anger chars its way up my throat. "I wouldn't have thought you were capable of this," I hiss.

She keeps her tone deceptively light. "Oh, I'm capable of a lot of things," she sing songs. "Even letting

441

your boyfriend get away with this heinous crime… under the right circumstances."

I cough a mirthless laugh. This can't be blackmail. She knows I don't have much. But the thought of handing over everything I own just to make her go away is suddenly very tempting. I can't let her ruin him. I can't let him go through that again.

"What do you want, Tori?" My voice is almost vicious. If Drew's safety depended on me physically fighting her, she'd be down in point five seconds.

She gives me a startled look. "I already told you. All I want is for you to break up with him."

"No."

The word rips from me like an animal's cry.

Tori puts on a disappointed face, her head tilting with weary patience. "Now, Evie. You know I only want what's best for you. How can I let you keep seeing someone who's so depraved, so unethical, he'd not only steal, but steal from *me?*" She flicks a palm toward her chest. "Me. Your own sister."

Angry tears blur my vision. "He didn't steal from you. You're just trying to hurt me."

Tori slowly shakes her head. "No, my love. And I'm sure the police, not to mention Mom and Dad, will see that." Her soft voice feels like razor wire to me now.

Razor wire. Like the kind that tops prison fences.
Oh God.

If she filed a police report — if there was an investigation with evidence — who would believe Drew? Who would believe us? If I told the police that Tori had staged all of this, would they even listen? Would Mom and Dad?

442

Tori seems to be reading my mind. "In the end, I can only hope a jury would serve justice, but now that you need a unanimous guilty verdict, it's hard to say," Tori says, still speaking like she's reciting a nursery rhyme. "But that might take... oh, I don't know... a year or more in the courts. And with Mr. Moroux's history, he probably wouldn't make bail, so he'd be in j—"

"Shut up." I turn away from her, unable to listen anymore.

But I know she's right. I know it in my bones. If she so much as files a report, Drew's freedom will be in jeopardy. And I have no doubt Tori will press charges. Even if he isn't convicted, Drew's life will be derailed once again.

Because of me.

I need to warn him. I need to tell him what she's done.

"You'd better not be thinking about leaving." For the first time since I walked inside, Tori sounds like herself. Angry. Biting. Vicious. I wheel around to face her. Tori's mouth is set in nasty scowl. I see at once the last thing she wants is for me to walk away. To deny her this victory.

I should just leave. Run across the street and tell Janine exactly what's going on. Maybe we could call the police together. Stop Tori before she can do anything.

"You walk out that door, and I pick up the phone. The police will be here in minutes." Threat is now clear in her voice. She's practically snarling.

So much for bolting across the street.

"You have one chance to protect your boyfriend, Evie. You will call him over here right now," she growls

443

through gritted teeth. "You will break up with him here. In this room where I can hear you."

My mouth falls open at this, but before I can protest she talks over me.

"And then you will write an email to Mom and Dad telling them you've broken up with him. That you're coming home, and that you want to take them up on their offer to travel as soon as possible."

"Tori, that's ridi—"

"I don't give a fuck where you go, but you will leave the country for no less than two months or I will turn him in."

"What?!" She's lost her mind. My sister has lost her mind. "You're telling me if I don't break up with my boyfriend, quit my job, and *leave the country*, you'll frame him?"

A glimmer of conscience ripples across her face, and for just a moment she looks startled to hear all of this out loud. But the look is gone just as quickly as it appeared. Smugness takes its place.

"I guess that depends on how much he means to you."

Everything.

Drew means everything to me.

But this is madness. Surely, I couldn't go through with this. And why does she want me to leave for two months?

I shake my head, confusion and distress threatening to turn my head inside out "Why two months? What happens in two months?"

Tori goes gimlet eyed, her smug smile still in place. "You owe me two months with a broken heart."

"What? Why?" Nothing makes sense. I feel like the longer we talk, the more lost I am.

Tori crosses her arms over chest and cocks her chin. "Ask me again why I'm applying to UT."

I've never wondered what it feels like to be a puppet on a string, but now I know. A sigh leaves me, taking with it almost all my strength.

"Why, Tori, why are you applying to UT?"

Her face twists into a vicious scowl. "Because, you idiot. Jason's there. He moved there this summer." Tori balls her fists, her shoulders shooting back as she seems to lever toward me. I step back on instinct. "He asked me to go with him. He wanted *me*. But I was chained here. Tethered to you, you ungrateful, spoiled bitch!"

Even though I shouldn't let them, the words sting anyway. But their meaning nearly knocks me over.

"Jason Watney?" I hear myself ask. Picturing the tan, sandy-haired software developer who liked outdoor concerts, *Riverdale,* and, apparently, Tori.

She sneers. "Have I brought any other Jasons home? My God, Evie, how dense could you be?"

I'm guessing pretty dense. I knew they were together. I knew, maybe too late, that Tori had been happy with him, but only because of how unhappy she'd seemed after he stopped coming around.

Because he'd moved. I'd had no idea. I just thought he'd broken it off. I wasn't even surprised.

He'd asked her to move with him? And she hadn't — couldn't — because of me? That's what all this is about. A good, old fashioned get even. I kept her away from her man. Now it's her turn.

Except it's not the same thing. Not at all.

445

I try to reason with her. "I didn't know, Tori," I say, trying to speak softly, still hoping to calm her. "I would have told you to go with him had I known."

Her scowl only cinches tighter. "It's not my fault you're stupid."

"Tori, I would have *wanted* you to go," I say, a pleading edge in my voice. "Because I want you to be happy."

She shakes her head with violence. "You just say things like that to make yourself sound better than everybody else," she hisses, bitterness spiking in her tone.

I've heard all this before. Accusations of pretense. Of perfection. I *do* want her to be happy. It would be such a relief, finally, to have a sister who is happy. Happy with her life. Happy with her family. Happy for me.

But I won't win her this way.

"I'm sorry about Jason. Have you been in touch with him? Does he know you've applied to UT?" I regret my questions almost as soon as I utter them.

"Oh he knows," she snaps. "But he's been seeing other people. Even if I get over there, I might not be able to get back what you took from me."

I press my lips together and breathe through this new layer. When I can keep my voice even, I try again. "I see that you blame me for this, and I can accept that," I say with a slow nod. "But Drew is innocent here. He never stole from you. He doesn't deserve this."

Her mouth hangs open with disdain. "Like I care what that felon deserves. Things *were* stolen from me." Her voice climbs with emotion. "And someone's going to pay for that."

Then Tori turns and grabs her phone from the coffee table. "And if you won't, he will."

"Tori—" I move toward her, but she gives me her back. I step around her to see she has the keypad open. Her thumb presses the nine and the one.

"What are you doing?!" I shriek, slapping the phone out of her hand. It clatters to Mom's polished wood floors, and Tori gives me a hard shove in the shoulder. I brace my core, years of balance postures keeping me upright.

"What does it look like? I'm turning in that thief, you little shit." She reaches for the phone, but I snatch it up first and clutch it to me.

"You don't have to do this," I plead.

She glares at me, eyes hard. "Break up with him, and I won't have too."

"Tori, please." I hold her phone, but it's useless. I can't stop her.

"I *will* call the police, and he *will* be arrested. Today."

Drew's at work right now. He texted me on his lunch break to say he missed me.

He missed me.

He'll go by the hospital tonight before he comes home. I can't let him be arrested. Not there. Not at the garage. Not in his home. Not again. And definitely not now as he's keeping vigil for Mrs. Vivian.

"Break up with him. Leave the country." Tori crosses her arms over her chest with a shrug. "If he still wants you in two months, hooray for you." And then an evil glint lights her eyes. "Of course, he might be seeing other people."

447

My mouth goes dry. The muscles in my quads are shaking as if my legs might give any moment.

"What's to stop me from telling him you put me up to this?"

She scowls at me like I'm an idiot. "Because the deal's off if you do."

A mirthless laugh leaves me. "How would you even know? It's not like you can watch me twenty-four seven."

"You're moving in where I can keep an eye on you until you leave. I watch his house. I watch you. I check your phone. I catch you even sending him so much as a text, and I call the police," she says with menace. "No warning. No second chance."

I clench my teeth but say nothing.

"If you want to protect your boyfriend, you'd better not contact him after today," she warns. "I've seen you come and go from his apartment. No one's invisible. Stay away from him. Leave for two months. Then he's safe."

Drew's safety and welfare are everything to me.

"How do I know you won't hurt him then?"

The corner of her mouth lifts, and I swear, she almost looks proud. As though she approves of my question. But she executes a coy shrug.

"Maybe he will find a way to return my stolen property, so then I'd have nothing to report."

I know what this means. In two months, she'll tell me — or Drew — where she's hidden whatever she planted in his apartment. There's no way I can stay away from him that long. There's no way I'm leaving the country. But I need time to figure this out, and Tori's not giving me any.

She reaches out and turns her palm up. "Give me the phone, or I use the house line." Holding onto her cell is pointless, so I hand it over. Saying nothing, she eyes me with an icy smile for perhaps a minute. "Now, Evie, times up. You call him, or I call the police. What's it going to be?"

I shake my head. "He won't believe it. I love him, and he knows it. People who love each other don't break up, Tori."

Her nostrils flare. "Yes. They. Do," she growls. "It happens all the time. And you'd better convince him if you know what's good for him."

The rage in her gaze shuts me up.

I draw my phone out of my back pocket and stare at it.

Drew.

I close my eyes and reach for him. Feel him. His essence. His energy. The Drew-ness of him. And it's there. Right there. All I have for him is love. It is whole. Pure. Unbroken and unblemished. I've never felt this much love for anyone. Not family. Not friends.

It pours from me. It blankets me. And right now, he's all I want.

How can I do this?

"Stop crying," Tori hisses.

I open my eyes and find my face soaked with tears. "Please, Tori. Please don't make me do this."

She shakes her head in disgust. "Have it your way." And she unlocks her screen again.

"No! No!" I shriek.

Tori throws up her hands in frustration. "Well, let's get on with it then."

449

Anguish tightens around my throat. I can't even see my phone's screen. Blindly, I tap in my passcode and then just stare at the swimming letters of Drew's last text.

I miss you.

"Oh, God," I mutter, sinking to the couch.

In a flash of movement, Tori rips the phone from me. "Give me that. I'll fucking do it."

"Tori!" I grab, but she bats me away. "Damn you! Give it back!" Panic and outrage overtake me. No fucking way. No way will I let him think her words are mine.

"Ow!" Surprised, Tori draws back her wrist, which now bears the mark of my nails, but I hold my phone. She's written *We need to talk,* but, thank God she didn't press send. I erase her words and begin with the only ones I want to tell him. Tori peers at my screen and makes a derisive noise, but says nothing.

Me: I love you, Drew.

A sob quakes through me. Even through my tears, I see his dots bouncing, his heart already answering mine.

Drew: I love you, Guppy. You okay?

Oh my God. How does he know? I break down completely. He is my love. I vow in this moment not to lie to him. I won't tell him what I can't tell him. But I refuse to lie.

Me: No. I'm not. Something's happened. Can you meet me after work? At my parents' house?

His response is immediate.

Drew: What's wrong?

I can feel his tension, his worry and protection for me, and I fall apart. *I have to protect him,* I remind myself. And it's only this thought that makes it possible to go on.

Me: I can't tell you now. Please come when you can. I'll be here.

"Good girl," Tori says, her voice dripping with satisfaction.

I say nothing. I will never speak to her again.

Drew: On my way.

I bury my face into the couch cushions, my heart an open wound.

CHAPTER THIRTY-TWO

DREW

I pull up to the Lalonde's house, confused as hell. I was in the middle of an oil change when Evie texted me. I finished up, clocked out, and scrubbed my hands in the bathroom for at least five minutes, but they're still dirty.

I glance down at my grimy nails once more before looking up at Evie's picture perfect home. Her parents should be on their way back to Nigeria. At least, they should have left a couple of hours ago. As I slam the heavy door of Grandma's Buick behind me, I wonder if plans have changed.

My eyes flick again to the grease-marked cracks in my calloused palms, and I wince. I'd rather not shake Evie's father's hand like this. With a sigh, I climb the steps to their front porch, remembering the other two times I was here. Once to tell off Dick Face Drake. The other to get an ass-chewing from Tori.

Yeah, no real positive associations here.

I mutter a curse under my breath and ring the doorbell. It echoes within the house, but only silence follows. I wait. Frowning, I ring it again. And then I hear a muffled voice. It sounds like Evie, but... different.

The door swings open, and Evie sags against the doorframe. At first I think she's doubled over with laughter, and then I think she's sick. She's a mess. Her face is blotchy, her eyes streaming. Her turned down mouth is open in a gasp, as though she's in pain. It's only when I reach for her and her sob breaks that I realize she's crying.

Uncontrollably crying.

I pull her to me and wrap her in my arms. Later, I'll realize that seeing her like this should have scared the hell out of me. But in this moment, it doesn't. Whatever is wrong, I'll take care of it. There's nothing I wouldn't do for her, so, as far as I'm concerned, this problem is solved. Whatever it is.

I've got this. I've got her.

So I hug her to me and just let her cry. Hot tears soak through my shirt. Her whole body radiates heat like a furnace. I raise a hand to her wet cheek and smooth the wispy curls away from her face. Her curls are damp from her tears as though she's been crying for a while.

She's clutching me with fierce strength. Like she's afraid of losing me. As if she ever could.

I lower my lips to the top of her head, kiss her reckless curls, and drop my mouth to her ear.

"Whatever it is, it's okay."

Evie shakes her head against me but keeps it buried. Her voice emerges in a squeak. "… Not okay."

She's in one piece. As far as I can tell, she doesn't have any scrapes or bruises, but too late, the thought occurs to me that someone may have harmed her.

My arms close tighter around her. "Did someone hurt you?" Anger like hot tar begins to boil in me. If anyone touched her—

But she's shaking her head against me, and more wet squeaks and sniffles emerge against my chest. "No. No." But then she fists my shirt in her hands. "Well, yes, but not like that."

I frown. "Like what?"

This question just kicks off another wave of tears, so I walk her further into the house, which, at first

453

glance, seems empty. There's no sign of her parents, and if Gemini were here, he'd be right at Evie's side. I think we're alone, but then the sound of a door squeak from the hall at the other end of the room makes me wonder.

Evie's parents' house is nice. Even nicer on the inside than it is on the outside. Still clutching her to me, I walk her to the expensive-looking couch. Who has a white couch? Isn't that just an accident waiting to happen?

I grew up in a household with three kids. The one time Ma actually bought a new couch when we were little, it was brown. And not even solid brown. But streaked with dark green and black. Nothing was showing up on that thing. No spilled Kool-Aid. No stray Sharpies. But this looks like a blank canvas ready for disaster.

I sit Evie down, but I don't try to peel her from me. She'll surface for air when she's ready, and then we can get this worked out. She's still clinging to me, hiding her face in my shirt, so I just run my hands up and down her back to make sure she knows she's not alone.

"It's alright," I whisper. "I'm here. Take your time. I'm not going anywhere."

But this, clearly, is the wrong thing to say because Evie smothers a cry of pure agony against me. And the sound of it stabs at something small and young inside of me.

"Baby, what's wrong?"

For a long moment, she is just silent, pressing so hard into me it's like she's trying to join me in my skin. And I'd let her if it would make her feel better. But then she pushes back from me. Her beautiful face is puffy and red from crying, her lips and nose raw.

454

With rough swipes, she brushes away her tears and blinks up at me, but then her face closes on another silent sob, and she hides it behind her hands.

"Evie, babe." I gently clasp each wrist. "What is it?"

I tug lightly, and she lets me pull her hands away. The look she wears behind them is one of complete heartbreak. It hits me that every time I've opened my mouth, I've made her cry harder, so I shut the hell up. She knows I'm listening. I watch her and wait.

This must work because she forces a deep inhale, blinking against fresh tears, and she looks me straight in the eyes. "I don't want to do this."

I frown in confusion. And then it hits me.

I once read that the worst feeling a human can experience is doom. Just ask anyone on death row. The certainty of annihilation surpasses simple fear, overrides dread. Doom is hopeless. It is destruction, death, and damnation all at once.

This is what I feel at Evie's words. Doom. And a full-body frostbite. She doesn't even have to say it. She's ending this. Ending us.

Just like I knew she would.

Her bottom lip is trembling, and she bites down on it before speaking again. "I don't want to do this," she says again, her voice barely above a whisper. "But I have to."

I can't feel my face. I hope my expression is even. Blank. I'd like to give her a look of understanding. Of acceptance. But I —

Damn.

Damn.

Damn.

Damn.

I knew this would happen. I tell myself I knew this would happen. But did it have to be so soon? I must have fooled myself into believing we'd have — I'd have months with her.

Evie breaks down again. I want to reach for her, but I can't. I held her just a moment ago, but if I touch her again, I'll lose it.

My throat tries to close, and I swallow hard against the choking loss. I can't. I can't show her what this will do to me. *Is* doing to me. I promised myself when the time came, I'd make this easy on her.

Evie, I love you.

I've never wanted to say the words so badly. I've said them, but not enough. Not nearly enough.

As I sit on this perfect, white couch that may as well be soaked in my blood, I promise myself I will say those words aloud every day for the rest of my life. Every goddamn day.

But I need to get the hell out of here.

Gritting my teeth, clenching my fists, I move to stand, but Evie clutches my wrist. "Wait. Wait," she says, her voice panicked. "D-do you know what I'm trying to say?"

I clear my throat and with everything I have, I force my voice to come out steady. "You're breaking up with me."

It's like she's been struck in the chest the sob shakes her so hard. "But I don't want to," she cries.

So it's her family. They're making her do it. I'm not surprised. And there's some part of her that knows they're right. Evie's too headstrong and unconventional just to cave to their wishes. I want to know what happened to make her do this now. What they told her that led her to see reason. But I won't ask. That would only make it harder for her.

My Evie.

I'd give her my life. I'd stand sentry outside her door until she's ninety-nine and I'm a hundred and four. I'd take a bullet, get hit by a bus, or throw myself on a landmine to protect her. I know she's crying now because she doesn't want to hurt me.

Me. The felon. The thug.

She's crying. Over me. And it just makes me love her even more. More than I ever thought I could love. I knew this would hurt like hell. It does. So goddamn much. And it'll hurt to keep loving her. But it's the best thing I've ever done, and I don't plan to stop.

Despite Evie's hand tight on my wrist, I stand. I need to howl for about three days, and I can't do it here.

"I get it," I mutter.

Silently, I vow: *I will love you beyond death.*

Unwelcome, the Audioslave lyrics we heard just weeks ago come back to me. If I died right now, would I know any lack of her? Would she already be in my heaven?

Knowing Evie and her magic, she would.

Okay, something to look forward to.

I let go a breath that's dangerously close to a sob, and I lock it down. "I gotta go, Evie."

Her hand slips from me, her eyes widening. "But you don't understand."

"Yeah, I do."

457

"No, you d-don't." Her voice breaks, and she reaches for me, but Christ almighty, I can't handle that, so I step back and lift my hands behind my head.

"No." It's all I can say because I'm about to fucking lose my shit. And maybe the word comes out harsher than I intend, but holy fuck, I won't be able to leave if I hold her. "I gotta go."

Her mouth falls open, and she stares at me like I've just struck her. "So that... that's *it?*"

This is my Evie. Emotional. Mystical. Spiritual. She wants closure and peace and harmony and all that shit. I wish I could give it to her, but I fucking can't. The temptation to drop to my knees and beg her to tell her family to go to hell is almost more than I can bear.

I blow a breath out my nose. "Evie, it's all I've got." This is both lie and truth. What I have for her, if I let it loose, would be like an avalanche. A fucking landslide that could wipe us both away. So the only truth I can give her is my control. My control is all I've got.

"Drew," she says, her chin quivering. "I love you." Tears flood her eyes again, and I'm ready to cave.

Fuck me.

Fuck control.

Fuck it all.

I'm about to kiss her like the sun is set to explode and we're the only things left to light the sky. Tell her that her family can't have her because she's mine now, and I'll never give her back. Tell her my sole purpose on this earth is to love her and I'll do it always whether she wants me or not.

I'm tearing through my own chains, just leaning in toward her, when the sound of my phone ringing grabs me back from the edge.

I lock eyes with Evie for a weighty moment. The floor in the hall creaks. I whip my head toward the sound, but no one's there. My phone rings again.

Ripping myself away from Evie, I reach for my phone. Annie. I answer.

"Yeah?"

"Drew?" Her voice is tight. Steady. Unbroken. But tight.

Grandma.

"I'm here."

"Oh Jesus. It's time. The nurses say it won't be long now," she says in a rush. She's talking fast. Trying not to let the fear and sadness leach into her voice. Because she's my sister through and through. "Can you come?"

"I'll be there." I back toward the door as I speak. "On my way."

Evie hasn't taken her eyes off me. They're wide. Worried. Full of pain. Full of love. Love I'll never get to keep.

"I'm sorry, Evie." I'm apologizing for not losing control. For not giving in to how much I feel. I'm apologizing for not being the kind of man she would do anything to keep. I'm sorry for all the anguish loving me is causing her. Because I know she loves me. I know it hurts. And I'm apologizing because I know I don't deserve any of it. "Goodbye."

I'd give anything to be numb.

459

It's nearly midnight. Grandma Quincy is gone. And we were all there. My aunts and uncles. Annie. Most of my cousins. Even a few of their children. We stood around her bed like a wreath of progeny. Ma was there, too, standing so far to my left I couldn't see her. I stayed between Annie and Aunt Josie, who both clutched me by the arm as if I'd escape.

As if I had anywhere else to go.

And I'm a piece of shit. I should have been thinking about Grandma and everything she's ever done for me. Feeling the loss of her. But the loss I feel, the one that overwhelms everything else, is Evie.

Besides, the still body that breathed its last breath encircled by all of us wasn't Grandma. I can't help but think that the essence of her was already embracing Grandpa Pete. And Anthony. And everyone else she'd wished to be reunited with.

I have Evie to thank for that. For even the possibility it might be so.

"Evie."

I'm driving alone in Grandma's Buick, and there's no one else to hear me say her name, so I say it again. And again.

"Why now, Evie?"

I'm crushed. Pulverized. But I'm not angry. I'm not bitter. She was never mine to keep. But I will keep her.

"You're mine, Evie." I tell the night, and there's nothing but shadows and the glow of street lamps on South College Road to hear the catch in my voice. "Everything you are, everything you gave me I'll keep."

And then I hit the brakes, swerving just in time to miss the dark shape that darts in front of the car.

Glancing in the rearview, I see no one's behind me, so I stop and scan the side of the road.

"I'll be damned."

The little black mutt with the scruffy coat stands on the sidewalk, eyeing me warily. I swear, it's the same dog Evie and I saw the other day. The one she asked me to look out for after I dropped her off at the yoga studio. This time, he's in front of the daycare instead of the complex where we saw him last time.

I check my rearview again before pulling into the daycare's driveway and killing the engine. The dog has taken a few steps further into the grass, but when I open the car door, he stops and lowers his head. He doesn't move as I step out of the car, and our eyes meet over the hood.

"Evie would want me to stop," I tell him. His ears bob, and he lifts his head just a little. "We saw you the other day. She was worried about you."

The little guy's tail is tucked, but at my words, I see it wag just a bit. In spite of everything that's happened tonight, this makes me smile.

I take two careful steps to the front of the car in the dog's direction. I watch him tense, but he doesn't move. Then, slowly, I drop into a squat.

"You look like you've had a rough day," I say, taking in the clots of mud that coat the dog's chest and forelegs. "Couldn't have been worse than mine."

I don't really know what the hell I'm doing, talking to a dog by the side of the road in the middle of the night, but it feels right. I know without even having to think about it, Evie would approve. So what else is there to do?

"She'd take you in." I chuckle when I say it, thinking of her sweet, soft heart. *Evie, I love you.* My throat closes around the chuckle, and my eyes sting. The dog just watches me without judgment. A moment later, my voice comes out raspy. "You wanna come with me? I don't have much, but it'd be better than this." I nod to the four lane road where this dog will surely be squashed if he keeps this up.

I pat my knee and hold out an open palm. The dog doesn't step closer, but I watch him sniff the air, trying to judge my scent.

"I won't hurt you. I can promise you that." I pat my knee again and try to make myself look smaller. I tuck my legs under me and sit on my heels. He wags a little more. "Oh, you like that, do ya?" I drop one hand to the ground, damp leaves and grass cool on my palm, and with the other hand I reach toward him.

"Come on, buddy. Come check me out."

The dog draws his nose from left to right, sniffing hard now. He takes one step. Two steps. His nose is now just inches from my fingers.

"That's it," I prompt softly. Then a wet nose brushes my knuckles and a tongue swipes my fingertips. I try to hold as still as I can while the little guy smells me. He's small. Maybe twenty-five pounds, and even though he's a mess I can tell with a haircut, he'd be pretty cute.

When I curl my fingers to scratch under his chin, he flinches, springing back just a little.

"Not gonna hurt ya," I promise, speaking as softly as I can. "Come on, bud."

And then he steps closer and lets me scratch him. I start under his chin, feeling clods of dried mud, and

462

when I move up under his ear, the dog lets out a gruff sigh.

"Good boy."

He lets me stroke his head and a moment or two later run a hand down his shoulder. His fur is so matted, I can tell he hasn't been cared for by human hands in a long, long while.

"We'll need to get you cleaned up, pup." Slowly, I rise up to kneeling, still stroking the dog. He's watching me, but he doesn't slip from my touch. He isn't wearing a collar, and I'm not about to pick him up in case he freaks out and tries to eat my face, so if he's going to come with me, it'll have to be his choice.

"Want to come home with me?" At my question, the little guy tilts his head, tipping his left ear up in such a cute pose, I grin. "You shouldn't be out here all by yourself. You need someone to look after you."

I rise up to my full height, the dog's gaze following me the whole time. I take two steps toward the car and pat my thigh. As if by magic, the dog takes two steps closer to me. I smother a chuckle and take two more steps, this time angling around the side of the car. More hesitant, the mutt just peers around the front of the car, watching me.

I've left the door open so this part would be easy. No noisy movements or scary swinging car parts, but as I creep closer to the open door, I don't know how I'll convince the little guy to jump inside.

But in the end, once he sees the open door and the interior light, he doesn't hesitate. He hops right up, and stands in the middle of the passenger seat like he belongs there.

And maybe he does.

"I'll be damned," I say again. I get in the car, pet him, and then start the engine, wanting nothing more in the world than to be able to tell Evie about this.

But that can't happen. Not now. Not ever.

"Evie, I love you." The words come out choked. "What am I supposed to do with all of this?"

I glance over at the dog to find him watching me, and then he scratches behind his ear. Then he lifts a leg and—

"Well, hello," I say, surprised. "You're not a boy."

The dog — *she* — appears unsurprised by this and gets busy cleaning her nether regions. And even though I've had one of the worst days of my life, even though I feel like weeping for days, I just have to laugh. Laughing at this little mutt might just be how I'm going to get through this.

I drive. My head so thick with memories I can barely keep my eyes on the road. But it's when I pull into Grandma Q's driveway and see the light burning in her living room that it really hits me.

She's gone.

The source of warmth and welcome, of love and forgiveness, of family is gone. Her house looks just the same, just as familiar and inviting, I can't believe she's not inside, standing at her stove or watching *Ellen* in her housecoat.

Did I thank her for what she did for me?

Did I ever tell her what it meant to be claimed? To be wanted after what I'd done?

Did she know how good it felt to be her grandson?

Did she know how much I loved her?

464

I look down at the little mutt. "Grandma Quincy knew how to make everyone feel at home. I should probably start by giving you a bath."

As soon as I open the door, she springs to her feet and follows me out. She sniffs the driveway, meanders to the grass, and squats to pee.

Definitely a girl dog.

I unlock Grandma's front door, and the dog stands on the front stoop, circling the air with her nose, sniffing prudently. I step inside.

"C'mon, girl. This is your home if you want it."

She puts a tentative paw over the threshold, her black nose angling left and right.

"It's okay. It's safe. I promise."

I know it's impossible for her to understand me, but something in my voice must reassure her because she steps lightly inside and doesn't flinch when I close the door behind her. She follows me into the hall bathroom, and I shut the door, plug the stopper into the drain, and turn on the water.

As if on instinct, the little charcoal colored dog backs into the corner.

"Ah, so you've had a bath before," I say. "Sorry, but you're not staying inside all caked in mud."

I scan the plastic bottles in Grandma's shower caddy. Suave and Head & Shoulders. I take out my phone and Google safe shampoos or soaps for dogs. After reading about skin infections and screwing up a dog's pH balance with harsh fragrances in human shampoo, I learn that Dawn dish soap is safe for dogs.

I shut off the water. "Hang tight, dog." I close her into the bathroom, head to the kitchen for the dish soap, and come back to find her hiding between the toilet and

465

the wall. Cowering like this, she looks even smaller, and my heart sort of melts.

I squat down in front of her. "C'mon, girl. You have to be brave," I tell her. She doesn't move. I pat my thigh. "C'mon dog... I can't keep calling you dog. What should I call you?" My eyes scan the bathroom for inspiration, landing on Grandma Q's floral print shower curtain, her tarnished sterling silver hairbrush, and a framed Quincy family coat of arms over the bathroom window. It's been there forever. I've seen the red and gold crest probably a thousand times. As a kid, I liked the silver knight's helmet above the diamond studded shield the best, but now what stands out to me is the Quincy name on the banner below. Grandma's name. Grandpa Pete's name. The family that claimed me more than any Moroux ever did. I look down at the charcoal mop of a dog.

"Okay, Quincy it is. Time for your bath. And you'd better not bite me if you know what's good for you."

She seems to take me seriously because even though she's trembling when I scoop her up, she doesn't make any noise or give any sign of violence. She splays out all four legs as I lower her to the tub, but when she finds no purchase to stop her from meeting the water's surface, Quincy just hangs her head and stands perfectly still.

I chuckle, grateful for her docile disposition. "Don't worry, Quincy. I'll hurry." The water reaches above her belly and watery plumes of dirt bloom from her. I work quickly, wetting her matted coat all over. I use one hand to hold her down and the other to squirt blue soap down her spine. Some of the mats come loose under my fingers, but the worst ones on her hindquarters are going to need to be cut out. For now, I just worry about getting her clean.

Minutes later when I lift her from the tub and wrap her in a towel, I see she's mostly hair. Her body is skinny, and her ribs plainly visible.

"We'll get you dried off, and then I'll find you something to eat, girl," I promise. As I scrub the towel over her, she seems to recover, wagging her tail, shaking off, and then grinding her face into the bath mat. She snorts, scoots, and wiggles her bottom until I laugh out loud. Finally, she gives a full-body shake and a lusty sneeze before looking up a me with an expression that seems to ask *what's next?*

"Food," I answer, and she follows me to the kitchen.

And, no, there's no dog food to be found, and I don't want to go searching for an open grocery store after midnight, so another Google search yields that scrambled eggs make an acceptable meal for dogs. So I grease a skillet and break four eggs into it.

I place a quarter of the steaming eggs into a cereal bowl and set it in front of her. She empties the thing before I even take my first bite, and then she looks up at me expectantly.

"More?" Her dark brown eyes and salt-and-pepper eyebrows are trained on me, unblinking. "Hell, yes, right?"

I scrape more egg into her bowl and quickly eat mine, but since she stares at me the whole time, I wind up giving her the last few bites. I think about leaving the dishes in the sink to soak, but I don't let myself.

Grandma Q would have hated that, so I hand wash everything and put the dishes in the cabinet.

"Okay, upstairs."

We walk out the kitchen door, and I lock it behind me. Quincy stays at my feet as we make our way around the house. When we reach the bottom of the stairs, I think I may need to carry her up, but before I can reach down for her, she shoots up the wrought iron steps like a black arrow. At the top, she looks down at me, tail wagging and mouth open as if smiling about showing me this trick. I laugh again.

I reach the top, let us into the apartment, and when I close the door behind us, all laughter dies in my throat.

It's after one in the morning. And across both backyards, for the first time in weeks, Evie's bedroom light is on.

468

CHAPTER THIRTY-THREE

EVIE

I've slept with the light on the last three nights.

It's not because I'm afraid or lonely, though I am both. It's not because I'm not sleeping much anyway, though I am not. It's because I know Drew can see the light from his window, and I need him to know I'm still here.

Tori is watching me like a hawk. She demands to see my phone at least five times a day, checking calls, texts, even emails. She'll find nothing there, but I have tried to call Drew from work.

He won't answer.

He may not know it's me, though I've left two voice messages. So if he does know it's me, he hasn't tried calling back. I've asked at the studio every day if there have been any messages for me. None.

I've even left him a letter in Mrs. Vivian's mailbox when I walked Gemini two nights ago, but the mailbox is stuffed full. I doubt anyone's checked it in a week. And why would they?

Mrs. Vivian is gone.

I saw it in the newspaper yesterday. And, damn her to hell, so did Tori. She's insisting we go to the burial. Not the funeral. The burial. She wants Drew to see me. She definitely wants me to see him. Watching us suffer would fit nicely into her revenge plan.

And no matter how much it will hurt, I do want to see him. Desperately.

So Tori is the one who drives us to Lafayette Memorial Park Thursday afternoon, but I'm the one craning in my seat as we park, trying to catch a glimpse of Drew before he spots me.

"Mrs. Vivian sure was popular," Tori remarks as we step out of the car.

"Yes," I say, emotion catching in my throat, thinking of Drew's sweet grandmother and what she'd said about us that day the ambulance came. "She was a wonderful person."

I don't say this for Tori, of course, but for Mrs. Vivian. For Drew. For the scores of family and friends who are making their way from the snake of cars parked along the cemetery drive to the plot that's clearly marked with a canopy and chairs for mourners.

When I leave the car, I don't fall in line next to my sister, but put distance between us. She's forcing me to be here, but that doesn't mean I have to stand beside her. But she is right. A lot of people have come to pay their respects. A couple dozen white-haired ladies and a few elderly couples who walk arm in arm make their way to the plot.

As soon I clear the branches of a spreading live oak, I see him. I've seen him in jeans, coveralls, and nothing at all, but the sight of him in that black suit takes my breath away. It's only been three days, but it feels like I haven't seen him in years. Grief is etched all over his face, between his brows, the line of his mouth, even in the way his throat works as though he's trying to keep his emotions in check.

How can he look so beautiful, even now?

He's standing on the edge of the line of family, next to his sister and his Aunt Josie, up near the head of the casket. But when I get close enough, I see that his gaze isn't on the skirted coffin, but anchored on the headstone just beyond it.

Anthony's.

470

I'm not close enough to read the engraving, but I know it. I just know. And I ache to go to him. To stand beside him as he walks through his grief, new and old. I should be with him, promising him a life we will share together, giving him something to hold onto as he has to let so much go.

I glance back over my shoulder and see Tori coming. Her eyes meet mine, and she gives me that smug little grin. I want to slap her. She's seen Drew, seen how much he's hurting, and she can probably read the ache in my face, and she's loving every minute of this.

I will *never* forgive her. For what she costs us on this day alone, not to mention the pain I've lived in the last three days. Or the hurt I put in Drew's eyes on Monday. When he wouldn't let me touch him. When he thought I was abandoning him.

Or the way she'd teased me after, recalling his words when he left. *Evie, it's all I've got.* She must have said them seven or eight times after mimicking me crying. Crying and telling Drew I loved him.

He didn't fight for me.

I know it's for the best. And, truly, I'm grateful he didn't fight because I don't think I could have handled it. I might have caved and told him everything. Everything about Tori's plan against us. Then she would have called the police, and Drew could be in jail right now.

But he didn't fight for me. For us. And he hasn't returned my calls.

I was the one who chased him. I was the one who wouldn't leave him alone. This is what I think about when I'm alone in my room with the lights on, not sleeping. Was I completely wrong about us?

471

I slip my hand into the pocket of my black cardigan and clasp the tightly folded square of paper.

I guess I'll know soon enough.

I angle around the gathering and tuck myself into the crowd so I can still see Drew in profile. He hasn't spotted me yet, and I'm hoping Annie and any relative who would recognize me hasn't either. I don't want my presence to upset him. I don't want to take anything away from this most sacred of family rites. If I can't be with him, holding his hand or wrapping my arm around him, I'd rather be invisible.

The priest officiating calls for everyone's attention and invites the family to sit in the single row of chairs. I listen to the man's words, but I can't take my eyes off Drew. His head is bowed, and I watch his shoulders move in the laughter that everyone shares when the priest calls Mrs. Vivian a mother hen to everyone.

"More than once," the priest shares, "she would come to the rectory with a plate she'd made for me — if I was lucky, it was her brisket—" When he says this, an appreciative murmur rolls over the crowd, and Drew closes his eyes as though he's lost in memory. "And she'd insist on watching me eat it."

Again, knowing laughter ripples around the gathering.

"You see, Vivian thought I didn't have enough meat on my bones." The middle-aged priest grips his thin arms in demonstration, a wistful smile claiming his face. "She always knew what everyone needed, and Vivian made it her vocation to give it to them."

The man's voice softens as his eyes move over Mrs. Vivian's family. I swallow against the knot in my

472

throat. "Some may look at Vivian Quincy's life and see that her purpose was to help others, but I ask you to look a little closer. If you knew Vivian even a little, then she also *taught you* how to help others."

The thin priest lets his eyes span over the gathered mourners. "She wasn't just a good person. She taught us all how to be better people." He brings his gaze back to the family. "The best way we can honor her memory is to care for each other the way she did. Fiercely. Boldly." He gives a little shrug. "Maybe even a little obnoxiously."

We all laugh, but beneath the sounds of everyone else, I can hear Drew's low chuckle. It touches me like a warm breeze, and my eyes find him again. Longing courses through me. And maybe he senses the force of it because with a swift jerk of his head, his gaze lands on me.

I freeze.

For the briefest of instants, I read naked surprise in his eyes. But it's gone in a flash, replaced by a mask of solid granite. The look doesn't hold anger or pain. Or love. It's just completely blank. But his eyes lock with mine for a long moment, and I know my own face holds nothing back.

Shame. Guilt. Desperation. And a love that is almost killing me with its power.

Is he protecting himself like I know he does? Does the face he's showing me hide a depth of feeling that matches my own? Or is he showing me nothing because he feels nothing?

Is he angry with me?

Breath leaves me with this thought. He has every right to be angry. Without knowing my reasons, how

473

could he think anything good about me? I gave him my love. I told him I wanted to be with him no matter what.

What if he hates me now?

A tear slides down my cheek. I didn't even know I was crying. Again. I know when Drew looks away that he's seen it.

I feel a million times the fool.

I close my eyes, willing myself to be steady and strong. I've done this to protect him. To save him from going back to prison. He's told me only a little of what it means to be locked up. The monotony. The indignity. The violence.

I'd do anything to keep him safe. I inhale deeply, holding that conviction in my chest, and then I can open my eyes, brush the tears from my lashes. When I do, I see an attendant with a basket on his arm, handing Drew and each member his family a single white flower. I blink away my tears, curious.

"While Vivian grew many fruits and vegetables in her treasured garden, peas among them, sweet peas aren't for eating," the priest says, lifting a crepe-blossomed flower to his nose and sniffing audibly. "Still, the flower is a symbol of departure, of fair well, and of thanks. The family welcomes you to come forward, take a flower, and make your own gesture of remembrance and adieu, knowing that we will see our friend, our mother, our grandmother Vivian in God's heavenly garden that knows no death nor separation."

The priest turns and nods to a plump woman in the crowd, and she steps forward, lifts her chin, and begins singing in a clear, operatic soprano.

"Morning has broken like the first morning…"

And as she sings, one of Drew's uncles walks up to the casket and places his flower, gently, reverently, on its polished wood surface, and stands aside. Drew's mother follows, and then his aunts, his cousins, and finally Annie and Drew. I watch as they walk up together, hand in hand.

The thin stemmed flower looks tiny in his grip, and the petals shake as he lays it with the others. I see his struggle to let go, but he does it and lines up beside the rest of his family, forming a kind of receiving queue.

The gathering of mourners falls in line. I glance over my shoulder, and find Tori's eyes on me. I quickly take my place so others fill in behind me before she can. As I approach the basket of sweet peas, I tuck my right hand into the pocket of my cardigan and squeeze the folded note tight against my palm.

The flower is almost weightless, its perfume light but sweet. I try to hold Mrs. Vivian in my mind as I walk in the slow-moving line to her coffin, but I can feel Drew's eyes on me the whole time, and all I can think about is my need to pass him the note without Tori seeing.

When I lay the flower down on the now spreading pile of flowers, I have one thought for Mrs. Vivian.

Please. Help me.

I have to make my way down the line of his relatives, awkwardly offering them my left hand because I don't dare let go of the letter now. But as I approach Annie, I know that even if Tori looks at me, she'll only have a view of my left side.

475

Drew's sister frowns as I step up to her. She knows. She knows I've broken his heart, and she hates me for it. He might too.

"Annie, I-I'm so sorry. I loved Mrs. Vivian." I draw the note from my pocket, so nervous I don't even hear her murmured response over the pounding in my ears.

Drew's eyes pierce me. I'm standing in front of him, and I don't even remember moving. The look he gives me is hard, guarded, and the weight in the pit of my stomach tells me he just wants me to leave him alone.

Shaking, I take his right hand with my left, and it's like touching a mannequin. He has absolutely no response to my touch.

"Please," I whisper. I have to make this work. I have to let him know what's happening. So before he can pull away, I lean into him, raise up on my tip toes, and brush a kiss against his cheek.

He smells like love.

I lift my lips to his right ear as my fingers find the right pocket of his pants. "Please just read it. But not here. It isn't safe." I slide the note inside the same moment that Drew's hand covers mine.

I meet his gaze to find lightning in his eyes. A sharp intelligence, alert but mystified fills his stare. He's looking at me like I've just landed a spaceship in front of him. His grip goes tight around my wrist, but I need to back away.

"Let me go," I murmur under my breath. "You have to let me go."

Drew's eyes narrow in confusion, but he releases me, and I'm relieved as I draw away from him. That relief grows as I see him slip his right hand into his pocket. He has the note. He'll read it later. He'll understand. He'll know I love him.

I only hope it's not too late.

CHAPTER THIRTY-FOUR

DREW

I finger the wad of paper in my pocket as I watch her go. What does she mean, it isn't safe? Is she in danger? My eyes scan the crowd for anyone threatening, but it's just a sea of Grandma Q's friends. Ladies from church. Her gardening society. Neighbors.

A thought occurs to me, and I do another sweep for any face I might recognize from Angola. Could someone I know have been released and be looking for me? Someone who couldn't contact me directly?

But if so, how would they know to go to Evie? No one from The Farm knows about her. The last time I talked to A.J., I told him I was seeing someone, but I left it at that. Didn't even tell him her name. So it can't be that.

"This must be a really hard time for you." I look down to find Tori Lalonde smirking up at me, and my spine tingles. She looks too fucking happy to be at a funeral. What the hell?

When I say nothing, the corner of her mouth crooks higher. "Of course, you know all about hard time."

Beside me, Annie's mouth falls open. She lunges forward, and I swing a restraining arm in front of her just in time. Still Tori flinches, and then she lets out a nasty snicker.

"Why are you here, Tori?" I mutter low. She's already upset my sister. I should just let her go, but the hair on the back of my neck is telling me to pay attention.

Tori shakes her head. "I wouldn't have missed it. Not for the world." I can't explain it, but I'm certain

478

she's not talking about Grandma's funeral. I squeeze the little note against my palm.

Please just read it. But not here. It isn't safe.

I've stared murderers and gang rapists in the face. I know a villain when I see one. The look in Tori Lalonde's eyes isn't just bitchy. It's plain evil.

I have no idea what she's up to, but I know it like I know the sound of a busted axle, she wants to hurt Evie.

My eyes narrow, and my nostrils flare. My blood might as well be gasoline. That look on her face is a spark.

I lean toward her and growl through gritted teeth. "You leave Evie alone."

Her chin notches back, and she bats her lashes at me. "What on earth are you talking about?"

"You heard me."

Annie's gaze is flicking from me to Evie's sister. She looks pissed but totally lost.

Tori keeps blinking like an imbecile. "You know, I think you're the one who needs to leave my sister alone," she says, her tone syrupy sweet. "If you know what's good for you."

I step into her space and glower down at her. "You know where I've been. You don't scare me." I tell her with a slow nod. "You watch yourself with Evie."

She drops the innocent act like a sack of shit. "Are you threatening me?" She pitches her voice loud enough for my whole family — and anyone else in this line — can hear.

And I don't fucking care.

But as I'm just about to tell her that, hell, yeah, I'm threatening her, Evie, looking terrified, pops up behind Tori and grabs her by the arm.

"C'mon, Tori. Let's go home." Her voice is pure panic, and she doesn't even look at me as she yanks her sister out of my reach.

And before Tori turns away, that wicked smile I've only seen on sociopaths slithers right back onto her face.

"Come after me," she taunts, her voice low again. "I dare you."

And this time it's Annie who restrains me. And it's a good thing she's a cheerleader who's essentially solid muscle or I might knock her down. But I grip my sister's shoulders to keep her on her feet and watch them go, Evie plowing through the crowd, practically dragging Tori behind her like death itself is after them.

Evie doesn't even look back.

"That bitch is crazy," Annie says, sounding out of breath. "No wonder I always hated her."

Aunt Josie walks over to us, frowning in confusion. "Was that your girlfriend and her sister?"

Annie's shaking her head before I can answer. "That was a psycho."

"She's not my girlfriend."

Josie's frame jolts with shock. "What? Of course she is, Andrew. That girl's crazy about you."

I look back in time to see Evie disappear behind a cluster of trees, and then I force myself to face my aunt.

"We broke up."

Annie makes a snarky noise in the back of her throat, and Josie looks like I've splashed a drink in her face.

"What?"

I shake my head. "Now's not the time."

But Annie chimes in. "She broke up with him the day—"

"Not. The. Time," I grind out, and the register of my voice must be just enough to check the meddling gene in both women. Annie and Josie share a look before stepping back into our line, but there's really no point. The last of the crowd is edging away, aiming for their cars. My guess is half of them will be joining us at the house. Them and an army of casseroles.

My bones feel heavy at the thought. The last thing I want to do is stand around talking to more people. And Evie's note is burning a hole in my pocket. But I'm not going to take it out while I have an audience.

So it isn't until the limo takes us back to Fountain Memorial Funeral Home and I get into Grandma Q's Buick that I allow myself to reach for the paper and unfold it. I've never seen Evie's handwriting before, but it's as though I recognize her anyway. It's a pretty hand. Not cutesy. Not elegant. But somewhere in between. Her letters curve with feminine grace, but there's a friendliness to them, too. An inextinguishable happiness. All Evie.

But the words on the page are anything but happy. They're desperate. Urgent. And as I read them, my heart quickens.

Drew, my love,

Please read this through to the end, and promise me you won't do anything stupid. None of this is what I want. I love you more than anything, I want to be with you, and I will be with you — if you'll still have me after all of this.

481

I frown at her words, back up, and read them again. What the hell? If I'll still have her? Is she kidding?

Please forgive me, but I did what I did on Monday because I had to. It's too hard to explain here, and I need to keep this short, but Tori forced me to do it. She wants to hurt me, and she's using you to get her way. I don't know when, but Tori snuck into your apartment and planted something of hers in there. I know this sounds crazy, but she wants to be able to make it look like you broke into our house and stole from her. And she knows what she's doing. I think she took hairs and fibers from your room to stage in hers as evidence.

My spine is a rod of rebar. I can hear my racing pulse in my ears and nothing else. I'm gripping the paper so tightly, one edge tears.

Drew, I can't even believe I'm writing this, but she's blackmailing me into staying away from you. She threatened to turn you in and have you sent back to prison if I didn't end things between us. I can't let that happen. I'll do anything to protect you, even let you go. But please know that I love you more than my own life.

This won't last forever. Is it too much to ask you to wait for me? You've already lost so much time. I'd understand if it is.

I make a noise of disgust. Is she serious?

Tori is moving in a few months. The danger will pass when she goes. Can you wait that long? Please don't text or call. Tori's checking my phone constantly. And please don't do anything rash. If you want to respond to this, go through Janine. She'll make sure I get word from you. I've included her number here.

I don't even read the number. I'm already keying the ignition when my eyes fall on her last words.

I'm so sorry about Mrs. Vivian. It's killing me not to be with you through all of this. Just know I'm not far. I leave my light on every night so you'll see I'm still here.

Love,

Evie

It's only the threat of arrest that keeps me from driving home like a mad man. I want to go to her, talk to her, but first I need to tear my apartment inside out and find whatever it is Tori could use against me.

They shouldn't, but cars lining the curb down St. Joseph Street throw me at first. Evie's letter has wiped all else from my head. Aunt Josie and Uncle Nelson have parked in the driveway, but they've left me a spot. I wonder if I can sneak around to the apartment before anyone notices. Even before I left the cemetery, I didn't want to have to see anyone.

But now I'm like a man possessed.

I think I'm going to make it to the apartment stairs, but as soon as I get past the kitchen door, it opens.

"Andrew?" It's Aunt Josie, but, I swear, the way she says my name sounds just like Grandma Q.

I turn slowly and face her, guilt hunching my shoulders. I should be inside, welcoming Grandma's friends and neighbors, extending the hospitality she always did in her honor.

But how can I shake hands and smile and drink coffee while I feel like my skin is on fire?

I need to be upstairs, tearing my apartment to shreds. It's small enough. It can't possibly take too long to find whatever belongs to Tori Lalonde. And if I do, maybe I could have Evie back tonight—

"I'm sorry, Aunt Josie. There's something I have to—"

"I've been wanting to talk to you," she says, ignoring my impatience. "The last few days have just been so trying. No other time felt right."

I let go a restless breath. "Now's not really—"

"She left you the house."

For an elastic moment, the words scatter like birdshot, soaring apart from each other with no hope of making sense. But their echo rings in my ear, pulling back their meaning, and I frown at my aunt, disbelieving.

"What'd you say?"

She's watching me with just a hint of a smile on her lips. Still, she looks pleased with herself. "I *told* Lottie you had nothing to do with it," she mutters.

My eyes bug. "*Do* with it? Josie, what are you talking about?"

Aunt Josie shakes her head, her smile growing. "About a week after you came home, I took Mama to see her lawyer." She arches a meaningful brow. "She made me stay in the waiting room, but she told me after that she was signing papers, making an adjustment to her will."

Blood fills my head. My ears and eyelids seem to swell with it.

Josie lays a hand on my elbow and gives it a little squeeze. "She wanted you to have the house, Andrew," she says. "She wanted you to be able to call this place home even after she was gone. We'll go to the lawyer's on Tuesday. The will will be read then, and it'll be yours. Just as she planned."

I close my eyes and picture my short, gray-haired, feisty, meddling Grandma, who had her way right up to the end.

"My God." I palm my forehead, still reeling at the thought. The house must be worth two hundred thousand at least. My eyes pop open. "But what about you guys? The house is your... your inheritance."

She cocks her brow at me again. "Do you really think any of us would want to deny Mama's last wish?" She glances over her shoulder and lowers her voice. "I wouldn't put it past her to haunt us if we did."

"Josie." She's making light of it, but I can't. "I'm good. We can just ignore her will. I don't want everyone to hate me."

All humor leaves her face. "Andrew, no one is going to hate you." She shakes her head, her mouth going tight. "I mean, was your mother happy about it when she found out? No. But it's not because she wants the house for herself or was even thinking about benefiting from its sale."

I huff. "Two hundred thousand split three ways is no small thing."

Josie rolls her eyes. "It's not worth that much. It needs a new roof. You'll be lucky if this one makes it through next spring."

"Josie—"

"Andrew, Lottie was upset because she's still trying to punish you, not because she wants cash," Josie says with a scowl. "Mama was always on her about doing right by you. Maybe this was her way of having the last word on that."

I don't doubt Grandma Quincy's ability to get the last word — even beyond the grave — but I don't deserve this. "I can't accept it," I say with finality.

Josie's face hardens in a way that makes her look more like Grandma Q than I've ever seen. "You can, and

485

you will. And you know what else you can do?" She crosses her arms over her chest and glares at me. "You can put up a fight for that girl of yours like the life you have actually matters, and when that's good and settled, the two of you can start planning for the holidays because I've never had Christmas dinner anywhere but inside this house, and I'm not ready for that to change."

Her lecture shuts me up for a second. Because she's just painted a picture of a future I'm almost too scared to hope for. Christmas? Here at Grandma Q's house — *my house* — with Evie? The memory of us laughing in the kitchen as we pickled okra flashes behind my eyes. It could be like that again. We could burn the apple pie. Spill gravy. Drop the bread. Any number of happy disasters.

She would make the walls and windows smile.

I look back at Aunt Josie. Her gaze is still hard, but now there's a glint in her eye. "That puts things in a different light, doesn't it?"

I say nothing, but I can't deny she's right. I could give Evie a home. Everything she needs. I'll never be completely worthy of her, but this would bring me closer at least.

"I saw her at the funeral. You can't tell me she's not head over heels for you," Josie says, her face softening. "Go to her. Right now, Drew."

How I wish I could. Just hop the fence and carry her home. I square my shoulders and meet Josie's gaze. "There's something I need to do first."

Jumping and twirling, Quincy greets me as I open the apartment door. I rake my eyes across the room as though I'll now see what I haven't noticed before, but of course whatever Tori Lalonde planted here is going to be tucked out of sight.

"C'mon, girl. Let's go down to the yard, and then you can help me search."

I don't even bother with the leash by the door. Quincy won't leave my side. She follows me down the stairs and makes a quick dash onto the grass, my eyes on the Lalonde house the entire time. I hurry Quincy back to the stairs. I'll take her for a long walk later as we've done the last two nights — if I can get to the bottom of this.

If I don't go mad first.

Which seems a real possibility. Because when I step over the threshold of the apartment door, I feel the malice. Tori's hatred of her sister — and of me — had to be epic for her to breech my space and leave her weapon of evidence. Like a fucking landmine.

And as I feel the chill of this calculated violation, I'm aware, too, of a sickening shame.

Is it really so different from the way I violated so many? I've broken into dozens of homes with intent to harm. Not bodily. Not personal. But to enter someone's home uninvited... in secret. How abused it must have made those victims — *my* victims — feel.

For a dizzying moment, I nearly convince myself that this is no less than what I deserve. To feel violated. To feel suspicious of every shadow in my apartment. To feel hunted.

But while I may deserve all of that, Evie does not.

Tori's plot has caused Evie pain. Taken away her liberty. Made her afraid. No matter what punishment I have earned, I cannot let that stand.

I start in the obvious places. Everything comes off the bookshelf. I sift through books and CD cases. Quincy eyes me warily from the bed, flinching as plastic cases knock together. I empty my clothes from the wardrobe, pour over the contents of the kitchen cabinets. A couple of dust bunnies greet me from behind the refrigerator, but nothing else. I over turn the table and chairs. Quincy *boofs* in protest, jumping to the floor as the mattress comes off the futon. I search beneath it and among the rungs of the frame.

Nothing.

The stolen TV and PlayStation have remained uncovered since I revealed them to Evie a few weeks ago. I pick up each, check beneath them, and set them down again, resolving that they won't stay here another night. As soon as I find the wicked treasure I'm searching for, those things will be returned.

The bathroom is so small, it takes me only a moment to inspect every nook and cranny. I even look beneath the lid of the toilet tank.

Nothing at all.

I stalk back to the main room and pace the floor, raking my fingers through my hair.

"Where would she put it?" I ask aloud. Quincy has taken cover under the table but her ears perk at the sound of my voice. Or maybe the frustration in it.

Could Tori have made the whole thing up? To mess with Evie's head? At this point, I'd put nothing past her, but I think about the look I saw in her eyes today, and it wasn't the look of someone whose bluff could be called.

She's been here. She's left something. Obviously, it has to be something small. And valuable. And personal. Jewelry, most likely.

I scan the ceilings and walls. All tongue-in-groove. No ceiling tiles to pop out. No central air vent. I narrow my eyes at the window unit and dive for it. A moment later, I've removed the cover, thrown the filter across the room, but the cavity is empty.

"Shit."

A niggling voice the the back of my head whispers that a pair of diamond earrings could be hidden nearly anywhere. Sewn into the lining of my coveralls. Dropped into the freezer's ice tray. Hidden behind an outlet cover.

"I'm going to lose my fucking mind."

Whatever it is, I can't find it. And if I can't find it, I can't have Evie.

And if I can't have Evie, what else is there?

I sink to the floor and catch my forehead in my hands. All I want is to go to her. Take her away from that hateful sister, and promise to protect her. To see her the way no one else does. To love her forever.

But how can I promise to protect her if I can't even stop her sister from throwing me in jail on false charges?

If I gave up on this search and went to her now, would Tori call the police as soon as she saw me? Would Evie have to watch as I was arrested? I wince at the thought of her seeing me behind bars. She'd come visit me even if I told her not to.

The other inmates would touch her with their eyes. Lick her with their words. Call her names and name her parts.

The thought makes me shudder.

"Never." I shake my head and get to my feet. Everything in my apartment has to go. Everything. Maybe I'll find the mystery weapon along the way. Maybe I won't. But it won't be here anymore. It won't have power over us, and as soon as every fucking thing is gone and this place is just an empty shell, I'm getting Evie.

I look over the mess that has become my apartment, and my eyes settle on the first things to go.

"Let's go, Quincy." The dog springs to her feet at the familiar command. "We have a delivery to make."

The Acadian-style house on Twin Oaks looks pretty much the same. The bricked driveway and the landscaping had spelled *money* back then, as did the king-sized fishing boat in the side lot. The boat's still there, and the landscaping is even nicer. The one obvious difference is the ADT security sign next to the brick mailbox.

That, and the not-so-hidden camera on the front porch.

Quincy gives a nervous whine from the seat beside me. I've pulled to a stop and killed the engine, but I haven't moved otherwise.

And, yeah, I'm nervous, and she can probably sense it.

I look down at the dog and pat her. The impulse that had spurred me to take her home had come from Evie. To live a way that would make her proud. The thought settles me.

"This would make her proud," I say, opening the Buick's door. "Stay put. I won't be long." The trunk squeaks as I open it, and the sound echoes off the front of the house. It's not dark yet, but twilight is gathering the light on the street. I feel its eyes watch me.

Are the people inside this house already peering through the blinds?

I hoist the TV and tuck it under one arm, grab the PlayStation and remotes, cradling them to my chest, and leave the trunk open. As I walk up the brick path, I have no damn idea what I'm going to say to these people. I reach the porch and push the brass-framed doorbell, debating just dropping the stuff and sprinting back to my car.

Anthony and I had chosen the street because it horseshoes with Oakview, giving us two exit points in case the raid had gone south. Both streets ended on Johnston so we could have slipped into traffic and been lost in a moment. The same is true right now.

But before I can make up my mind, the door swings open, and a kid of about twelve glares up at me.

"Yeah?" he asks, his eyes darting from my face to the booty in my arms. He does a double take at the gaming relic in my hands. "Whoa, is that a PlayStation 2?"

The room we broke into way back when was a kid's room. But not this kid's room. He would have been in nursery school. The room we'd robbed had been covered with Nickelback posters and smelled like jiz.

Adrenaline and euphoria make you remember shit like that.

I clear my throat. "It's a 3," I say, answering his question. "Hey, uh, do you have an older brother?"

The kid frowns. "Zack? He doesn't live here anymore," he says. "You know him?"

I consider just pushing the stuff into his arms and taking off, but I don't think that would make Evie very proud.

I scan the hallway behind the kid, but no one else is in sight. I make up my mind.

"Look, uh, I don't know your brother, but a long time ago, I did some pretty stupid shit—" His eyes widen. "I-I mean stuff, and one of them was breaking into your house."

The kid takes a step back, his lips going white.

I shake my head. "I don't mean to scare you." I shrug my shoulders to indicate what I carry. "I just want to return this."

The kid blinks at me. "I-I'm not letting you in."

"No," I say, shaking my head again. "I don't want to come in." Awkwardly, I lower the TV to the ground before handing him the gaming device and remote.

He eyes the bundle with interest. "I think there's still some games for this in Zack's old room," he says almost to himself.

I take a step back, ready to get the hell out of there. "Great. Tell your brother — tell Zack I'm sorry."

The kid doesn't look up. "I wonder if the batteries still work." I turn toward the car and hear a plastic *click*. "Hey, what's this?"

I keep walking. It's done. He'll tell his brother. He'll tell his parents. End of story.

"Who's Victoria?"

I halt. Turn around. *"What?"* The word comes out a croak.

492

Something gold glints from his fingers. "Is that your girlfriend?"

I can't blame the kid for nearly bolting when I charge back up the porch like a bull. I only just stop myself from grabbing his wrist. But instead, I throw my hands up like someone's pointed a gun in my face.

"Please… Could you j-just please show that to me?" I ask, my voice shaking. My whole body is shaking.

The kid looks at me like I'm Pennywise the Clown, and without taking his eyes off me, he stretches out his hand. Pooled in his palm is a gold chain and a locket in the shape of a heart bearing a name.

Victoria.

It takes a good five seconds before I can fill my lungs and another three before my voice works. "Could I… Could I please have that back?"

The kid stares at me for a minute, confused disgust shaping his brow. "Man, you are *wack.*"

But he drops the locket in my hand, and without another word, he steps back inside and slams the door in my face. The TV is still at my feet.

I don't care. I sprint back to the car, but I'm pretty sure my feet don't touch the ground.

CHAPTER THIRTY-FIVE

EVIE

The knock at the door makes my stomach drop. It's him. I know it's him.

I have to send him away. Now.

Tori's upstairs. But Gem's already barking. She'll hear him. She'll know.

Gemini races me to the door. Is she already calling the police? How long do we have?

I know the blood has drained from my face because Drew's eyes widen as soon as he sees me.

"Evie." He steps inside, grabs my arm.

"Please," I manage in a hoarse whisper. "You can't be here."

His grip tightens. "Where's your sister?" The gray of his eyes has never looked more like thunder clouds. •

My heart becomes a bird in a snare, fluttering madly. Already doomed. "Drew, go now. Please," I beg.

He moves slowly, stepping close, filling my vision. Drew dips his head, and his warm mouth seals over mine. I hear the door close behind him. Dimly, I know Tori's heard it too. But instead of puzzling out what that means, I'm overcome with the reunion. With his heat. His scent. The way he tastes like belonging.

My arms lift and settle over his shoulders, and I press closer to him, his gravitational field calling my name.

It's when I hear Tori's footfalls on the stairs that alarms go off again. I jerk back, push against his chest.

"You have to leave now," I hiss. *"Now."*

But his body is solid as oak, his stubborn nature rooting him to the ground. Cursing myself, I hear Tori's steps in the hall. I should have known he'd be like this. His loyalty, his bullheadedness leaving no room for caution. For self-preservation.

I look over my shoulder to see Tori, phone in hand, her face a mask of menacing triumph.

"Well, well, well," she sneers, her eye teeth glistening.

Fear nearly takes me under. In mere minutes, I'll have to watch the police take Drew away.

And for one suspended moment, the world goes still.

Like hell I will.

Power girds my core, and I turn. The room seems to rotate slowly as I face my sister, my body now a shield between her and the person I love most in the world.

I plant my feet in mountain pose, and I've never felt more mountainous. Energy courses up my spine like a geyser, making my every nerve tingle. My eyes lock with Tori's, and I witness the instant she realizes I am no longer the little sister she can control.

"I won't let you do this to him." My voice comes out steady and cold, like iron. If she raises that phone, I will charge. Take her down. I can tell she sees I mean it.

But Drew must too because I feel his hand land on my shoulder, easing but also holding me in place.

"She can't do anything to me, Guppy." His voice is smooth, sure, and I wonder at its certainty when a flash of gold cuts through the air and lands at Tori's feet.

A shocked cry tears from her throat. Then she makes a noise of frustration through her clenched teeth.

I look down and read her name in the spill of gold on the floor. I recognize the necklace instantly.

495

Mom and Dad gave that to her for her sixteenth birthday. Just like the one I got on mine.

How could she use something so innocent, something given in love, to hurt us?

Anger pulls at me like an undertow. For a dangerous moment, I want to let it take me. To lose myself in it and barrel into her with all I have.

But I don't want to be that person. I really don't. So I won't give her the key to turn me into that person. If I had the power to tackle her a moment ago, I have the power to control myself now.

I'm not so sure about Drew.

He steps out from behind me but doesn't move closer to Tori. He doesn't have to. As soon as he moves, Tori's eyes go wide with alarm. I give him a quick glance, and while the V between his brows may not stand for *vendetta*, I hope he never looks at me the way he's looking at her.

"That's the last time you threaten Evie or me." His voice rumbles with warning. "The last time you step foot on my property. And the last time you get away with any act of malice toward us."

My sister, who I now understand doesn't know what's good for her and has probably never known, has the gaul to glare at him.

"You think you scare me?" she spits, crossing her arms over her chest.

I look back at Drew to see a muscle tick in his jaw.

"Yeah. I do. What you did was criminal, but you're not hardened like me." The words come out so soft and low they're even scarier than if he'd shouted them. "I wouldn't have to touch you myself. Got plenty of those that'd do it for me. Without a trace."

His words send a chill down my spine. They are true, and it's obvious all of us know it. I'm sure Tori knows it because of the way her eyes are fast blinking now. And then, without a word, she turns and runs from the room. I don't move until I hear her speed up the stairs and slam her bedroom door.

I turn to Drew, but he's already reaching for me.

His arms are around me, and my mouth opens under his. The kiss is quick, but deep. Urgent. A declaration, but also a promise.

Drew pulls back and releases me. "Pack a bag for tonight," he tells me. "We'll get the rest in the morning."

I blink at him. "W-where are we going?"

The non-smile I love marks his mouth. "To my house."

Our bodies are only inches apart, and I wonder if he can feel the question that must pulse from my being.

"For... now?"

His gray eyes glint. "For always."

Happiness ripples through me as if every cell — bone, blood, beating heart — is bathed in it.

"We — I mean, um, my stuff won't... won't fit in your apart..." My words trail off as I watch his expression change to one I've never seen, the look in his eyes scoring into me. It's somber... tender... lost and found.

Drew shakes his head, as if to clear it. "Pack a bag, Guppy. I'll get Gem together and explain later."

I point him in the direction of Gemini's harness, leash, and food before dashing upstairs. I only spare Tori's door a glance and see it's shut. I hear nothing behind it, but I don't care to listen either. I only hope she doesn't come out before I have a chance to gather things for tonight.

I haven't slept much the last three nights, but I also haven't exactly unpacked since leaving Janine's. I've been living out of a suitcase since Monday, returning to Janine's to rifle through one of my plastic bins in search of the dress I wore to Mrs. Vivian's funeral.

When I got back this afternoon, I'd been so emotionally raw, so stirred by seeing Drew again, I'd immediately changed into comfort clothes, so the dress joined the heap that spills out of the suitcase. I shake my head at the mess, grab a bag, and move to the bathroom for my toothbrush and face wash.

I look up at the mirror and meet my own gaze.

"Did Drew just ask me to move in with him?" I ask my reflection.

Seeing him today — touching him and watching him suffer — had left me a weeping mess. The signs are still there — my eyes bloodshot, my nose red. But right now? Honest to God, I've never looked happier.

I turn back to my room and rifle through the pile, pulling out clothes for class tomorrow. I'll figure the rest out later. I'll get a storage unit if I have to. And I'll need to explain everything to my parents. At some point. That isn't going to be an easy conversation, and I'm already guessing they'll make excuses for Tori. Downplay what she's done.

But that's not happening right now.

Right now, I'm slinging a bag over my shoulder and bouncing down the stairs. And Drew is there waiting for me, holding Gem's leash in one hand and his bag of dog food in the other.

And Gemini is leaping, spinning, dancing in midair as though he can sense my happiness. My eagerness not just to walk out of here and never look back, but to walk straight ahead with this man who just saved me by saving himself. And then saved me again by claiming me.

"Let's get out of here."

The corner of his mouth lifts. "You won't get any arguments from me."

As soon as we're out the door and into the night, Drew shifts the dog food into the arm that holds Gem's leash, and he clasps my hand with his free one.

When we hit the circle of light under a streetlamp, Drew stops. I'm on such a cloud I only notice when our hands go taut, and I halt like an anchored skiff. I look back to find Drew's arched brow bearing down on me. He doesn't exactly look angry, but he's not thrilled either.

"What?"

"Should have told me, Evie."

I blink. The joy I feel at having him back — having us back — is so rich, I am existing only in the present. It takes a couple of seconds to process what he's saying. Then I do.

"I tried," I tell him. "Every way I could think of that was safe."

He frowns in question but doesn't speak.

Such a Taurus.

"She was checking my phone thirty times a day. I tried calling you from the studio," I say, shrugging, a tightness in my stomach elbowing its way into my joy. "You never answered. I even left voicemails... I figured you didn't want to talk to me."

I can't help the hurt that comes through my voice, and Drew doesn't miss it. His grip on my hand firms before he lets me go.

"Voicemails?" He reaches into his pocket and wakes up his phone. Its glow spotlights his face as he taps and glares at the screen. His eyes shift to me. "The two-three-two number?"

I nod.

Now he's frowning for a completely different reason. "I thought that was the funeral home. Same prefix."

My eyes bug. "You mean you didn't listen to them?"

Drew's mouth opens. Then closes. Even in the halflight, he looks a little sick. "Why listen to a voicemail if you're just gonna call someone back?"

He taps the screen and my strained voice issues from the tiny speaker. *"Drew, it's Evie.* Please *call me back at this number. Don't call my cell. We need to talk—"*

I wince and shake my head. "Turn it off. I don't want to be back there." I want the pain of the last three days as far away from me as possible. Since his hand isn't free, I grip Drew's arm. "All that matters now is it's over."

With a tap, the recording of my plea cuts off. He looks down at me, brows furrowed, mouth hard. "You left that yesterday."

I want to speak but there's now a knot in my throat. I nod instead.

Drew's next words come out in a growl. "I could have had you back yesterday."

I swallow hard. I know my eyes are filling with tears, but through their blur, I watch Drew shove his phone into his pocket. He sweeps me into his embrace and holds me tight against him.

He's lost the jacket, but he's still dressed in his funeral clothes, and I grip the crisp white shirt and bury my face against his chest. I don't want to cry right now. I could have skipped on air a moment ago.

But the feelings of relief, the release of worry and heartache are too much.

Drew's arm is like a steel bar, trapping me to him, but his fingers brush in gentle caresses on my shoulder. "She can't hurt us anymore," he murmurs.

I fight for control and shake my head. "It isn't that. I just—" I hiccup as my voice catches, and I make myself look up at him. "The thought of losing you. It—"

"You're not gonna lose me, Guppy." His eyes are so fierce, unconquerable. I want so badly to believe him.

"But..." What happened is not his fault. This whole nightmare ended so much better than it could have. But I have to say it. "You didn't even fight for me."

Did I say he looked unconquerable? I was wrong. That strong facade just crumbled.

"Evie," he says my name in a rasp, anguish in his eyes. "I was a fool."

The bag of Purina One drops to the street, and both his arms close around me. I couldn't move if I wanted to.

And I don't.

"I told myself from the beginning that when you left me, I'd make it easy." His chin tips up to the night sky. "My God." Are his words a prayer? A curse? I can't tell which. He brings his gaze back down to me. "I was so sure you'd leave. It was just a matter of *when*. Not *if*."

"How could I leave you?" I ask, incredulous. My spine straightens, but the movement doesn't come close to giving me the height I need to stare him down. "You see me, Drew. That's what you said. And you're the only person who does. The only one who ever has."

Leave him? How could he be so hard-headed. *Such a Taurus.* I love him more than anything. And, in truth, it was best he didn't fight for me. But right now, I just want to shove him.

He must read all this in my face because if it's even possible, he pulls me closer. "I fucked up, Evie. I thought, no matter what, I didn't deserve you."

I've heard this before, and hearing it again doesn't make me feel any better. "So what's changed?"

His slow nod doesn't make me feel better either. "That's... that's a good question." His voice is so low, the words almost get lost in the night air.

My abs tense. If he still doesn't believe in himself, how can he believe in us?

His arms around me loosen, but he still doesn't drop them. "Can we..." He pauses, and I think I hear him swallow. "Can we keep walking? I'll try to put it in words, but I should... we should get back to Grandma Quincy's."

A jolt goes through me and I gasp. "Shit! I forgot," I blurt, feeling like an idiot. "Let's go." I squat down and grab the Purina, but Drew wrests it from me and tucks it back under his arm so he can take my hand again. We walk, this time moving faster.

But then I look down at myself and frown. "I-I'm not... dressed appropriately," I say to my pullover and yoga pants. I glance over. Drew may have lost his jacket, but with shirt, tie, and slacks, he still looks as formal as ever.

Beautiful, too.

He gives me a quick shake of his head as we walk. "You look great."

I stop. "But Drew... she was your grandmother. I want to show her respe—"

He squeezes my hand and looks down into my eyes. "Exactly. She was my grandmother. And she wanted you at my side, no matter what you're wearing." He gives me rueful smile. "Besides. It's after dark. Most of her friends have probably gone home. It'll mostly be the family."

I know what this means. His mother will be there. Screw my clothes. I'm not about to let him face her alone.

"Fair enough," I say, moving in step with him again.

"Oh," Drew says a moment later. "Does Gemini get along with other dogs?"

"He loves other dogs," I gush. "Did one of your cousins bring theirs?"

"No." He says nothing else. I glance up at him, and see the corner of his mouth has turned up. I'm curious, still I don't press.

Mrs. Vivian's driveway is full of cars. Even if it's just family, the house is going to be bursting at the seams.

"C'mon. We'll get this upstairs and then join them," Drew says, leading me around the side of the house.

But as soon as we reach the stairs, Gem stops, tail erect, nose to the ground. And the moment after that, I hear scratching and whimpering behind the apartment door. I look up as Drew turns Gemini loose, and my dog scrambles up the steps in record time.

"You have a dog?" I look at Drew, and he just shrugs, grinning.

It's the grin that makes my heart start *thump-thump-thumping* in my chest. I climb the stairs almost as fast as Gemini, who's now wagging and wiggling with impatience, nose firmly wedged to the door jamb. He's sniffing and snuffling, blind to everything else in the world. Scratching and excited whining comes from inside.

Drew joins me on the landing and lifts his chin to the door. "Open up, Guppy."

I turn the knob and push the door open to see a little black nose at the tip of a charcoal muzzle before the open doorway becomes a blur of gold and dark gray swirls.

"Oh my goodness!" I squeal. "He's so little!"

Gemini and the little scrap circle each other, tails high, nose to hindquarters in a spirited dog greeting.

"She," Drew mutters over the rapid *clickety-clack* of dog nails on the hardwood.

But I can't process what he's said because I've looked from the dogs to the rest of his apartment. "Oh my God," I breathe. The futon frame is empty, its mattress leaning against the overturned table. Chairs lie on their sides. His armoire stands open, a sweatshirt hanging half out of it and clothes in a heap on the floor as if the dresser has coughed everything up. Books and CD cases are opened and scattered everywhere.

"Yeah," Drew says simply. This is what he did after reading my letter. Tore his apartment to bits looking for something of Tori's.

So he could come for me.

"Oh, Drew," I whisper, my voice choking off. I lean into him, unable to take my eyes off the disaster in front of us. "I'm so sorry."

His arm glides around my waist and pulls me close. "Not your fault, babe."

The dogs, seemingly satisfied with their sniff-fest, gambol over to us, open-mouthed and panting. The little salt-and pepper dog stands on her hindquarters and places her front paws on Drew's knees, looking up at him with undisguised adoration.

He leans down and scratches her on the head. "Good girl, Quincy," he murmurs, low and sweet.

My smile is immediate. *Quincy.* And then it hits me. "D-Drew…?"

He straightens and grins down at me. "Yeah, Guppy?" The grin is knowing and amused, and a rush of chills break out over my whole body.

"I-Is… Is that…"

He nods, his grin on the verge of becoming an all-out beam. "I saw her. Late Monday night. Might have been Tuesday morning," he says with a shrug. "Right where we spotted her before. Damn near ran her over."

"Oh my God." I can barely hear my own voice. "The paper said Mrs. Vivian… passed away on Monday…"

Drew nods again. "I'd just left the hospital. Thought I'd lose my mind without the two of you. And there she was." His smile goes wistful.

Wistful on Drew Moroux is as beautiful and sublime as the starlit sky.

The playful shriek of a child greets us as we enter the small kitchen.

"Peter. Mary Margaret. Stop running in the house." The tight space is crammed with people, but I see it's Drew's Aunt Josie who has done the scolding. She is leaning against Mrs. Vivian's counter, holding a cup of coffee and talking to a girl I think is one of Drew's cousins.

"There you are," she says in hushed excitement as we come through the kitchen door. She puts down the cup and makes her way through the crowd with a tentative smile, her eyes searching Drew's face.

Then they flick to mine. "I'm so glad to see you, Evie," she says, leaning in to hug me, but as she does, she tries to catch Drew's eye again, and I can tell she's attempting to figure out where things stand with us.

I don't let her wonder long. As soon as she releases me, I slide an arm around Drew's waist and seal myself to his side. She doesn't miss it, and the polite smile she greeted me with now becomes warm and genuine.

Aunt Josie turns her attention to Drew. "Have y'all had a chance to talk?" She eyes him with meaning enough to make me look up at him.

Old Stone Face is back. "About some things... Not everything," he says cryptically.

Aunt Josie looks back at me, a benign but absolutely controlled smile on her mouth, and nods quickly. "Plenty of time," she says, and then touches my elbow. "Evie, honey, can I get you a cup of coffee or some tea? And there's quite a spread. Drew, why don't you take Evie to make a plate. You must be starved."

And with that, we are dismissed to the dining room. The space is empty, but I can hear chatter from the living room and the sound of kids playing. Drew saunters to the dining table. All of its chairs are gone, likely having been dragged into the front room, but the table's surface is packed with platters and casseroles. Drew hands me a paper plate but says nothing.

"So what was that about?" I ask, gesturing back toward this kitchen. I watch him scoop up a spoonful of potato salad.

His eyes meet mine. "You like potato salad?"

"Yes," I say flatly. "You going to tell me what's going on?"

"Yes," he says, non-smiling. Then he spoons potato salad onto my plate before serving himself. "What about ham?"

I drop my chin and eye him under my brows. "Yes. I like ham. What's going on?"

He slides a slice of ham onto my plate and then one onto his. "Well, right now, I'm serving you some dinner, and then we're gonna sit down somewhere out of the way and talk for a minute," he says, looking almost amused now.

I blink. "Oh... Okay."

He serves us both a croissant and then eyes a rectangular dish that's half empty. It's full of a golden brown crispy topped concoction dotted here and there with bits of red, either peppers or tomatoes. I can't tell.

"I have no idea what this is," Drew says, pointing to it.

"Looks good," I say.

Footsteps approach behind us. "It's chicken zucchini casserole, and it is good." I turn to find Annie peering at the dish. "Mrs. Troxclair brought it."

Mrs.Troxclair has been my next door neighbor for my whole life. "Aww. She's so sweet. She used to let me come over and play with her cat Mustard when I was little," I say, smiling at Annie.

She doesn't smile back.

Drew digs the serving spoon into the chicken zucchini casserole. "Mrs. Troxclair and Grandma were gardening friends," Drew says, casually enough, but I don't miss the way his eyes move between me and his sister.

Annie doesn't respond, and I can't either. I'm no longer thinking about Mrs. Troxclair or Mrs. Vivian, but the hostile vibe that's rolling off Annie and aimed unmistakably on me.

She knows I've hurt Drew. And she doesn't trust I won't do it again. It's as plain to me as if it was written on her forehead. I need to clear the air.

"Um… A-Annie," I stammer, nerves taking over. This is Drew's sister. His closest living family member. If she hates me, I don't—

"Annie, drop the attitude," Drew levels, easy but firm. "Evie and I are together. For good. What she did this week she did to protect me."

Annie Moroux is almost a foot shorter than her brother, but the frown of confusion that crowds her brow makes her look so much like him it's uncanny.

"Protect you?" Her eyes dart to me, still distrustful. Still angry. "What's he talking about?"

508

I take a lungful of breath, ready to tell her everything. "My s—"

"It's a long story, sis," Drew says. He's talking to her, but his eyes are on me. "I'm not in the mood to go over it again. But suffice it to say, Evie put up with a lot to keep me safe. And it's all good now. We're solid. Nothing's coming between us, so be nice."

The look in his eyes is all mine. I feel it. His love. His conviction. My nerves dissolve. It's going to be okay, even if Annie doesn't see it.

But one glance at her tells me she does. She's watching Drew with what looks like a little bit of awe, and I wonder if that's the same look I'm wearing. Annie shifts her gaze to me and she ducks her head.

"I'm sorry, Evie, if I—"

"Don't apologize." I shake my head and reach for her hand. She lets me take it with a nervous smile. "I'm glad he has you in his corner. I promise, I won't ever leave it."

Annie may look like her brother when she frowns, but when she smiles, unlike him, she hides nothing. No non-smile for her. She bounces on her toes, and the next thing I know, she's hugging me. And squealing.

"Jesus Christ," Drew mutters under his breath, but I hand him my plate and hug his sister right back. Over her shoulder, Drew may be fighting a grin, but I can see happiness in every feature of his face. The lines around his eyes. The tug of muscle high on his cheeks. The upward tilt of his brow.

He's about as happy as any Taurus could be.

"Evie and I need to talk," Drew says as soon as Annie and I untangle from each other.

509

His sister gives him an arch look. "Yeah, I figured," she says with a smirk. "If you want peace and quiet, you might try Florida." Then Annie grabs a croissant off the table and she's gone.

"She figured?" I ask.

Drew just gives me a silent eye roll and hands me a plastic fork. "C'mon."

I follow him, but instead of moving toward the living room and the buzz of voices, we enter a hall, pass a bathroom, and end up at the bottom of the stairs, opposite the front door. The sounds of people are still audible but less distinct.

Drew nods toward the staircase. "Let's go up."

I follow him, stairs creaking as we ascend. "This house is huge," I whisper, as we reach the landing, and the staircase turns to the left.

"Four bedrooms."

When Drew reaches the top step, he turns and sits. When he tilts his head down to the spot beside him, I sit too. But I can't help but look around. There's a bedroom at my right shoulder, a bathroom across the hall to my left, and more beyond the staircase wall.

Drew is watching me with a look of scrutiny. "Is that too many?"

I face him, blinking. "Too many what?"

His lips draw together, a smile trapped between them. "Bedrooms."

"I mean... no," I titter, narrowing my eyes at him. "Why would that be too many? Didn't your grandparents have like three kids?"

He watches me for a moment, and I feel him taking in my whole face. His, as usual, is impossible to read. "Four bedrooms wasn't too much for them," he

510

says, finally, his voice going softer than I think I've ever heard it. "But I'm talking about us."

My heartbeat takes off. I have no idea what he means, but my body seems to recognize its importance. "Us?" I sound like an idiot, but it's the only word I can manage.

Drew frees his smile. "Yeah, Guppy. Us," he says, with a tease in his rich voice. "Grandma left me this house. Will you live in it with me?"

I blink once. Twice. Force a swallow.

Live here? With Drew? In the Quincy Family home? But, now, it would be... *our home.*

"Yes," I vow, finding my voice at last. "I'd love to."

Drew's shoulders relax, and his smile grows. "Good," he says on an exhale. And it's only then I realize he was nervous to ask me.

I gape at him. "Were you afraid I'd say no?"

His barely there shrug is all I need. I set down the plate in my hands on the step below me before taking his and doing the same. And then I launch myself into his arms, planting a kiss on his mouth that can leave no room for doubt.

I kiss him, and he kisses back. And in his kiss I taste both relief and joy. And hunger. His hands settle along my ribs, trace down the curve of my waist, meeting my flared hips before making their way up again. I go loose under his touch, but before I let myself forget where we are and what's happening in the house just down the stairs, I pull back, but gently, taking my time.

I keep my arms in the cradle of his when I look up into his eyes. "So this," I say, casting my gaze along the walls and ceiling surrounding us, "is yours now?"

He's looking at me with a hazy desire in his eyes, but my question sharpens his focus. "Yeah," he says. "According to Aunt Josie, it'll be official on Tuesday when we meet with Grandma's attorney, but everyone already knows."

"Then, Drew," I say, a hint of worry edging in my voice. "Don't you think you should be down there? With your family? Instead of hiding up here with me."

He arches a brow and gives me a stern look. "We're not hiding. We're taking a much needed moment." He reaches down and grabs my plate. "And we'll join everybody in a minute. Right now, we both need to eat something."

I take my plate from him. About this, there's no sense in arguing. I recognize that signature stubbornness of his, and I'll readily admit that I sort of love it. Plus, I've eaten almost nothing in the last three days, but now that I'm here, my appetite seems to have made a full recovery. So I take a bite of the chicken zucchini casserole.

"Mmm… Annie was right."

Drew seems surprised at my acquiescence, so when he picks up his own plate, he does it without his eyes leaving me. Then he takes his own bite and makes a startled grunt of satisfaction.

"Maybe Mrs. Troxclair will share her recipe," he mutters, making me grin.

"With me or you?"

He shrugs, but his own grin turns teasing. "I don't know, but your zucchini bread is pretty good. Maybe you could take a crack at it."

Laugher bubbles up from my middle. "Yeah, but that was with your grandma's zucchini. You gonna keep her garden growing?"

Drew's gray eyes turn soft and thoughtful. "Worth a try," he says, his voice going hoarse.

I lay my hand on his knee. "I think she'd like that," I whisper.

He nods, holding my gaze, not looking away.

I smile, even though my bottom lip might quiver just a little. "You grow the zucchini. I'll make the casserole."

Drew clears his throat and forks another bite into his mouth. "Deal."

We're picking up our empty plates a few minutes later, when we hear someone approach at the foot of the stairs.

"Andrew?"

Beside me, Drew freezes. In his profile, I see wariness.

"Who is it?" I whisper.

Drew turns his confused gaze to me. "My mother."

Without another word, I grip his hand, and together we descend the stairs. When we make the turn at the landing, she's there at the bottom, looking up at us, and I see exactly where Drew gets the ability to hide his thoughts.

Lottie Moroux's expression is perfectly blank as she watches us come down. But I well remember the look she gave me at the hospital a few weeks ago, and worse than that, the look of devastation Drew wore after she'd spoken to him.

I squeeze his hand. He squeezes back.

I'm ready to be strong for him. To weather with him anything hurtful she might say. So I'm surprised when she addresses me first.

"You're Evie?" she asks, her face giving nothing away.

"Yes, ma'am. Evie Lalonde." I'm proud of the way my voice comes out even despite my jangling nerves. Saying it's nice to meet her wouldn't really be the truth, so I go for the obvious. "And you're Mrs. Moroux."

The corners of her mouth might twitch. "Lottie," she says. And I don't want to get my hopes up, but that sounds like an offering, and I'm not about to dismiss it, so I nod.

"Hi, Mrs. Lottie."

"Just Lottie," she says flatly, and I see again the resemblance in manner between her and Drew. At once, I soften toward her. She is, after all, the woman who gave him life.

"Very nice to meet you, Lottie."

This time she nods. "Evie, I have something to ask Andrew. Would you give us a minute or two alone?"

My face goes hot. I can't refuse her, but I don't want to leave him. And quite suddenly, I'm remembering the morning my parents arrived home on their surprise visit weeks ago. He didn't want to leave me then either.

But he did.

I swallow. "Sure, I'll just—"

514

"She stays," Drew says, squeezing my hand tighter. I look up at him, expecting to see hostility, but his features are perfectly calm. "We're together, Lottie. And this will be her home, too. Whatever you need to say to me, she can hear it."

I'm sure my eyes are about to bug out of my head. I look back at Drew's mother, but mostly so I can be ready if she goes for my throat.

Instead, for the first time, her mask of detached coolness wobbles. She suddenly looks unsure of herself. Her gaze snaps to mine.

"I just..." She looks down, and I see now that she's struggling with shame. She lifts her face to meet Drew's eyes again, but she fails and lets her gaze fall to the floor between us. "I just need to know if I'll be welcome here... Now that the house is yours."

I feel the tremor that passes over Drew.

He squeezes it once and drops my hand before stepping closer to his mother. His movements are slow, tentative, as he lifts a hand and just barely touches his fingertips to her elbow. I'm holding my breath, praying she won't pull away.

She doesn't, but the lines around her eyes speak of anguish and uncertainty.

"You will always be welcome here." His words are low and soft, but I hear the root of hope in them. He wants this so desperately, it hurts me.

Conflict wars in Lottie's eyes. For a moment, I'm not sure if she's going to slap him or hug him.

She does neither.

"I don't know if I can forgive you, Andrew."

The man I love takes this on the chin, the clenching of his jaw the only sign of how bad it hurts. I

515

want to wrap my arms around him, but I don't dare move. This isn't my crisis. All I can do is invite healing.

I mentally fan through my library of gods and goddesses, in search of one to appeal to for Drew, but then I remember where I am, the ground on which I stand. Mrs. Vivian's house. And the answer is clear.

Raphael the Archangel.

For Catholics, even though he's an angel, he's the patron saint of healing. I close my eyes for a moment and send up a silent prayer asking him to help Drew's mother find forgiveness so this relationship may be healed. As I breathe through my plea, peace steals over me, and I open my eyes with the distinct feeling that Mrs. Vivian would approve.

Drew is looking at his mother, his eyes soft and unguarded. "For a long time, I didn't want you to," Drew says. Lottie blinks, and I can see this admission surprises her. "But now, I want forgiveness. Yours... Anthony's... My own. Whatever I don't have now, I'll work to earn it."

She narrows her eyes, looking skeptical but curious. "How will you aim to do that?"

Drew doesn't hesitate. "By living the kind of life Anthony would have." At the mention of her lost son's name, Lottie winces in pain, but Drew keeps talking. "Working hard... living right..." He reaches back for my hand, takes it and pulls me against him. "Raising a family and taking care of it."

Lottie glances to me and then back at Drew, and I can't be sure, but I think I see something new in her eyes. Something like possibility. But she doesn't speak.

Somehow, Drew knows exactly how to read her silence.

"I'm learning that if I forgive myself, it doesn't mean I forget him," he says, and I know immediately this is exactly what needs to be said. What he needs to say and what she needs to hear because when the words are spoken, Lottie's eyes well with tears. "And maybe it'll even help me to remember him."

She holds his gaze for a moment, her mouth bunched tight as she fights to keep her face from collapsing, and then she looks down, gives a quick nod, and then turns on her heel. We hear the front door open and close.

Drew doesn't move. Doesn't speak. So I don't either.

But I do press into him, wanting only for him to feel me. To know I'm here and I always will be.

At last, his arm around my waist holds me tighter. "That was... unexpected." I can't tell if he sounds encouraged or disappointed.

"She wants a relationship with you. That's something."

His hand pats me on the hip. "I don't know about that," Drew says flatly. "But maybe she *wants* to want to have a relationship with me. That *is* something, and I'll take it."

I settle my right hand on his chest. His heart beats beneath it, steady and sure. "Well, if she never gets around to actually wanting one, it'll be her loss." I speak lightly, but my words are still defensive, and I can't help my frown.

When the laughter purrs from deep in his chest, I feel it. "Glad you see it that way, Guppy."

I let the hand at his chest travel up to his collarbone, along his neck, and rest at his cheek. He

517

looks down into my eyes, and I run my thumb over the terrain of his smile.

"I love you," I whisper.

His mouth opens, and the tip of my thumb disappears between his teeth. Lips and tongue claim my flesh with a hard suck that pulls a gasp from my throat.

"I love you, too, Evie," he mumbles around the digit.

And this is how his Aunt Josie finds us, wrapped in each others arms and my thumb in his mouth.

"I was — Oh!" I jump away as she stops just inside the foyer, eyes wide and immediately amused. "Sorry, I didn't mean to interrupt—"

"S'okay, Aunt Josie," Drew says, pulling me back against him despite my effort to keep just a little space between us. But I give in when my front meets his. No point in pretending right?

And I suppose this is our home now, so...

"I just wanted to tell you that we're starting the clean-up. Nelson and Shelly are getting ready to leave. Is it okay if they take the rest of the ham?"

"They can have whatever they want," Drew says, before meeting my eyes. Then he smirks. "Except maybe that zuchinni casserole."

Josie grins. "I'll leave that here and one of the pecan pies. I know you like those. I, uh..." She checks me over, seeming to hesitate over her next words. I return her smile. "I took the liberty of making up the big bedroom upstairs. I figured if y'all wanted to stay in the house tonight, it might be too soon to use Mama's room."

Drew's spine stiffens. "You figured right."

518

Josie's look turns wistful, and she reaches forward and pats Drew on the arm. "Well, give it a little while, but don't treat it like sacred ground," she says gently. "Nelson and I will set aside some time to go through her clothes and things and donate what we can to Goodwill—"

"I can help with that," I offer, "i-if it's okay, I mean."

With her other hand she grabs my elbow, so the three of us are now linked. "Of course it's okay. You being here with Andrew was exactly what she wanted," Josie tells me, eyes going misty. She looks up at her nephew. "After we get her things sorted, you two should pick out some drapes, put on a new coat of paint, and make the room yours."

Drew watches her for a moment, and at first, I'm not sure how this is going to go. He may not be ready to think about this. I'm about to reassure him there's no rush when he speaks up.

"That could work," he says, his brows lowered in thought.

Josie seems pleased with this, and her face brightens. "By then, it'll be just about time to decorate for Christmas."

At this, Drew arches a brow at his aunt, stares at her for a second, and then swings his focus to me. "Apparently, we are hosting Christmas. Comes with the territory. You up for that, Guppy?"

At the same time I nod, Josie squints in confusion. "*Guppy?*"

I can't help but giggle, even though my cheeks flame.

Drew might go a little pink too. "Inside joke, Aunt Josie."

She blinks at him like she's never seen him before, but she looks pretty darn happy about it. "Whatever you say, Andrew," she says with a bewildered smile. She stands on tiptoes and presses a kiss to his cheek before coming down on her heels and doing the same to me. "Like I said, we're getting things cleaned up and hitting the road. We'll see you on Tuesday."

Drew nods, but then almost as an afterthought, he grabs his aunt by the arm and kisses her on the cheek. "Thanks, Aunt Josie," he says, meeting her eyes again. "Thanks for everything."

Two hours later, the food is put away, the house is empty, and Gemini and Quincy have made the rounds, upstairs and down, sniffing every corner and crevice of the house.

Drew is locking up downstairs, and the dogs are with me, making a final sweep of the bedroom Josie made up for us. I'm standing in the doorway, taking in the space. The room is spotless. I don't know how Mrs. Vivian did it, but there's not a speck of dust on the dresser, the night stand, or the window seats on this side of the two dormers that face the front yard.

It's a great room.

Of course, I'm pretty sure the light blush wall paint and darker pink trim is circa 1985, but I can't wait to see sunlight through those windows.

Drew's steps creak on the stairs, and then he's standing behind me. His arm wraps around my middle, and his hand presses flat against my belly as his lips meet the side of my neck.

I shiver under the thrill of his touch.

"Whose room was this?" I ask, laying my arm over his and leaning back against him.

He doesn't answer me at once. Instead, his mouth leaves slow kisses up my neck until his lips brush my ear. A sigh escapes me.

"I'm thinking Josie's," he whispers, his words a breathy tickle on my skin. "Definitely not Nelson's, and Lottie never liked pink..."

Somehow, this doesn't surprise me. Pink seems too cheerful for anyone who could turn their back on Drew. I realize this is not a generous thought, but I don't think I'll ever be able to be unbiased where he's concerned.

I reach back and let my free hand find its way into his hair. He pauses in his attention to my neck to place a kiss on the inside of my wrist as if in greeting. "It was nice of Josie to make up the room for us. I really like her."

"Mmm hmm." The tip of Drew's tongue traces the shell of my ear, and it's a good thing I'm leaning back against him because I doubt I can stand by myself. His arms tighten around me. "Don't want to talk about my family... Don't want to talk about your family."

I turn slowly in his arms. "Oh?" I look up at him with pretend innocence. "What do you want to do?"

Drew narrows his gaze, his gray eyes smoldering. Without a word, he walks me backward until we collapse onto the pink-on-pink bedspread.

And both dogs spring onto the bed to investigate, Gemini sniffing me with concern.

"I'm okay," I say, pushing him away.

"Down," Drew says, pointing to the floor.

Quincy and Gem both hear the authority in his voice, and they obey at once, springing to the floor.

Drew's weight presses into me. Real. Solid. And male. Unmistakably male, in fact. And as good as that feels, it's nothing compared to the certainty he's given me. About him. About us.

I'm so grateful, I want to thank God. Thank every god.

"I missed you," I whisper, running my hands down his back.

He makes a gruff noise and brushes his lips above the V of my top. "I don't think I could have missed my own skin more than I missed you."

Drew angles his hips, and I feel him hard and glorious against me. I wrap my legs around him, wanting to fall into this bliss, but needing him to know how sorry I am.

"I should have been with you," I murmur into his hair. "Monday night... Today..."

His hands slip under my top, moving up to my ribs, his thumbs sweeping the skin just below my breasts.

"You're with me now." He places a kiss right above my cleavage. I shiver. "That's all that matters."

I know he's right. The now is all that matters. But the last three days still have me in their grip. I need to make peace with them, and the only way I can do that is to make sure he has made peace with them.

"I hated what I did to you. I've never been so miserable. You've suffered so much." His lips still against my skin. "I hate that I added to that."

522

Drew lifts his face and locks eyes with mine. "Evie." He says my name like a vow. His gaze is intent. Bottomless. "Loving you's the best thing I've ever done. And I kept loving you the last three days because I wasn't about to stop doing the best thing I've ever done. Yeah, the last three days hurt. They hurt a lot. But you were still with me."

His words don't erase the guilt, but something eases in me. He's watching, and I think he sees it happen because his eyes soften.

"Was I with *you?*" he asks, a knowing grin shaping his mouth.

I grip the fabric at the back of his shirt. "Of course you were with me!" I cry. "I thought of nothing but you. I couldn't sleep. I couldn't eat. I meditated in my love for you. I held you in my heart—"

I stop this little rant when I feel him shaking, laughing silently, on top of me.

Squeezing his hips with my legs, I glare at him. "It's so not funny."

Drew shakes his head. "Not laughing at you, Guppy." He slides one hand out of my shirt before pressing it to my cheek. It's rough, huge, and warm. I stop glaring. "You were doing your magic, like you always do. Making it safe for me. Turning evil into good right in my backyard."

I blink at him. "What do you mean?"

His eyes shine as he looks down at me. "Evie, you turn everything around. My guilt. My shame. The way I see myself." His thumb sweeps up and down my cheek. "Hell, even this house. Grandma left it to me, and I didn't want to take it until I thought of bringing you here. And then it went from an empty house to our home."

I'm so glad Drew is lying on top of me. Otherwise, happiness, golden and weightless, might just carry me away.

"You have any idea where I found Tori's necklace?"

I shake my head, tensing at the sound of my sister's name.

Drew quirks a brow at me. "You remember that piece of shit PlayStation I stole?"

I nod. "The one under the sheet."

He nods, too, slowly. "I decided to take it back today after I'd searched and searched and couldn't find anything that could have belonged to your sister." His eyes narrow and I watch him swallow. "But I brought it back to the house where I'd stolen it because I knew you'd approve of that. And then this kid — this middle school kid — opens up the battery slot and pulls out her necklace."

My eyes bug. "You're kidding."

Drew shakes his head. "No. I keep thinking about it. I mean, what are the odds? As soon as I righted that wrong, I got you back." The light in his eyes is now tinged with awe. An awe that I now share. "I'm not an innocent man, Evie. But loving you is teaching me I can be a good man."

My nose stings. My throat goes hot with ready tears. "Drew..." I say his name because it's the only thing I can manage.

His thumb glides up and catches the lone tear that slips from my eye. "So stop worrying about the last three days, huh?"

I bite my lip and manage a nod, the unease I felt before has melted completely, leaving nothing but joy in its place.

"It's the same for me, you know," I rasp.

The fingers at my cheek move with a gentle caress, and then the hand under my top echoes it. "What is?" Drew asks. His smile is easy, but heat has returned to his eyes.

"Loving you... and you loving me... It's changed me." And then I struggle to put it into words. Because what I feel is immense. And the way he's touching me scatters my thoughts. "Or it's changed the way I see myself. Who I am? What I want? It's enough."

"Evie," he says, the word jagged and full of need. And then his mouth is on mine. It's as though we haven't already kissed half a dozen times tonight. As if this is the first kiss of our reunion. The first kiss of discovery. And I'm ready for it to last another hour or two, but Drew breaks it, panting, and gazes down at me. "It's not just *enough*," he says. "It's everything."

EPILOGUE

DREW

One year later

"So, they're going to board Quincy and Gem *for free?*" I ask as I pull the Supra into the parking lot of Loftin Veterinary Clinic. It's in Youngsville, a hike from the Saint Streets, but I can't argue with free.

"Well, it's more like bartering," Evie says with a shrug. "Ten days of boarding for ten private yoga lessons."

Last spring, I helped Evie convert the apartment into a studio. It's not big, but she can hold private lessons and small group classes there. She still teaches at the Yoga Garden and gives free lessons in the park, but her clientele is growing. I can see her opening up her own place one day. Someplace cool...New Age...sacred. Just like her.

I kill the engine. "And Dr. Loftin practices yoga?"

She gives me a sassy smile. "His wife Sarah does." She scoots out, flips the front seat, and ducks her head in to unbuckle Gemini. "Good thing, too, because Bertrand's was going to charge us twenty bucks a night. Each."

"Each?" That's twice what the apartment in Greece is costing us. How the hell Evie found an apartment on Zakynthos Island at twenty bucks a night, I'll never know. But the woman likes to travel, and she knows how to do it cheap. We used her dad's points for the plane tickets, so we're going for next to nothing. A part of me still can't believe we're going at all. Or, rather, that *I'm* going.

I get out and work on unclipping Quincy. Nervous as hell, she's pacing on the backseat and trying

526

to twirl around, and generally making the job harder than it needs to be. "Easy girl. You'll be alright."

I lay a hand on her back and she stills. Quincy's a good girl, but when she rides in the car, she gets antsy. My guess is she's afraid she won't go home again. I glance up at Evie. "You think she's gonna be alright? For ten days?"

Her green eyes soften as she looks at me. "I made sure she and Gem will share a kennel. They'll sleep right by each other just like they do at home. She'll be fine."

Of course, she'll be fine. And, of course, Evie has already looked out for her. Because that's what she does.

"You heard her," I say and gesture for Quincy to jump from the car. She obeys, but then she presses her little body to the side of my leg, her tail tucked up so tight it's probably tickling her ribs. Evie comes around the car with Gem to find her just like that.

"A-ww," she says, the word breaking on a giggle. "She's pitiful."

I huff. "We can't have that, Quincy," I say, nudging the dog gently. "Show no fear. Just look at Gem."

The Rhodesian Ridgeback has pulled his leash taut, sniffing the sidewalk and trying with all his might to reach the patch of grass that probably holds the smells of a thousand different dogs.

Some of his enthusiasm must impress Quincy because she decides to step closer to him.

"Atta girl," Evie says, and when she leads Gemini to the entrance, Quincy follows. And the scene inside the lobby erases any of my lingering concerns.

"Dr. Delacroix loves you...and Dr. Delacroix loves you...Yes, she does." A redhead in a white coat is sprawled on the lobby floor while two ecstatic lab puppies jostle for a spot on her lap, trying to lick her in the face.

Clearly, the temptation is too great to resist because Gemini charges up to them, sticking his nose in the vet's face, and wagging his tail just like one of the puppies.

"Ooph!" the vet exclaims before getting a hand up to brace Gem. "Well, hi there. You're new," she says, scratching him under the chin.

Beside me, Quincy watches this whole exchange with cautious curiosity, but her tail is wagging. Just a little.

Evie manages to pull Gem out of the woman's lap. "Hi, I'm Evie. This is Gemini. That's Quincy," she says, pointing down at my feet, and then she reaches back for my hand. I take it with a squeeze. "And this is Drew."

The vet scrambles to her feet and offers Evie her hand. "Hi, I'm Millie Delacroix." She shakes both our hands and then gestures to the puppies who still leap against her legs. "This is Jazz, and this is Disco. They belong to our receptionist."

I glance over to the receptionist's window, but the space is empty.

"She just ran to Twin's to get us some lunch," Dr. Delacroix says, bending down and scooping up a pup under each arm. She tilts her head toward our dogs. "Are these are our boarders?"

"Yep, they'll be here until the twenty-ninth," Evie says.

Dr. Delacroix glances at Quincy, and then at me. "The little one's kinda shy, isn't she?"

528

I nod. "She is. We've had her about a year, but she was a stray before that."

Her chin bobs in understanding. "She'll warm up. You can tell she wants to play, but she just isn't sure it's safe yet. In a day or two, she'll be ready."

Dr. Delacroix has sized up Quincy right off the bat. I like that. And I like that she has gone out of her way to reassure us. I don't think anything could keep me from enjoying Evie in her bikini on a Grecian beach, but I'm glad worrying about Quincy won't be a factor.

The vet takes her squirming cargo through a side door and then reappears with them in the reception office. She sets down the pups before moving to the computer. As Evie and I approach the window, Gemini springs up on hind legs and puts his front paws on the counter so he can keep an eye on what's happening. Quincy trots up behind him, sniffing the air, trying to figure out what's going on.

While the vet taps away on the computer, Evie drops into a squat between our dogs. She tugs at my hand. "Come down here."

"What for?"

She tugs again. "Family hug."

I squat down, already grinning. I've never heard her say *family hug* before, but Evie and these two dogs are without a doubt my immediate family, and I won't miss an opportunity to pull them all into a hug.

She puts an arm over each dog, so I do the same, and our hands clasp over canine backs.

"Okay, dogs, Dad and I are going on a trip, and you need to wait for us here until we get back," she looks between the dogs as she speaks. They don't really listen. Gem is nosing her face, and Quincy starts sniffing my right shoe. "Since we're going to Greece, we're gonna call on the Greek goddess Hestia, protector of home, hearth, and four-legged animals, to watch over you while we are gone."

"Oh, Guppy," I mutter and tamp down my smile.

"Shh!" She shoots me a playful glare. "You know better than to naysay a goddess, Drew."

I lift the hand off Quincy's back to signal my apologies. "No offense, Hestia."

Evie nods, appeased. "Hestia, keep Quincy and Gemini safe while we travel, and protect our home in our absence. Amen." She tilts to the side and kisses Gem. "I love you… I love you…" She leans the other way and kisses Quincy on the back of the head. "And I love you."

It's a good thing we're lower than the counter because when she presses in to kiss me, I hook an arm behind her neck and make it a real one. Laughter. Magic. Love. Evie has given me all of this. And now I get a family hug.

I let her go and find her blushing, but her eyes meet mine with a secret joy. Like we've just gotten away with something.

But I have my own secret.

Evie being Evie, I've let her plan most of our trip to Zakynthos. Beaches, boat tours, scuba diving with sea turtles. We're going to do whatever she wants, but on our last full day, I'm taking her up to the Cliffs of Keri. If the view is even half as good as it looks online — and the water below even half as blue — it'll still make a great spot for me to drop to one knee and ask if she'll have me.

530

And the fact that someone like me has the chance to propose to someone like Evie on a fucking Grecian isle just blows my mind.

She'll say yes. I'm sure because she's made me sure. And that blows my mind, too. Every damn day.

From the moment we got back together, the day she moved in, Evie has let everyone in our lives know — in no uncertain terms — that we're a package deal. The day after Grandma Q's funeral, Evie Skyped her parents to tell them as much and to fill them in on all the shit that went down with Tori.

I expected them to be shocked and sad, and they were. What I didn't expect was for them to apologize to me. And not just for Tori's actions, but for how they had seen me. For their judgment.

These were apologies I accepted. For Evie's sake as well as my own. Her dad's planning to retire in a couple of years, and that means my future in-laws will also be my backdoor neighbors. When they came home for Christmas last year and again in June, both Sondra and Elliot made it plain that they were looking forward to this future. They didn't go so far as to list the eventual arrival of grandchildren, but I didn't miss the hopeful glint in Sondra's eyes that could only have meant that.

So I'm thinking they see me as more than a grease monkey ex-con. Four-bedroom houses in the Saint Streets aren't exactly a dime a dozen. And watching your grandchildren grow up right in your back yard isn't something most folks get to enjoy. That's something I can give them. It's something I can give Evie. And it's something I can give to the kids I hope we have.

And I have Grandma Q to thank for that. Every damn day.

And maybe I should give Sondra and Elliot Lalonde a little more credit. When they're in the states, they always spend a little time in Austin, where Tori is now. Evie and I don't ask about her, but the Lalondes have hinted that she hasn't changed much. She's unhappy, and she blames other people for her unhappiness. So maybe Evie's parents like me for more than just the house. Maybe they see that Evie *is* happy, and that's the most important thing.

I sure as hell think it is.

And to make sure she has everything she needs — not just a roof over her head, but health insurance, dental, a 401K, and all that shit — I left C&C six months ago for the lead mechanic position at the Southwest Volkswagen dealership.

And I have my cousin Chip to thank for that since he knew the guy I replaced, and that guy got to make the recommendation. And, yeah, working for a dealership pays a lot better than working as a junior mechanic at a local garage. The only way I'd make more was if I owned my own place and it did well.

Maybe that'll come one day, but for right now, I'm lucky. So damn lucky.

Evie would say it's destiny. That it's in the stars. She told me on my birthday that Taurus and Pisces are well matched — that she knew she was meant to be with me that day when we talked over the fence.

The first time she made me laugh.

And maybe she's right. I'd be lying if I said I didn't feel something shift in my own life that day. But that's Evie. She changes everything.

532

I watch my destiny rise to her feet. She answers a few of the vet's questions and then we're patting the dogs goodbye.

As we leave the vet clinic, Evie slips her hand in mine, her green eyes shining like sunset on a Grecian sea.

"Ready for an adventure?" she asks, smiling wide at me.

I squeeze her hand, lean in, and brush my lips against hers. "With you, Guppy, always."

Acknowledgements

I have so many people to thank for their inspiration, encouragement, and expertise that helped me deliver Evie and Drew's love story. I don't think anyone could match Bria Lozada's encouragement and enthusiasm as an alpha reader. I count myself very lucky to have her on my team, and I hope she'll continue giving my drafts her eager attention.

For answering all my legal questions and giving me the term "good-timed out," I want to thank my brother-in-law, Jason Robideaux, criminal defense attorney extraordinaire. My dear friend Shane Breaux needs a shout-out just for being a saint among mortals (once coming to the rescue after my car was totaled AND when the roof started leaking during a thunderstorm). But he also gets the credit for much of Drew's automotive know-how. Without him, I wouldn't have known where to begin with an abandoned 1992 Toyota Supra.

Adriene Mishler and her Yoga With Adriene YouTube channel have been an influence in my life for a couple of years now, and her gentle, loving, and quirky demeanor definitely found its way into Evie's yoga practice and into certain aspects of her character. Relatedly, I'd like to thank Chuck St. Romain for everything he has taught me about insight meditation. Evie learned from the best.

All of my full-length novels are set in my hometown of Lafayette, Louisiana, and while my stories are complete fiction, some of the places that pop up exist in real life. The Yoga Garden is one such place, and anyone who follows me on Instagram or Facebook knows I am guilty of succumbing to the almond milk latte and vegan, gluten-free strawberry cake doughnut at Tribe Collective almost every Saturday. In fact, Evie and Drew's order is our usual. The folks at Loftin Veterinary Hospital are the best, and they've been taking care of my dogs for years. To these local treasures, I thank you for your inspiration and your service to our community.

To fellow romance writer and friend Kimberley O'Malley, thank you for answering all my questions and for all of the good advice as I ventured back into the realm of self-publication. I continue to be grateful for Jena Brignola's artistic sense and her patience with me. She always manages to give me such beautiful covers. To the amazing and ever-thorough Kathleen Payne, thank you for your editing, your honesty, and your help with tying up loose ends. Evie would especially like to thank you for the suggestion to turn the apartment into a yoga studio! For marketing, PA services, and formatting, thank you to Mary Ann Clarkson and Michelle Bowman at WLK Media.

To my daughter Hannah, thank you for helping me with the big decisions like titles and cover fonts. I can't wait to return the favor. To my dogs Gladys and Mabel, who are never far when I'm writing, thank you for keeping my feet warm and making me get up from time to time. These two make their way into the antics and personalities of my canine characters. In fact, Quincy is a dead ringer for my sweet Mabel. To my husband John, who, as I write this is making taco salad so we don't starve tonight, thank you for everything. For reading, for holding me when I'm scared, for cheering me on and being proud of me, and for staying married to me these twenty-five years. I sure do love you.

Finally, dear reader, thank you so much for reading this book. I truly hope you enjoyed it, and I humbly ask that you post a review. Honest reviews matter so much. It's one of the best things you can do to support writers.

As for what's next, the hint is in the Epilogue.

Happy reading!

About the Author

Stephanie Fournet, author of eight novels including *Leave a Mark, Shelter,* and *Someone Like Me,* lives in Lafayette, Louisiana—not far from the Saint Streets where her novels are set. She shares her home with her husband John and their needy dogs Gladys and Mabel, and sometimes their daughter Hannah even comes home from college to visit them. When she isn't writing romance novels, Stephanie is usually helping students get into college or running. She loves hearing from fans, so look for her on Facebook, Twitter, Instagram, Goodreads, and stephaniefournet.com.

Books by Stephanie Fournet
Fall Semester
Legacy
Butterfly Ginger
Leave a Mark
You First
Drive
Shelter

Anthology:
Block & Tackle

Turn the page to read a sample from Stephanie
Fournet's novel *Legacy*.

February

Chapter One

Corinne Granger felt about 100 years old.

It didn't matter that she had only been alive for two and a half decades; the last two and a half months had made her an old woman.

She taped up the last box of Michael's clothes—the ones she could bear to part with—and carried it out to the front porch. Mr. Roush, Michael's father, would pick them up in an hour and take them to Goodwill. He and Mrs. Roush had offered to help her pack up everything, but Corinne had refused. She really didn't want anyone inside the house. Before this morning, she hadn't gotten out of her pajamas in two days, and the two-bedroom rent house that she and Michael had shared for the last year and a half was a wasteland of unwashed dishes and empty take-out boxes.

Of course, the only reason they *were* empty and not yet attracting vermin was because of Buck. Michael's three-year-old black lab saw to it no morsel of pizza or drop of soy sauce remained on Corinne's dishes or delivery containers.

Buck followed her out to the front porch and sniffed the stack of boxes. He gave a short whine, and Corinne reached down automatically and caressed his left ear, rubbing the warm flap between her thumb and fingers. It was a gesture Michael used to do, and now she did it countless times a day—almost without noticing.

Corinne looked at the dog's soft, glossy head and allowed herself a sad smile. Without him, she might not even get out of bed on some days, but Buck—at the very least—had to be fed, and he had to be let out. The lab often stood expectantly by the coat rack near the front door where Michael kept his leash, but Corinne hadn't walked him since the last time Michael asked her to—three days before he died. And that was eight weeks ago.

The memory of Michael in the hospital bed flashed before her mind, and she closed her eyes and scrubbed them with her knuckles until she saw stars behind her lids.

"It's cold," she told Buck. "Let's go back inside."

He followed her in, as she knew he would, staying right at her hip. She closed the door behind them, looked around the small living room, and sighed. The place was a disaster. A disgusting disaster.

Perhaps she could pick up the trash. She bent down and collected a pizza box, a China One bag, and some soiled napkins. Corinne's back and hamstrings protested with the ache that had become part of her body's essence. She carried these items to the kitchen where she faced an overflowing trash can that smelled faintly sour. When had she last emptied it?

Her shoulders slumped at the prospect. That would have to wait. She waded back to the living room, found the remote in the couch cushions, and flopped down. Buck scooted in between her and the coffee table and leaned against her legs as she turned on the TV.

The DVR was full of shows she and Michael watched together. *Elementary. Agents of Shield. The Daily Show.* Corinne bit her lip against its trembling and found the Food Network instead.

Giada de Laurentiis was making pancetta and cinnamon waffles in her bright kitchen, explaining in her soothing way how the warmth of fresh ground cinnamon made all the difference. Corinne sunk back into the couch and gave her mind over. The morning had been emotionally and physically exhausting, and watching the innocuous mixing of batter was like a morphine drip.

In the moments when he wasn't awake, Corinne had been jealous of Michael's IV drugs. Why had no one thought to give her some? Was there any worse pain than witnessing the love of your life die a slow and agonizing death? One that was so senseless and unfair?

As Corinne watched Giada pour her velvety batter into the waffle iron, she thought about how the anger had energized her before the end. Her anger had been her strength, making her ready to fight Michael back to health after the accident, ready to drag him out of hell. To push him through months of physical therapy. To help him walk again. To do whatever it took.

She never got the chance.

And then—*after*—the anger that had fueled her converted into a soul-crushing grief so violent and all-consuming, Corinne believed it would have to bring him back. Of course, it didn't. It simply took her heart with him. And now, she was hollowed out. Shucked clean of her will, of her energy.

Corinne's eyelids felt heavy as Giada drizzled melted butter onto her golden brown waffles. It was easy to fall asleep. She never stayed asleep for long now, but the feeling of fatigue never left her, so she dozed off all the time.

And sometimes, Michael would be there...

She was in their bed, aware of the morning sun on her face and Michael kissing her ear.

"I'm going to work. I'll see you tonight, love," he whispered.

"Mmmmm. Why do you have to leave so early?" she muttered, refusing to open her eyes.

Michael laughed quietly, tickling her ear, and brushed his lips against her temple.

"Because I'm not the artist in this operation. Real job and all."

"Real jobs are stupid," she said, reaching for him.

"Yes, terribly silly," he said, letting her tug him into her arms. His clean, pressed shirt was cool against her neck, and he smelled like pine needles and cocoa. "You're so beautiful."

"Be late today," she tempted.

"Can't. Meeting." He pulled away, but gently, and tucked the covers around her again. "Bye, love."

The sound of the door rattling stirred her, but in the Neverland of her dream it was only Michael leaving for work.

But Michael's gone, she reminded herself.

And Corinne opened her eyes. It was always like this. An assault of truth waiting for her each time she awoke. If she could keep sleeping, would she be able to stay with him?

The sound repeated itself, and this time Corinne heard it for what it was: knocking. Michael's dad.

Shit.

Buck was already prancing by the door and whimpering with excitement. She pulled herself up from the couch and tried to comb her fingers through her dark hair as she made her way to the door. Her hair felt oily, and with her hands up at her head, she could smell the tang of her armpits.

"Damn you, Michael," she muttered for the hundredth time and unbolted the door.

543

Corinne tried to paste on a semblance of a smile as she swung the door open, but the smile caved in when her chin trembled. When she looked into Mr. Roush's sad eyes, she saw Michael's, and Corinne had to grip the doorjamb before her knees could give out.

It wasn't until she forced herself to look away that she saw that Wes Clarkson, Michael's best friend, stood on her porch as well.

"Hi..." she croaked past the lump in her throat. Both men took her in, and Corinne was keenly aware that she looked as though she could have stepped from a horror show. Mr. Roush's face registered pity. Corinne thought Wes seemed faintly grossed out.

"Hi, Corinne," Mr. Roush offered, patting her elbow by way of greeting. Wes said nothing.

"Is this all of it?" Michael's father asked, gesturing to the stack of boxes by the door. Corinne nodded, not daring to speak if it could be helped.

"Is there anything else you'd like us to take right now?" His voice softened, making him sound even more like Michael. It felt like a longsword had pierced her in the center of her chest and anchored her to the floor.

"No, Mr. Roush," she whispered, hoping that if they left, she wouldn't have an audience to watch her collapse.

"Please, Corinne...it's Dan," he reminded her, gently.

"Dan...Right...No, I'm good," she lied.

"There's something else," Wes spoke up, stepping forward. "If you don't mind..."

Wes picked up the first box in his stupid, hairless Hulk arms, and Corinne remembered Michael frowning the first time she'd called his friend "Maximum

544

Density."

"What?" she asked, feeling a little irritated that he had come along.

"I was wondering if it would be okay if I took his bike," Wes said, eyeing her evenly. For a second, Corinne hated him. He didn't look destroyed. He didn't even look hobbled like Michael's father. He looked like he always looked—like a meathead. Glossy faux hawk, such a dark brown it was almost black, gray Under Armor t-shirt clinging to his marbled torso, ever-present black gym shorts. In February.

"What's the matter? Yours isn't fast enough?" She spoke softly, trying to make it sound like a joke, but his brown eyes hardened, and Corinne suddenly remembered him weeping at the funeral. She shook her head and took a breath to apologize.

"Actually, it's not for me," he answered, raising a brow at her. "There's a tri guy I know who teaches high school history. His bike is a piece of crap, and I figured Michael would want someone to use his Pinarello, especially—you know—a teacher who'd never be able to afford one."

Corinne knew she deserved the punch in the stomach that seemed to come with his words. Of course, Michael would want that—something good to come from his death. He might even have chosen to donate the bike to this history teacher while he was still alive.

Corinne nodded.

"It's in the spare room. I can get it if you load these," she said, pointing to the boxes. She turned back inside, letting Buck out onto the porch and listening to the men greet the dog as she walked away.

She stopped in the doorway of the spare room

545

and flicked on the overhead light. Corinne hadn't been in the space since Michael's office sent someone to collect his laptop more than a month ago. The room held a queen-sized bed for the rare times they'd had overnight guests, but it was also where Michael had kept his desk, his bike, and a weight bench.

The black and red Pinarello Dogma 2 stood in its stand, Michael's matching helmet on a shelf above, along with finisher's medals from the MS150, the Rouge Roubaix, and La Vuelta.

Corinne stared at the bike and considered the irony. She'd always been so afraid of Michael wiping out in a race and breaking his neck or being hit by a car on a training ride. She'd never thought to worry about a head-on collision with a drunk driver at 9 p.m. on a Thursday.

She crossed the room and picked up his helmet and was only vaguely surprised when she saw tears splash onto it. Memories erupted in her mind. The time they had camped at Lake Lincoln State Park so Michael could ride in the Mississippi Gran Prix. They'd sat by the fire with the other racers from Lafayette, but instead of trading stories about the road race, Michael had whispered the names of the stars in her ear. He later proved to her that sleeping naked in their two-person bag really was warmer than sleeping with clothes.

He had never tried to hide how much he loved her. He'd told her first—just weeks after they'd been together—and he didn't rush her to say it back; Michael had already figured out that declarations of any kind did not come naturally to her. But he had opened her. He had filled her. He had loved her more purely, more completely than anyone else. And she would never know that again.

She cradled the helmet to her chest and shook with sobs. Corinne had learned in the last two months that she might be able to keep from crying now and then, but once the dam broke, she was lost. There was no stopping it until she'd wrung herself out. Weeping was a full-body endeavor, a cardio workout that doubled her over and took everything.

Which is why she didn't hear the front door or the steps in the hallway.

"Aw, crap," Wes muttered behind her.

Corinne wheeled around to face him, shock and shame checking her sobs. She slashed a sleeve across her eyes and under her nose, instantly outraged at his intrusion.

"What are you doing?" She flung the words at him, wanting to launch the bike helmet at him instead.

Wes threw his hands up with exaggerated innocence. A look of caution in his eyes replaced something else. Was it...*regret*?

"I just came in to see if you needed help," he said, eyeing the bike. "I...didn't mean to...Are you alright?"

Corinne felt her eyes bug before she scowled.

"Uh...*No?!* Do I look alright?"

Wes folded his arms across his chest and set his jaw. The muscles in his face signaled his teeth clenching.

"Actually, you look like shit," he said, blankly.

Corinne startled at the stinging words. Not the truth in them—she knew she must have looked like shit—but the fact that someone would say them to her. Didn't she deserve to fall apart? What happened to her should be a free pass to be left alone without ridicule, without judgment.

"Well, we all know how important appearances are to you, Mr. Personal Trainer," she spat. "I wouldn't want to offend your aesthetic sensibility anymore, so, by all means, get the fucking bike and let yourself out."

She tore past him, but not before his shoulders sagged and a frown crimped his brow.

"Corinne, wait—"

"Always a pleasure, Wes," she said, stepping into her bedroom and slamming the door behind her. Corinne locked it for good measure, tossed the helmet to the floor, and flopped face down on the bed. She expected another onslaught of tears, but her anger at Michael's best friend seemed to keep them at bay.

"He's such an asshole, Michael," she spoke into her pillow. Not for the first time. Just the first time he couldn't contradict her.

She could hear Wes messing with the bike, and she hoped that he and Mr. Roush would simply go without seeking her out. Surely, they would put Buck back inside and just leave her in peace.

She curled onto her side, listening. The sound of clicking gears crept under the door, and it was so easy for her to imagine Michael at home, getting ready to go out for a ride.

The house had grown so quiet without him.

Corinne closed her eyes and let herself pretend just for a moment. Sleep would come again, and perhaps her dreams would be merciful.